Praise for Richard Bausch
and *Mr. Field's Daughter*

"Richard Bausch is a master."   —Louise Erdrich

"Bausch's clean, strong prose, and his wise seeing, his powerful affection for his characters who labor to love one another—these are the banners Bausch's genius flies. **I know of few writers who write so movingly about children and parents in their mutual darkness, mutual need** . . . few who celebrate the big defeats and little victories of the human spirit with such sure humor and certain sense of shape."   —Frederick Busch

"Richard Bausch is one of the few writers today who has the guts, intelligent compassion, and clarity of vision to write about the modern evil of slipshod drift and the mundane burden of the love that can defeat it—*Mr. Field's Daughter* is a book of all the fathers who wonder what to do."   —Mary Lee Settle

"Among the best we have. . . . Bausch has created over the last several years a body of uncommonly good work, stories that stick in the mind like a personal memory."
                    —Tom DeHaven, *The Philadelphia Inquirer*

"Unusually rich and v      a study— deeply felt but thoroug   ate web of emotions that constitu
                                                        .gton Times*

"Fine fiction. . . . *Mr. Field's Daughter* is a complex novel, skillfully told. . . . grown-up in its telling and what it tells us."
    —William L. Tazewell, *The Virginian-Pilot and The Ledger-Star*

Books by Richard Bausch
REAL PRESENCE
TAKE ME BACK
THE LAST GOOD TIME
SPIRITS AND OTHER STORIES
MR. FIELD'S DAUGHTER

MR. FIELD'S
DAUGHTER

MR. FIELD'S DAUGHTER

A Novel

Richard Bausch

COLLIER BOOKS
Macmillan Publishing Company
New York

ACKNOWLEDGMENTS
to Harriet Wasserman and Allen H. Peacock,
there when it counted

Copyright © 1989 by Richard Bausch
Originally published in hardcover by The Linden Press/Simon & Schuster,
1989. Published by arrangement with Simon & Schuster, Inc.

Collier Books
Macmillan Publishing Company
866 Third Avenue, New York, NY 10022
Collier Macmillan Canada, Inc.

Library of Congress Cataloging-in-Publication Data

Bausch, Richard, 1945–
Mr. Field's daughter : a novel / Richard Bausch.—1st Collier
Books ed.
p. cm.
ISBN 0-02-028145-5
I. Title.
[PS3552.A846M6   1990]
813'.54—dc20   89-28196   CIP

Cover design © by Laura Glazer

Cover illustration © by John Collier

First Collier Books Edition 1990

10 9 8 7 6 5 4 3 2 1

Printed in the United States of America

THIS BOOK IS FOR KAREN, WESLEY,
EMILY, PAUL, AND MAGGIE
ALL IN LOVE

PROLOGUE
Mr. Field All Alone

In early June of 1976, in the weeks after his one daughter and only child, at the age of nineteen, walked out of the house with someone like Cole Gilbertson—undoing, he believed, everything he had tried to accomplish in the years of raising her by himself, and heading with unbelievable placid recklessness toward disaster—James Field began drinking in the evenings just to get himself calm enough to sleep. He sat in his living room with a bottle of vodka on the coffee table before him, in the sound, that he mostly didn't hear, of the television, all the way through the late news, which seemed as distant and irrelevant as the weather of another planet. When he finally made his unsteady way to the bedroom he was often drunk to the point of sickness—often enough, in fact, he had no memory of the last few minutes of consciousness, and would wake in the hours before dawn, still clothed, slouched in one of the easy chairs in his room, facing a window, the familiar view of his adopted city before him in deep shadow, the scattered pre-dawn lights of Duluth, Minnesota, shining like facets of something leaking at him through the dark, and, far and wide below, the shimmer and sparkle of Lake Superior lying in a vast bowl of moonlight. These nights, the nights of the northern summer he had always loved, with its cool breezes and clear, bright-starred sky, he was oblivious to everything but the need to go to sleep, to get out of himself, out of the noise of his own mind, where he was constantly replaying the fact of his daughter speeding south in Cole Gilbertson's souped-up Cutlass, with its weighted back end and its bald tires, its thundering engine, its trunk full of old army uniforms, dirty clothes, and dope.

My God, Annie. Do I have to report you to the police to stop you?

What gives you the power to do that? Just because you're my father and your drug happens to be legal?

For God's sake. For God's sweet sake. This is me you're talking to.

I'm sorry, Daddy. But you just don't understand. We're getting married. It's not against the law to get married. How we choose to live is our own business

There was of course little room for worry about the fact that he was no longer functioning very well in his duties at the bank. On some days he had to fake his way through all the required gestures and words, like a man wearing a disguise, a man portraying James Field, the tall, portly gentleman, considerate and kind and gently reserved, senior loan officer—the steady, dignified Mr. Field, father of Annie Field, recently married and residing in Savoy, Illinois, with her new husband.

Some mornings he didn't go in at all. He lay in bed, claiming a flu he couldn't shake, and resolving to get himself back to some sort of order and control. But rage smoldered in his heart, and by nightfall he felt like a man in the grip of a huge desperation. He stood in the doorway of her room and looked at the familiar pictures on the walls, the open closet door, and when he moved through the house, he was aware of himself as the only sound, a ghost, someone waiting for an idea to occur to him, as though it would come from memory, some earlier version of himself in the rooms.

In a way, it was like a kind of riddle to him—and when it

came to him that he wasn't going to be able to let her go, it came exactly like the surprisingly simple answer to a riddle: he could not stand by and wait for her to come crashing down out of the clouds of dreamy infatuation that had carried her away from him; he loved her too much, had put too much into the raising of her. What he believed he had allowed to happen as a function of understanding her youth and the need to be on her own, what he believed he had permitted, aching in his own helpless wish to trust her, now all seemed like cowardice to him. Trying to let go gracefully, he told himself, he had let go too easily, had given her room to reach the point where his word and his ire meant nothing, and she could make this prodigious mistake.

Sodden, bleary-eyed, and dazed—trying to think through all of this—he became rather oddly energetic and agitated. Past nine o'clock of a cloudless July night, and he was pacing, trying to think of practical details—at first simply wanting to moor himself to the reasonable things that surrounded him and then beginning to realize that this new agitation was part of something else. And quite suddenly he was deciding to take charge, he was setting himself into motion. He would have to take off work for a few days, get a little money together, pack some things. He wasn't even sure what he would finally do, and then he was simply doing it.

Somehow managing to keep a steady, calm tone in his voice, he made the necessary phone call asking for a few days to restore himself, then he stuffed some old jeans and T-shirts and a few toilet articles into a small duffel bag and headed south, still drunk. He drove more than a hundred miles that way, down Highway 53 in Wisconsin—two lanes, mostly, flanked by stands of dark trees and hilly fields of grass with the lights of farmhouses in them, all of it gliding by on either side of him like something quite patiently awaiting his attention—and when he reached the divided lanes of the interstate, he stopped along the shoulder, turned the car off, and put his head on the backs of his hands where they gripped the steering wheel. He intended only to take a moment's pause to breathe and think. But in the quiet, after the steady loud droning of two hours' speeding through the dark, he fell asleep. He was no one and nowhere until, in the first glimmer of dawn, he woke blinking into a band of pain across his forehead, and experienced a terrible moment of disorientation and fright, sitting straight in the seat and looking through the misted windshield at the filmy image of the road going on into the dimness. He coughed, gasped into his own trembling fingers, cried out in the chilly confinement of the car. Then he was just sitting there remembering, at first with relief and then with something like the sense that to think at all was to aggravate the already fierce throbbing behind his eyes, that he had been driving south, actually meaning to travel the thousand miles to Savoy, to stand before a young woman and demand that she hear again his objections to her husband. He had actually been about to do a thing so preposterous. This went through his mind like a stab of grief, and even so he started the car, continued south. For a while he told himself that he must look for an exit, a place to turn around. But the exit came and he didn't take it.

In the middle of the morning he stopped for gas. He was a few miles above Madison, Wisconsin. The day had become chilly and rainy, like a day in late fall, but now and then sunlight leaked through the screen of gray clouds to the east. There were travelers, vacationers, in the gas station, families in the easy attitudes of summer. They gazed out at him from leisure vans and RVs, the open windows of smaller vehicles crammed with luggage and gear. James Field gassed up and thought again about turning around. He had no idea at all what might happen if he kept on. But he kept on. He knew that Savoy was in Champaign County, just south of the city of Champaign. He would stop somewhere in the town and ask for the Gilbertson place, and then he would see. Vaguely he entertained the fantastic idea that if she saw him, saw how desperate he was—if she understood the extremity of his anguish over her—she might have a change of heart, might decide to come back home with him. In the same moment that he knew the full absurdity of such a hopelessly childish daydream, he was visited with the strange, elated conviction that no other outcome was possible. It made him quite eerily happy, and he tried to hard to calm himself down, to concentrate on the road ahead, the shifting traffic around him.

He drove past the clotted tributaries of the Chicago Freeway system, down Interstate 57, the fields on either side of him spreading out, widening, growing flat—row upon row of soybeans and corn: a vast monotonous open scape going on into the pale blue distance, where the chilly rain was breaking up into separate showers and wider and wider pools of spilling sun—land shadowless and green, interrupted by silos and grain elevators and the occasional ring of big trees surrounding white clapboard houses and tall, tin-roofed barns.

He followed the signs into Champaign, then stopped at a gas station and asked for directions to Savoy. The station attendant was a tall, wispy-haired blond boy with small blackened teeth, who seemed puzzled by the question.

"Savoy," he said, reaching under his small striped cap and scratching the back of his head.

"Savoy, right," Field said, and waited.

"Savoy."

"Come on, son," Field said.

The boy looked off down the road. "Lot of turns."

"What?"

"Is there something wrong, mister?"

Field stared at him.

"You all right?"

"Just tell me how to get to Savoy."

"It's on Highway 45. You know how to get to Highway 45?"

"I'll find it," said Field, and pulled away from him. The boy stood watching; Field looked at him in the side-view mirror.

The mirror moved slightly as the car rumbled over the un-
evenness in the road, and Mr. Field shivered, receiving the
uneasy impression that he was growing dizzy and feverish. He
drove slowly through the streets of Champaign, concentrating,
trying to be calm. The sidewalks were crowded with students
from the University of Illinois. They carried books and guitars
and satchels, and they stood along the curb, where open cars
waited, trunks packed with belongings. They embraced, and
smiled, and chased after Frisbees in the damp grass of the college
lawns, and they all looked disheveled, unwashed. Field stopped
at a liquor store and bought two bottles of vodka, and he asked
the liquor clerk, a skinny little cirrhotic old man with evil-
looking yellow eyes, how to get to Highway 45.

The man pointed out the window of the store. "Down there
at the end of Green Street."

"Savoy?" Field said to him.

"Turn left."

Field walked out into the sun, and made his way to the car.
Across the street, two young women in denim shorts walked
through a band of shade. They were blond, and lithe, and happy-
sounding, speaking in shrill, excited voices. The school year was
over. One of them was going to Europe, to Oxford, to study.
She began talking animatedly about studying drama with a tutor.
Field sat behind the wheel of his car thinking about his daughter,
nineteen years old and already thrown away on Cole Gilbertson,
on good looks and the stupid charm of a boy. He opened the
vodka and drank, then started the car, raced the engine. The
girls looked back at him, and he returned their staring. They
shrugged, walked on. He pulled out, turned, headed himself to
the end of the street.

Highway 45 was two lanes, running parallel to the raised bed
of the Illinois Central railroad tracks heading south. He passed
a car dealership and a golf course, a few houses set back off the
road behind billboards and tall oak trees waving in the wind.
He had sped through what there was of Savoy and was out in

the country again before he realized it, and so he had to turn around and come back. He stopped at the one motel along 45 and rented a room. He paid for a week. The room was musty and stale-smelling and very small, and the air conditioner in the one window was too weak to really cool it off. But he would not be spending much of his time there anyway. He showered, changed, then poured some vodka into one of the little conelike paper cups provided for coffee. With the vodka burning in his gullet, he stood at the window, gazing through parted, dust-soiled drapes at the highway and the fields beyond. The weather was clear now, the sky a brilliant blue, with a single stupendous escarpment of smoky cloud rolling off to the west. Watching it change and flicker deep in its folds with lightning, he felt almost confident. He was acting out of love, and worry. Outside, in the sunlight, the little breezes of a summer day, he went about the business of finding the house where his daughter now chose to live.

In 1976, Savoy was a small cluster of buildings along 45. There were grain silos along the railroad track, and several crossing streets. Off in the green distance of one flat field were the low white beginnings of what would soon be a group of new houses. Mr. Field took one of the crossing streets, over the railroad tracks, and stopped at a small hardware store to ask about the Gilbertson place. There were two men in the store with almost identical sunburned, leathery faces and drowsy eyes, neither of whom could tell him anything. They didn't know any Gilbertson. Field detected something faintly guarded about their reaction to him: they wanted to know who he was, what his business was. He left them without answering, and drove back to the motel room. It was simple enough to find someone if a man could calm down and know what to do, and after pouring himself another slug of vodka, he sat on the bed in the motel room and paged through the telephone directory, looking for the name. He had the cup to his lips, sipping the burning liquid, when he found what he was looking for: Gilbertson, S. #2

Route 6. He tore the page out and put it in his shirt pocket, then changed his mind and brought it out again. He would call her. He would dial the number, and perhaps Annie would answer the phone.

My little girl. My baby

He felt a pressure now in his chest. He waited, breathing. Then he dialed the number. The buzz on the other end seemed to travel along the nerves of his neck and shoulders, and it occurred to him that he might be having a heart attack. Finally the receiver of the other end was lifted. "Yes?"

He waited. It was not Annie's voice.

"Hello? Anybody there?" A murmurous, nervous-sounding contralto.

"Is—" he began.

"Yes?"

"Is Annie Field there, please?"

"Annie who?"

Field repeated the name into the silence that followed.

"Oh—yes. For God's sake. I don't know what's the matter with me. Just a minute, please."

Again, he waited.

"Hello?"

"Annie."

"Daddy?"

He couldn't speak.

"Daddy, where are you?"

"Annie, it's a mistake. You have to see that now."

She said nothing.

"Annie?"

"Where are you?"

He lied. "Home."

"Well don't call if you're just going to start on me again."

"Is everything all right?" he said, too quickly.

"Everything is not all right, no." Her voice broke. "You can't say these things to me and expect it to be all right."

"Honey. Everything can change, I swear."

"You're going to be a grandfather," she said.

He was again unable to speak.

"Did you hear?" She had become steady again.

"My God," Field said. "Oh Christ."

"No—you don't understand. I *want* to be pregnant."

"Annie, you're only nineteen years old. My God."

"I'm married, now," she said.

"No," he told her, insisting. "It's a mistake. You don't know your own mind."

"I have to go now," she said. "Good-bye, Daddy."

"Annie, he's a goddamn dope-pusher!" Field screamed.

But the connection had been broken.

Route 6 was an east-west road, the crossing road he had taken when he visited the hardware store. He took it again across the tracks, heading east for a mile or so, feeling the pressure in his chest, barely able to breathe, and when he saw that the numbers on the mailboxes were all in the teens, he turned around again and headed west, back past the hardware store, the tracks, Route 45, and on. Number 2 Route 6 was no more than a mile past the turnoff of 45. He stopped on the side of the road opposite the house and looked at it—an old, paint-peeling place, set back amid wild, uncut grass and shaded by tall, drooping willows. He'd found it. He had come here—*was* here. He parked the car a few yards up the road, around the bend, in an overgrown driveway, then walked back, keeping close to the deep, weedy shoulder. A sparse, wild-looking hedge bordered the edge of the property; a man could place himself there next to the telephone pole and remain unseen by anyone in the house. It was a perfect spot for keeping a watch. Getting down in the grass there, off the road and out of sight, he waited for some sight of Annie. Occasionally he lifted himself enough to look at the field beyond the house, but mostly he was just staring through the brittle leaves of the hedge at the house itself. An old, rusted-out Chevrolet was parked in the drive next to the porch. Wash hung from a line in the side yard, and when a stray breeze moved it slightly, he saw something he recognized with a sickening sense of loss as belonging to his daughter—a sky-blue sleeveless dress with a white collar. Getting down on his stomach, he put his hands to his face and tried to keep from crying aloud. All his life he had done and delivered what was expected of him; he had been a man of mostly calm temper and moderate habits, with some culture, reserved and kind and concerned with the dignity of others as well as his own. Some people may have found him a trifle stiff, a bit standoffish—some people may have wondered why he spent so much time at home, why he never remarried. Some must surely have considered him rather predictable and dull. But that was all gone now.

Now, in the increasing, bug-swarming heat of evening, amid the smell of witch grass and manure from the field on the other side of the road, he lay waiting, the effects of the vodka beginning to wear off again, his stomach churning with hunger, with having been given nothing but straight liquor to digest. He stayed where he was, and perhaps an hour later, as the sky faded toward twilight, he was surprised to see a car that had come along the road from the east turn into the driveway. It was Gilbertson's shining Oldsmobile. It pulled fast down the drive, stopped in a cloud of yellow dust, and Gilbertson got out, slammed the car door, then bounded up the porch steps and into the house, the wooden screen door clapping shut with a rickety sound. For a while everything was still again, and then Annie came out of the house with a woman in a flowery, baggy dress. Slowly, almost lazily, the two women began to pull wash from the line. Field watched this. His whole mind hurt. He couldn't bring himself to move or look away. The older woman was gray and thin, but her movements were somehow not those of an old woman, and her laugh was young. Annie chattered at her, looked happy. They were laughing at something: two women in the somnolent beginning of summer twilight, taking wash from a line. And then Annie's eyes wandered to the hedge. She seemed to look right at him. For an instant, he thought of ducking down, but then he couldn't move. It was a kind of paralyzed hesitation, and it had worked to his advantage: for in the next moment it seemed possible that she was seeing nothing at all but the moving leaf and leaf-shadow of the hedge. Even so, the pressure in his chest had grown worse, and something in the attitude of her body, something in the languid, curious tilt of her head as she stared, made him tremble as if from a sudden deep chill. She stared for another moment, her face showing no alarm at all but only a kind of questioning, as though she were trying to remember a name, or distinguish a sound from the chorus of sounds the birds were making in the huge, drooping willows of the yard. She wasn't seeing him, quite. He was certain of it now. He was a shadow, a shape of shadow and leaf.

A moment later, she turned to the other woman, and their talk continued. They filled two baskets with clothes and carried the baskets into the house. James Field waited awhile, then eased back away from the hedge and made his way down the road to his car. He got in, gripped the wheel, and waited for his breathing to return to normal, for the pressure in his chest to subside a little. It let go of him, but it was replaced by something far worse, something not quite physical, yet powerful as any physical pang or ache: for he now found himself encased in the desolating sense of having indulged himself in something so badly and pathologically mistaken that, if she were to find out about it—if indeed she didn't already know about it, hadn't in fact recognized the shadow in the little leaves at the edge of the yard—it would drive her farther away than he could ever hope to bring her back.

Annie, don't you see? I knew from the first minute you brought him into the house that he was a predator, that for all his charm and his good looks and his glib, ingratiating manner he was someone for whom others lack an essential reality or substance . . . knew it by the way he looked at you when he didn't know I was watching,

*and by the things he said and did not say. Forgive me, Annie. I
could tell, even before you started to change, and I could tell that
half the time he was on something, coming into my house*

Back in the motel room on Route 45, not even a mile away
from his daughter, Field lay on the bed in the sick haziness of
what he'd had to drink, and thought about going home. Outside,
the crickets made their turmoil in the dark. The air was sodden
with humidity. He drifted, slept, dreamed. The dreams were
exhausting, and when he woke he had no memory of any of it,
yet felt as though he had bodily endured it all. The light around
the edges of the door was from the motel sign, which buzzed
like a long complaint, and drew swarming clouds of moths. It
was still early—not even midnight. Not even near the hours of
night when Annie would come home glassy-eyed with whatever
she had been ingesting, confident of some new idea of herself,
some fabrication she had come up with in the dreamy excitement
of being in love, of being certain of how much of a fool her
father was—the doddering, old, innocent man with the wool
over his eyes: the one she could no longer bring herself to care
about, or give the commonest consideration of the truth to. There
were the smiles she had turned on him, cloudy and giddy.

Annie, what is he giving you . . . what has he done

Field went out to the motel diner and ordered coffee. It was
important to do something ordinary and simple. His hands
shook. He folded them before him and looked out at the night.
There weren't any other customers in the diner, and the waitress
wanted to talk. She was a woman in early middle age, whose
hair was dyed and teased, and whose white uniform was pulled
tightly across her chest like a sort of binding that she kept shifting
under, trying to get more comfortable than she apparently was.
She went on about the hot weather and the air conditioners that
didn't work and the trouble of running a motel with just a
husband and a sister to help. Field nodded and was polite, and
when she asked him where he was headed, he told her he didn't
know.

"Seems if you were going to head somewhere," she told him, "you'd want to know where it was."

He thanked her for the coffee and said he was going home.

"I guess you know where that is," she said.

He drove back past the house, to the same overgrown driveway, and pulled farther into it this time, the hood of the car dividing dense growth, until he came upon a crossing chain hung from two big oaks. A rusted-out sign proclaimed that the property was under the jurisdiction of the court of Champaign County. When he turned the engine off, the silence felt like a muffled something heavy on his eardrums. Then he began to hear the racket the night bugs were making all around. He got out of the car, leaving the door open a crack, and stealthily, as though a footfall would be heard by anyone, crept out to the road and along it to the ragged hedge.

All the lights were on in the house. Watching the windows, he could hear the faint strains of music: rock 'n' roll. Nothing moved. All he wanted was one more look. Just to see her once more. He knelt down, put his arm around his own middle, suffering his helplessness. And then abruptly a light was on him, as if to show him to the world—a blinding white illumination that spilled over him and was gone: the headlights of an automobile turning somewhere on the other side of the field across the road from where he lay. He got back down in the grass, and now another car was coming toward him. It seemed to veer at him before going on around the bend. He lay waiting for the sound to die away. It was quiet now; even the crickets seemed to have hushed. Minutes passed. For a while he was simply a pair of eyes hidden in the dark, watching a house.

Presently the old woman appeared in the yellow space of one of the windows. She was doing dishes, talking to someone, but her words were garbled by distance, by the sound of rushing water, the small clatter of china. Somewhere a dog barked and whined, then was silent. There was a ringing, or seemed to be a ringing. Field was too far away from the house to tell. He imagined the driver of the car that had seemed to veer at him calling the house to say a prowler was outside. Mr. Field lay perfectly still, and now the lights began to go out. They went out in a systematic way, one by one. Mr. Field watched this, half believing that he had been discovered. The house receded into the moony dark, and when the front door opened, he had to resist the urge to get up and run. A figure, a tall shadow, was coming down off the porch. It was Cole Gilbertson, crossing the yard, crouching, wary, pausing now and again to look around himself, something held tight in his left hand—a stick or a club. He came forward another pace or two, and Field gathered himself to get up and run. But then Annie stood in the light of the doorway.

"Cole," she called out. "Wait. I called the state police."

She came down the steps and ran to him, and the two of them stood very close together, whispering, arguing, Annie pulling at his wrists, apparently trying to get him to return to the house. James Field edged carefully away, staying on his belly until he was below the level of the shoulder of the road, then scrambling along it as soundlessly as he could—through the knife grass and brambles and clouds of mosquitoes—until he had enough distance, could climb up onto the road surface and make his way, running to the overgrown drive. The car door, when he closed it, made a sound that seemed to carry far from him, and he started the car and pulled out, heading back past his hiding place, speeding. He did not look at it as he went by, though he had the feeling that if he had, he would have seen them still standing and arguing in the yard.

Back at the motel room, he locked himself in. He had the rest of the vodka, and the knowledge that he'd sped past them in full awareness that they would see him, would recognize him, if they were where he thought they might still be. He drank a little of the vodka, and then lay on the bed in the oppressive heat, staring at the television, resolving that he must end this now, must collect his strength and his senses and turn himself toward home.

Sometime toward dawn, long after there wasn't any more television to watch, he dropped off to sleep. He was a blank, then; a dreamless quiet. A stillness—which was now broken by what seemed a booming explosion. The explosion brought him bolt upright in the bed, and almost immediately it sounded again. Someone was banging on the door. Field—dazed, still groggy with sleep, thinking he was home—had made his way to the door before realizing where he actually was, before it came to him that he was hearing Annie's voice, that it was Annie on the other side. He ran his hands over his scalp, hearing her, and then opened the door just enough to see out, and be seen. Peering through the sliver of space at his daughter, he saw that she was wearing the blue dress with the white collar. He almost remarked about it. "I knew it," she said. "I knew it. I saw you go by us last night. It was you watching the house—and yesterday behind the hedge. Wasn't it. My God. My God."

She was crying. He tried to open the door all the way but the chain was on; it stopped him. She had turned and was walking away.

"Annie," he said. "Annie. Wait a minute—Annie." He got the door open. She had gone out into the blinding sunlight of the parking lot. Following her, shirtlesss, he was suddenly, painfully conscious of how he must look, and he pulled at the waistline of his pants. "Annie, listen to me."

She faced him. "You go home! Do you hear me? Go home. Leave me and my husband alone."

"Annie," he said, taking hold of her wrists. "I was worried—"

"You get out of here and leave us alone!" Wrenching herself free, she turned and almost broke into a run, crossing the lot to where Gilbertson waited in the low roar of the Cutlass. She got in on the passenger side and closed the door, and Field, coming on her heels, put his hands on the closed window.

"Annie." He stood back and pleaded with her as the car began to move. His daughter was just a shape now behind the reflected glare of his own supplicating figure on the glass. But then she rolled the window down.

"Look at you," she said. "For God's sake, I just got married."

He looked past her and saw Gilbertson's calm, observant, intelligent face, with that calculating, almost measuring expression on it, and he couldn't help himself, was already starting around the front of the car.

"All I did was get married—Daddy, Daddy—"

He stopped, pointed at Gilbertson through the windshield, and screamed, "I'll kill you!"

Gilbertson backed the car up, pulled around him. The tires squealed. The car roared out onto the highway, made a wide, shrieking turn north, and raced away. Field watched until it disappeared into the melting distance of the road—a long, horizontal column of thin blue dust rising in its wake. Then he went back into the room and sat on the bed, looking out the open door at the sunlight. Some nerve in his head throbbed, as if to count seconds, and in an odd, murky way it also tipped him, stage by hurting stage, over the edge of consciousness. In a little while he was lying on his side, gone, the room door open to the heat and the noise of the highway. He was beaten.

Sometime later that morning he began to decide about going home, though later he would not be able to remember exactly when he picked up the pieces of himself enough to make the journey that followed. He didn't go home. Or, that is, he didn't go back to Duluth. Instead, he headed east, to Point Royal, Virginia, to visit for a few days with his sister Ellen, who counseled against trying anything else, counseled patience, letting go, learning to trust his daughter's strengths and resources. He tried to listen to this, tried to keep himself busy: he spent a few days going to the places of his youth and young manhood—Charlottesville, Demera, Roanoke, Point Royal itself. Everything had changed, of course. The houses were all new. The woods were taken over by shopping malls and housing developments. The little country house where he had met his wife was gone, had been razed to the ground to make another lane for the highway that skirted Point Royal, heading on to the mountains and Route 81. The house he and Ellen had grown up in had been turned into a bicycle shop, and all the downstairs walls were gone. Field thought of the delicately elegant look of those rooms as they had been when his mother kept them—the careful and subtle placement of pictures and knickknacks and figurines. And he thought of his own father sitting in a chair by the front window, reading the evening newspaper, smoking a cigarette and blowing the smoke out the open screen. Bikes now hung where that window had been. Field stood out on the walk and stared in at the men waiting behind the counter, and his heart was breaking even as he nodded at them and smiled, and turned to walk away. He was not drinking so heavily now, and so it was very soberly that he thought of dying as some consoling thing, a way of leaving the unrecognizable world he now found himself in.

When he said good-bye to his sister and started north and west, a part of him believed he would never see her again. But the days took their slow course through his heart, and he simply kept on. He took a month getting back to Duluth, across the northern route, past Mackinac Island. He opened the doors of his house and walked through the rooms, putting things away, tidying up. There were things to do. He returned to work, steadied himself, a man nursing an unhealable wound. Everyone understood. Everyone was good to him. Perhaps there were remarks about how quiet he had become; how much more reserved. He sent postcards to Savoy, a letter or two. In the letters, he tried to talk about safe things: the weather he was living in, books, Aunt Ellen, Uncle Billy and the kids. But he ended by asking her to call him, write, come home for a visit.

All is forgiven, he wrote.

She never answered specifically. He received a card on his birthday, another one at Christmas. Still another when his grand-

daughter was born. She sent a picture of the baby, and he wrote
asking for others. Months later he received a family portrait—
Cole Gilbertson, arms folded, smiling, staring out from a wall
of leatherbound books, the fake background of some photog-
rapher's studio, while Annie sat in an easy chair with the baby
on her lap, her own smile somehow qualified, as though even
in the moment of being photographed she wanted to emphasize
the distance between them. When he tried calling her, Gilbertson
answered the phone, and Field hung up. He tried again a few
days later, and again he got Gilbertson.

"Who the hell is this," Gilbertson said into the line, and by
now it was too late for Field to speak. He simply waited until
Gilbertson hung up.

Finally, one afternoon, it was Annie who answered.

"I just wanted to see how you are," he told her.

"I'm fine. The baby's fine. I've got a job."

"What's he doing?"

"Cole is going to school, Daddy."

"What's he studying?"

"You really want to know?"

Field said nothing.

"He's taking some music courses, actually."

"Music."

"He wants to learn how to play guitar."

"What's he going to do with guitar lessons?"

"You don't have to *do* anything with them, right?"

"What else is he studying?"

"Accounting," she said. "Does that make you happy?"

"My happiness is not important," said Field.

"Daddy, if you only knew how you sound."

"I know how I sound."

She said, "I have to go now."

"You could give an old man a call once in a while," he said.

"Daddy, you can't call here just to talk to me and nobody
else. I'm part of another family now."

"Yes," he said.

He phoned Ellen, who explained to him that the poor girl was probably doing all she could do, given the circumstances. He must put himself in his daughter's place, must understand that she needed time, it would take time. And so at last he had cultivated the resolve to think of himself as someone waiting for something, abiding, keeping a vigil. He went on with things in this way, and time began to blur. There were days when he had a little trouble with the loneliness, and with the tendency to drink the feeling away, but that was mostly under control, and when his sister was widowed, and moved north to live with him, she provided a daily order, the semblance of a household. They spent many quiet evenings trading memories and speculations about people they had known in Point Royal, old friendships and marriages, the grown children of mutual friends, the fate of hopes and wishes; they remarked on the progress of various lives, and they almost never talked about his daughter, for that was a subject he kept to himself. . . .

By the time Annie returned to the house, he had all but abandoned the hope that she would ever do so.

When she did arrive with his grandchild, out of a ruined marriage, four years after his crazy chase down the face of the continent in search of her, he discovered in himself a sense of the world returning to symmetry again, things fitting together and showing the old ordered shape, the look of his old life, even with the complicated turmoil of her divorce to help her through. Through it all, through the days and weeks of helping her settle things with the divorce, of being there for her when she needed him, of understanding everything and being the good father, the one who supported her and listened to her and never recriminated with her or reminded her of past difficulties, he found that there were times when he could not think of her, could not imagine what she must be feeling. *He* was feeling glad again, alive again, and a part of him took a guilty sort of pleasure in it, in secret. He was sorry for everything, but there could be nothing too deeply wrong, could there, with being grateful to have work to do and a family, and an understanding of the import of each day's gestures—to be once again in the middle of living, in the clear, settled shape of things as they were supposed to be. And later, if there was always the residue of the bad time, it was all now a kind of blur in his memory; it was livable, a thing he had befriended in himself, and that Annie had mostly forgiven him for. It was a story he liked to think had ended.

He had learned to believe what he could see with the luxury of hindsight: when he looked at himself in a mirror, the reflection gave back a man who, having raised himself out of unhappiness, could plumb its depths and recall its signature with something like relish—certainly with the pride of accomplishment. What he recalled now of Annie's flight, he recalled like elements of a story he could repeat to himself when he had the inclination to do so: *he raises a daughter, he loses her, he suffers her absence. He waits patiently, with love. And one day she returns with her own daughter, his grandaughter. Again, there is a little girl in his house. He has a family once more. He is again a happy man. All the trouble is a thing of memory at last. It is behind him. He thinks of it as a part of his life that is over. Years pass.*

PART ONE

The Magic Machine

On a cool morning earlier this year, Selena Gilbertson called the rescue squad and reported that there was a dead man in a bed in one of the upstairs rooms of her house. She had apparently come upon the body while she was cleaning. Cole Gilbertson, half asleep in the room upstairs, heard her talking on the telephone, heard the note of horror in her voice, and knew he should get up to see what had disturbed her; but he kept putting it off, dozing, waiting for the trouble, whatever it was, to come to him, and finally she had grown quiet. He relaxed, drifted into a hazy flying dream, and awakened to find four rescue workers and a policeman standing over his bed. The policeman was holding a very large white helmet, and Gilbertson looked at the handcuffs on his belt. He thought of trying to run, sat up, pulling the blanket around himself. There was a vial of coke in the travel bag on his dresser; a razor blade and mirror were lying on the bedstand.

"Oh, goddamn," he said. "Jesus, God."

The officer, a youngish-looking man with blond hair and a cherub's round, pink-cheeked features, said, "Okay, nobody's dead here."

"Dead," Gilbertson said. "Who's dead?"

"Are you all right, sir?" one of the rescue workers said. He was a wiry-looking, hook-nosed man with pouches under his eyes, who looked irritable and deeply bored with everything.

"What's going on?" Gilbertson said. "Who's dead?"

"Well, *I* sure don't know what to make of it," said the police officer.

And then all of them—Gilbertson following, wrapping himself in the thick, blue-flowered blanket from the bed—filed down to the room off the kitchen, where Selena Gilbertson sat doing needlepoint, with the television on loud, and a portable fan on the cedar chest across from her, stirring the air up, whirring like some ongoing protest no one was listening to. In a moment, they had figured it all out; they had taken in the information that Selena was slipping, and, forgetting that her son was still living in the house, came upon him asleep in mid-morning, and reached the conclusion that he was a corpse. "I slept late," Gilbertson said, humiliated. "Man, oh man." He pulled the blanket tight around himself. "I took a day off work. You know."

The police officer shook his head slightly. "Okay," he said to the others. "Let's go."

They all went quietly away.

Gilbertson went to his room and dressed, then closed the door and stayed there. He wasn't really working anything like a job, now, and he couldn't think of facing Selena in her fog, so he did a little of the coke, just to get himself at a level, and then spent the afternoon watching soaps on the small portable television she'd bought him for his privacy. It was a thing he had insisted on, if he was to go on living in the house with her, constantly being humiliated and constantly having to worry about her. When he heard her talking again, he hurried in to her, angry, meaning to tear the phone out of the wall. But she was just sitting there mumbling to herself.

"Jesus, Selena," he said.

· · ·

A week later she disappeared. Gilbertson woke up in the early afternoon to find the house empty, a pot of coffee perked away to almost nothing on the stove. He called neighbors, friends of his mother's; he drove through the streets of Champaign and out into the country, looking for her. He even called the police. No one could do anything to help him. There were procedures, forms to fill out, but mostly one simply had to wait. So he waited, and after the second day he came to the realization that he enjoyed the house on his own. The thought crossed his mind, and he entertained it, that it would be all right if Selena was gone for good. There was something wrong with the logic of the whole thing, but he didn't examine it much. He was keeping himself fairly well, portioning the coke out, rationing it. And then toward the end of the week, Selena wandered into a department store in Urbana and began to put baby toys in the pockets of her coat. She was shopping for her son, she told the store detective, shopping for Cole. The store detective told Gilbertson this, and Gilbertson thanked him. He took her home, put her to bed, then drank whiskey until it dimmed everything and he could sleep. He slept deeply, but not very long, and when he got up, she was gone again. He found her out in the fallow fields across from the house, sitting on the trunk of a dead tree at the edge of Dyer Creek, hands on her thighs, staring into the green spaces beyond the little trickle of muddy water as though waiting for someone to return from there. He took her by the arm, led her back to the house, and put her to bed again. He explained to her that she must stay in the house. She must not go outside under any circumstances at all. She nodded at him, seemed puzzled that he could be so concerned. "I'll spend the day playing gin with Annie."

"Annie's not here," he said. "Annie took the baby and went back to Duluth. It was years ago."

There were provisions to get; business to take care of. And he was afraid to leave her alone. Three times during the course of the day, as he had been preparing to do a line of the coke, he heard her begin to dial the phone, and had to hurry it, worrying about who she might be calling. Some part of him was aware that he was growing more and more paranoid, and lately he'd had episodes in which he felt it as an almost unbearable pressure behind his eyes. For a long time he had been without work, living off Selena, hiding in the house and worrying only about ways to keep replenishing the supply of coke. He had scored most of his present supply from a man named Brewer, who had very recently been arrested, and was therefore out of commission indefinitely. There was a need to get out and move around a little, work up some new connection, and Selena, the source of income, was proving impossible to handle, had to be watched almost every waking hour. Gilbertson stayed with her, and felt himself growing bizarre. His fascination with the process of her decline was boundless, and he kept having to remind himself that this was his mother.

One morning toward the end of September, he woke from a series of bad, drug-vivid dreams to find her lying on the living room floor in her nightgown, curled up like a child, asleep with her thumb in her mouth. He stared at her for a long time, frozen in his own strange enthrallment, and then he made himself kneel down at her side, to see if she was breathing. She was. She opened her eyes and looked at him. "Cole," she said, "that's you, isn't it."

He helped her to her room, into bed, and sat watching her while she drifted off to sleep. When she began snoring, he padded silently to his own room, took the pillow from his bed, and returned to stand over her, holding the pillow in both hands, staring at the pale, closed line of her lips. It looked like such a peaceful, undisturbed sleep. He put the pillow over her face, and then pulled it back. Somehow, it hadn't waked her. His hands were trembling now, and sweating, and he made his way back to his bedroom, trying not to gasp or cough. The travel bag was in the top drawer of his bureau. He set it all up and did three lines, then sat back on the bed and took the rush, bracing himself and holding on as it came over him. In the other room, she slept peacefully, her hands folded across her chest. He watched her for a few minutes, then shut her door and took himself back into the living room, and the television set. His heart was racing; he had gone over some threshold in himself. The high seemed to be veering off too quickly into something else, and so it was with mounting fear that he opened the whiskey and set about trying to offset the coke a little. His fear only grew worse.

Through the gloomy hours of that afternoon—while a blustery, wintry wind swept rain incessantly at the windows of the house, and seemed somehow to move at the heart of fright— he sat straight-backed on the sofa, in the meaningless hilarity of the television set, watching one game show after another, exhausted, unable to bring himself to rest, his stash dwindled almost to nothing, his heart beating in his neck and throat. Near dark, his mother walked through the room and out the front door, and it was only through the chill of outside air reaching him that he realized she had stirred. Once again, she had wandered down to Dyer Creek, but this time she had gone across the creek, into the woods and brush above the opposite bank. She was moving among the fallen branches and tangled weeds, looking for something, bending to pick up twigs or pieces of bark or stones, now and again stopping to look around herself, turning in a small circle, confused, scared, and sad. He watched her through the interstices of bare, dripping branches, watched her with an empty, curious attention, shivering, the rain pouring down his face. She was moving away from him.

"Selena," he said, staring after her.

And then abruptly he had turned, was running wildly back across the field in the direction of the house. It was as if something had come crashing out of the woods to pursue him; all he knew for certain was that he had an overriding need to get back into the house. When he had crossed the road and come up the steps of the porch, he stopped and looked back toward the creek. Daylight was fading quickly, and the raw rain and wind hadn't slowed at all. The thought occurred to him, like something from another mind, that he could say he had been unable to find her; he could let nature take its course. Crossing the porch, he entered the house, closed the door, and stood with his head against it, hearing the rain soughing at the windows. He was drenched. His heart was booming in his chest. In the watery light of the living room, he poured himself a glass of whiskey and drank it down. He dried off and changed his clothes, and sat in front of the television, using the remote control to flick nervously through the channels. It was growing later all the time. As he took still another long drink of the whiskey, he lost his resolve, and soon he was stumbling through the dark beyond Dyer Creek, calling her name, flailing at the tangled, water-logged undergrowth, and trying to see in what was now pitch dark. It took a long time to get to her, and it took a longer time getting her back to the house.

"You know what I did wrong, sweetie?" she said, while he helped her out of her clothes. "I gave in to you all the time. I let you have anything you wanted from me."

"You got a chill," he said to her.

"Go ahead and drug yourself," she told him. "You think I don't know it?"

He looked at her, and then he was looking at the room. He had an eerie moment of feeling that the very objects around him were bending toward chaos: the books lying on her bureau seemed tossed or dropped as if by someone in reasonless flight; the skin over her bones looked like the distraught work of fugitive, hurrying hands. And the rain still beat at the windows, as though the whole sky were breaking up. She lay down on the bed, quiet and seemingly calm and yet clearly wary of something too, her eyes taking everything in as if this were a sort of contest, and she knew what was at stake—what might happen if she failed to notice something, if she allowed the smallest detail to escape her. She was gazing at him now and she smiled, almost as though she wanted to reassure him. "My boy," she said, her voice soft and confident and kindly. She closed her eyes, then opened them again, and stopped breathing.

He was on the phone, talking, shouting. It seemed impossibly necessary to try everything to save her now. He got into the bed with her and blew into her mouth, and when the rescue workers pulled up in the ambulance, he ran out onto the puddled lawn, crying, calling them to him. They loomed out of the darkness, splashing toward him, and he was telling them how she had simply closed her eyes and then opened them and stopped. He was begging them to be careful, go slow, don't hurt her, don't wake her, don't frighten her. They worked over her for a time, and then they lifted her onto a stretcher. The thought traveled through him that she didn't weigh any more than a handful of sticks.

In the waiting room of the emergency ward, he sat with his hands folded into tight fists on his lap, and shivered. His clothes were still damp from the rain. There were several other people in the room—a man holding a cut finger up; a woman with a swollen foot; an old couple, huddling together on a bench along the wall—and he saw that they were all staring at him. He couldn't stop shaking. When they came to tell him it was over, he walked out into the dark. Before him was the dimly lighted street outside the hospital; and beyond, the stillness of the middle of the night on the plains, a clearing, black sky, the vastness of midwest midnight. The world seemed to have acquired a deeper silence than anything he could have imagined, and he thought of Annie and his daughter, so many miles away, so far north.

Somehow, he got through the business of getting Selena's funeral and burial taken care of. Only a few neighbors came to the service—old women his mother had known for years, who had been through their own losses, and who had apparently been the auditors of her worries about him. They all seemed to

know that he had been out of work a long time, that his marriage
had collapsed; they all seemed to know he had been in trouble.
They offered their condolences, and talked about what a dear
friend Selena was, and at one point he overheard two of them
talking about how reclusive she had become toward the end.
They all looked at him with frankly wondering eyes. Several
of them asked him what he planned to do now. He thought it
was best to try and be truthful about it; the truth was that he
didn't know. He was fortifying himself with the coke, suffering
from swollen sinuses, a bad cold. Selena had left twelve thousand
dollars in an account at the bank. The morning she died, he
had gone over there with her ATM card, and drawn out two
hundred. It was the way he and Selena had done things over
the last two years, and he saw no reason to alter it now. The
money was his, to live on in increments. The week of the funeral,
he drew two hundred a day, hoarding it for the time when it
became necessary to make the next purchase.

After the funeral, he drove to Peoria, to look up an old
connection—a scabrous, rail-thin, medallion-wearing punk who
styled himself as some sort of kingpin. His name was Tenchley.
Tenchley had had the good fortune of being the son of someone
who owned the patent on an important aircraft part which the
military had paid—and was continuing to pay—millions for.
He lived in a high-rise apartment building off Highway 74, and
was fond of pointing out his various possessions to his visitors
as visible evidence of their tax dollars at work. "Your tax dollars
at work," he would say, indicating the little fountain with
nymphs and mermaids he had bought for one corner of his
apartment; the trickling sound it made would serve as a reminder all night. Tenchley would never lack for the money to
support his various bad habits, or to provide the circumstances
he liked best, being, as he put it, the sort of person who greatly
enjoyed having the upper hand. He liked dealing drugs because
of the purity of upper-handedness he felt doing it. He had told

Gilbertson this more than once, back when Gilbertson had done business with him regularly.

On this occasion he was enjoying the fact that Gilbertson's source in Champaign had dried up. He smiled and took a lazy drag on his cigarette, and then said, "I've procured some Quaaludes, old pal. Would you like to cool out a little? You seem a teensy bit overstimulated."

He told Gilbertson to wait in the hall, then closed the door. A few moments later, he opened the door again.

"You still here?" he said.

"Come on," said Gilbertson.

"I'm alone this evening," Tenchley said. "I don't like to have company when I'm unguarded." This was true. Tenchley usually had two or three goons around.

"Where is everybody?" Gilbertson asked him.

"Errands, let's say." Tenchley liked to sound vague and threatening.

"Thought I'd stop by and say hello," said Gilbertson.

Tenchley smiled. With a nervous, almost cowardly kind of relish, he made it clear that Gilbertson was going to have to spend the evening with him as a condition of the sale. It was Tenchley's habit—born, no doubt, out of necessity—to require the society of those who needed something from him. It was, he'd once told Gilbertson, all he would ever know of true friendship; he said this and laughed. He had always seemed exactly aware of just how repugnant he was, and he never seemed to mind at all. As long as he had the power to compel people, as of course he was compelling Gilbertson. It was all what Gilbertson expected, like a ritual they played out. Tenchley put music on, and fixed whiskey for them both. He was apparently sailing on some of his own stuff. Gilbertson knew that now and again the other man liked to cook heroin and shoot up, and he wondered about it as Tenchley handed him the whiskey.

"Here," Tenchley said. "A little something to ease off with."

Gilbertson sipped the whiskey. It was sour mash bourbon, with a sweet aftertaste. "I thought you said you had some Ludes."

"Let's be sociable on a higher scale, first."

"I'm kind of fucked up here," Gilbertson began.

"Have a seat," Tenchley said.

It was ridiculous. Gilbertson watched him settle back on the couch, his white shirt spreading where it was open at the chest. Now there was going to be the whole interminable evening to go through.

For a few minutes, they were just sitting there, sipping the drinks politely while the stereo played. Tenchley had put on the best of Steppenwolf. "Magic Carpet Ride." "Like this?" he said.

Gilbertson nodded, and raised his drink.

"I made a tape—all sixties stuff. Beatles and Lovin' Spoonful and Dylan. You remember the Fugs?"

"The Fugs."

"Yeah. You remember them?"

Gilbertson shook his head.

"I've got stuff by the Fugs."

"I don't think I ever heard of the Fugs."

"Sure you have. You just don't remember."

"Maybe," Gilbertson said.

"The Fugs are the quintessential group of the sixties. They said it all just by being what they were. Simple indulgence and outrageousness."

Gilbertson took more of the drink. He was beginning to feel very shaky and sick. He swallowed the whiskey, and it burned in his stomach.

"I figured it all out," Tenchley said. "The sixties. It was all leading here. It had nothing to do with politics at all. It was just the first step leading here."

"I don't remember much about the sixties," said Gilbertson. "The Kennedys getting shot. Martin Luther King getting shot. The war."

"I was in the war. Do you believe that? I really was, man. I was in the motherfucking war."

"I don't remember much about it."

"Man, it was a fucking war."

"I was in junior high school," Gilbertson said, "when King got shot and they burned the cities."

"The human destructive urge. You can't beat it."

"I guess not."

"You look strung out," Tenchley said.

Gilbertson sipped the whiskey.

"It was just a binge. And this is where it leads." Tenchley indicated the room, which was all metal angles and abstract-looking furniture. There was a painting on one wall of an eyeball with hundreds of nude figures crowded into the iris of it, like a tangle of facets, and the dark center, the pupil, was a deep hole into which the bodies were all about to tumble. Above the couch was a glowing pastel of a man holding a cat by its tail, as though it were a weapon of some kind, crouching above a deep gorge or canyon. The man was extremely muscular and was wearing some sort of body armor.

"Look," Gilbertson said, "if it's all the same to you, Tenchley, I'm in a hurry."

"No hurry," Tenchley told him. "You like The Who?"

"Is this who we're listening to?"

Tenchley shook his head.

"Okay, yeah—whatever."

"Yes, sir." Tenchley leaned back, took a swallow of his drink, and rattled the ice in the glass. "I have some good clean stuff, too. Very good quality."

Gilbertson waited for him to go on.

"You know what I figured out?"

"You told me."

Tenchley went on. "I figure it's all a part of the course of civilization. And there's no sense trying to stop it."

"I guess so," Gilbertson said, and drank his whiskey down.

"Do you know what I'm talking about?"

He nodded.

"Tell me."

"I think you've got it scoped out pretty good," he said.

"Shit, man. You're humoring me. Don't humor me. Take part."

Gilbertson swallowed more of the drink.

"How's your wife doing?" Tenchley asked him.

"My wife."

"You used to come around with her. I just wondered."

"We broke up four years ago."

"She left you, didn't she."

He drank.

"Tell me about it," Tenchley said, smiling.

"Why don't you go fuck yourself, Tenchley."

"I always liked her—what was her name. Annie."

"Look, I'm telling you to shut up about it. Okay?"

"Well, it's a subject that interests both of us," Tenchley said.

"I'm telling you," said Gilbertson, "I'm not in the mood for this."

"The mood? You? Look at you, man. You can't stop shaking."

He took the money out of his pocket and put it on the glass coffee table between them. "That's five hundred dollars, Tenchley. What'll it buy me?"

"Diddly-shit," Tenchley told him. "Get out."

Gilbertson looked at him. "Somebody ought to choke the life out of you now and then, just for exercise."

"He's threatening me now. I don't believe it."

"Look, you want the money or not?"

"Piss on your money."

"I'm not fucking around," Gilbertson said.

"I believe you're just leaving," said Tenchley. "If you want to stay healthy."

"All right, look. Come on—let's talk. Let's have a goddamn evening."

"I've changed my mind. If you could get your hot little ex-wife to come see me, now that might help out a great deal."

Gilbertson stood. It dawned on him that Tenchley, alone, was behaving as if he were surrounded by his hirelings. In the next instant, this knowledge gave him the backhanded insult that it was—the other man thought so lightly of him that he could be secure in this attitude of disdain, using this casual obscenity with him about something as personal as his ex-wife—and before he knew he would do anything, he had lunged at Tenchley, had got his hands around his throat, holding on tight, almost from reflex, looking into Tenchley's bugged eyes and feeling a kind of rapturously satisfying sense of power. Tenchley's tongue came out, bluish and dry. Gilbertson walked him across the room, and now felt himself giving over to the idea of carrying things out to the end, staring into the desperation in the man's eyes. He said, "You know what this is, Tenchley? This is justice happening to you." Tenchley looked back at him. It was pitiful. It wasn't even worth the aggravation. Gilbertson pushed and let go, and the other man fell through the coffee table in an explosion of shattering glass. He lay there, not moving, his tongue out, and then he was coughing and gasping, trying to get up. The broken glass had cut him badly on one elbow; he looked at it, blinked, made an effort to sit up, then set about stanching the flow of blood with a part of his shirtsleeve. He tried to talk but couldn't.

Gilbertson took the money from where it had fallen on the floor.

"I'm bleeding," Tenchley managed in a rasping croak. "I'm bleeding bad, here." He lay back down in the glass. "You're dead. A dead man." His eyes rolled back.

Gilbertson stood over him for a moment, and when he was sure the other man had passed out, left him there, and made his way into the bedroom. It was a bare place, with only a bed and a night table, under a single hanging lamp, and even so it gave the impression of some artist's intentions: the walls were

white, as were the bedstand and night table, the lampshade, the
window blinds, and curtains—everything was white. Except
that the floor was littered with old newspapers and books, and
with piles of dirty clothing, which gave off a strong mildewy
odor. On the night table were Tenchley's works, and two vials
of coke. Gilbertson looked in the drawer and found another,
folded up in a paper bag. He put everything in the bag, looked
around the room for whatever else he could find, and, finding
nothing, returned to the living room. Tenchley lay in a pool of
blood, but he was breathing, and it looked as though the bleeding
had mostly stopped. Gilbertson left him there, drove back to
Champaign, and closed himself in the house. Somewhere in the
back of his mind was the concern for what Tenchley might try
to pull, but he put it off—whatever happened, he would deal
with it.

He had the five hundred dollars in cash, and the coke, and
he felt as though he had accomplished something. After doing
two lines of the coke, he went into the living room and sat
under Selena's old reading lamp, feeling its light like a kind of
warmth, and the prospect of the days and weeks ahead opened
out before him like vast, cloudless distances. But he was not
content to sit still, so he did one more line, then wandered
through the house, looking at things—his mother's belongings,
all the accumulations of a life. He had everything to himself.
In the attic, he found boxes of photographs of Selena as a child;
Selena with her sisters, all so much older than she was, and all
looking like members of a different family; Selena in attitudes
of satisfaction and happiness, holding her baby and looking into
the sunlight of three decades ago. One photograph showed Selena standing arm in arm with a tall, skinny boy in a tight
starched collar and bow tie—Gilbertson's father, younger than
Gilbertson was now, smiling and looking happy, benign, all
sorts of sunny goodwill shining forth in his expression, and no
trace or hint of the violence in the man, the angers lurking
under the smile. He tore the photograph in two, saving the half

that was Selena. Then he collected what he wanted of everything and took it with him to his room. There were letters, fading and yellow with age, busy with the concerns of 1935. He even found schoolwork she had done when she was seven years old. Apparently, she had saved everything. It fascinated him. Looking at it all, he thought he could feel time move back.

Days passed in this way.

The mail came and he put it in the wicker basket above the kitchen sink, where it had always gone; it was all bills and advertisements and fund-raising ploys addressed to Selena Gilbertson and he wasn't interested. Sometimes the phone rang, and sometimes he answered it. Once it was a man selling light bulbs; another time it was someone from the insurance company: his mother's policy would be paid, but it was only two thousand dollars after the expense of the funeral. That was all right. There was a lot of money in the machine.

One day near the end of the month, a man from the Internal Revenue Service came to the door—a small, round, florid-faced man, who smelled of cigars and wore a gray suit with threadbare patches on the elbows. He came in carrying a briefcase, and sat down on the couch, arranging himself, opening the briefcase, asking if Gilbertson minded if he smoked.

"Yeah, I mind," Gilbertson said, thinking of Tenchley.

"Well," said the man, "I can certainly understand that."

"Look, what is all this." He had just been free-basing in the bedroom, and knew his eyes weren't on straight. It occured to him in this way: that they were crooked. He sat across from the man and shivered with paranoia.

"Mr. Gilbertson, we've been in contact with your mother several times by registered letter since June, and I'm afraid things have come to a rather unfortunate pass. Have you been domiciled here during the last year?"

Gilbertson simply stared at him.

"Have you Mr. Gilbertson?"

"Yes."

"Well, then you must know about this. You must know your mother was tax delinquent and that we've been seeking some resolution of the problem through the courts."

"No," Gilbertson said.

Now the man stared back. After a pause, he said. "You mean to say you didn't know your mother was behind on her taxes?"

"That's right."

"Well, sir. She was. Seventy thousand dollars, counting penalties and interest."

"Just say what you want," Gilbertson said.

"Why, the money."

"You—" Gilbertson began. "From me?" he said.

"From the estate. Your mother's property, sir. I'm sorry—I thought you might know about it. And in any case, I really am sorry."

"You're going to take the house," Gilbertson said. "The machine."

The man looked puzzled. "The machine?"

"You're just going to take the goddamn money like that, huh."

"Well, I'm afraid so, yes. What there is of it. I mean it'll still leave us thirty or forty thousand short of full recovery on the debt."

"Did Tenchley send you?"

Again the man was puzzled. "I'm sorry?"

"Get out of here, pal."

The man quickly gathered the papers and put them in the briefcase. "I wish there were some other way, sir. I understand how you feel. You'll be hearing from us."

"You're from Tenchley, right? Tenchley sent you."

"I'm afraid I don't know that name."

When the man had driven away, Gilbertson sat on the porch steps in a brooding, furious silence, his hands resting on his knees, his head pounding with the effects of the drug wearing off. The sun was high, and it was cool and breezy. Wind murmured in the tops of the trees. The shade moved. He looked at the yard, the brightness of the sun on the grass, the mottled, sunny color of the leaves that were collecting against the hedge. It all seemed to mock him; it was all just the simple pleasantness of an afternoon in the world and it had nothing to do with him—as, he realized now, this house and the magic machine would soon no longer have anything to do with him. The authorities were going to take it all.

He drove to the bank in Champaign and put Selena's card into the machine, pressed the buttons, asked for the limit of two hundred, and the machine issued the money. Apparently, the IRS hadn't gotten around to doing whatever it would do. With almost seven hundred dollars in his pocket, he went into one of the bars in Urbana and ordered a whiskey. It felt good to be out among people for a change. Nearby, in an upstairs apartment off Green Street, lived a young woman he had spent time with over the course of last autumn, and he thought he might go see her again. Her name was Alice Minneford, and she had attached herself to him in a way. He had made love to her, and had considered it casual enough, but there had been in her attitude and thus in their relationship something vaguely matrimonial, as if each gesture of his, however affectionate or indifferent, were somehow sealing him into the fabric of her life: she had taken to calling him *honey,* and *dear,* and had begun to talk about the future as though they would both be old together. It had reminded him of being married in a pleasant way, at first, and now when he thought about it, he imagined how it would be to see her once more. But after two whiskeys, he had begun to feel a little shaky, and he headed back to Savoy. It was still bright when he pulled into the driveway, though the dappled places in the yard had begun to soften toward the slanting blue shades of evening. He sat in the car for a while hearing the small tick of the engine as it cooled. At last, he stirred, made his way back into the house. Mail had come, and he took it in with him, dropped it on the table. The kitchen smelled of garbage. He went into his bedroom, brought out the travel bag.

There was just the sound of him in the rooms, and this made him nervous. Sitting at the kitchen table, he chopped some of the coke, concentrating, trying to keep his hands from shaking. He snorted two lines, and two more, and then grew worried that he might've done too much, so he poured some whiskey and drank it down. Wanting to busy himself with something, wanting not to think about how he felt, he began distractedly looking through the day's junk and occupant mail. Tucked in the middle of it all he found a postcard from someone his mother had been writing in Indiana, and two letters—one from the IRS, the contents of which he knew, and one from Duluth. He recognized the handwriting on the envelope, and tore it open.

Dear Cole:
This is not about the money, or anything we still have between us in the way of trouble, nor about Linda, except in a tangential way. I'm writing you to let you in on something that you should have expected all along, of course— though I have the feeling it will come as a surprise to you— I can hear you saying it, Cole, what a surprise it is, and I can hear Selena agreeing with you. What I'm writing you about is this: I've met a very nice man who wants to marry me, and I'm planning to take him up on it. He owns an antique record shop, and he's an older man—he has a grown son—but he loves me, and he's good for me, and he's very good with Linda. In fact, he wants to adopt Linda. And Cole, I think I'm going to go along with him. Because the fact is he's already supporting us in a way you haven't done for a long time now.

I told you once that I would never stop you from seeing Linda, as long as you kept up with your part of the agreement. Well, since my father has been providing the support you've failed so consistently to provide, and since I now have someone who wants to provide it as a husband and father, I think it's time for some things to change where you're concerned. I think you ought to remember it was trouble you made that got in the way of your seeing Linda. The fact is, I have to get on with life, and with raising Linda in the best possible circumstances. I'm sorry. I hope things are going better for you (I really do) and I hope you'll be able to see in your heart that this is the right thing to do. Try to understand.

Annie

The way he looked at it, he had been through a lot of misery trying to be the husband she wanted, trying to catch on in one job after another: years of a kind of aimless pitting of himself against overwhelming odds, of struggling with bosses and rules and people wanting him to do things he lacked the spirit for: wanting him to smile and bow at customers, or spend all day punching one button, or sit all night with nothing to read or listen to and no one to keep him company. Everything looked like bullshit to him, all the daily transactions, the common concerns of others, those people who drove to work early and came home late and watched television and were anxious about bills, insurance, savings accounts, the yearly vacation, going to church and having children—it had always seemed to him that such things were part of some big lie. He didn't know where this feeling came from; he hadn't questioned it or looked at it. The fact was, he couldn't bring himself to feel that anything at all was of much importance, finally. And finally this was what Annie hadn't been able to take; she hadn't understood his basic nature. His memory now was filled with images of her walking away from him, failing to support him or give him the benefit of the doubt; believing her father, a man filled with hate. There she was in his mind, taking his little girl out of his life, heading away from him, the baby staring at him over her shoulder, going going gone, simple as the truth. . . .

. . .

He got up from the table, and went outside again. It was all just restless motion. Outside, the air was sweet with the odor of honeysuckle and willow and pine, and the soft early evening breezes were stirring. The sky was deep blue and cloudless, only itself. In the road, a big white car passed, then seemed to slow. Gilbertson stood on the porch and thought of the IRS. The car had gone on around the curve, but a small rising cloud of dust there kept him watching; apparently it was turning around, and turning around fast. Instinct made him duck off the porch, and crouch down at the side of the house, where he could peer through the latticed wood over the crawl space and get a good, protected view of the road. It was the white car all right, pulling up on the other side of the hedge and stopping with a rocking motion, as two men got out. One of them was wearing a suit, the other a light gray cloth jacket and jeans. The one in the suit was heavy around the middle, and sloppy-looking, the rumpled pants of the suit giving him the appearance of someone at the end of a long workday. He had his tie thrust over his shoulder, and as he crossed the lawn, coming casually as though he were keeping an appointment, he took a quick glance back at the road, then brought a pistol out of the side pocket of the suit. Behind him, his companion had also produced one. They went together up onto the porch, and into the house.

"Hey, man," one of them called. "Hello. You got company."

Gilbertson crawled along the base of the house to the backyard, and then made a run for the shed, hearing his own footsteps as thundering announcements of his whereabouts. Any second he would be shot down. But nothing happened, and he had made it all the way to the small rise behind the shed. He lay on his stomach there, perhaps fifty feet from the back of the house. His own breathing made it difficult to hear anything, but he was too winded to hold his breath. The house was partly in the shade of a willow on one side, and through the drooping branches of this tree he could see the parked white car with its open doors. The car was idling, and its radio was on low—voices arguing. In the house came the sound of something breaking—a glass falling, or a small picture frame. Then it was silent again. Perhaps five minutes went by. And then one of the men—the one in the suit—came out off the porch in front and walked across the lawn to the car. Gilbertson watched him close the door on one side, then start around to the other. The man was tall, and looked very calm and competent. Gilbertson's heart was beating against the ground, and slowly he pushed back from his vantage point, trying to make his way along the ground away from the house. The ground was uneven and rough, but very soon he was in tall grass. A few yards to his right was a branch of the creek, and he got to it without any trouble. There, he could travel in either direction and be carried farther from the house; he decided to move toward Route 45, where the growth was thicker and the depth of the creekbed was steeper. His clothes were soaked with sweat, and with effort, and his chest and abdomen were besmirched in a fine coating of wet black earth. Everywhere was the smell of the stagnant water, the clammy feel of the place. He had scrambled almost wildly along the muddy overgrown bank, and now he crouched, quite still, in a pool of yellow-streaked water and slime, while mosquitoes buzzed around him and settled in his ears and on his neck and arms. He was waiting, wanting to listen, certain that one of them would be following his trail along the weed-choked branch. But there was nothing.

He waited there, in that state of wariness and expectation, until dark. Then he crawled through the mire to the culvert that ran under Route 45. Two trucks went over the culvert, then all was silent—just the distant sound of traffic in Champaign, and the whine of an approaching train out of the south. The tracks were parallel to Route 45, and when the train rolled past, its light going on ahead of it, Gilbertson climbed out of the ditch and hurried across the road, to the tall weeds there.

It was a freight train, many cars, going very slow. Gilbertson knelt by the side of the road and watched it, a moving shadow that kept coming out of the south. He had been staring at it for some time before the thought struck him that he could scramble up the railroad bed and latch on to one of the cars. He saw himself doing this, and then the last cars had come into sight, were even now gliding toward the place in the tracks parallel to where he was. It was going to be too late. He looked around at the road, stood up, and ran along the bank, starting up at an angle, gravel sliding off below him, slowing his ascent. The train cars were enormous; no amount of thinking could have prepared him for the sheer weight and size of them, or the suffocating iron smell of the wheels. But now he had come abreast of the second to last car, a big red boxcar with CHESSIE SYSTEM painted in large white letters on its side. He reached up, closed his fingers around the iron grip, and it was as though the train were pulling him now. One leg gave way, but he had ahold of the grip, and he hung on, trying to pull himself up. The gravel and ties below him were moving faster it seemed; the whole train seemed to have picked up speed, and abruptly the gravel gave way to air— the train car had come onto a bridge overlooking a farm road. In only a moment, there was gravel again, solid ground, but Gilbertson had let out a scream, had managed in his fright to pull himself up onto the ladder, so that he was standing now, riding along in the night toward Champaign.

The train slowed to a stop just as his car was crossing another trestle. He waited a moment, then climbed down. He was in the city, not far from Green Street. Behind him was the wide field of the Assembly Hall and the stadium of the University of Illinois. They made huge darker shades on the dark sky. The trestle gave off onto an open area of grass and asphalt—one of the university's parking lots. He crossed this, hurrying, wanting to keep out of the light. Everything—every bush, every small tree, every configuration of shadow and light—seemed to offer the possibility of ambush. Every car was something to duck away from.

When he reached Green Street, he felt safer; it was well lighted and crowded with traffic, with knots of students standing outside the bars and the cafes. He went along the sidewalk, heading deeper into the campus. For a moment, he entertained the thought of returning to the bar where he had spent part of the early afternoon, but then he changed his mind. What he needed was a place to hide until he could get his thoughts straight.

He had come to the boardinghouse where Alice Minneford lived. It was directly across the street from the Red Lion Lounge, where she worked as a waitress, usually into the early morning hours. You could stand in the window of her room in the house and look into the bar, and sometimes he had lain in her bed and watched her moving among the tables. Now he stood outside on the street, shivering in the wind, watching the windows under the blinking sign. There was a blood-colored glow in the light, a cast to it that made him vaguely sick. A few yards up the street, a group of young men were standing around under a street lamp, talking and jostling each other. From the bar came the low beating of drums, the screech of guitars, a rock band starting up. These people were assuming they would be all right; they were all going on as if nothing could harm them. After a few minutes, he crossed the street and ducked into the bushes that lined the front of the house. He was beginning to come apart. His hands shook, and he couldn't seem to manage them. In the dark of the pine-smelling bush, he crawled toward the side yard, and then bolted into the uncut grass there, around to the back stairs and up to the door of her room. He knocked and waited, itching, holding on, looking out into the night—the backyards of other houses, and their lighted windows. Everyone was at home. It was quiet. The wind murmured in the little spaces under the stairs. He couldn't believe it. His heart was hitting his chest bone, and there wasn't enough air. The night air was very bad, very much overwhelmed by the odor of creosote and engines. Finally, almost as if trying to break out of some suffocating element, he slipped the lock on the door with a jack-knife, and edged inside. The air here was no better—heavy with the faintly medicinal flower-fragrance of her perfume. It was as though she were hiding somewhere in the dark. He turned the overhead light on, saw that he was alone, then shut the light off again, feeling that it took away the breathable oxygen. He stood there gasping, trying to stop himself from unraveling. The afterimage of the room's clutter seemed to rush at him from every direction.

"Oh, Jesus," he said. "Alice?"

Nothing moved or stirred. Carefully, he moved through to the bathroom, turned the light on there, and washed his face. The mirror, behind flecks of toothpaste and smears of moisture, showed him his own strange, dirt-smudged countenance in the light. He wet his hands and ran them through his hair, and then he went on a search for anything she might have in the way of drugs. To his great joy he found a small bag of coke. He put some on his gums, and when he felt the rush, turned all the lights on, walked through her mess with a certain pro-prietary satisfaction. In her closet, he found some clothes he had left with her—a pair of jeans and a shirt, an old denim jacket. He donned the shirt and jeans, stashed the money in the elastic of the sock on his left foot at the ankle, then went into the bathroom and had some more of the coke, using the blue cap of a Bic pen. When he had ingested three hits, he put everything away, turned the lights off again, and lay on her bed, gazing out the window, watching the street. The perfume smell was very strong here, but it didn't bother him as much now; it was a vague irritation very much like the feeling she had engendered in him when he was with her. He had not thought about the possibility that over the months she might have taken up with someone else; he didn't let himself think about that now. He would not have believed she could attract men very easily, in any case: she was tall, ungainly, and she had something of a skin problem about which she was unnecessarily sensitive: it was not readily apparent that anything had gone wrong. Her eyes were clear and dark, a shade of brown that made him think of the deep tan of Annie's skin in summer. She had a pretty smile, a good laugh. At first there hadn't seemed to be anything she expected from anybody; she liked a good time. She had come south from Chicago, from parents who worried about her too much, and were always making up pretexts to call her on the telephone. Gilbertson had spoken to her mother once or twice, a gravel-voiced, distraught woman talking threats to him because he was divorced and older and because he was obviously on something.

He watched the street. Probably she would come home with somebody, another man, a new boyfriend. Somebody he couldn't handle. A college boy, or a farm kid with dirt under his fingernails. His imagination had already begun to believe in this possibility, and so the next matter for consideration was where to hide—he could get into her closet, or into the shower stall in the bathroom; he could crawl under her bed. He was trying to decide where to put himself, and then he was staring at the room in the dimness. The disheveled look of it—clothes draped over chairs and strewn on the small couch against the wall; dirty dishes on the table and in the sink; ashtrays overflowing—all gave him a sense of hopelessness and fatigue. It seemed too much to manage. He stared at the shapes and shadows around the bed, the flat gray walls, without paintings or photographs, the single light bulb hanging from the ceiling, the lamp on the table, tarnished and dusty, shade-peeling, crooked. And now he was hearing her climb the stairs. He lay still. She was fumbling with her keys outside the door, and she gave forth a little gasp— apparently she had noticed something. She turned the key in the lock and opened the door a slit, peered in.

"It's me," he said.

She came in and turned the overhead light on, then slammed the door and faced him. "Jesus Christ, Cole."

He sat up, swung his legs around, and set his feet on the floor. "Honey, I had nowhere else to go."

She put her purse on the table, slipped out of the sweater she wore. Underneath it, she had the waitressing uniform on—a sleeveless black dress with a wide red belt and gold buckle.

"Selena died," he said. And was surprised at his own pain, hearing the words.

"Who?"

"My mother."

"I never got to meet her." She moved to the refrigerator and brought out a beer. "You want something to drink? You want to slow down a little?"

"Not now."

Sitting at the table, she opened the beer, took a long drink from it, and, swallowing, gazed at him. There were faint smears of makeup on either side of the top of her nose, where she had rubbed the sleepiness out of her eyes. She gave a slight toss of her head, breathed something out, words he couldn't distinguish.

"What?" he said.

"Nothing. I said I knew it."

"Knew what?"

"Nothing. It's been months since you've been anywhere near me. I mean we were going along fine and then just like that you might as well be in interstellar space—no complaints, no arguments, nothing I can put my finger on. Boom. Nice knowing you. And now you come here all jazzed up and break into the place."

He got up from the bed and stood with his back to her at the window. Outside, in the blustery dark, the street looked desolate; everyone had gone from it. The wind shook the street lamps, and the light moved, seemed to swoon. He stared at the crossed shadows of the trees and tried to think. "They're taking my daughter away from me."

"I don't understand," Alice said.

He wiped his jaw and turned to look at her. "I need to think."

"Jesus," she said.

"I missed you," Gilbertson told her.

"Bullshit, Cole."

"It's true."

She took another long pull of the beer. "Look, I work for a living. I just put in six hours of hard labor and I'm not in the mood for a lot of fucking around. Two guys came into the Red Lion earlier today, and they were looking for you. Is that why you're here?"

"I need to stay out of sight awhile."

"Jesus, I knew it."

"Alice, I was coming to see you anyway. I'm lost."

"You're lost," she said. "Good one. You're here like a load on my mind, and you're lost."

"Listen," he said, sitting down on the edge of the bed. "I swear."

She said, "Get the hell off my bed."

He stood. "I just need a friend."

She lay down, one arm flung across her eyes. "I don't feel like it. Friends, no friends—sincerely yours and hugs and kisses. You know what I mean? I've got mustard and onions and pizza and beer in my breathing passages. I don't feel like it, and I don't feel like you. You know what the day before yesterday was?"

He waited.

She moved, looked at him, then lay back again. "Never mind." She lay there with her arm across her eyes.

"Those men were coming to fuck me up," he told her. "They were armed." His own rhetoric sounded strange to him. "They were looking to hurt me." She didn't move. He wasn't certain that she was even still awake. "Tenchley sent them."

"Jesus," she said. "Tenchley."

"I'm telling you. We had some trouble."

"Tenchley," she said. "Jesus. You mean those two assholes were killers? Them?"

"They came after me." He started to sit on the bed again, but she stopped him with a look.

"Take a chair."

He did so, and for a moment they were quiet.

"Well," she said. "they'll be back, then. Won't they?"

He was exhausted, and when he closed his eyes he could feel his nerves gearing up. The coke he had ingested wasn't enough. Looking at her again, he wasn't sure that this was the next moment.

"Right?" she said.

He didn't answer.

"God, Cole—did it ever strike you what a waste you are?" As she spoke, she got off the bed—she seemed to storm off it— and commenced straightening the room, moving around with a certain nervous alacrity, almost as though he weren't there and she was hurrying to get the place in order for his, or someone's, arrival. "Well, I'll tell you right now, I don't want any part of this. I'm not getting myself into this."

"Just forget it," he said. "You're right."

She was on the other side of the room now. She had started cramming dirty clothes into a laundry bag, and for a moment she paused, saying nothing, standing there considering, working something out in her mind. Her features had taken on the frowning, vaguely troubled look of concentration, and he knew the look. Then she shrugged her shoulders, and when she spoke again there was a kind of sadness in her voice. In some obscure way, he was gaining the upper hand.

She said. "I don't guess it makes much goddamn difference what I want, though, does it."

He waited a moment. "So what was the day before yesterday?"

"Nothing. I don't want to talk about it."

"Alice, I need us to be friends again."

"Is that what we were? Friends?"

"We were friendly, weren't we?"

"The day before yesterday was my birthday."

"Happy birthday," he said.

One side of her mouth moved, and she gave forth a little rueful laughing sound that was also somehow dismissive. "Jesus, not to be believed."

"I can't help what happened before," he said. "I'm in some shit, here. Come on, Alice. What do you want?"

"Do you know what I want?" she said.

He thought she would go on and tell him.

"Do you?"

"Tell me what it is," he said. "I'll try to do it if I can."

"I want you to get out of here and stay far away."

He reached down and brought the money in its tight roll out of his sock. "See this? This is seven hundred dollars, and I can get my hands on a lot more of it since Selena's gone. Maybe as much as ten or twelve thousand if I can get to the bank in the morning. We can take it all and head out of here, Alice." The idea had come to him like a lie he was telling, something to convince her to let him stay, and then it seemed to dawn on him that it was what he wanted; it was what the two of them could do. "Listen," he told her. "We can leave the state. They're taking my little girl away from me up in Minnesota. You see what I mean? We could go there and put a stop to it. We could start over."

She stared at him. He could see his own persuasion taking hold.

"Well?"

"Start over," she mumbled.

"We'd have some money to tide us over. We could get a place."

"Jesus Christ," she said. "Tenchley'll never believe I don't know where you are. I told those two assholes where you lived."

He was silent.

"I'll tell you something, Cole. Something amazing. People actually think you can see them, like anybody else. They actually think you believe they exist."

During the time they had spent together, it had been one of her propensities to analyze him in this nebulous, phenomenological way, as though he represented a species separate from her own. And if he could not have exactly described this tack of hers, he understood it clearly enough, and was immediately on guard, fidgeting, looking away from her. She seemed to be mulling over it all aloud: "Maybe it's the looks. Maybe that's it. Because you're so good to look at, even starting to get a beer gut, you look like—like somebody couldn't have dreamed you up. And all that goofing, too. It makes people believe you, I guess. It makes them believe you're possible."

There was nothing he could think of to tell her.

"I'm tired of being a character in your movie, Cole."

"What movie—what're you talking about."

"Let me finish."

"I want to know what you mean about the movie. What is that?"

"I can't believe nobody ever said this to you before."

"Why don't you get it off your chest," he said.

"I can't stay here, Cole. Think."

He said nothing.

She let the laundry bag fall, and simply seemed to wait.

"You're saying you'll come with me?"

"I'm saying I can't stay here. Not in this situation."

Gilbertson stood. He was holding the money in the palm of one hand, and with the other he opened the folds of it, looked at it, then creased it tight and bent down to put it back in his sock. When he had straightened, she was stuffing the clothes into the laundry bag again, not looking at him.

"I've got relatives in Duluth," she said. "My uncle Ellis lives there."

"You coming with me, then. Right?"

"Just like that."

"I don't think I can go back to the house—do you?"

She shook her head. "What about Tenchley?"

"He'll take what he wants from the house and think he's hurting me. And the house will belong to the IRS."

"Well," she said, "I'm not staying here and waiting for them to come back, that's for sure."

"Hey," said Gilbertson, "you can be a waitress anywhere."

A Ride on the Queen of the North

The man in the dark blue captain's uniform rang the bell, and then stood with his arms folded, his stance slightly piratical, while the big engine chuffed and the *Queen of the North* headed out onto Lake Superior. James Field and his granddaughter, Linda, were seated along the railing overlooking the big turning wheels, and they turned their attention from the captain to watch the swells of water cascade over the blades. It was cold here; a chilly column of air seemed to rise from the water. Field took his coat off and put it over the child's shoulders. He had promised her a ride on the *Queen of the North* before the weather turned, and because things had been confusing and awkward in the house, he had put it off. Now he was keeping that promise. The weather was already turning, though. He shivered, and, seeing this, she offered his coat back.

"I'm all right," he said. "You keep it."

"You're cold," Linda said.

"I'm fine." He put his arm around her. He would not put things off anymore. He would take her places, show her the good things to do and see in her native city, and he hadn't appreciated her enough. He hadn't used his time as well as he should have. He sat in the cold, moist rush of wind from the water and thought about how it was going to be when she and her mother lived elsewhere—how it would feel in the mornings, waking up to the quiet, the absence; just he and his sister again, heading through the days.

"You can feel the spray when the wind blows," Linda said. "We're getting soaked."

"I'm not cold," she said. "I like it."

"It's awful cold," Mr. Field said.

There were others along the railing—a young couple, and three high school boys in letter jackets and baseball caps. In the benches that were set in mid-deck, only an old woman sat, her coat wrapped tightly about her. She seemed not to be interested in the view of the shoreline, the sailing shadows of clouds on the fading, sunny distances of the water. She sat muttering to herself, and the high school boys seemed to be engaged in some sort of game involving her, making jokes about her, watching her with the rude expectancy of children playing a prank. Beyond this deck, elevated and reachable by stairs on either side, was the captain's deck. He stood there as though attending to a summer crowd, though the disheveled look of his coat and the unbuttoned collar of his shirt were clear enough indications that this was the last run of the season. He rang the bell again, turned the wheel. They were riding the choppy waters of the lake in a big circle, and would come back around to the North Shore.

"Granddad," Linda said.

He leaned down to listen.

"Can we come back?"

"Sure," he said.

"Can we come here every day next summer?"

"We'll come back a lot," he said.

"Every day?"

"We'll find other things to do, too."

"Every day?"

He looked at her. It was easy enough for adults to decide to get married again, and upset everything in a child's life. "Every day," he told her.

She shook her head. "I know we won't."

He kissed her hair. "You're going to wish I'd go home."

Apparently the strangeness of this remark was working on her as well. He pulled her closer, and felt sad.

"I want to *stay* home," she said.

"It's a change," he told her.

"Why can't Louis move in with us?"

The answer to this was simple enough, except that it could not be adequately explained to a girl eight years old. At least he didn't think it could. "Louis wants his own family. Your mother and you. He—he wants to provide for you and love you like a father."

She stared off at the water, and the high bluffs of the Minnesota side of the lake. Field reflected that she had not had much in the way of fatherly love.

"What're you thinking?" he said.

"Nothing."

"I'll come see you all the time," he told her.

She seemed to brighten a little. "Aunt Ellen, too?"

"Aunt Ellen, too."

The wind was very strong now, picking up a mist of the water churning in the wheels. It was beading up on her face and hair.

"You're getting soaked," he said. "So am I."

"It feels nice."

"Let's move to the other side, honey."

She was sitting back with her eyes closed. "I like it here."

A moment later, she said, "Louis is so much older than my father."

"Yes," he said, and waited for whatever she would tell him about this fact. But she just leaned forward a little, and looked over the side. The lake water below them was green and foamy, roiling.

"We're heading back now, aren't we," she said.

Again, he simply agreed.

Ahead was the shoreline of the city of Superior, a sprawling of houses and marinas and old buildings, and to the left, seeming to rise from the cloudy surface of the lake itself, the metal supports of the lifting bridge made their tall rickety shadow on the sky. The high bluffs of Duluth shone in a wild array of autumn colors.

"I wish it was last year," she said, staring off.

"Have to go along with things," he said lamely.

A little later, he took her hand and walked with her across the deck to the rows of benches where the old woman sat. The old woman, he saw, was not much older or younger than Field himself, and he had an odd moment of thinking of his wife, twenty-six years dead, as having lived to attain this age; how strange to think of her as old. It always brought him up with a jolt, and reminded him unpleasantly of his own age. He nodded at her, and she leaned down to speak to Linda.

"What's your name?"

Linda told her.

"A nice name."

"Thank you."

"How old are you?"

"Eight."

"My, my. Such a big girl."

"Not so big," Linda said.

Mr. Field wanted to hide her in the folds of the coat—his darling, so conscious of her size, her heaviness.

"You're a very grown-up young lady," the old woman said.

"I am that." Linda's eyes were bright, and showed the complication of worry, of hurt; it was in the quick movement of her gaze from point to point on the horizon.

"A very pretty girl," the old woman said to Mr. Field.

"Not me," said Linda.

"Of course you are," Field told her.

"I can read on a twelfth-grade level," she said to the old woman.

"Well, that is just wonderful."

Across from them, two of the high school boys were throwing the third one's cap around, keeping it from him. They were wrestling and tugging at each other.

"Boys," the old woman said.

Field said nothing.

"I raised five of them, you know. And they're all alike—wrestle and fight over everything, like a lot of bear cubs."

"I read *Gone With the Wind*," Linda said.

The woman looked at Field. "You let her read that?"

"Her mother—" Field began.

"My mother lets me read anything I want," said Linda.

When the woman looked at Field, he felt the need to shrug slightly, and explain. "My daughter likes to encourage her." He went on to say, as if to seek some sort of approval, "It's in the school library."

The woman shrugged. "Things change."

A moment later, she said, "You have boys?"

"Just the one daughter," Field answered.

She looked at Linda. "Do you have brothers?"

"No."

"All ruffians, the whole bunch of them. You can't control them."

"I never could control my daughter," Field said.

On the elevated deck, the captain rang the bell again, and signaled for the boys to sit down.

"You heard the man," said the woman. And it dawned on Mr. Field that these rough boys were with her. Apparently she had seen the recognition of this in his face, for she smiled at him and said, "Grandchildren."

"Yes," he answered, patting Linda's shoulders.

"I would like to have one granddaughter," said the woman. Mr. Field nodded in reply.

He hadn't realized how wet they'd gotten. When the boat pulled up to the dock and they got off, they found that they were leaving a trail of water across the parking lot to the car. He got an old army blanket out of the trunk and put it on the seat, but they soaked through it. The air here was warmer, but it was beginning to get dark, and the wind came breathing out of the north. He put the heater on, and held her while she shivered. The sun had dropped behind the hills to the west, and everything was gray. He drove slowly, feeling the heat come. She turned the radio on, then flicked it off again.

"Warmer?" he said.

"Yeah."

"I'm glad I have my granddaughter," he said, referring to what the woman had said.

Linda snuggled closer to him.

As he pulled the car along the curb in front of the house, she said, "Why don't you move in with mommy and Louis and me?"

"What would I do with Aunt Ellen?"

"She could move in, too."

"There wouldn't be any room," he said. "And what about Louis's boy?"

"Roger'll be my brother now, won't he."

"Your half brother."

She sat there with his coat wrapped about her shoulders. There were so many things a child had to keep up with in such arrangements. A child had to learn to divide herself up, just to get along. Apparently Linda was already thinking about having to separate from this house in whose shadow they were now parked.

"You'll see," Field said to her. "It's going to work out just fine."

"Can I come stay with you a lot?" she said.

"Of course you can."

She was quiet. Field wondered if perhaps she was not thinking about her father now, and quite suddenly he was struck by the possibility that she was worrying about the new situation in light of what she had already been through.

"Linda," he said. "We won't be far away, honey. Not ever."

She looked at him. Her face was still creased with worry.

"I promise you," he said.

She said, "I'm freezing."

She'd caught a chill. He went with her up the walk and onto the porch, and her mother opened the door, already wearing a bathrobe and slippers, her hair tied back in a red bandanna.

"It was crazy to go out there," Annie said. "Look at you. Look at both of you." She took Linda by the arm and smoothed the matted hair back from the child's forehead. "Come on, baby. I'll draw you a hot bath."

"I'm sorry," Field said.

"You too," his daughter told him. "Go get under a hot shower or something. I'll have Ellen make some hot chocolate and coffee."

"There's coffee," Ellen called from the kitchen.

Field was staring at Annie.

"What?" she said.

"Aren't you and Louis going out tonight?"

"I'm tired tonight," she said.

He went up to his own room and closed the door. Another door on the opposite side of the room led into a small bath, and he padded in there, started the hot water running and steaming. He was past sixty, and he still liked to stand and watch the steam displace him in the mirror. There were many things he did idly, without thinking about them, and perhaps Annie was right that his old, staid, banker's reserve was unnatural.

He undressed, adjusted the flow of water, and stepped into the shower. So many things were going to happen so fast. Standing under the hot steam of water, he let his mind wander to Cole Gilbertson. It was never quite possible to forget him, or to forget that he was still somewhere out there in the huge distances of the plains, the wide shade of the coming night.

He turned the water off, stepped out, and pulled a towel from the rack. It was easy enough to imagine Gilbertson watching the house, or standing in the foyer downstairs, waiting to talk to him.

Annie knocked on his door. "Are you okay?"

"Sure," he said.

"No chill?"

"I'll live."

"Aunt Ellen says dinner's ready."

"I thought I was going to cook Chinese," Mr. Field said.

"I guess not."

He put a robe on and opened the door. "You're not mad at me are you, Annie?"

"I'm just afraid she'll get sick now," Annie said.

Linda was lying under an electric blanket on the sofa down in the living room. He kissed the side of her face, noted that she was still trembling, and wondered if it might be more nervousness than the chill. In the kitchen, his sister, Ellen, was putting hamburgers on a tray for Linda.

"Why not give her one, and see if she wants another later," he said.

"She asked for two."

He went back through to the living room, where Annie was working to start a fire in the fireplace. "It's not that cold out yet, is it?"

"It's going to freeze tonight," she said.

He thought she looked pale in the light. "Are *you* feeling all right?" he asked.

"I'm fine," she told him. But she seemed agitated by the question.

"Did I say something wrong?"

She gave him a look. "Go eat."

"You're not eating?"

"I'm tired. I'm going to bed."

"You *do* look pale," Mr. Field said.

She waved this away, and a moment later she had taken a book with her and gone upstairs. Field watched Ellen give the tray of food to Linda, who hadn't moved from the sofa. Ellen put the television on, then went back into the kitchen. He followed.

"So," he said.

"You want cheese on your hamburger?" she asked.

"Does Annie look pale to you?"

Ellen paused. "I think she's fighting something off. She's tired a lot."

He sat down to the meal she had prepared. Out the window at his side, the far lights of Superior winked in and out of the moving branches of the trees. Tomorrow, they would all be bare.

Arriving

The bank manager at Selena's savings and loan, a man with fluffy white tufts of hair above his ears and little whiskerlike tufts jutting from his nose, told Gilbertson that it was his regretful duty to have to inform him that the account was no longer accessible to him. The IRS had notified the bank of a lien on all property and assets of Selena H. Gilbertson. Nothing could be done about it. There was no one else to speak to about it. Gilbertson would have to contact the IRS, work it out with them. Outside, in the pouring rain, he tried the card in the magic machine, and the machine took the card. He cursed, turned to see Alice staring at him from the front seat of her car, like a wife. When he got in, she said, "Great. Twelve thousand dollars. So where is it?"

"Goddamn this government," he said, hitting the steering wheel. Then he opened the window and shouted into the rain. "I hate the fucking government of the United States!" When he had rolled the window up, he shifted around in the seat to see her sitting there staring at him. He put the car in gear. "Well, they damn sure won't get seven hundred of it."

"Great," she said.

They drove back to Green Street, but one of the men from

Tenchley was standing out in front of the Red Lion, and Gilbertson drove on.

"Oh, that's just wonderful," Alice said. "How the hell am I going to get my things? I don't even have a toothbrush."

"You should've packed before we went on to the bank," Gilbertson told her. "Jesus." He was heading north. He had put some of her coke on his gums, but he wanted a little more. The road ahead was all rain and puddles of rain, shimmering with the lighted reflections of the backs of cars and the fluorescent windows of the buildings along Green Street, and the wipers were smearing the glass of the windshield. He held tight to the wheel, peering out, wanting the coke and feeling her peevishness at his side. When they reached Lincoln Avenue, he turned left, toward the interstate, and there was less traffic. She had hunched down in the seat, her arms folded, staring out at the sidewalk and the tall aluminum-sided dormitories in their fields of drenched grass and fall flowers. He pulled into a gas station near the interstate and, reaching for his coat, in which he had stashed her supply of coke, started out of the car.

"Where're you going?" she asked.

"Wait here."

The bathroom walls were covered with graffiti and grease, and the floor was littered with piles of dried toilet paper. There was the suffocating, urinous odor of months of neglect. He sat on the commode with the lid down, and brought the coke out. It became necessary to hurry, because someone was apparently outside, waiting to use the facility. He took two hits, then rubbed the residue on his gums. When he opened the door, he thought of Tenchley's men, but it was just a boy in a baseball cap with a badge pinned to the bill. The boy looked at him, and seemed to be paying a sort of unusual attention, as though there were something obviously wrong with his clothing or his stance.

"Well?" he said.

"Are you through?" said the boy impatiently.

Gilbertson stepped past him, and ambled back to the car. She was still sitting with her arms folded tight, and she didn't move when he got in. "So," he said.

"How much is left?" she asked.

"How much what?"

"Don't shit me, Cole."

"There's some. You want some?"

"I know there's some. It's my little stash, right?"

"You want some or not?"

She shook her head. "I think I should drive."

He put the car in gear and pulled out into the road. "No way," he said. The rain was letting up. There was just a tiny drizzle now on the windshield. Off to the north, great blue holes had opened in the cloud cover, the sun pouring through them in soft, liquid shafts of gold, and Gilbertson, driving toward all this, thought of psalms and churches and his mother's old belief in visible manifestations of the love of God for humankind. He felt young now, confident, invincible, as though somehow the gravity around him had failed, and made him feather-light. Alice began talking, at first bitterly about birthdays, and the failures of observance in love and friendship. Evidently she had experienced a rough time on her job, where no one seemed to care much about anyone else. The miles rolled away and he pretended to listen, and gradually the notes in her voice grew lighter. She even laughed once or twice. His mind was mostly filled with images of his ex-wife and baby: he was heading back to them, and he felt imbued with an almost breathless sense that he was going to accomplish some final, overwhelming thing, though he had no idea at all what it might be.

"You're not hearing me," Alice said.

"Yes, I am."

"All right—what did I just say?"

"You've been talking for the last seventy miles."

"I asked you what I just said."

"I don't remember."

"You don't remember because you didn't hear it. I said I don't want to stop and see my mother in Chicago."

"Did I say we were stopping?"

"You'd stop if I wanted to, wouldn't you?"

He didn't feel like talking. He didn't feel like listening to her. She had begun to go on about wanting to leave Champaign and feeling liberated, even from the things she'd accumulated over the time of her residence there. She started naming these things: a record player, a lamp, a few books, some clothes. A table and a bed. A chest of drawers. This car. She told him all this, reciting it all, counting off on her fingers, her voice taking on an odd, formal quality, as though she were speaking into a microphone to strangers. As if this were an occasion for her to confess everything about herself: and now she began describing her reasons for moving south in the first place—something about worry and morbid expectations, her mother's nervous obsessive devotion—and for not wanting to stop in Chicago. He stared out at the road, growing more restless all the time, and finally he turned the radio on.

"I'm curious," she said, "what do you want me along for?"

He had turned the radio up loud.

"I might as well be alone," she said.

They rode in the din of the radio. Country music. From time to time she sang along with one of the songs: "Blind Love" and "Heart of Mine." She brought cigarettes out of her purse and smoked, and then she used the rearview mirror to brush and primp her hair. It was getting dark. Reaching into her purse again, she looked at him with one raised eyebrow and said, "You know what I've got in here?"

He regarded her for a few seconds, then stared out at the road.

"Well?"

"Money."

"Ha."

He said nothing.

"That little stash isn't everything."

"Pills," he said, "Right?" She had always taken a lot of different kinds of pills.

"Pills," she said. "Sure. And some more blow, too."

Gilbertson looked at her.

"I've got it in some gift wrapping paper," she said. "It needs to be chopped."

"We're rich," said Gilbertson.

"I've had it for a month," she told him. "I haven't been using it. I've been keeping it around."

He wondered if she expected him to say anything in particular in answer to this, and before he could think of anything, she said, "I've been walking away from that kind of life, Cole."

He said, "You've been carrying it around with you."

"I packed it," she said. "For you."

He was silent. She seemed to be waiting for him to speak. "What do you want me to say?" he asked.

"You could thank me."

"I thank you from the bottom of my heart."

Somewhere above Madison, after the second stop for gas, he pulled over and asked her to drive, which she did with a kind of eagerness, like a girl getting to do so for the first time. In her excitement she began talking about herself again, telling him about some of the men she'd gone out with in the time he had neglected her. She used this word, and he lighted a cigarette, blew smoke at the windshield, feeling held back and crowded. When he was finished with the cigarette, he folded his arms and sank down in the seat, wanting to feign sleep. But sleep had come. When he awoke, they were sitting in front of her uncle's house in Superior, and no one was home. Gilbertson looked out and saw fat shrubs on either side of a closed, darkened entryway, and tall, curtained windows. The roof of the house was outlined in a bank of snowy clouds through the top edges of which the moon shone.

"We'll go down to Park Point," she said.

"What's in Park Point?"

"I don't know. The lake. It's something to do. I always loved to go there when I was a kid."

"Let's get a room."

"We can stay here. There's no need to spend money on a room. We're going to need money." She had pulled out, and was heading back down the road.

"Jesus," he said. "I'm tired."

"You slept four hours."

"I'm in need of a little something."

"We'll get ripped at the beach," she said.

At last, he talked her into renting a room in a motel. The one he directed her to was familiar, and hadn't changed much over the years. It was a row of cottages connected by a sidewalk in a semicircle, perched on the highest hill in Duluth, overlooking the widening prospect of the two cities skirting St. Louis Bay and the harbor. Each cottage was furnished with two queen-sized beds, a table and chairs, and a wide, low bureau with a mirror attached to it. There was a color television set, with a faint, snowy signal from a local channel; everything else was apparently scrambled.

"Our own little ivy-covered house," she said, falling across the bed.

They had both done some of the coke. He had brought it out, and she'd said, "Let me have a little." This was of concern to him, since if they were both going to be using it the supply would run out more quickly, and in any case, he was restless. He put the room key in his pocket and stood in the doorway.

"What're you doing?" she said.

"You sleep. I'm going to drive around a little."

"You're not going to leave me here without any money," she said.

"You going to spend it in your sleep?"

She stared at him.

"Okay," he said, and took out the bills. He gave her a twenty.

"Give me another one," she said.

He did so. "You wouldn't know where we can score some blow, would you?"

She shook her head, stuffing the bills in her blouse. "I'm coming with you."

"Do you know someplace?"

"I wasn't doing that stuff when I lived here."

"You lived here?"

"Summers. I told you in the car."

"I'll be back," he said.

"If you don't—" she began. She had lowered her head, and was looking at him as if to threaten him.

He closed the door on that look.

In the car, he took what was left in the vial of coke—the residue was all—and rubbed it on his gums. It wouldn't nearly be enough. The streets were quiet, and familiar, and he drove down to the harbor, looking at everything, this place where he had come fresh out of the army, having picked the name off the map and headed here with some obscure idea of going on to Canada, though—back then—he'd had a friend he knew from basic training, who gave him a room to sleep in, and introduced him to Annie Field.

What he did, finally, on this night, was make his slow way back to the street in front of her house, and park there across the road, watching the front door and the porch, though it was still a long time before daybreak. The windows were dark. One light burned somewhere off in one of the rooms facing away from where he was. He waited, thinking about his daughter and about Annie still living in the house. Then he drove off, heading back across to Superior. He thought for a while of going on, going anywhere away, hauling the trouble of himself—his condition, his badness, and the bad men who were probably still pursuing him—someplace away from where his little girl now lived her life. His heart was pounding in his chest, and it was clear that he was going to need some whiskey to calm himself down.

He slowed the car; he had been gripping the steering wheel so hard it hurt his palms. Before him the road curved off into a confusion of lights and crossing streets and signs. A little to the left, on the other side of the exit ramp from the bridge into the city, was a bar he had liked to spend time in during the days when he lived here. It was called The Empire. He took the turn toward it, toward the far-off glow of the neon facade, and when he got to the parking lot, saw that it was a different place now. A family restaurant. Above a glass wall, the absurd figure of a smiling steer sat with legs crossed and a knife and fork in its front hoofs. The sign blinked at him, and there seemed something angry, almost sinister, in the smile of the cartoon steer. He drove on, gripping the wheel, and finally he came to a side street, on the corner of which was a bar. Steve's. He parked the car in front of the place and got out. It was quiet. He could hear the faint sound of the jukebox. The windows were red, and a Miller High Life sign shone in the window. The sign buzzed, and made him think of insects and summer nights. Inside was a low-ceilinged room with booths crowding the walls on either side, and the bar itself ranged along the back. Two women sat in a booth nearest the door, and several men were seated at the bar. Gilbertson walked over and stood near the group of men, pretending an interest in the thicket of shelved bottles across from him. The men were talking about the World Series. They were all wearing Minnesota Twins T-shirts and baseball caps, and they were a little drunk. Gilbertson ordered a bourbon from the bartender, who looked vaguely familiar, and sat quietly drinking for a few minutes. Finally, when one of the men glanced at him, he said, "I'm not from around here."

"Hey," the man said. "Great."

"You?"

"No, man—I'm not from around here either."

"So I guess we're strangers," Gilbertson said. He was beginning to feel very bad, and he drank the rest of his whiskey in a gulp. When the bartender looked at him, he nodded, tried to sit quite still while the bartender fixed him another.

The other man had turned to his friends. "Says he's not from around here."

One of them, a small, wiry, dark-haired, almost effeminate-looking man, leaned toward him from the other end of the bar and said, "Hey, man—you look like someone I know."

"Who's that." Gilbertson managed to raise his drink and smile at him.

"Guy name of Trig. Hey, you guys know Trig."

"Trig," the first one said. "Hell, man—Trig is ugly."

"Would Trig know where I could score some blow?" Gilbertson asked them.

Now they stared at him. It seemed to Gilbertson that, save the small, effeminate one, they were all blond and tan, and blue-eyed. The blond hair stood out on their arms, and showed above the collar-line of their T-shirts.

"Blow?" the little one said.

Gilbertson smiled again. "Sure."

"Blow."

"That's right."

"You hear this, fellas? Man says he wants to score some blow."

"Blow," said the first one. "No kidding."

"You mean, like, blow?" the little one said to Gilbertson.

"Okay," he said. "Thanks anyway."

"Man, I mean you are not talking about weed, right?"

Gilbertson shook his head. "Naw, man. That stuff's bad for your lungs, right?"

The other seemed to ponder this a moment. Then his face broke into a smile. "Oh, yeah—right, man. What you want is blow, as in blow—right?"

"Right."

"And say you found out where you could score some—you got the money for it. Right?"

Gilbertson tried a joke: "I was sort of hoping I could depend on friendliness and generosity."

The other stared at him. They were all staring at him. Then the small one's face broke into a smile again. "Oh, that's great. Friendliness. I like that. No, I *love* that, man. I really do."

"Friendliness," Gilbertson said, and lifted his glass again.

"Hey, friendliness. Right. And let's not forget generosity."

"Right."

"Man, where exactly are you from?"

"All over," said Gilbertson.

"Yeah. A lot of friendliness and generosity, too, huh?"

"Everywhere I go."

"Sunshine and light," the little man said.

"Friendliness and hospitality," said Gilbertson. He ordered another whiskey, and drank part of it, feeling their eyes on him. Finally he was feeling calm enough that he might be able to contend with whatever this was going to be. "So," he said, "I guess even if I had some money for it, there's nothing shaking. Because it just so happens that I can get my hands on some funds."

"You came to the wrong place," the little man said. He seemed surly now, only vaguely interested.

"Just asking," Gilbertson told him.

"Listen," said the little man, "say I knew somebody who would know where some goods might be hiding?"

"That might be interesting."

"I mean, we're all clean upstanding citizens. But say I could get a little dope."

"Naw, man. No dope."

"You desire something very specific."

"Right. If it's available." Cole kept smiling at him.

"Well, I'll tell you what. See, we're all police officers, sort of. Off duty, you know."

"You're joking," Gilbertson said. "Right?"

"Joking. Right—yeah. That's good."

"You don't look big enough to be a cop."

"Isn't that something," the little man said.

"But you are, right?"

"Hey, right."

"Right," Gilbertson said.

"And you know they don't like it in city hall when we pass shit around to the citizens."

"Absolutely."

"You see how embarrassing it could get."

"No question," said Gilbertson.

"So what if we just search your car for you or something like that?"

"No problem, man."

The other man shook his head and smiled. "Hell, I've got a better idea. You know, because I don't feel like the hassle tonight. Not tonight, celebrating and all, you know how it is. So what about this." He put his arm around Gilbertson's neck and began walking him toward the door. Then he stopped. "You pay for your drinks?"

"No."

And the man walked him back to the bar. Gilbertson put a twenty on the smooth, polished surface.

"Very generous."

"I'm supposed to get some change," said Gilbertson.

The others laughed, and the one with the arm over his neck squeezed, cutting his air off for a moment. "Man, what about generosity and friendship?"

"It's not fair," Gilbertson choked the words. The others were all around him now, and so he could only stand there and take it. The little man held him a moment longer, while they all laughed, then gave him a little shove toward the door. "What about this now," he said. "What about you take your useless ass out of here and just get about as far away from this region of the country as you can get? Say, in the spirit of friendship and generosity."

Gilbertson held his neck, standing between two booths, looking at them.

"Well?" the little man said.

"I'm going," he told them.

"If we see you around, man, we're going to put you away, all right?"

Gilbertson pushed out into the night. He felt the need to hurry now, felt them thinking of following him, troubling him further. He got into the car and got it started and was on his way, throwing gravel, and he made several turns in order to make any attempt to chase him implausible. When he got out into the country he was careful not to speed, careful to look casual, on his way to a simple and reasonable destination. But the whiskey had worked something other than calm on him, even as the trouble began in the bar, and his blood was coursing through the veins of his face and neck. He was heading south. The signs said the names of towns in Wisconsin. At a wider place in the road, he turned the car around, and pulled over to try and get ahold of himself. He could feel his eyes beginning to swell as if with the sudden expanding force of something hot in his soul. Oddly, he thought of the hours of the night when his father came home drunk and wanted to talk to him. His father would wake the house up, wake Selena up, wanting to expound his opinions of the world and the goings-on in the newspaper. It was always the goings-on in the newspaper that got him started. He would come thudding into the house and when Selena didn't want to talk, he'd wake Cole up. There were things he wanted to teach him. He would sit the boy down in the kitchen and begin talking to him, pacing back and forth in the room, making enormous shadows, angry, giving forth rhetoric and gesticulation and the wrath of his disagreement with the goings-on. He wanted his son to be involved in the world; wanted to raise him a man of affairs, he said. None of this farm talk for him or for his boy. And the talk went on; the boy was someone to listen to him. The boy fought sleep with his whole being, fearful of displeasing him, and in the end he simply couldn't keep awake. The voice of his father terrified him, and even so he was put to sleep by it. Every time. Sleep stole over him like death, a thing no one could stop, no amount of will or fear or resisting could prevent.

Thinking about him in the hours near dawn, parked on the side of Highway 53 in Wisconsin, Gilbertson began to cry. Other cars came by him, and the lights went on into the grayness ahead, illuminating trees and tall fronds and stones. Then it would be dark again. But light was stealing into the sky like stealth itself. He got himself back onto the road and headed into the harbor, and was sitting at a stoplight when a police car pulled alongside him. The two cars idled quietly. Gilbertson could hear the policeman's radio hissing with static. He held the wheel, and when the light changed, he let the policeman pull ahead.

Something was in the process of snapping inside him; it was breaking, the last straw, the whole goddamned thing, his life, his bad luck, and the big lie always killing the warmth in his heart, and all the bullshit about which he could only stew in this helpless, searing rage.

He drove back to the motel, let himself into the room where Alice slept with her mouth wide open and her legs and arms flung across the bed. He got into her purse, being stealthy, looking for the gift wrapping paper. She had taken some pills. Several of them were lying out on the bureau against the wall. He found the coke and he took it into the bathroom and closed the door. Sitting on the edge of the bathtub, he opened the folds of brightly colored paper, and poured a little of the powder out

on the closed toilet seat. It was a disappointing amount. His
hands shook. There wasn't anything to chop it with. Out in the
room, he went through her purse again, and found a little metal
nail file. He got it to work as well as it would, and ingested
what amounted to a fairly large dose. The rush took a strange
long time getting to him. And then it kicked in, sending him
off. He had performed everything with precision, he told himself, sitting there with his hands over his face. His whole mind
was burning. It was all one thing, extending outward like ra-
diance from the source of illumination; James Field had ruined
him; James Field's hatred had wrung everything down. He
looked at this thought in his mind, and then got to his feet,
folded the wrapping paper and stashed it in his pocket, wiped
up the evidence and put it on his gums, ran water in the sink
and stood gazing at it. A moment later, he turned it off, coughed,
flushed the toilet, then opened the door and stepped out. The
sun was pouring through the window. Alice lay sprawled in
sleep. He opened the nearly transparent curtain and looked
through the blinding part of the morning to the shadows of the
trees across the road, thinking of himself as a man who had
come to claim what was rightfully his: a wife, a child.

Certain Testimony

I have a memory of buying a dozen roses from a sidewalk vendor on Lake View. Late summer, 1960. A presidential campaign going on, and one could feel that everything was about to change. I was just thirty-three, and I remember being happy and confident in the clear, uncomplicated way that the young can be. It was a brilliant, sunny day, and all along Park Point there were beach umbrellas and crowds of bathers lying on their blankets or floundering in the cold shallows of the lake. I remarked to the sidewalk vendor that Park Point, from this distance and from this high angle, could be Miami Beach. "Look how white the sand is," I said. I had a little baby daughter, and a wife I loved. I was thinking about having more children, someday sitting at a table rounded with the people we had given to the world, though of course it wasn't as intellectual as all that: I wanted a large family. I wanted to live long enough to see them all grown. I had no reason to believe I would not be granted this wish. On this day, my wife was to come home from the hospital after a routine tonsillectomy. I had already stocked the freezer with her favorite flavors of ice cream—strawberry and peach and butter almond. I had been teasing her for days, talking to her in the babble of babies, because *she was having to get this child's operation. Even the doctor—a nice Scottish gentleman who liked to play to his patients, and who had a good and loving soul—had teased her about it, and about all the ice cream she was going to be eating. I was on my way over to the hospital to pick her up, and I had bought the roses on an impulse.*

I remember how it felt to be a man in love, at the beginning of things. The day shone like a new coin, and I walked up the street in the soft breezes, feeling as though something in my good mood had produced them, or were contributing to them: it has occurred to me that in extremes of happiness or pain, all things appear to be linked somehow, like folds of the same cloth.

I strolled whistling with my new-bought roses into the hospital, and down the wide, clean corridor to my wife's room on the first floor—and found two nurses wrapping her body in a sheet.

They stood there with her half turned on the bed, the cloth not quite covering her face yet.

"Mr. Field," one of them said. She was the younger one, no more than twenty years old. She held on, while the other one stepped away from the bed.

"Sir," this one said, advancing on me. I remember that I thought it strange, she had wrinkles in the skin just below her ears. "Sir," she said, "if you'll just come with me."

I let the roses drop to the floor, and the nurse had now put her hands on my arms. She was talking to me, though I couldn't make out what she meant. I was looking at my wife's face—the bluish cast to it, and the eyes not quite holding shut. .

"Happens so rarely," the nurse was saying to me, trying to move out of the room. ". . . sthetic shock. So sorry . . ." Something of the kind: there was pity and horror and a barren kind of sorrow in her voice. She had seen this sort of thing before, perhaps, no matter how rare she said it was.

I pulled myself from her grip and stepped back. And then, in some abrupt shift of position and stance that I did not perceive, I found myself on the other side of the bed, facing both of them, holding my wife away from them. I just seemed to wake up there, holding tight, and seeing nearby the signs of some violence. Apparently, I had knocked a chair over. There was broken glass on the floor at my feet.

"Get out," I said to them.

"I'm so sorry," the older one was saying, and the younger one was pulling at her arm.

"Get out!" I screamed. And when they were gone I went and put a chair under the doorknob, so that I could be alone. I remember that I stood for a long time in the room without going near her. There were people outside the door, and there was a general uproar that I came to realize was me. I broke a few more things. I stood at the window and looked out on a parking lot and a row of dumpsters, and at that sky with its perfect white clouds as though God were brandishing them at me. Then I turned and went to the bed and began to understand the facts of the matter, which were that I was at the beginning of something awful, and I began to cry, holding her. I didn't even know her. It came to me there that I hadn't even had the opportunity to really get to know her, twenty-nine years old, with dark, dark eyes, and a gorgeous note in her laughter and in her voice; a lovely young women with a clear, straight-on way of looking at you, and with soft features—pretty and intelligent and possessed of an affectionate, sympathetic heart. I sat on the bed and held her, and bellowed, and heard the efforts of the hospital staff to get me to open the door. Heard them begin the process of breaking it down. And even when they had, they had to wait for me to let go of her. They had to wait for my anger to die down. . . .

That Thursday night, late, I stopped reading and listened to the sounds: Annie was moving around in her room. Linda was stirring in her bed, warm at last, turning the pages of a book. Ellen was playing her music. Often enough, I was the last person awake in my house, and I almost always knew what everyone else was doing. It wasn't as though I made it my business to know, but when you have lived in a house for more than thirty years, you come to know its little shifts and sounds. I had come to like the knowledge of others awake, contesting with their own nighttime worries, or indulging in their own nighttime fancies: this night, I was wakeful because in a way the whole house was wakeful.

I heard Annie go down for more milk, and when she was quiet, I heard Ellen come out and start down. Normally, my sister sleeps deeply, with her earphones attached and Muzak playing softly through her dreams. When she went back to bed I waited a minute, then snuck out into the hall and listened at my granddaughter's door. I opened it carefully, and something resisted me. I thought for a moment that she might be leaning on the other side; but it was a bath towel. I had been after her about picking up after herself, the way I used to get after her mother about it; but lately I had tried not to say much. They were leaving: in a few weeks, after the wedding, they would be living with Louis Wolfe. The job, I said to myself, was not going to be mine to do anymore. My sister had taken to explaining for me, as though I needed instruction about it, that I was going to be free to travel a little, to have some of the leisure time I deserved; I could enter my retirement years without the encumberment of a family. And my answer to this—not quite joking—was that if Annie were marrying a man twice her age merely to do me the favor of guaranteeing my freedom after sixty-five, I wasn't interested in the favor. I was careful not to parade such feelings in front of Annie, of course, since I had in fact already presented her with my objections and received my answer—with a look that said: not again. *We have already been through this,* my daughter said with a little elevation of her left eyebrow and an abrupt set to her lips, as though she were steeling herself for a fight. Well, we would not fight.

Now I picked up the bath towel—it was dry—and stood for a moment watching my granddaughter sleep. The book was open, facedown on her chest, and her hands were folded across the top of it. I moved her hands, and she stretched, rolled over just as I got the book out. Settling, she moaned in the back of her throat, was quiet. *Oh, my girl.* I bent down and lightly kissed the moist side of her face, then turned the light out and left the room. Alone in the hall, I thought of the day when they would leave—I know: I was tightening the screws of my own pain—and finally I snuck down to the kitchen, thinking I'd have a drink of bourbon. The bottle was in the cabinet above the refrigerator. I brought it down, set it on the table in the breakfast nook, fetched a shot glass from the hutch in the dining room, and I was ready.

It was past one o'clock.

I poured a little into the bottom of the shot glass, sipped it down. I was being very careful, knowing what a bad mixture sadness and alcohol were for me. The whiskey burned unpleasantly, and I put the bottle away.

Climbing the stairs again, I had another unexpected moment of feeling the house as it would be when my sister and I were alone in it again. It was always coming up behind me to surprise me. It burned in my chest like the whiskey. Again, I listened at Linda's door, and finally I paused at my own, having heard movement in the house. Annie was up. I came close to knocking on her door, but decided against it, finally. Whatever we could say to each other at this hour could be said in the morning, and if she had wanted to talk, she would have opened the door at the sound of me in the hallway.

．　．　．

When I brought Cole into the house the first time, he was just out of the army, and so they talked about that. He wanted to know what Cole's plans were: college, a field of study, a career. He said: "They have the GI bill now. Without college, there's not much out there." Cole listened, looked almost eager. Yes, sir. Yes, sir. He couldn't really identify for himself what his interest might be, and he was very polite and sweet—a bright young man, beautifully put together, with the kind of charm you read about.

"Well," my father wanted to know, "what're you interested in right now?"

"Right now?" Cole said, and, smiling that crooked boy's smile, looked at me. "I guess you could say I'm interested in having a good time, basically."

I guess after a stint in the army, you've earned that," my father said.

"Actually I never thought of it that way," said Cole.

"What way?"

"That a good time had to be earned."

"I hate to sound like a puritan," my father said, "but everything's got its cost."

"Daddy was in the army, too," I said. I was nineteen, and head over heels.

"What was that like?" Cole said.

My father looked at him. "What was it like?"

"Did you see any action?"

"I served during Korea. But I didn't go overseas."

"Must've been nice," said Cole.

"I wanted to go," my father said.

"You must've been crazy."

I remember that he laughed at this, looking at Cole and laughing, I thought, with him. But the rest of the evening was odd, and when I came in from seeing Cole off, we went very quietly about the business of cleaning the dishes and the dirty ashes from Cole's cigarettes, and then he went on up to his room. I waited awhile, then went up and stood leaning on the frame of the bedroom door, *watching him lie there on his side, his back to me. In the bath of light from his lamp the hair on his arms was gold. He had a book open and was staring at it, but of course he could see me out of the corner of his eye. "Well?" I said.*

He looked at me. "What?"

"Are you going to tell me what's wrong?"

"Nothing," he said. "What's wrong with you?"

"I'm fine," I said. "I couldn't be better."

"Well, then, that's fine, isn't it."

"Something's wrong," I said.

"Nothing's wrong."

"You didn't like him, did you."

"Annie, what are your plans?"

"What do you mean, what are my plans? Are you asking if my intentions are honorable, for God's sake?"

He was looking at me over his shoulder. "I'm asking what your plans are."

"I don't know what my plans are. What's the matter with you?"

"Look," he said, "just don't—jump into anything, all right?"

"I'm thinking of jumping into bed with him," I said. "He's gorgeous and interesting, and I'm falling in love with him."

He moved on the bed and arranged the pillows, and I stood square in the doorway, in the light from the hall. My shadow was all over the room. It struck me that I had told him the truth, and that it had been something like an assault, something I meant to hurt him with. "You'll have to forgive me," he said. "It's just my nature to worry—and to project, and frankly I don't see much of a future for that boy. I don't suppose I can talk you into going slow."

"God," I said, and left him there. And then that night, very late, Cole called the house. He wanted to talk to me, wanted, I suppose, to reassure himself about the way the evening had gone; he was drunk, and it was my father who answered the phone. "You're drunk, young man. Go home and sleep it off. Annie's asleep." I had opened my bedroom door and was staring at him, just a shape off in the dark of the hallway.

"Daddy?" I said. I couldn't make out the features of his face. But then he spoke, and I didn't have to.

"That was your gorgeous, interesting friend, and he sounded neither gorgeous nor very goddamned interesting."

The phone rang again. He picked it up. "Young man," he said. Then he was listening.

"Daddy," I said, "let me talk to him."

"Well, now, Cole—let me tell you something. As long as my daughter lives in this house she'll abide by the rules—and one of the rules is no phone calls in the middle of the night from stupid, drunken babies who can't hold their liquor. And you are absolutely right about it, boy, to sense my disapproval." He slammed the phone down again.

"Daddy," I said.

"Do you know what your gorgeous friend had to tell me?"

I waited. Our eyes were accustomed to the darkness, and still we were like two gray shades at either end of the hallway.

"He thinks he might want to get married. Now. He thinks he might want to drive to Illinois and get married and he senses my disapproval."

I said nothing.

"Annie, are you talking about marriage now? You haven't even known him a month yet."

"We've talked about it," I said.

"I went with your mother for three years before I married her."

"That was you—and anyway I can't help that."

"What kind of answer are you giving me here? You can't help it. Is that our life together now? You can't help it?"

"I don't want to talk about it now," I said. "It's late. I'm going to bed."

"Annie, don't throw yourself away."

"I haven't said I was going to do anything, have I?"

"Jesus Christ," he said, and went into his room and closed the door.

Later that week, in a motel room off Highway 51, Cole and I

consummated things. And did cocaine together. It was a party. Glory
and clouds trailing shafts of sunlight, Cole said, laughing, lying back
on the bed with his eyes wide and luminous and offering me his
hand. Nothing like it when you've had some blow, he said, so pretty.
Everything was happening at once, and I was panicky somewhere
under all the lighthearted talk and the flying, as if some part of me
knew what I was heading for and was already cringing; and even
so I sometimes remember that cheap, unreal time with a kind of
aching. When this happens, it leaves me empty, alone, marooned
inside myself, fearing—everything. It's almost as if I'm running after
myself in my mind. . . .

It wasn't even full dark when I went up to my room, feeling
tired again, feeling the weight of what I was worried about, and
knowing that the next morning I would have to get up and go
to work at the library, just as if things were normal. I got into
bed with a book, and the noise of Linda watching television
began to get on my nerves, so I went to the door and called
down to her. But by now Linda was in her room. It was Aunt
Ellen, sitting in an easy chair with her popcorn and her drink
on her lap; she was reluctant to move. I stood at the top of the
stairs, leaning down to look at her, pleading for quiet, and my
father came in from the porch.

"Really chilly," he said.

"Annie wants the television turned down," Aunt Ellen said.

He walked over and touched the knob, then stood back to
watch.

"It's still a little loud," I said.

Neither of them heard me. I started back down the hall, and
Linda caught up to me, wanting a kiss goodnight. I hugged her,
and when she sighed "Goodnight," the odor of the hamburgers
she'd had for dinner nearly took my breath away. "Honey, you
didn't clean your teeth."

"Yes, I did."

"Well, do it again." I turned her around and gave her a light smack on the rear end, thinking, in spite of myself, that with her weight and her sensitivity about it, she could at least be careful about her teeth. It was a poor, mean little thought, and I made my way to bed like someone injured, wishing myself asleep. Earlier, I had begged off going out with Louis, promising that we'd sneak off together the next night, which was Friday, which happened to be the night he and I had agreed would be a family night: we were to take everyone out to a movie. So I told him we'd sneak away after the movie, feeling the whole prospect like another deep ache. And of course, I knew what these symptoms were—the sore breasts, the getting up all night to pee, the fatigue, the sickness in the morning. All day I felt as though I were wading through mud. I was as depressed as I was frightened.

Linda went into the bathroom and was in there a long time, with the water running, and somehow, downstairs, the sound on the television crept upward again. Aunt Ellen was hiding the remote control somewhere in the folds of her robe. I went down to the kitchen, fixed myself a glass of milk, and carried it up to my room. With the milk in one hand, and my book in the other, I read for a while, then put it all aside and, wrapping the pillows around my head, began to try for sleep. The room wasn't quite dark, and then it was. I had slept a little, I knew, because the television program had changed. I lay there hearing it, knowing I wouldn't sleep. I thought of Louis, looked at him in my mind's eye, and was tempted to call him. But it seemed necessary to be sure. So I just lay there with my eyes closed, and soon the television was off, Ellen was climbing the stairs to bed, my father coughed in the bathroom. I turned my light on and sat up reading. But I kept looking at the same sentence over and over. *It struck Wilson as odd that she came to the wedding.* Over and over I read the line. *It struck Wilson as odd . . .*

At midnight, I put my robe on and went down to the kitchen for some more milk. The house was quiet. There was light under my father's door, but he wasn't stirring. From Ellen's room I heard the faintest strains of music. I drank the milk down and went back up to my room, closing the door on a dark house. Tomorrow, I told myself, I'll see. And then I thought about how tomorrow was here.

PART TWO

PART TWO

Peaceable
Arrangements

Field awoke in the still hour before sunrise on Friday morning, and, as had become his habit in these pre-dawn stirrings, lay on his left side with his knees up, facing the door and the window, hands over his face, enjoying the calm, and wanting to doze if he could. He hadn't slept well; his bones ached. Perhaps he'd caught cold out on the lake. He'd had dreams of falling into darkness, dreams that had caused him to come jerking awake, and had left him lying there in the quiet, aware of the slow procession of minutes, the yellow numbers on his clock radio turning while he watched. Now he was too anxious to lie still for very long, and after a few minutes he got up, put his robe on, and made his way downstairs for his newspaper. The chill of the air when he opened the front door disheartened him. For almost thirty years he had lived in Duluth, and always the first signs of seasonable change engendered in him a kind of bewildered unreadiness, the odd feeling that this transformation was a thing he had never undergone before. (As it was impossible for some people to fathom the ageless variations in the planet's centrifugal flight through space, which led to such radical shifts in the weather, it was somehow beyond Field's capacity to quite imagine the shifts themselves: he was always experiencing the vague sensation of being boggled by the season he happened to be entering as if, once established, a weather pattern ought to continue, like a stage of evolution.)

Chilly, shivering slightly, and unable to quite believe the change, he closed the door as if turning away from a disagreeable caller and padded into the kitchen, where he sat in the white light of a small table lamp, reading the newspaper—or, more accurately, trying to concentrate on it. He was thinking about the coming winter. This was not a household which adjusted very well to any sort of change. The unease that surrounded everything now, the tension and irritability, had upset routines and altered the feel of time in the house: everything seemed somehow backed against the coming shift, the new arrangements: it was difficult to think beyond the day Annie and Linda would leave the house, as it was increasingly difficult to think about anything else.

He went on trying to read, and when light began to outline the windows, he commenced with the preparation of breakfast. Annie's alarm had gone off, bringing a long moan out of her, and a curse. She had silenced the alarm, had come down the hall to wake Linda for school, and to get a bath towel out of the linen closet. In a little while, there was the sound of water running in the tub. Field poured three bowls of dry cereal, put coffee on, buttered English muffins, and these simple tasks provided him with something other than his daughter's second marriage to think about. He had finished and was sitting at the table in the breakfast nook, waiting for them to come down— as he did every weekday morning—when the telephone rang. The sound of it at this hour startled him, made him hurry to answer it, and the fact that it was Louis Wolfe irritated him, as if the whole thing were a sort of unfunny practical joke. He did not feel like talking to Louis, and in the space of the next moment or two it cost him some effort to keep the aggravation out of his voice. "Annie isn't down yet," he said. "I'll get her."

"No," said Louis, "don't wake her. I'll catch her at work."

"She's taking a bath, Louis."

"Well, don't disturb her, really."

Field was tempted to say that he himself had been asleep; and in any case he didn't resist the impulse to give him a little reminder of the hour: "If it's important enough to call this early, I'll get her."

"I'm sorry about the call, James. I should've waited and called her at work."

"I'll tell her you called," said Field.

They spoke for a polite moment or two about the Canadian air outside, agreeing that they dreaded the snow more each year, and each year it seemed to get worse—the storms blew longer and more harshly than in earlier years. When Field put the receiver back on the hook, he reflected that he had been speaking to his future son-in-law about the weather of the forties and fifties, and once again experienced the unpleasant awareness that Louis was nearer his own age than Annie's.

From the kitchen window, he looked out at the twin towers of the lifting bridge on Park Point, the low hills of Wisconsin across St. Louis Bay, which was scintillate with early sunlight. It was going to be a windy, wintry day; he could feel it in his joints, watching the shadow of wind move on the lake. Upstairs, Annie crossed the hall from her bedroom to the bathroom and back, getting ready. He went up and dressed for work, then came back to the empty kitchen and waited. It was the same every day: breakfast getting cold on the table while everyone tried to catch up from sleeping late. Finally he went through the downstairs hall to the base of the stairs, to call to them, but Linda was coming down, one plump hand on the railing, the other primping the curls at the back of her neck, each motion contributing to the immediate sense of her as a girl too painfully conscious of her own size and weight—the heaviness of her legs, the thickness of her hips. She was wearing her plaid skirt,

Field noticed; it was the same skirt she had worn yesterday, and the day before.

"Linda," he said. "Honey."

"What?"

"You have so many things to wear."

"Aunt Ellen washed and dried it for me."

"But you don't want to wear the same clothes every day."

"It's clean," she said. "I like it."

The truth was that the plaid skirt disguised, to some extent, the bulkiness of her hips; the hem reached below her knees. Field patted her shoulders, allowing himself the momentary indulgence in an old wish: that she could have inherited her mother's small frame. "You don't want people to think this skirt is all you've got to wear, do you?" he said, following her into the kitchen. "You have a lot of nice things to wear."

Sitting down at the table, she bit off a little of the edge of a muffin, not looking at him.

"Linda?"

"This is fine," she said, chewing.

For a moment, they were quiet. They heard the wind moan outside. Field had busied himself with pouring coffee, and now Annie walked in, dressed and made up and ready to leave for work, though her eyes were a little puffy with sleep. She had brushed her hair back and tied it with a white ribbon; its color next to the ribbon and in the light of the lamp was a vivid black, with shades of almost-blue in it. Field was never able to shake the twinge of astonishment at how much she resembled her dead mother in such moments: when she was dressed and prepared to meet the world outside the house; when she had brushed her hair back like this, and was fresh from a fragrance-scented bath. She took the cup of coffee Field offered her, turned and leaned on the counter, looking at her daughter, and then at Field. "Who was that on the phone?"

Field told her.

"Didn't want to talk to me?"

"He didn't want to disturb you, Annie. You know how he is."

This seemed to confuse her a little, and her father saw in her expression a kind of subterfuge: as though she meant to deny the things she could not have failed to notice about Louis: his essential shyness, a shyness Field might've said was timid. But now she had focused her attention on her daughter's choice of clothing for the day. "When you're finished with breakfast, sweetheart, I want you to put something else on."

"I don't have anything else," Linda whined.

"Scoot," said Annie.

The child wrenched herself from the table and marched out of the room. In a moment, her door slammed. Annie hesitated a moment, as though she were trying to decide about something, then moved to the table and sat down. Field sat across from her. "Annie," he said, "she thinks the plaid skirt hides things."

"I can't let her wear the same skirt all year."

"I just mean it's painful for her."

She shook her head. "I know."

In the years since her return, they had acquired something like a system of gestures and phrases which warned each other off certain subjects; it was an arrangement which provided for a kind of empathy between them, like that of a couple trying to keep their complications from children. "I don't mean to butt in," Field said.

She had put her hands to her eyes. "It's too early in the day," she said. "Linda will find something else to wear, and I'll have to deal with her about it. And I don't have the energy right now." She blew across the surface of her coffee, then took a small, careful sip.

"You and Louis have plans?" Field asked her.

She nodded.

"Anything special?" He meant to seem conversational, and he kept his eyes from hers.

"Daddy, you don't have to work it, you know."

"I'm not working anything," Field said.

"Well," she told him, smiling wearily, "remember—we're all going to the movies. Louis and I are taking everybody." She poured more coffee for herself. "A movie party."

"Sounds like a good time," he said.

For a while, they occupied themselves with the muffins and the cereal. Field took the opportunity to study his daughter's face, and what he saw there was a strain that drew the lines of her mouth down, and made the skin around her eyes look a shade darker than it should. Her hands went to her hair and smoothed it, trembling, and her interest in breakfast had clearly begun to flag.

"Honey, it's nothing to worry about," he said.

Her face registered mild surprise. "What?"

"It's mostly baby fat. A lot of little girls lose it when they reach their teens."

"Oh, I know."

He watched her sip the coffee, watched the daydreaming look come into her eyes, a look of distraction and worry. It occurred to him that something else was the matter. "Annie, what is it?"

"Nothing."

He said, "All right."

She appeared to be taking in the room now, as if trying to commit the look of it all to memory, and something about her expression made him feel uncomfortably mutable and temporary: he had a moment of feeling himself already deep in her past—the dimmest recollection. "I love this old kitchen," she said.

He said, "At least this time you won't be so far away."

"No—right."

Presently, she said, "I wrote Cole and told him. I told him I'm going to let Louis adopt Linda."

Mr. Field sipped his coffee and said nothing.

"I thought he deserved a letter, anyway."

"Oh, what *does* he deserve, Annie. You haven't heard from

him in almost five years. He's more than seven thousand dollars behind on support payments. How much deserving is in that?"

"Okay, then maybe deserving isn't the word."

"Sometimes I wonder what goes through your head."

"Don't you wish you could read my mind," she said evenly. They were quiet.

A moment later, she said, "I'm sorry."

He took a bite of a muffin and sat chewing it, not looking at her. In spite of all his best intentions, he could not help thinking that after four years of being a father to her child he, Field, would be cast in the roll of someone coming to visit, waiting to be visited; someone fading out of a girl's life while the new relation, the new life, took over. And even as he inwardly accused himself of being petty and childish, he felt wronged, somehow, couldn't shake the unhappy conviction that all his help and his worry and concern had been taken only in the light of their use.

Annie had put her coffee down. She stood, eased the chair back under the table. "I'm not hungry."

"I'll stay here with Linda tonight," he said, trying to master the edge of bitterness in his voice.

"Sure you don't want to come along?"

"Not interested," he said.

"Listen," she said, "why don't we start over." She went out of the room, down the hall to the stairs, then came walking back, faking a yawn, feigning sleepiness, rubbing her eyes and blinking. "Morning, pal." She bent down and kissed him on the side of the face. "Sleep okay?"

"No."

"I heard you pacing. Me, too, it seems. Seems like everybody can't sleep these days. Seems like everybody's nervous in the service."

"Something like that," he said, feeling very forlorn and unhappy.

"I wish there weren't any bad nights to be had out there,"

she said, crossing the room to the sink, turning and coming back to him. "I wish everybody could have what they wanted all the time—the right clothes and the right body structure and the ability to take back mistakes. That especially."

"Annie, stop it."

"I'm just trying to get along," she said, smiling only with her mouth. "I'm just trying to get through the morning without hurting anybody's feelings too much."

"All right," he said. "Let's stop it, now."

She said nothing for a time, but she was staring at him, going over something in her mind. "Dad, if I marry Louis, it's—it won't be the way it was with Cole. Louis lives right here in Duluth. We'll be over here all the time. You like him and he likes you. What's the problem?"

"*If* you marry Louis."

She looked at him.

"You said *if*."

"*When* I marry Louis. Okay?"

They were quiet a moment.

"There's no problem with your marrying him," Mr. Field said.

She said, "I didn't say there was."

"All right," he told her.

"I thought it might be bothering you that we're moving out."

"Of course it's *bothering* me, Annie."

She moved to the sink and poured herself a glass of water.

"I'm going to miss you," said Field. "That's all. And I do worry that you might be making another mistake."

"You think I'm throwing myself away again."

"I think you're old enough to know what you want," he said.

"Thank you."

"Maybe I just wish I understood you better."

At this, she appeared to give in to some mild exasperation. "I'm an open book," she said, irritably.

He was silent, watching her face. She seemed to consider a

moment, seemed in the thrall of another thought altogether, and then she shrugged, obviously putting her irritation aside. There had seldom been anything furtive in the way she behaved with people, including her father, and yet now he had the distinct feeling that she was withholding something, that there was a species of dissembling in the cheerful way she approached him, put her hands on his shoulders, and kissed his forehead, as if the morning's tension had been broken by the mere gesture of shrugging it all off. In spite of himself, he remembered the days when, because she was running around with Cole Gilbertson, everything she told him was a lie, or in some way amounted to a lie.

But now Linda was coming down the hall from the stairs, having changed into the one dress that most accentuated her girth; it rode up over the knees, and there were rucks in it where the cloth stretched across her abdomen. She had been crying. She advanced into the kitchen slowly, as though it were painful to move, and stood before her mother. "Is that what you want to wear?" Annie said.

"No." The child was fighting tears.

"All right, sweetie—let's go find you something to wear." They walked, hand in hand, to the stairs, and again it went through Mr. Field's mind that soon they would be doing this in another house, apart from him, all their comings and goings and their voices in the rooms. "We'll go shopping this weekend," he called after them, his voice almost quavering. "We'll get some new clothes." But they had gone up, were already closing the door to Linda's room, and he was alone in this part of the house.

He began to clear away the mostly uneaten breakfast, leaving some muffins for his sister, who had stirred, and put her radio on—an easy listening station, and she liked it loud. There were a few morning tasks that needed doing, and he set about it all with the faint sensation of merely trying to keep his mind occupied: he watered the plants, dusted the surfaces in the living room, and straightened the pillows on the couch. Ellen came down in her bathrobe and poured herself a cup of coffee, then took it back up to her room. Field went into the kitchen and sat down with his newspaper, and through the walls came the strains of Ferrante and Teicher. Annie had said once that the house was like a dentist's office in the mornings, with Aunt Ellen's music piping in through the heat vents and down the halls. It was a joke between them, though there were times, like now, when Mr. Field wished for quiet. Now Ellen came back in and picked up an English muffin. "Cold," she said.

"It was ready almost an hour ago."

She took a bite of it. "Tastes fine cold."

"Please—Ellen—" he began.

"Don't even say it. Music's bothering you. It's not that loud, James." She stood there chewing. She was a tall, energetic woman with wispy, young-looking blond hair and light, light blue eyes—eyes such a light shade of blue they appeared to be fading even as one looked into them. They were the most striking thing about her, and they were buried in a network of wrinkles in her ruddy, lined, sunny face. She was three years older than Field, and had been living with him long enough to feel quite at home in his house.

"Ellen," he said, "if I can hear your music, it's too loud."

"I swear," she said, walking away. "The most unmusical man in the world."

"You don't pretend to believe that's music," he called after her.

A little while later, she wandered back and stood in the doorway. "James, I wonder if I'm not losing my hearing or something. I swear everything sounds muffled to me."

"You're not losing your hearing, Ellen."

"Pardon?"

He gave her a sardonic look. "You're joking, right?"

"No," she said. "Honestly, I didn't hear you."

He said, "Did you know Annie wrote Cole?"

"I guess I did, yes."

"I just heard about it this morning."

"Is that what you were arguing about?"

"We weren't arguing, exactly," Mr. Field said.

She shrugged. "Sounded like it to me."

"Do you think he'll do anything?"

"Cole? I assure you I don't have any clue as to what he might or might not do. How does Annie know he even got the letter?"

"I guess she doesn't. I mean I didn't ask her."

"She sent it to Savoy," Ellen said. "But who knows if they still even live there."

"I guess so," Field said.

"You aren't worried about it, are you?"

He nodded. "I'm worried about everything."

"What'll he do, contest the marriage? I mean he *can't* contest the adoption." She took another muffin from the plate on the table and began to nibble at it, leaning against the door frame. "You know," she said, chewing, "I bet I've got wax buildup or something like that. Will you look in my ear, James, and tell me what you see?"

"Why don't you go see a doctor?"

"Doctors." She shuddered.

"Well," he said, "I don't have a medical degree. I wouldn't know what to look for."

"You'd look for wax buildup."

"No, thanks," he said.

She frowned. "Everything seems muffled. I swear I can barely hear you."

"I said, no thanks."

"I heard *that*."

"I didn't say anything else," he said.

She turned a little and looked back down the hall toward the stairs. She was always imagining what might be going wrong with her health, always hinting that something permanent might be under way. Almost four years ago, she had walked into the downstairs bathroom of her house in Point Royal, Virginia, and found her husband lying on the floor in front of the sink, dead of a heart attack at sixty-four. He had been down with the flu, had got up to dress and shave: she had gone out to get him some cough medicine and antihistamine for the symptoms. He'd lathered his face, and made one or two strokes with the razor, then simply died where he stood. The razor was still in his hand, and one leg was bent back rather awfully, as if some weight had come down from the ceiling and pressed him to the floor. There had been no warning, no sign of heart trouble, and the suddenness of it all had caused Ellen, since his death, to begin to interpret every minor ache or change in her body as the onset of disease. It was something she couldn't help. She had never been the sort of person who felt very comfortable talking about ailments and illnesses, and so quite often she couched her anxieties in casual remarks about the symptoms, as though there could be no question of her continuing health. Of course, Field knew all the time—because she was his sister and because he knew her as well as anyone—that she was inwardly convinced of the seriousness of her condition. He tried to reassure her by reporting his own, often similar symptoms, and sometimes this worked. Sometimes, though, nothing worked, and poor Ellen went about her daily business in a state of dread, talking garrulously and sad-eyed at whoever would listen, convinced that she would soon be gone, and that nothing could help or save her. It was difficult to watch her bearing up under the strain of this belief, because there was something finally rather comic about it; and in spite of his best efforts to keep in mind that her suffering was real, he and Annie had often enough made jokes about her.

Now she shifted slightly in the doorway, still eating the muffin, and wondered aloud if it might not be best to let Linda wear the clothes she felt most comfortable in each day, even if it was the same skirt. "I wouldn't mind washing it every day, you know."

He said, "Every other girl her age wants to wear three different outfits in the *same* day."

"She's not like other girls," Ellen said.

"No child wants to be different, Ellen."

"I don't know. I guess *I* didn't mind."

Presently Field said, "You didn't advise against writing Cole, did you?"

"I wasn't asked," she said. She looked back down the hall.

"I don't suppose you'd turn the music down," he said.

"I already did."

"I can still hear it, Ellen."

"I wish I could get rid of this muffled feeling with everything," she said, starting off down the hall.

He watched her go, and in a moment the noise of the radio was less. He ate another muffin, then stood at the window looking out. Lake Superior was gray and moving with wind-shadows, and the northerly sky had grown white, like a snow-field. The idea of another winter made him feel as though the months ahead were something palpable and heavy—a thing he would have to carry over great distance, without help.

"Dad."

He turned. Annie was standing, with her coat on, by the table. "Where's Linda?" he said.

"Getting dressed. We found something she can stand." She had her coat collar turned up, so that it touched the lobes of her ears; her dark hair was tangled over it. She might have been her mother's twin. He looked at her, felt the similarity with a pang that changed his heartbeat, and then he looked away.

"Good," he managed.

"Dad," she said.

"Yes," said Field.

"I haven't told Ellen, or anybody—" She halted.

"You haven't told anybody," he said, looking at her again. "I'm listening."

"Nothing."

He waited. He had learned to be patient, and to try not to expect anything. "Annie, what is it," he said at last.

"Nothing," she said, straightening a little. "I just wanted to say—you know, that I didn't mean to cause any tension this morning."

"That isn't what you wanted to tell me, is it."

"Yes, it is."

"Why would you have to keep that from anyone?"

"I don't know what you're talking about now," she said.

"You told me you hadn't said anything to Ellen, or anybody else."

She paused. "I have to get to work," she said finally. "Are you walking Linda to school?"

"You know I am, Annie."

She came to him and kissed him on the cheek, her lips barely brushing the side of his face, and then she had turned and was on her way out. "See you this afternoon."

"Annie, is it something to do with Louis?"

"Stop guessing," she said. "This isn't a game."

"It is about Louis, though, isn't it. You don't have to marry anyone, you know." He had followed her down the hallway, past the stairs, to the front door, where she paused to gaze into the mirror above the hall telephone stand. "Well?" he said.

"It isn't that," she said. "Please."

He had the feeling that anything he could find to say to her—words of advice or reassurance or consolation or support—would be so far removed from what was really bothering her that he would make himself ridiculous, even in the moment of most wanting simply to be whatever she needed, of most wanting to let go of his pride and his old anger about past troubles, tensions, disappointments. Oddly, in this instant, he believed he sensed something of what they might truly be to each other. He almost spoke about it aloud, almost said it out, like a confession of love. But he couldn't find the words. He watched her go down the front steps and the cracked sidewalk to the street— this grown woman who looked so much like her mother that it took his breath away—heading out to her day's work.

The Window of
Her Childhood Room

Linda watches her mother get into the little Volkswagen
and begin the usual struggle to start it, pumping the gas pedal,
waiting, trying and failing, and then trying again. The car starts
finally. Her mother waits for it to warm up, sits staring out the
windshield, lightly tapping out some rhythm with the palm of
her hand on the wheel, as if counting up the seconds. She will
not look back at the house. Always, it seems to Linda, her mother
is headed straight ahead; whatever Annie Field does, she does
with a kind of headlong straightforwardness, without the slightest hesitation. Linda watches her, knowing all of this without
words, and wishing she could be thin, and quick-moving, and
certain. When the car pulls away, she leans close to the cold
window to keep it in sight—up the hill it goes, toward school,
past all the parked cars along the curb. At night, while everyone
is asleep, Linda watches the street, gazes out at the moon-
haunted row of houses on the other side, tries to see into every
pocket of shadow, and past the little ponds of light created by
the street lamps; she looks for any movement in the dark, and
watches every passing car for the one that will slow down, pause,
then go on. It has happened several times in the past four years
that something moves out of the periphery of light, or a car

does come that pauses, slows as it passes the house. And she imagines that it is always the same car. This morning she waits, dressed, wearing her second favorite outfit, the one that makes her look taller. She doesn't want to live with Louis Wolfe or his son. And sometimes she doesn't want to stay here, either. What she wants is to be like everyone else, with a father and a mother about the same age—and she very much wants to look at her father once more: simply to stare at his eyes and make him answer with his own. She hasn't voiced this wish to herself; she merely imagines the moment when she is with him, and his eyes answer back. In her mind, it is the moment before he comes to sweep her up in his arms and cover her face with kisses. Sometimes she pretends she's a princess locked away in a castle, whose real father is searching for her. And while she's old enough and has been through enough to know this is day-dreamy and a little immature—she prides herself on her ma-turity—there are nights when, drifting toward sleep, she lets herself dwell on it all the same. It seems to her that the moments before sleep are just private enough for this small indulgence of childish fancy, as she might call it (she keeps a thesaurus by her bed, and is hoping that when she grows up she'll be a writer) and besides, there's always the chance that she'll go on dreaming while she sleeps: one can't be called to account for what happens in sleep.

She has known almost from the beginning that her mother and Louis Wolfe would decide to get married. She knew early last summer, when her mother and Louis took her to Park Point to swim. That day, Louis—who always insists that she call him Louis, or Lou, for God's sake, though as anyone can plainly see it makes her nervous—that day Louis packed a big picnic with-out telling anyone, and showed up at the house with beach plans already set in his mind. A Saturday afternoon, there was a matinee downtown, and Linda's mother had promised she could

take a friend to see *Back to the Future*. Because Louis had packed
the basket and made his plans, the movie was ruled out, and
the friend—Jane Sellers—was ruled out, too. Jane Sellers is not
a person who can be disappointed so casually.

"Tell Jane we'll all go tomorrow," Linda's mother said.

And Linda repeated this into the phone.

"I can't go tomorrow," said Jane. (Now, when Jane, who is
always with six or seven other girls, sees her in the hallway at
school, she makes a big fuss about greeting her, as if there could
be no more generous act than to bother speaking to her.)

"She can't go tomorrow," Linda said to her mother.

"Well then tell her some other time."

Linda stared, and put on her most pained look.

"Do it," her mother said.

"I didn't mean to cause trouble," said Louis.

Linda waited, hearing Jane say her name impatiently on the
other end of the line.

"Tell her," Annie said.

So they had gone to the beach, and Jane Sellers put Linda on
the anathema list, the list of untouchables, people to be kind to,
and noble about.

At Park Point, her mother and Louis set a blanket down in
the shade of a big, floppy beach umbrella that Louis had brought
with him. It had the word "Cinzano" on it, and the edges of it
were tattered and frayed—most of the fringe was gone. Louis
was very proud of it. He'd got it from a friend years ago, he
said, and Linda thought about how *that* could mean as far back
as the forties. He had pulled his shirt off, and she was looking
at the white hair on his chest, the way the skin at his neck hung
a little and was wrinkled. Her mother had lain back, resting
her head on her clasped hands. Perhaps twenty other people
were on the beach, but no one was swimming. A few yards
down from the umbrella, a little boy was digging with a small
plastic shovel in the wet sand. Linda sat with her hands folded
over her knees, feeling bored and mad and thwarted (she liked

the word; she had been looking for an opportunity to use it aloud), and Louis asked her if she was going to swim.

"No," she said.

"Go get your feet wet, anyway," her mother said.

"I don't want to."

"Go play."

"I'm fine right here."

Her mother raised her head and looked at her, then lay back again. "At least take the jeans and blouse off. You must be burning up under all those clothes."

Because her mother had told her to, she had put a bathing suit on under her clothes, but she had known all along she would never walk outside in such a getup. "I'm fine," she said.

"Don't you want to get a tan?" Louis said.

"Let her do what she wants," said her mother.

"It's so hot," he said.

Then they were quiet for a time. Others arrived, carrying blankets and food and inflatable rafts. Up the way, several people had gone into the water. They splashed and shouted and exclaimed about how cold it was. Someone had lighted a grill nearby, and the odor of cooking meat came to them on the little stirrings of air. Louis was trying to get some music on the transistor radio he'd brought with him, and when he caught Linda looking at him, he smiled almost sheepishly. "I come prepared," he said.

"What?" her mother said.

"I was telling Linda I come prepared."

Linda's mother lifted her head and shaded her eyes to look at him. "Oh." She lay back down.

Linda watched him go on turning the dial, and then she looked out at the beach. It was a hot, white day, and it was getting hotter all the time. The lake was a light, sky blue, turning to green closer in. It went on and on, into the washed deeper blue bottom of the sky. On the radio, there was only static.

"Louis," Annie said, "for God's sake."

And that was when Linda knew it—knew they would probably get married. She looked at Louis, turning the radio off and
storing it in the picnic bag, then clasping his own hands over
his folded knees, almost as if to ape the way Linda was sitting,
and she knew it. She said, "Some fun."

Her mother said, "Relax, and shut up." And lay there with
her eyes closed. The only part of her that moved was her toes.
Linda got up and wandered out to the edge of the water, where
a little boy was digging in the sand. In the brightness, his red
hair looked as though it might burst into flame. He was intent
on what he was doing, and didn't see her. She stood watching
him. Finally he looked up at her, seemed about to speak, then
went on about what he was doing—digging a hole in the wet
sand and watching it fill with water. Linda turned and looked
back at her mother and Louis Wolfe under the beach umbrella.
Louis was talking, still sitting with his hands clasping his knees.
Annie lay on her stomach, her toes digging into the sand. She
might as well have been asleep. They were going to get married,
and it was even possible that they themselves didn't know it yet.
Linda realized that she had come away from them because she
was embarrassed for them, needed to get away from them—it
was almost as if her embarrassment had closed off certain passages in her lungs, and she had to get out of the shade to breathe.
Now she tried to put the whole thing out of her mind. She
stooped to help the boy scoop sand out of the hole. He said,
"Quit it."

"Just trying to help," she said.

"Get out of here."'

"Your mommy and daddy ought to teach you some manners."

"Up yours."

She stood. "Where are your mommy and daddy? Maybe I'll
just tell them what you said."

He worked on, using the little plastic shovel now.

"You little brat," she said.

"Stuff it," said the boy.

She walked down the beach, looked once over her shoulder at the boy's red back, then went on, keeping to the wet part of the sand. There were three ships out on the lake, blue shadows that seemed not to be moving. Gulls wheeled and soared and cried all along this part of the shoreline, and she watched them with a sense of the ease of their flight; they made her aware of her own heavy tread, her own large feet and unwieldy body. Before her now, a very big woman in a black bathing suit went lumbering toward the water, complaining that the hot sand was burning the soles of her feet. She splashed into the shallows and then flopped down and disappeared like a big seal, graceful and sure, like that. When she reappeared she had turned to face the beach, and was swimming backward. She spat water. Her companion, a man almost as heavy as she was, walked in a few feet and stood shivering. His white back was all gooseflesh.

"Come on," the woman said.

"It's so cold," said the man.

Linda watched him work his way, by shivering stages, into the water. Then the two of them lolled and wrestled and played, and it was hard to believe they could see anything to like in each other. They were both fat and ugly. At school, all she ever got were jokes about her size. No one was kind, at school, even other kids who were heavy. And when did people stop hitting you where you were sensitive? She turned from the couple gliding and splashing in the lake, and saw Louis walking down toward the little boy and his hole in the sand. Louis was thin, but his belly stuck out, and his legs looked like old, brown twigs. He went past the boy and stepped into the shallows, then took a few running paces and glided under. When he came up he shook water from himself and then went down again. On the blanket under the umbrella, her mother sat staring off. She could have been someone in a painting. Linda made her way up to where she was, and sat down on the blanket.

"Honey, why don't you at least take the blouse off."

"You're going to get married, huh."

"What?"

"You heard me."

"When you get older you can say things like that, and you won't sound like what you now are, young lady. And that's impertinent. Do you know what that is?"

"I don't care, I'm right," Linda said. "You're getting married."

"And you're still impertinent."

"I don't remember what that means."

"It means you have a loose tongue, and no respect for your elders."

"Just because I say you're getting married?"

"Listen, girlie, this is something you and I might talk about in a few weeks. But not now. Do you understand? I don't wish to discuss it now."

They said nothing for a few moments. They watched Louis swim easily across their line of vision, from left to right, and then right to left.

"I guess you don't like him much, do you," her mother said.

"He's all right." She reached between her knees and got a handful of sand, then dropped it into her palm and let it sift through her fingers.

"Don't you want me to be happy, Linda?"

"Yes."

"But you're not happy."

"I don't know." She felt like crying now, and she was angry with herself for feeling it. A few feet away a young man carried a baby on his shoulders down to the water. She thought of her father, watched the man's young back as he lifted the baby high. It seemed to her then that being happy was simple: it was just being like that: strong and lean and healthy and good-looking. The man put the child down and gently laved the water over the small back.

"Why aren't you happy?" her mother asked. "Is it because we didn't go to the movies?"

"Mom," she said.

"All right. I didn't think so, really. Maybe I hoped that was it."

"Why?"

"You're too grown-up for your age, sweetheart."

Linda said nothing.

"I like Louis," her mother said. "I like him a lot."

"I know, and you're getting married."

"Maybe. Yes—maybe we are."

Louis was coming now, moving quickly across the sand, his arms wrapped around himself. He took a towel from the bag and worked it over his head and shoulders. "Water's great," he said. "Cold, but great."

"I'm hungry," said Linda's mother.

"Lots of good stuff to eat," he said, kneeling down. The sand adhered to his knees, just as it had adhered to the fat little knees of the boy. There was something so odd about him—a strange gentle unawareness of the way he struck others, though she could not have expressed this. She only sensed it, and knew that it made her feel sorry for him somehow, as though he had done nothing to deserve the complicated people she and her mother were. He had draped the towel over his neck, and was reaching into the bag. Linda's mother put her hand on his wrist, then, and he stopped. "You're a dear man, you know it?" she said.

He glanced at Linda, seemed embarrassed and puzzled at the same time. "Is this the judgment of the committee?"

Linda said, "Leave me out of this, you guys." She smiled to show she was teasing.

"Well, I thank you both anyway," Louis said.

Linda gazed off at the gulls pinwheeling in the sky, and thought about how it would be to live in his house, with its walls lined with record albums and books, and its heavy, over-erfancy furniture, as if he had chosen everything from some stuffy old hotel that was about to be torn down. She was certain that she would feel *buried* there, like something stuck away in the attic of a museum. And she wished Louis would find someone else to marry. Wished it even as she felt strangely sorry for him, watching the clumsy way his fingers went along her mother's wrist as he tried to take her hand.

Now, waiting in her room for her grandfather to come collect her for the walk to school, she thinks of that day in July, and wonders what she might have said to keep things from changing so much, so quickly. Perhaps if she had said something about her father, it might've awakened them a little, and made them stop traveling toward each other so fast. But she can't be certain of anything. She has planned all along that her father would come back, and it's been hard watching everybody learn to forget him. Though she hasn't seen him for a very long time, she still tries to see his face in her mind, still conjures him, like a ghost, in the hours by her window at night. She senses without having to put it into words that when she can no longer see him in memory, she'll lose him. She knows this has already begun to happen, for whenever she tries to picture him now, parts of the image grow dim, and then it all falls apart: she can't *see* all of him the way she wants to, and it bothers her sometimes at night, when she stares into the dark and wishes herself back to him. The nights are often bad for her, because she sleeps too lightly, and, once awakened, finds it almost impossible to go back to sleep. Her imagination plays tricks on her, convinces her of shapes in the dark, movement in the deep shadows of the room. She hates waking up in the dark, yet she can't sleep with a light on, and so she sometimes simply decides to stay awake. Sometimes, when she knows she'll have trouble, she plans things to help herself through: she smuggles a towel in from the linen closet, and puts it along the bottom of her bedroom door, so no one will see that she has her light on, and she reads into the late, late hours, even after her grandfather has gone to bed. A part of her understands that she shares this with him—this night-walking, and sleeplessness—and though she derives some pleasure from the reading, though she experiences a kind of guilty thrill when she's the only person left awake in the house, she spends much of each day wishing the night wouldn't come. She spends most of her waking hours dreading it, in fact, and there's nothing quite so rare or wonderful as the realization that at some point in the long trial of a day's end she's dropped off to sleep, and the hours of the night have missed her, have allowed her to escape, to reach morning in a blissful, dreamless slumber.

This morning, like every recent morning, there's another source of anxiety: she's always been nervous about school, but the prospect of going off to it from Louis Wolfe's house, of doing her nights there, fills her with dread. She's standing at her mirror, holding her stomach, when her grandfather calls to her from the stairs. He's just getting to the top step when she opens the door of her room. "Telephone for you," he says with all sorts of questions in his voice. She gives him a puzzled look.

"It's a woman—maybe from school?"

Downstairs in the hall, she picks up the receiver and puts it to her ear. Her grandfather has come partway down, and stands waiting. "Hello?" she says.

There is a shuffling sound on the other end.

"Hello?" she says again.

"Sweetie." A man's voice. "Don't say anything. Let's keep it a secret for now, okay? Can you hear me?"

"Yes?" Linda says, her heart clamoring up her gullet.

"It's me. It's your daddy. Don't let on."

She stands there holding the receiver to her ear.

"You know, don't you," the voice says.

"Yes," says Linda.

"Who is it?" asks her grandfather from the stairs.

"From school," she mutters.

"Sweetie," says the voice of her father. "I've missed you something terrible."

"Where—" she begins. She can't speak. Her hands are trembling; her knees feel as though they might buckle.

"Don't tell them, okay?" the voice says. "I'll see you soon."

"I have to go to school now," Linda says.

"Keep a secret," says the voice. "Hear?"

"Yes."

"Now say good-bye and hang up like it's somebody from school."

"Good-bye," Linda says, and puts the phone down.

Her grandfather is standing above her, one hand on the stair railing. He's peering at her, as if something in her face might tell him what he wants to know. "Who was it, honey?"

"Nobody," she says. "Somebody from school."

"Well, who." He's watching her.

She looks for a name and can't find it. Her lungs feel swollen, dry as bones buried in dust.

"Linda."

She thinks of the name of a friend. "Stephanie," she says.

"It didn't sound like her," says her grandfather.

"It was her mother."

"Oh."

She knows she should say more—but her mind is blank again. It's hard to believe he can't see everything in her face, which is burning hot, and seems about to twist into the shape of some other face—the face of a stranger, deep red and twitching under the eyes. "Stephanie and I are doing a project at school."

"You look upset."

"Stephanie's moving away."

"You knew that, honey."

"She can't do the project with me." This is the truth, but it is also something she has known since Wednesday.

"I'm sorry." He stares at her a moment longer, then stirs and begins to make his way upstairs. "We have to go soon."

"I'm ready," she says, following him.

He goes down the upstairs hall, hits Aunt Ellen's door once, hard. "Ellen, for Christ's sake," he says, going on. When he closes his bedroom door, Linda hurries into her room and pulls her window curtains all the way back. She stands in the sunlight that is pouring hotly through the glass, and gazes up and down the street. Everything is still; there's no traffic. The yards are all trim and sprinkled with flowers, and the sidewalks are empty. She watches the door of one house open: a woman steps out to pick up the morning paper. The door closes, and Linda feels suddenly quite alone and frightened, as though the woman has somehow left her stranded on this high perch, in this blazing second-story window. She pulls the curtain shut and gets down on her bed, arms wrapped tightly about herself, shivering. It requires all her strength to keep from crying out, but she manages. She even resists the temptation to pull the blankets over her for comfort. She's very still—simply waiting for whatever happens next. When she hears Aunt Ellen's door opening on the music, she gets out of the bed and pretends to be primping her hair in the mirror next to her closet. Quite suddenly she's aware of herself as someone harboring a secret, and in the next moment a new feeling begins to come over her, like something traveling along the surface of her skin. She looks at herself in the mirror, combs the soft strands of her hair, and basks in the delicious, dizzying sense of having begun an adventure.

Dancing at the
Royal Duluth Hotel

The Star Dust Record Store was on the first floor of the last building in a row of tall, Victorian buildings on Michigan Street, each with its own facade, either of brick or clapboard, and each in some different stage of disrepair and decline. This block had once been a part of the business center—the dry goods and general stores, the bank and the hotel and a saloon—of the old mining town Duluth had been when the iron range was booming. The buildings faced Michigan Street and Lake View, and one could stand at the rear windows and see a panoramic view of St. Louis Harbor and the lake. At one time, store owners and their families could sit on lawn chairs in the backyards and watch the tankers coming in from the northerly rivers; no doubt they dreamed of the money pouring in. They were mostly gone now, and two of the buildings were empty; one was condemned; still another housed a travel agency and a division of the Department of Motor Vehicles; and one—the one next to the record store—was occupied by a rickety savings and loan company whose employees all looked vaguely dishonorable and tired. Walking down Lake View to the end of the block and the intersection, one saw this row of buildings standing in full perspective, casting a serrated band of shade on the other side of the street, and it was easy enough to get a feeling about how it all had looked in the earlier time: something about it made one imagine a street where scoundrels and gunmen had walked, in the days of the old outlaws and the rough-and-tumble miners. Louis Wolfe liked to imagine it as he crossed the street every morning, having parked his car in the lot on Lake View. Sometimes, he saw himself as a man who would have been more at home in the last century—and in any case, the sense of history in these old buildings always made him feel vaguely denied something: he would have liked to walk these streets in, say, 1869.

On this particular morning, he waited at the intersection and thought of not crossing, thought of turning around and going back to his car. He wanted very badly to talk to Annie, and not over the telephone. Yet he did not want to appear desperate, or worried. He was worried. He crossed the street, opened the store, turned the lights on, and then stood for a moment in the odor of old cardboard and dust that was always on the air in this small, stuffy place. The store was arranged in narrow aisles between large wooden stalls, each with its own tightly jammed group of albums—jazz, swing, rock 'n roll, blues, folk and country, almost all of it from ten and fifteen years ago. Along one wall there were posters from old movies that he had ordered through a specialty house last year in an effort to give the place a little color. The posters were finally a little out of place here, with their smiling, glamorous faces and their bright shades of red and blue and gold. In the window that looked out onto the street, his son, Roger, had placed a selection of the albums in stock, and from time to time people walking by on the sidewalk would stop and browse. They made Louis feel as though he were under some scrutiny, like a zoo animal; but now and again one of these sidewalk browsers would come in and buy something, so he left things as they were. Of course, there were never enough customers to make this more than a marginally expensive avocation (Louis had a monthly income from the federal government, having retired from the Air Force at the rank of colonel).

At the back of the store, an open passageway led to a windowless room with a single light bulb hanging from the ceiling, a bed along one wall and a desk against the other. He went back there, shuffling in the quiet, feeling old and discouraged. Lately, it seemed to him that she had been restive, distracted, and distant. At one point during dinner, two nights ago, he'd reached across the table to take her hand.

"Want to talk about it?" he said.

She gazed at him with those astonishing black eyes, but said nothing.

"Annie?"

"I'm sorry," she said, smiling. "I didn't hear you."

"I said do you want to talk about it."

"Talk about what?"

"Something's on your mind."

"No," she said. "Really—I'm just kind of sleepy."

But it was clear to him that she wanted an end to the evening. When he left her, after an hour of sitting on the porch of the house on Superior Street with James Field, she merely touched his elbow, sent him on his way like an old friend, someone other than a lover.

He'd had all day yesterday to stew about this, and last night had been very, very long. Now, sitting at the desk in the little room, trying to keep his mind on counting out the money for the cash register to begin his day's business, he found himself unable to keep the numbers in his head, unable to shake the uncomfortable feeling that something important had gone wrong. He started over, counted out thirty dollars and change. And then he was sitting there holding the rest of the money, staring off, thinking.

He knew what the real source of his unease was: from the very beginning of his affair with Annie, he had been unable to believe his own luck, had worried all the time that she would change her mind about him, come to her senses. He was fifty-two years old, he had a grown son, and these days he felt most of the time like a high school kid. His heart raced; his nerves were jangled; he sometimes felt that he couldn't stand straight for the trembling in his knees. Everything upset him, though it was all somehow brighter, too, more vivid. The palms of his hands grew sweaty, and sometimes his voice actually cracked, actually jumped an octave. All of this was doubly embarrassing because he was perfectly, painfully aware of how ridiculous it sometimes made him. There were times when he thought he could see it even in his son's face. Yet none of this made any difference beside the fact that Annie had said she would marry him.

To begin with, he was not the sort of older man that a young woman was likely to feel any attraction for. He'd never deceived himself about this—he'd always had a horror of being that person who unwittingly humiliated himself in the act of trying to be someone other than himself. The mirror in the morning showed him a balding, squarish, big-shouldered man, neither particularly handsome nor particularly distinguished-looking, with kind, light brown eyes and an expression that in his own estimation was more trusting than simple, but which could be taken for something less then extravagantly intelligent. He had a photographic memory; he was good with people. And perhaps beyond this he was not endowed with much else. He was a man who had done well enough commanding other men, had gained respect if not love generally, in all his dealings with those responsible to him—he had administered an entire supply base for the last six years of his commission, and he had conducted a business for the more than five years since his retirement. He owned a specific knowledge and enthusiasm about a certain thing—the popular music of the forties and fifties—and was possessed of a certain gentleness and stability that one young woman had learned to feel the need for. Moreover, he was shrewd enough to know that her affection for him was perhaps a little temperamental, and that this had oddly to do with his age and the timbre of his voice, with the fact that he had a pacifying effect on the turmoil of her emotions. He was willing to accept these things as they were. What mattered was that she wanted to be with him, and as for the rest of it, he worked to put it out of his mind.

Last night, all night, this morning, he had been unable to do so.

It wasn't eight o'clock yet, and he was already tired with worry. He counted the money yet again, and again lost count. Finally he went to the front and put the closed sign up. He would take the loss of the two or three sales it might cost him for the time to think, and to talk with Annie.

Back at his desk, he sat down, picked up the phone and put it on his lap, lifted the receiver, dialed the number at the library, then hung up before anyone could answer. Perhaps a minute ticked by, and he didn't move. His hands were clasped before him on the desk. There was no quiet like this. He looked at the room—the pictures of places he had been in the world, of people he had known in the air force, of citations he had won, and of his wife and son—and then he put his head on his arms and closed his eyes. Another minute or two passed. He stood, then sat down again, then picked up the phone and dialed the number, waited.

"Circulation," came the voice.

"Annie Field, please. This is Louis Wolfe."

"She's away from her desk."

"Could you tell her I called?"

He opened the store, sat behind the counter, working a crossword puzzle, waiting for the phone to ring. Outside, the street was draped in shadow, and little knots of people walked by, hurrying in the chill. Finally he couldn't take the quiet, so he turned the radio on, and listened to music. One man came in and looked around for a few minutes, but didn't buy anything.

Louis walked back to the little room and his desk, and again dialed the number.

"Circulation." It was Annie.

"Hey," he said.

She said, "Hey."

"You okay?"

"I was awake when you called the house."

"Well," he said.

"Louis?"

"I'm right here," he said.

"Can I call you later on?"

"Sure, I'll be here."

"I've got a lot to get done today."

"Right," he said.

"I'll see you this evening."

"You bet."

"I haven't forgotten that we're supposed to make a night of it after the movie."

"Right," he said.

"I've got to go now," she said.

"Well, you know where I'll be," said Louis.

When she had hung up, he sat for a long time in the meager light of the room, hearing the faint sound of the radio out front. At last he got to his feet and shuffled out to sweep the floor of the shop. He would spend the morning putting the place in order.

He had met Annie in a roundabout way through her father, who had been an occasional customer at the store. One evening last spring, he ran into Mr. Field at a meeting of the local widowers' club. As was the custom for visitors or new members of the group, Field stood up to speak during the proceedings, and Louis, recognizing him right away, decided to introduce himself after the meeting.

The actual name of the club was The Chessmen, and noboby knew where or how the name came about, except that none of the members wanted particularly to be called widower. It met every two weeks in the home economics room of the city's oldest high school, Saint Mark's, an enormous red-brick building with gabled eaves and tall, gothic spires, whose leaded windows looked out on a stand of birches. The meetings comprised games, and drinks, and a short program, usually a talk by one kind of expert or another, followed by questions and answers. The group had been formed from a chapter of a single parents' club, and the bond they all shared was the loss of their wives. Louis had learned all this on his first visit, at the invitation of a friend, not long before he attended the meeting at which Field was asked to introduce himself, and, in response to the evening's presentation—a talk from a child psychologist about raising children alone—said a few words about his own experience. He explained to the group that his wife had been gone for many years, and that this was the first time he had ever done anything like talking to other men about it. "I don't know why I've come," he said, though he thanked another member for inviting him. "But I'm glad I got the chance to hear," he went on, "from anybody who knows anything about how it is to raise children alone. My daughter and granddaughter are living with me, have been for some time. And I raised my daughter by myself. She fought me every step of the way. I don't think I learned much."

This had brought an appreciative—a commiserative—laugh from the group. But Louis, even as he joined in the laughter, had the sense that laughter was not what was wanted: he sat watching the other man smile and nod, and knew that Field had intended something else. He could see it in the man's sad, shadowed eyes, in the way he looked down as the laughter continued around him. Louis felt for him.

Field went on:

"I'm not fool enough to think my troubles with raising my

daughter alone are so singular. I've had trouble being patient sometimes, and sometimes I've probably been too patient. I did some things to enforce my will when I thought it had to be enforced, for her safety and well-being. I tried to be a friend to her, when that was called for, and a lot of the time, probably when it was not. I listened to her as much as I could, and I think I did as well as anyone does under the circumstances. I mean I tried to be a good father, and give her everything she needed to grow up and be whatever she wanted to be, and the result of all that was that she ran off with the first pretty-looking kid who came along. I mean I did everything according to the books, and she just—well, she just ran off. It was like everything I'd tried to teach her and everything we'd been to each other— it just all—it—none of it mattered. And this kid—the kid she ran off with—well, he was exactly what I feared—I loathe him."

At this, there was more laughter, and Field looked around with a look of puzzlement and dismay. The laughter subsided. At the front of the room, behind the podium, stood the evening's speaker, still smiling, apparently amused. The speaker was a young man, no more than thirty-five, and he had written a book on the subject of raising a child alone.

"What I meant to ask," Mr. Field said, "was this. My daughter came home a while back—it's been more than four years actually—and brought her baby daughter with her. I don't want to repeat any mistakes, and I'm not sure what you can tell me about it. With my granddaughter, I feel much more reluctant to discipline her or show any displeasure at all."

"How did you show displeasure before?" the speaker said.

Field shrugged. "I guess most of the ways there are to show it."

"Did you spank your daughter when she displeased you?"

"Three or four times, yes," Field said. "When she was younger and needed it."

The speaker folded his thin hands on the podium and looked down, as if suddenly weighted down with sadness.

"Did you want to say something about that?" Louis asked him, turning slightly and nodding at Field to indicate that he meant no rudeness by stepping in.

"Well," the young man said, shifting his weight at the podium. "As you'll find in my book, I really don't believe in using any form of violence with children."

"I said I spanked her," Field said. "I didn't say I beat her."

"What kinds of things did you spank her for?"

Field thought a moment. "I remember once she got into the laundry soap. And another time she was playing in the street after I said she mustn't do that."

"Does she remember what you spanked her for?" the speaker asked.

"What's your point," Louis put in. Now he and Mr. Field were both standing. They were in different rows, but they could see each other, and they exchanged a glance.

"My point is," said the speaker, "that all the child remembers is the violence—the spanking."

"That may be so," Field said, "but after I spanked my daughter for getting into the laundry soap, she didn't get into the laundry soap again. I don't think I was trying to teach her any life lessons."

"Yes, but you can always use these things to do that—to teach lessons—"

"You have any children of your own?" Field said.

And there was a silence.

"My wife is expecting," said the young man.

Field shook his head and sat down, then got up and walked out of the room. A moment later, Louis followed, and caught up to him in the hallway near the door. Field had recognized him, remembered him from the store. They shook hands, and then they were standing out on the sidewalk in the wind and cold of late spring, talking about the failures of expert knowledge. Finally, Louis suggested they go across the street, to a little bratwurst house he knew, for something to drink. Mr. Field went along with a deference that made Louis wonder if the other man were not merely being polite. The restaurant was a very dim and narrow room, with heavy, urn-shaped candles on the tables, and alpine mountain scenes in paintings on the walls. It was not a very artfully designed place, but the food was always good, and Louis remarked about this as they settled themselves at a table near the back.

"Looks all right to me," Field said. He seemed a little restive.

Louis said, "If you have something else to do, of course I understand."

"No," Field said. He folded his hands and gazed at the other tables, at the walls, the mirror behind the bar. "Nice place," he said finally. "I've never been here before."

Louis said, "I found what you said very interesting, you know. Because I raised my son by myself. You've seen my son in the store, I'm sure."

Field looked doubtful.

"Well," said Louis, "he works there on Fridays and Saturdays sometimes, and I pay him a little salary. He's going to UMD now."

"I wanted my daughter to go to college, but she wasn't interested," Field said, rubbing the back of his neck as though this information had caused an ache there. "I saved all those years."

"Well," said Louis, "my son's failed out of a couple of schools. I can't seem to get him to focus on anything definite—he just drifts from course to course. Getting by. These kids, it's as if they think everything's going to take care of itself."

"Yeah, or someone else will take care of things," Field said. "Your daughter still lives with you?"

"There's my granddaughter. It's just easier that way."

The waitress came over and they ordered hot dogs and mugs of beer. There wasn't anyone else in the place. Field kept looking at the door, as if he were expecting someone.

"My wife was killed in an automobile accident," Louis said.

The other man stared at him.

"She was on her way to buy a dozen eggs because she wanted to bake a cake and we were out of eggs. She didn't even like baking or cooking that much. She just got an urge to try a Dutch chocolate cake, and we were out of eggs. So she went out to pick up a dozen, and I never saw her awake again. Kid from the high school, driving a brand-new Dodge a hundred miles an hour. He came down this hill behind her where she was waiting to make a left turn into the Stop 'n' Shop. She never woke up. She hung on three days—barely breathing. Then she just stopped. The kid didn't even get a bruise. Got thrown from the car and landed in shrubbery on the other side of the road. A juvenile joyriding around in his father's car while his father was down in St. Paul on business, so of course there wasn't much anybody could do in the way of making the little son of a bitch pay for what he'd done. His parents took him to Washington State to live the next summer. He's in his thirties by now, and sometimes I wonder what he sees in his sleep at night, if he sees anything at all."

The waitress brought two mugs and set them down. The beer was a little warm, and Louis watched the other man's face for a reaction. There was none. Field drank, then set the mug down and regarded him.

"What about you?" Louis said.

"My daughter was only a month or two past her second birthday. It was a long time ago."

"Ever think of remarrying?" Louis asked.

"A few times."

"I did get married again, but it didn't work out and I think it was probably my fault. I kept making comparisons—little mental notes to myself. Stupid, of course. But I couldn't stop doing it, and after a while things just fell apart. She lives in St. Paul now—a very nice lady who deserved better I guess."

"I had a daughter to raise," Field said. "I think I gave women the impression that I was auditioning them as prospective mothers for her." He shifted in his seat, then took a long pull of beer. "Anyway, my daughter was in your store for the first time last week, and she thought it was a very nice idea—a record store based on nostalgia."

"You should tell her that if she comes in again, to say hello."

"I will," Field said.

They finished their beer, and the waitress brought the hot dogs, and more beer. It was a pleasant evening snack, though for a while they didn't have much more to say to each other. They talked about the renovation of the downtown area of the city, and about the university's hockey team. When they paid the bill, Field was very precise, counting out pennies, and then insisting on leaving the tip. They shook hands again outside the restaurant.

"Well," Field said, "take care of yourself."

"Maybe I'll see you at the next meeting."

"I'm not much of a joiner."

"Well," Louis said.

He watched Field go across the street and up the block, hands deep in the pockets of his coat, body thrust slightly forward, as though he were walking into a strong wind. Louis wondered what he would find to say to the man the next time he came into the Stardust.

One morning perhaps a week after this, Louis was tending the store alone when a young woman strolled in and bought a recording of Patti Page's "Old Cape Cod." He was ringing up the purchase when she said, "I think this is a good idea, this shop."

"Thank you," he said. "I like it."

She nodded at the record as he put it into one of the small, envelopelike paper sacks he used for singles. "That's for my father."

"You don't care for Patti Page."

"Actually, I love this song. My father used to play it when he wanted me to drift off to sleep at night."

"It's a lovely song."

"I think you met my father recently," she said.

He nodded, gazing at her. He believed he would have remembered her if he had ever seen her before: a lovely, almost
fragile-looking woman, with wonderful dark eyes, and skin that
had something of the sun in it, as though she had just walked
in from the beach. "Yes, y-yes," he stumbled. "Your father talks
about you—" He felt absurd. There seemed nothing whatever
else to say.

"Where do you get all your records?" she said.

"Oh, people auction them off sometimes. People come in and
trade. And there are estate sales. I buy and sell them—you'd
be surprised."

"Does it—is it—what sort of—" she hesitated.

"There's not a lot of profit in it," said Louis. "Not really."

She smiled. There was something quite extraordinary about
her eyes—some energy or animation, like light—but not light,
since they were so deeply black that you couldn't see where the
pupil ended and the iris began. He realized that he was staring
at her, and so he broke off, picked up the Patti Page in its paper
sack. "You must let me give you this record."

"Well, but it's a gift for my father, for my birthday."

"Your father's having a birthday?"

"It's *my* birthday," she said. "I always get him a little something on my own birthday, too. It's something he and his sister
used to do for his mother and father, when I was growing up.
Sort of a family tradition."

"Then you must let me give it to you for your birthday."

"All right," she said, smiling pleasantly.

He handed her the record.

"How long have you had the store?"

"This is my sixth year. I got it right after I retired from the
Air Force."

"Oh, you were in the Air Force."

"Listen," he said, "I was thinking of taking lunch early today. Would you—have you got any plans for lunch?"

"I'm supposed to meet my father."

"Oh." He almost winced at the stupid, automatic sound of this."

"Would you like to come along?"

This surprised him. "Well—" he said, but couldn't follow it with anything.

"I'm sure my father would be happy to see you again."

"I should probably stay here," he said. "Get some work done." He looked away, and found something to do with his hands, stacking a pile of 45s and setting them before him to be cataloged and put in their respective boxes on the counter. When he glanced back at her he saw that she was studying him, that an expression of concern had come into her face. It occurred to him, with all the absurd, illogical force of the shifts of reality in a dream, that her expression was exactly what it might have been had she witnessed someone struggling with a coughing fit.

"I can have dinner with you," she said.

"Dinner," he said, stumbling.

"Sure," she said, "why not."

"Wonderful, yes—yes we can. Very good," he said.

"Good," she said.

Then the two of them were laughing, as if the whole conversation had been a joke. They laughed, and the moment passed, and she subsided even as he heard himself continuing, laughing far too loud. He put his hand to his mouth, feeling abruptly clumsy and buffoonish, hopelessly awkward—the old familiar sensations—and yet she was regarding him with such friendliness that none of it worried him quite so deeply. He was sure he had noticed an element of self-deprecation in the way she raised her eyebrows, as though frustrated with her own clumsiness. It seemed to Louis that they were already friends.

Later that night, while they rode in his car along the edge of the lake, going toward St. Louis Bay and the restaurant he intended to take her to, he mentioned this to her.

"I feel that, too," she said. "It's the truth."

It was a cold, snowy night, the snowflakes drifting down out of the clouds like many individual live things, each flying in its own direction. They sat quiet, watching it as he drove. Presently she began to talk about living in the north, how it made a person strong against the elements, at least. She was obviously talking just to talk.

He said, "Where do you work anyway?"

She left a pause. "The library."

"I'm sorry," he said. "I thought you were finished talking."

"I work in the circulation department."

"You must know Tina Bradford, then. She comes into the store a lot."

"Yes," she said. "I work for Mrs. Bradford."

They were quiet again.

He had heard a note of displeasure in her voice when she said the name. He decided to gamble a little. "I never liked Tina Bradford."

She reached quickly over and touched his elbow. "What a relief."

They laughed.

"She's just so disdainful of people."

"I never thought of it like that, but yes," he said.

And again they were quiet.

"Do you like your job?" he asked. He was afraid of the quiet.

"Not particularly—it's a job. You know."

"I like working in the store," said Louis. "But I get lonely sometimes. My son helps out on weekends. It's something he does too cheerfully, if you know what I mean."

"You'd rather he do something else."

"Exactly."

"How old is he?"

"Almost twenty-one."

"It's hard to know much at that age, I guess."

A moment later, she said, "You know, I have an eight-year-old daughter."

"In fact, I did know."

She gave forth a lovely, soft laugh. "What else did my father tell you?"

"He just said you were living with him."

"His sister is living with him, too. We're all living with him, and that's the way he wants it. Did he seem like somebody who's getting what he wants?"

"I didn't really notice anything that specific," Louis said. "How long have you worked at the library?"

Again she laughed softly. It was a wonderful musical, throaty little sound. "A deft change of subject. I've been working at the library for three and a half years. Before that I was getting a divorce, and before that I was married."

"Your husband from Duluth?"

"Illinois." She gazed out the side window, then sighed, shifted slightly, as if to gather her coat about her. "I guess my real job now is my daughter. I mean I'm hoping to have enough money put aside soon to get a place of our own."

He pulled the car onto the lifting bridge, toward Park Point. Out on the lake, lights flashed and blinked in the dark panorama of moonless water and sky. The snow swirled and glinted in his headlamps. Ahead, to the right, the restaurant windows shone like meager flames. "Ever eaten here?" Louis said.

"No."

"It's a nice place—an atmosphere like the thirties."

"Sounds fun."

He pulled into the lot, and found a place to park. When he'd turned the ignition off, she said, "I didn't mean to go on about my father like that earlier."

Louis looked at her.

"You were very gracious about it, too," she said.

"There's been nothing that required any graciousness," he said.

The words sounded oddly like something that could be mistaken for a rude remark, so he added, "I'm enjoying myself, really."

She arranged the folds of her coat over her legs. "He didn't want me to go out with you tonight, and it felt like old times a little."

"It's my age, of course," Louis said.

She sat there in the ghostly light of the front seat and stared at him. Then she leaned over, put her arms around his neck, and kissed him. It was a long, tender, deeply arousing kiss. He breathed in her mouth, lightly caressed the back of her head. When she pulled away, she patted the side of his face, and said, "Don't think about your age."

"I never worry about it, really," he lied. "Can't be helped, right?"

"Right," she said.

"Right," Louis said. He got out of the car and looked at the falling snow. He was thinking that he could bound across the lot if he wanted to. He walked around the car and opened the door for her, held her hand as she got out.

"I've embarrassed you," she said.

"No."

They went on across the lot, arm in arm, and when they pushed through the heavy wooden doors of the restaurant he saw that there was a dust of snow on her shoulders, her hair. He was suddenly filled with an aching sense of having already lived through what he would ever have of romance: her kiss now seemed merely the kindness of a young woman, an act of graciousness, freely given because it was not important, did not signify. As they sat down in a little booth along one wall, in a dark alcove of the place, he felt the absurdity of his own chain of thought over a thing small as a kiss, and a little tremor began in his stomach. He took a sharp breath, trying to get control of his suddenly rampaging nerves. She was getting out of her coat, having some trouble with one of the sleeves, and as he leapt to his feet to help her, his hip struck the table. One of the wine glasses toppled over on its side and shattered.

"Oh, hell," Louis said.

She was standing with the coat draped over one shoulder, and then the waiter was there. The waiter was young; a tall, thin handsome man with jet black hair and blue eyes. He helped Annie out of the coat, cleared away the broken glass, while Louis simply sat across the table and watched, mumbling apologies and trying to make jokes about his clumsiness. The younger man held Annie's chair for her, and the smile she gave him was appreciative and somehow collusive: they were both young. They probably liked the same music and the same movies; no doubt there were parts of speech, fashions, body language, articles of faith, magazines, and books they had experienced in common, and could talk about. "My name is Terrence," the young man said, putting menus down. "I'll be your waiter for this evening." He left them with the menus, which were enclosed in tall, leather folders rimmed with gilt. Annie opened hers, then reached in her purse and brought a cigarette out. He breathed, gazed at her while she lighted the cigarette. She was staring at the menu. The waiter came back and poured water for them. "Can I get you something to drink before your meal?" he said.

Annie had the menu open before her. She leaned forward a little to look at the wine list, holding her cigarette off at a slight angle. Louis wondered why he had never in his life been able to summon the ease—the placid, confident grace—that was in the way she held her cigarette, and mused over what she might order to drink. In the next instant, as she started to say what she would have, she gulped, lost a syllable in having to swallow, put the tips of two fingers to her lips, said, "Excuse me," and started again. "I'll have Chablis."

Louis wanted to reach over and take her hand. He said, "Me, too."

When the waiter had gone, he sipped his water, and his hands shook.

"I know I shouldn't smoke," she said.

Something in the way she now looked at him made him feel that he could tell her anything. "I'm nervous," he said.

She put one hand to her chest. "Me, too."

"I wonder what it is," he said. Then: "That's a lie. I know what it is."

She was simply gazing at him.

"Too easy to lie about these things," he said. He had no clear idea what his own words meant—if she had asked him to define *these things* he believed he might have to excuse himself. He almost blurted this out in the mood of honesty that was on him.

"You know," she said, "there's a wonderful sad kindness in your eyes."

"You, too," he said, and realized how wooden—how ridiculous *that* was. "I mean, I like what I see in your eyes, too."

"What do you see there?" Her slight smile was almost a challenge.

He said, "Vibrancy."

"I'm a librarian," she said.

"Since when has occupation had anything to do with what's in a person's eyes?"

She sat back, took a deep draw on the cigarette. "I sometimes think I'm getting beady-eyed."

"It hasn't happened yet," Louis said, and felt curiously at ease. A few moments later, after the wine had been poured, he was calm enough to offer a toast, holding his glass out, his hand good and steady.

"To friendship," he said.

"Friendship."

"Happy birthday," he told her, and they drank to that.

When the waiter returned, they ordered dinner. Louis was surprised to find that he was ravenously hungry: all his nervousness was gone. They ate a big meal and they ordered champagne and brandy. They were both a little tipsy by the time they were through, and as they crossed the parking lot in the snow, she began to hum softly—a happy little tuneless cantillation.

When they reached the car, she said, "Let's go dancing."

"Is it allowed?"

"Whether or not it's allowed."

He held the car door open for her, then tried to close it too soon.

"Oops," she said. "Ow."

He had caught her ankle. "Good Lord," he said.

"It's okay," she said, "you just squeezed it a little. You didn't push hard."

"I'm so sorry, Annie."

"Come on," she said. "It won't even bruise."

Letting her close the door, he trudged around to the driver's side and got in. They were sitting in the clouds of their own breathing.

"Cold," she said.

"Jesus," said Louis. "I don't believe I did that."

"Will you stop it? We were talking about dancing. Let's go dancing."

"You can dance on that ankle?"

"I told you it's fine. Really."

They were quiet a moment. He started the car and gunned the engine, put the defroster on. He had to get out and wipe the snow off the windshield, and in the few moments it took to do this, he tried to regain his composure. She was a shape in ᴉne window, but he knew she was watching him.

When he had settled behind the wheel again, she said, "Do people call you Lou?"

"Sometimes," he said.

"There's dancing at the Royal Duluth, isn't there?"

"I don't know."

"There's a lounge, and they have dancing. I'm sure of it."

"At the Royal Duluth?"

She nodded.

"Let's go," he said, putting the car in gear.

The snow was coming like a full-fledged storm now, but they drove through it. The lights of the city made a bright gold glow on the frosty dark, and the dim windows of closed shops gave them back their own gliding car in a swirling curtain of snow. The hotel stood alone in one city block, just up from the old Palace Theatre on Front Street. They parked along the curb and made their way across the huge shadow of the building to the entrance. When they strolled under the heavy gilt arches of the lobby, they were singing "Old Cape Cod" out of tune, and the porter there—a tall, gloomy-looking man in an ugly burgundy suit—informed them that the lounge was closed, that there was no dancing on any night of the week (or of the year, for that matter, save New Year's Eve), that it was past ten o'clock of a Wednesday in March, and that they were waking up the hotel's few guests with their singing.

"Sorry," Annie said. "I guess this isn't the *old* Royal Duluth. In the *old* Royal Duluth there was dancing every night, and a girl could get some sparkling wine to drink out of her high-heeled shoes if she wanted to." She took a few steps into the enormous, dark-wood-paneled, marble-columned lobby, then turned, put her hands up as though to stretch in sunlight, and said, "I'll bet you could in 1940." She fixed the porter with a dark look. "Do you have any rooms?"

"We have rooms," he said, and went by her to take his place behind the gothic altar of a front desk.

Now she was looking at Louis.

"It's late," he said, his heart racing. "I'd better get you home."

She did nothing for a moment, then simply strolled by him, holding her purse by its strap over one shoulder, and seeming to daydream. He followed her outside, and held the car door open for her. The snow had let up, was just tiny grains of ice now. When he got in behind the wheel, she was staring out at the facade of the hotel. He started the car, and then let it idle for a time. There wasn't anything he could think of to say.

She sighed, leaned back in the seat.

"It's been a lovely time," he managed.

"I didn't mean to embarrass you," she said.

"You haven't."

"We were having a good time and I didn't want to stop."

"Yes," he said, reaching for her. But in the gently pliant way she accepted his kiss, he had the feeling that this was the wrong thing to do, just now. He touched the side of her face, then shifted to his side of the seat and put his hands on the wheel.

"You remember telling me you already felt as if we were friends?" she said.

He said, "Yes."

"Do you still feel that way?"

"Yes."

She folded her arms and seemed to nestle in the folds of her coat. "Me, too."

He drove her back to her father's house, and walked with her up onto the porch. There, she turned and looked out at the prodigious white expanse of the moonless lake, at one end of which the far lamps of Superior winked like little minute traces of fire in the deep, gray distances. "Looks like it just goes on forever," she said. "Doesn't it?"

When he put his arms around her, she laid her head against his chest. The windows of the house were dark, but then the porch light came on. He breathed the damp fragrance of her hair, standing in the light. The wind was cold, and groaned in the eaves of the porch.

"Annie," he said. He couldn't believe this was happening.

She looked at him, smiled, then kissed him. It was a kiss that left him with a sense of just how meager his life had been over the past few years. Abruptly he felt starved, deprived. An old, unfortunate man. He held tight, kissing her neck, the side of her face.

"Do you want to come in for a nightcap?" she asked.

He said, "I think we woke your father."

"I don't think he was asleep."

"Well, there's no sense disturbing him."

"Goodnight," she said.

"I'd like to see you again," he said. "I'd like to meet your daughter."

"Yes."

"We'll have fun," he told her.

She nodded. "Goodnight."

He walked out to the car and then stood gazing at the shape of her, framed in the light of the front door. She waved, and he waved back. She closed the door, was gone. Something about the way the house had seemed to surround and contain her—the looming, shadowed walls and lightless windows, the jutting, snow-covered eaves and the heavy curve of the roof—made him think of everything he would have to learn about her, all the facets of her life that he couldn't know yet, but might come to know. All the times he had driven past this house: all the times he had missed it in the blur of passing houses, as he moved through his city. In the dark, he still gazed for a time at the dark shape of it, and then he got into the car and drove himself home.

They made love for the first time one evening at his house while Roger was out on a weekend with friends from the university. The television was on, they had been staring at it, talking quietly, and then they had begun. A few moments later, quite as if this were the pleasant and comfortable habit of years, they went upstairs to his bedroom. It seemed to Louis that they had both known it would happen. In the dark of his bedroom, he undressed her—she had to help him with her bra—and then she lay back on his bed while he got out of his own clothes. She was very slender except for the soft fleshy swelling of her lower abdomen—the ripe feel of the skin there, where she had carried her child—and the gentle roundness of her hips. He thought she was more beautiful than he could have imagined, and the fact that she lay there before him, perfectly happy to have him gaze upon her, made him tremble.

"My love," he said, lying down at her side.

Her breasts were small and firm; the nipples stood out when he kissed them. She was utterly quiet, yet her hands seemed to guide him. It seemed that she met every slight turn or change of motion or rhythm he made with something of her own. At one point, while she meditated above him, moving only inside, so that her body seemed to pulse on him, her hands down on his chest to support her weight, he lay staring at the rapt, wondering expression on her face, and thought of calling to her, as though she were somewhere away from him; but in the next instant she looked down at him and smiled. "Oh," she said. "Mmmm."

It put him over the edge. "Annie," he said, reaching to pull her down to him, to kiss her breathless mouth.

"My darling," she said afterward.

"Yes," he said. "Those words exactly."

"You were very gentle. I never felt so—*cared for,* making love."

"I hope that's good," he said.

"It's good."

"Annie, I think you're beautiful."

She kissed his shoulder.

"I've been so miserable," he said.

"Don't talk like that." She sat up, stretched her arms, like someone waking from a long sleep. Then she turned, began kissing his chest. He breathed, sighed. In the dimness, her hair looked as though it were made of a kind of light. She rested her chin on his chest and smiled. "No more miserable," she said.

· · ·

There followed weeks of seeing each other in the evenings,
of brief meetings in the middle of the day, sometimes at the
Royal Duluth Hotel, and sometimes at Louis's house. It was
like an affair—as if they were adulterers, and though Louis
found this exhausting and in some way puzzling, he was also
willing to admit that there was something delicious about keeping to themselves the secret of their relation. It had continued
in that way until the middle of the summer, when they started
going on outings together, and she would bring Linda. This
seemed a kind of signal from her, and in any case he had wanted
to bring everything out in the open, being, as he was, proud of
her love. Through July and August, it became a sort of unac-
knowledged fact that they were seeing each other. Louis and
Mr. Field worked at being friendly, and had in fact become
cautiously fond of each other—they had even spent a few evenings in each other's company without Annie being there. She
seemed to be orchestrating everything, getting ready for the
change that was approaching, and at the end of August, Louis,
considering the change was well enough prepared for, made his
proposal. At the time, he experienced something like a twinge
of incompleteness, as if he were reciting part of a script and the
words were not his own, but he attributed this to the rattled
state of his nerves. Annie had responded with the amused, interested, friendly look that had started him on the way to love
in the first place. "I'd love to," she said.

He said, "When."

"When do you want to?"

"Now."

"This minute?"

"Today."

"What's your hurry."

"I think I'm pregnant," he said.

She laughed.

"Will you marry me," he said again.

"I told you I would, yes."

"When."

"Let's announce it first, all right? Let's be fiancés for a while."

"How long is a while?"

She shrugged. "A month. Two months."

"Two months."

"You already have me, Lou. What's two months?"

"I want us living together. I want to take you to Europe. I've got a little money put away, Annie. And I'm—I'm not getting any younger."

"Two months is not such a long wait," she said.

Over the weeks of the turn of the season, things had settled into the old patterns of the summer. There were outings—to the beach at Park Point, to the rocks up on the north shore, to Superior and the smaller lakes west and south, to Minneapolis, for theater and concerts—and often Linda came along, or Roger and the young girl he was seeing, whose name was Fran, and who struck Louis as being quite unable to enjoy herself, quite uneasy in the company of Louis and his young fiancée. Once or twice, James Field had come, too. Or they had spent the day at the house: Field's sister would cook something, and later Field and Louis would sit in the living room staring at chess while Annie and her aunt Ellen played cards at the dining room table. Everything was calm and friendly and domestic, and seemed the logical end of love to Louis, and yet he felt something slipping out of his connection to Annie. Lately all of their time alone together was somehow freighted with what would become of them in the heart of the family they were going to make. Linda had her demands, her troubles with the coming change, and Roger did, too. This was precisely what they had expected, of course, and yet what Louis had not expected was that it would alter the way Annie came to him, would upset the lovely balance of her passion and make him feel always a little deprived of her, of any time in true intimacy with her, free of the lingering concerns and worries of daughter, father, aunt—his own son. Lately he had labored under the continuing suspicion that something else was happening, something else was changing for her, calling her into distances he couldn't bridge with talk, or with kindness, or with passion.

Paris Is in France

Field walked his granddaughter to school. They strolled hand in hand up the shady, broken sidewalk, the long incline away from the lake, and today the distance left him feeling a little winded, a little arthritic—his knees aching, his hip catching him with each step. It was the sort of exercise he needed, and in any case he didn't mind. This was one of the daily tasks that defined him in a way. Linda walked along beside him, looking around, as if seeing these lawns and houses for the first time, and he had the old familiar feeling of wanting to shield her. Very lightly, he touched the back of Linda's head, smoothed the curls there. "Why so quiet?" he said.

"I don't know."

"Did Stephanie's mother put Stephanie on?"

"What?"

"Did you talk to Stephanie?"

She nodded.

"I'm sorry she can't do the project with you."

"She's moving away," Linda said.

They walked on a few paces.

"You're awful quiet," he said.

"I'm tired of school," she announced.

"Well, now and then everybody gets tired of school."

"This is permanent."

He laughed and lightly squeezed her hand. They went quietly along the sun-dappled sidewalk under the trees. When a chilly little stirring of air raised a swarm of dry red leaves around them, they crossed the street. Out of the shade, it was warmer. Linda turned to look over her shoulder.

"What's wrong," he said. "Did you forget something?"

"No."

"You keep looking back."

"I just did that once."

He watched her for a few paces. "Is there something going on?"

"What?" she said.

They had come to an intersection, a crossing light. They waited, and she began to hum something, staring off toward the school.

He thought he recognized the tune. "'What is that?" he said, as the light changed.

"What?"

They were crossing the street.

"What you were whistling."

"'Santa Maria.'" There was a way she pursed her lips when she spoke. He thought it was an unfriendly-seeming expression, almost flippant, and it was a thing he had seen other girls her age do; he wanted to find some way to discourage her from it. He couldn't imagine where to begin, without embarrassing her by calling attention to it.

"Where'd you learn 'Santa Maria'?"

"What?"

"Never mind," he said, irritated.

"I learned it from Aunt Ellen."

A moment later, he said, "Do you know how old that song is?"

"Aunt Ellen says she's got slides from when she went to

Europe, and she'll show them to me before Louis takes us there. After they get married."

"That'll be fine." Field had heard the note of displeasure in her voice. "Wouldn't you like that?" he asked.

"Sure."

They went on for a time without speaking. She was now staring at the sidewalk ahead, and he took a moment to gaze at her. Annie had put a red skirt and blue blazer on her, and she seemed comfortable enough. Watching her, Mr. Field experienced a pang of recognition, an almost visceral sense of his own genes in her blood, the weight and bulk of his flesh. In time, perhaps, she would lose all of her baby fat, and maybe she would have the shapeliness—the slender, fine-boned look—of her mother. And her mother's mother. But he didn't think so: in the ovoid shape of her face, the uncomplicated set of its features, he saw his own features, his own oddly expectant, rounded face.

"So," he said when she turned to look at him. "Where would you like to go in Europe?"

"I don't want to go there."

He stopped her. "Why not?"

She shrugged, looking away. "I don't know."

"Well, that's just silly."

"I don't want to go," she said.

"Is it because you'd have to fly?" He himself was afraid of flying, and he knew Annie was. He assumed the child must be.

"I'd like to fly in a plane," she said.

"Well, then, why don't you want to go?"

"I don't know."

"Linda, that is not an intelligent answer."

"I just don't," she said.

He took her hand and they started forward again. "Europe is—" he began. "It's—thousands of kids your age would love to get the chance to go there and see it—see France and Paris. Paris. My God."

"I know where Paris is," she said. "I saw it on television anyway."

"Television is nothing. Less than nothing. You have to stand on the street and see the cars and the buildings and the people. You have to *be* there."

She was silent.

"Is it because you'd be going with Louis?"

She considered for a moment. "No."

"It is Louis—isn't it."

"No," she said.

Ahead of them, in a wide green field, was the school and the playground, with its monkey bars and swings, and the tall sliding board from which, last year, she'd fallen and fractured her collarbone. Field never looked at it without thinking that she might have broken her spine or her neck. He squeezed her hand lightly, then let go. They went on up the sidewalk to the entrance of the building. Five buses were lined up in front, and children were streaming out of them. Others were crossing the field. There was a lot of horseplay, a lot of running and grappling in the grass. Cars slowed and stopped, and children got out. Mr. Field walked his granddaughter up to the door where, all those years ago, he had walked Annie. He bent down to kiss Linda on the cheek. "Do well," he said, as always.

Her answer was automatic: "I will."

And she joined the throng of others filing into the building.

The walk back to the house, downhill, was somehow more of a strain on his legs. The sun was so bright now that its reflection on the lake, even at this distance, was blinding. In the house, Ellen had her music going again. She was in Linda's room, making the bed.

"Why would someone from school call Linda *before* school?" Field said, watching her tuck the spread under the pillow. She stood back and put her hands on her hips, then looked at him.

"Well?" he said.

"Someone called her before school?"

"I just said so, Ellen."

She moved to pick up the plaid skirt, which Linda had left in a heap on the floor next to the closet. "It happens," she said.

"I don't remember it happening."

"All right," she said, standing there with the skirt folded over her arm. "What then?"

"I don't know."

"Go on to work and stop fretting about everything, will you?"

"I'm sorry—am I fretting?"

She gave him a commiserating smile. "Runs in the family, I know."

"Did Annie say anything to you this morning?" he asked.

"She was preoccupied with Linda."

"You didn't get the feeling that she was preoccupied with something else?"

"What about?"

"I was asking you."

"I don't know," Ellen said. "Annie doesn't confide in me the way she used to." She paused, looked down, seemed about to cry. Quietly she turned from him and busied herself with tidying up the room.

"Ellen," he said.

Her children, five boys, were scattered all across the country— two in Florida, in different parts of the state; one in Ohio; another in Texas; still another in California. They were all working jobs and raising families, and she never saw them anymore. When she'd decided to move north to live with her brother, there were hurt feelings. No one could understand why she would want to live in Duluth. She had wanted to be independent, not to depend on anyone for anything. Her husband, with whom she had made a difficult marriage over almost thirty years, had left her enough money to pay all the bills and have some left over to provide a small monthly income. If there was

anything to say about Billy, it was that he was thorough. He
had been dead now almost six years, and she thought of him
as from a great distance, from long ago and far away. If she
missed him, she never spoke of it; but she never spoke ill of
him, either. He was just the man who had been her husband,
the father of her children, whom everyone called Billy, even his
sons, and he was gone now. Whatever his weaknesses, they had
traveled with him to the grave. Mr. Field believed privately that
during the last years of his brother-in-law's life, Ellen had
changed somehow, had outdistanced the man in some way that
was puzzling and perhaps vaguely angering: in any case, staying
with them, recuperating after the wild, drunken, sick pursuit
of Annie, he had noted a reserve between them, a politeness
born of distance, as though they were somehow making do with
a situation neither of them could fully understand. Their boys
were mostly grown, and had begun to leave them, Billy had
retired from his job at the county court, and perhaps they were
having trouble finding things to do in the days. Mr. Field had
imagined that some of the unease he'd noticed—or all of it—
might be the result of his presence in their house, but when he
mentioned this to Ellen, her response was definite and quick.
"Are you kidding?" she said. "Billy's glad you're here. He's got
somebody to talk to and argue with now." And perhaps it was
just that the fury had gone out of their love—for even when
they were courting, back when James Field was still in high
school, they had made everyone wonder at the sudden violence
of their disagreements, and the quickness of their temper with
each other. Ellen, after they had been storming at each other
and breaking things in their house for a decade, was fond of
saying that no one had expected them to last a year. And, well,
they had in fact gone twenty-nine years, and raised five robust,
healthy boys. And if the ending years were different for them
both, it was a thing she would not seem to regret, or question.
In a way, it was as if she were allowing him his dignity in death:

one tended to remember his towering rages, and not the man sitting quietly in a chair, beginning to suspect that he would die soon.

Mr. Field often thought that if his wife had lived, they would have had more children—sons and daughters—and that their children would remember them being in love, and passionate about each other, as Ellen and Billy had been. The end, then, couldn't matter as much. For a long time now he had understood why his sister had decided to come north rather than move in with one of her sons: here, she could live with and among the memories *she* chose.

Now, watching her close his granddaughter's bureau drawer, Mr. Field tried to soothe her. "Annie *never* confided in me."

A moment later, she said, "Here." And walking over to him, turned and lifted the thick, pepper and salt hair away from the back of her neck, as though she wore a necklace and wanted him to clasp it. "See anything?" she said.

He said, "What?"

"There's a sore place. Is it a mole?"

"I don't see a mole," he said.

She touched the skin just below the hairline at the base of the skull. "Right there. It's very sore."

"Ellen," he said, "there's nothing wrong with you."

"I know that," she said irritably, stepping away from him. "Good Lord. I was just wondering if there was any possible connection between this and the muffled sensation I'm getting."

"You mean with your hearing? I don't see how there could be."

She said, "I don't either. I was just wondering." Moving by him, she went out into the hallway, to the stairs and down. He followed, gazing at her there before him in the stairwell, his one sister, aged sixty-four—a woman who, in one famous instance of her impulsive nature when young, once knocked her husband over a chair and broke one of his ribs, and who was now rather sadly careful and tentative, holding onto the rail, concentrating, descending. "Think you can stand living alone with me again?" he asked.

"I can stand anything," she said.

He went out onto the porch and lighted a cigarette. The sun was almost summer-warm here. She had turned the television on. In a minute, he would have to leave for work.

He smoked, and the wind picked up, reached him under the eave of the porch, carrying with it the morning's chill. He was thinking about the absurdity of Louis Wolfe as his son-in-law, and then he was thinking about the fact that Annie had written Cole Gilbertson.

"James," Ellen said from the door, "it's late."

"You don't suppose he'd show up here again, do you?"

"Who?"

"You know very well who, Ellen."

"All right. No, I don't suppose he'll show up."

"I wish Annie hadn't written him."

"Yes."

"I just have this feeling," Mr. Field said.

"Is it the feeling that you're late?"

"I'm going," he said.

"Pardon?"

"I said I'm going."

"Well, go."

When a car came down the street, he caught himself staring through the glare of the windshield, trying to decide who it was, and feeling unpleasantly that he would not be surprised to see a face he knew all too well.

Spy

Alice Minneford lay back on the motel bed and complained about his mood. She wasn't wearing anything, and with one leisurely finger she traced a line from her breasts to her navel. They had made love, and now Gilbertson was sitting in the chair opposite the bed, a towel in his lap. His eyes burned. He felt woozy and faintly sick to his stomach. She had ordered breakfast from room service, and it had been lying out on the bureau, on one big tray—cold eggs and limp bacon; glasses of milk and cups of coffee—when he came in from the morning's action.

While she slept, he had driven back to the house, had parked almost a block away, and had seen Annie walk out and get into her car. Annie looked the same, and it struck him oddly that it was as if she had forgotten everything between them. His mind reeled. It seemed incredible that she should look so much as she always had, that she should show no sign of having fought to put him behind her. He couldn't imagine what such a sign might be; it was just that she appeared so calm and comfortable, working to start the car, turning the wheel and checking for oncoming traffic. She drove past him, staring ahead. He watched her car go on out of sight, and then he saw his daughter leaning into the glass of the upstairs window, following the progress of the car—his daughter, so much bigger. A chubby, round, baby-looking face that sent a thrill of recognition and resentment through him. She was a little fat girl. They had made a fat girl out of her.

He returned to the motel in a white rage, to find the litter of breakfast and Alice lying on the bed, sleepy, pill-drunk, and wanting sex.

"Not yet," he said. "You're going to make a little phone call for me."

"Who am I calling?"

He was dialing the number; he hadn't ever forgotten it. "Ask for Linda. Tell whoever answers that you want to talk to Linda. Say you're from her school or something."

When he heard the ringing, he handed her the phone.

She said, "Hello, is Linda there, please?" She stood there and waited.

"Who answered?" he muttered.

"Some man." A moment later, she handed him the receiver and lay back on the bed, opening her legs, smiling at him.

After he hung up, he became frightened that he might have done the wrong thing. "What if she tells them it was me?"

Alice shrugged. "They have to know you're here sometime, don't they?"

"There's no telling what they've told her about me."

"Like maybe you're a coke head without a job?"

"Annie promised once not to set her against me."

"Well," Alice said, "why don't you come over here and get some fun out of life?"

He had obliged her, working himself up, going at her with an urge to hurt, and finding that she was equal to his every move. For a moment, he was glad of her, kissing the smoothness of her pale shoulder, forgetting everything, riding the slow un-dulation of her hips.

Now, she was just troublesome.

"You know," she said, "I think you actually have a crummy disposition. I think that's what your problem is." She kept tracing the flesh of her abdomen.

"Stop it," he said. "Stop doing that with your hand."

"You don't find it sexy?"

"Just lay off it."

She pulled the spread over herself.

"What the hell are they feeding her," he muttered. "She's a fat kid. I don't believe it. Can't they see it? Why don't they put her on a diet or something."

"It's probably baby fat."

"Bullshit. You didn't see her."

"Poor Cole."

He was going to need more coke. He felt like death now. When he closed his eyes there were stabs of pain, and his throat burned—a poisonous, blistery feeling that made swallowing dreadful.

"I want to see my uncle Ellis," she said, lying back and stretching her arms to the ceiling. "I want to get off the shit. I was off it until you showed up. I had coke and pills all over the apartment from the last time, and I hadn't used any of it."

He had bought another travel bag, and the coke was safely stored there. It was in the back of the car.

"So what are we going to do," Alice said. "Just spy on her?"

"Maybe."

She got out of the bed and went into the bathroom, closing the door. He sat and waited, thinking of possible courses of action. There were things he needed to get straight in his mind, and he had an idea of himself as being concerned as a father, of worrying about the welfare of his child. It seemed incredibly unfair that Field could be the way he had been about Annie, and that he, Gilbertson, should not be permitted the same furious protectiveness. When he thought of Annie, he caught himself wringing his hands with rage. She had taken Linda away, and now they were going to make sure of it; they were going to let some stranger have her.

He put his pants on and went out to the car and got the travel bag. Alice was showering. He sat at the bureau and prepared the drug amid the piled dishes. He knew he should eat, but the thought of food made him queasy. When he finished with the coke, he put the travel bag under the bed, and sat in the chair again, feeling the rush, thinking about how they had all been conspiring against him from the start. Then he thought about Tenchley, and this sent him to the window to peer out. Sunlight was beating down on the parking lot, and high, sunny alps of cloud were visible off to the north. Everything looked peaceful. Cars went by on the road. Birds darted through the fall colors in the trees that lined the left side of the parking lot. In front of the end cottage, two teenaged boys were arguing and tugging at each other over a baby stroller they had apparently unloaded from the back of a leisure van. A woman stood by with her hands on her hips, looking exasperated and tired. Gilbertson told himself it was inconceivable that Tenchley could know his whereabouts, and yet he couldn't bring himself to believe it.

When Alice came out of the bathroom he was sitting on the edge of the bed staring at the television screen. "Leave It to Beaver." He wasn't really watching it. She came out, and he looked up from the screen, saw the imperfections of her face, the odd, low-slung, tall curve of her hips, and it dawned on him that he had never even felt quite friendly toward her.

"What," she said.

He went into the bathroom.

"Hey," she said on the other side of the door. "What was that about?"

"Nothing," he said. "Get dressed."

"I don't feel like getting dressed."

"All right," he said.

"Hey, Cole?"

"What?"

"Where'd you put the travel bag?"

He said nothing.

"Fuck it, Cole. I know all about it."

"You said you wanted to get off the shit."

"Fuck it," she said.

He looked at himself in the mirror. He had come in here to get away from her. "Jesus," he said. Then, loud enough for her to hear him: "Just get dressed."

"Cole?"

"I'll be out in a minute."

"You've got it in there with you, don't you."

He said nothing—she could believe what she wanted.

A moment later, she whined, "It's lonely out here."

"Shit," he muttered. He was just hiding from her.

"Hey—Cole?"

"Yeah—I said I'd be out in a minute."

"You see how I can adjust, Cole? I don't even care."

He was silent.

"I just wanted to dabble a little."

Turning in the closed space, he began to feel locked in.

"Not like you, Cole."

He put the shower water on, got out of his pants, and stepped in under the spray. It was cold, getting hot. He stepped back and adjusted it.

"Cole?"

He didn't answer.

"Are you taking a shower? Don't you want to take it to-gether?"

He hesitated a moment, then reached around and opened the door. She was letting herself in for trouble, coming in on him like this, when he was in this mood. She stood before him, hands at her sides.

"Want to wash me?"

"Sure," he said. He watched her step into the tub with him,

and it was as though he had a kind of mastery over her—as though she were someone he had made up in his mind, and could therefore do anything with.

"What's wrong, Cole?"

The feeling was dissolving, washing from him like the coating of grime from travel and sleeplessness and sweat. Something seemed to be altering in her face, the skin bleaching and twisting slightly, the eyes widening and changing color. "Wait," he said.

"You got a headache? You got too much shit? Stuff'll kill you, lover."

He had put his head under the spray, and she was putting her arms around his middle.

"Poor Cole."

He strove to find the feeling of mastery, and here it was, waiting for him, like victory in a dream. Opening his eyes into the water, he let her touch him, let her do what she wanted to do. He was in control again, turning, so that she could kneel in the spray and take him into her mouth. Finally she lifted her head, the shower water splattering on her blinking eyes, and smiled. "Better?" she said.

He said, "Better."

Later, sitting in the late morning light from the open window, he began to entertain ideas about how he might visit retribution on all of them—all these people going on as if he had never existed. He sat rubbing his own thighs, believing himself to be possessed of some new amazing clarity of mind, even as he was aware that his nerves were going batshit on him. He turned and looked at Alice, sprawled like the aftermath of violence in the bed. For an eerie, panicky instant, he thought he remembered killing her, but she moaned sleepily, rolled lazily over on her back. The room was too bright. It hurt his eyes to look at anything. Closing them, he heard the rush and whoosh of traffic on the road outside, only it seemed to be veering through the veins in his head, somehow. He took three of Alice's pills, and lay down in the other bed. It was awful waiting for something to change. His heart thrummed in his chest, as if trying to run from the deep, stomach-wrenching, chilly sense of terror that now took hold of him. Shivering, as if with fever, he pulled the blankets over himself, and curled up in the dark hollow of his own ragged breathing.

Tourists in the Stardust Shop

In the middle of the afternoon, Louis's son entered the store, and the tiny bell above the door frame gave its cheerful little ding. The bell had been the boy's idea; there were so many small things he was clever at, and yet whenever Louis looked at him he felt something go out to him—a protective, hopeful ache, and the suspicion that his son was and would remain a kind of amiable failure.

"I need some salary," Roger said. He was wearing a bright imitation-silk jacket and baggy black pants, and there was something almost clownish about the way he walked, a Chaplinesque little swagger in each step. "Can you manage it?"

Louis opened the register and gave him ten dollars.

"I was hoping for more than that."

"How much more?"

"I need fifty."

Louis stared at him.

"Come on, Dad."

"Son, you haven't earned that much this week. And there's fall tuition to make yet."

The boy shuffled a little, looking down. It was too easy to make him feel shame. Louis gave him the money, felt it as a way of buying him off, and was abruptly ashamed of himself. Lately nothing had been easy between them.

"I'll need it for tonight," Roger said. "We're all still going to the movies, right?"

"That's the plan," said Louis.

"I'm taking Fran to a late dinner afterward. Or she's taking me. I mean it's her car."

"I don't suppose you feel like minding this place for a couple hours."

"Why don't you just close it up for a while—how much business can we lose?"

"I wouldn't want a regular customer to find us closed."

"I'll watch it tomorrow morning," Roger said. "Really."

Louis nodded at him but he was already turning to go.

"Thanks for the pay, Dad."

"Right," Louis said.

During the first fifteen years of his son's life, they had traveled the world together, living in plush officer's quarters in Madrid and Amsterdam and Berlin, and Roger had grown accustomed to the idea of privilege where his father was concerned. In England, and in Japan, he had gone to expensive private schools, had lived in an essentially segregated society, where officers' children were not encouraged to associate with children of en-listed men. Often, this had meant that the boy's only companion was his father. They spent afternoons together looking at the various things there were to see in the cities where Louis was stationed, and in the evenings they would do their respective tasks together—Roger his schoolwork, and Louis the work he had brought home from his office on base—sitting side by side at the big oak dining table that had belonged to Louis's mother. In several of the places they were stationed, they'd had servants, paid for by the Department of the Air Force, and on one or two assignments Roger's schooling was conducted by tutors. The advantage of all this was that the boy had very early exhibited a precociousness: at eleven years of age he could discuss with some insight the politics of the divided city of Berlin, and he knew the names of certain generals of the European theater of the Second World War. By the time his father retired, there was a bond between them, a deep allegiance to each other that held the rest of the world at a remove. They spoke and argued and disputed like brothers, and of course the older man, in his extravagant pride, was happily anticipating wonderful things.

It was clear to them both by now that nothing could have prepared Louis for the series of failures which followed.

Disciplinary problems, problems of attention and concentration, of will. Roger, trudging up the hill to St. Mark's High School in the middle of a Duluth winter, had apparently found himself unable to bear the idea of the people inside, with their authority and their narrow concerns and their badly over-crowded rooms. The boy had confessed to feeling cast adrift, forced to spend his days with people who would never understand him, never give him the interest and attention he needed. And Louis, trying to make up for what he had come to see were mistakes of indulgence and familiarity, had been forced into the role of taskmaster, requiring the boy to perform certain daily exercises of discipline and study, watching him like a jailer, trying to keep him from associations and habits that might make matters worse. In this way, they had got through Roger's high school years, and since then there had been bad stumbles at three different colleges. Now, of course, the problem was no longer one of attitude—now, in some mysterious way, the ability to concentrate fully seemed to have got beyond Roger; Louis had come to think that his son just couldn't bring it out of himself: what had come effortlessly when he was fifteen, now came rarely indeed if it came at all.

Father and son were divided by their mutual discomfort over the change.

Moreover, since Louis had begun with Annie, there had developed an even deeper sense of some essential distance between them, as if Louis, in his continuing disappointment and embarrassment at his son's failure to live up to earlier hopes and expectations, were subtly edging him out of his rightful place in their house.

Now, as Louis sat behind the counter in the Stardust Shop and waited for the afternoon to pass—thinking with the old ache, the old, sad guilt, of his badly raised son—a man and a woman entered, and began to browse among the bins. The woman had her hair tied back, and she was showing the signs of being in some sort of haze. Her hands moved nervously around her eyes and over her nose and mouth. She glanced at Louis and then seemed to hesitate. Behind her, the man was standing at the second bin, his hands in the pockets of his denim jacket. He looked like someone's idea of an itinerant ranch hand or cowboy—he wore faded jeans, a workshirt, and a wide leather belt with an embossed gold buckle. It took Louis a moment to notice that his clothes were soiled and tattered, that his face had an odd gray cast to it, and that he was apparently quite shaky.

"Hi-dee," the man said, smiling at him.

"Welcome," said Louis.

"You the owner of this store?"

He nodded.

"This the only antique record store in Duluth, isn't it."

"As far as I know," Louis said.

The woman fidgeted, while her companion appeared to browse. His hands shook when he picked up one of the albums in the bin.

"Old records," he said.

"Can I help you find something?" Louis asked him.

"Just looking."

Now the woman turned and faced him. There was nothing at all unfriendly in her demeanor, and yet Louis felt as though she were about to start something. "You got any aspirin?" she said.

"I might, in back."

"I got a headache."

Louis made his way to the back and opened the desk drawer. He had put a small tin of Tylenol there a week or so ago, but it was gone now. He moved the pencils and folded pieces of paper, looking for it, then decided the young woman would have to get relief elsewhere. When he returned to the front, the man was standing by the counter, hands in the pockets of the jacket, staring at the posters on the wall. The woman had moved to the door. They appeared to have been at odds about something, and they were not looking at each other.

"I'm sorry," Louis said. "I guess I don't have anything."

"You got a lot of money," the man said. "That's what you got."

Louis stared at him. The eyes were a deep, extravagant blue; the features were classically chiseled, sharp. He could see that this had at one time been an extremely handsome face—and there was still a kind of faded attractiveness about it, though the color was unhealthy, and the edges were obviously in the process of losing definition, so that even in this brief time it had already suggested corruption, self-indulgence, a kind of voluptuous decay. "I'm afraid I don't have a lot of money," Louis said, looking into the blue clarity of the eyes.

"You're poor," the other said with a snickering turn of his head.

"I get by."

The man's gaze wandered to the walls again, the crowded aisles. He sighed. "Must be nice being a storekeeper." He said the word with a sardonic twist of his mouth.

"Can I get anything for you today, sir," Louis said, stepping around behind the counter again.

"I doubt it," said the man, and ambled over to the doorway.

"Bye," the woman said, as they went out.

Louis watched them go, and for a second something glimmered under the surface of his mind—an odd pulse of light, an inkling that this visit had not been casual. There had been something quite purposeful about the way the stranger had questioned him. He thought of robbers, casing an establishment before actually hitting it. But the idea was absurd. There wasn't enough money in the Stardust Shop to be worth a robbery attempt.

The afternoon was waning, and a wind was blowing from the bald hills on the other side of the coal dump to the east; pieces of paper and leaves skipped by in gusts through the blue shade outside the shop window. He went to the door, opened it, heard the little bell, and thought of his son. He stood out on the sidewalk and looked up and down the street. There were no pedestrians at this hour, and few cars. The shadows slanted down from the buildings on the other side of the street now. The sun was bright in the windows behind him. Overhead, a jet unscrolled its white trail in the highest part of the sky. He watched it, cupping his hand like a visor over his eyes, thinking about how he should be happy, and feeling his own doubt like a kind of grief, weighing on his heart.

Certain Testimony

When I was small, he read books about raising a child—he consulted them, lived by them. They said: Keep a consistent schedule. They said: Be predictable. They said: Never punish physically. Keep a clear set of expectations that are realistic. He tried to follow it all. He worked at it. When I was eleven, and very precocious, I went into his room and picked up one of the books and sat on the floor reading it. There was dust, and the smell of his cologne, and the nightstand was piled with his books and newspapers. His room was never as orderly as the rest of the house, and I believe that even then I had some vague notion that he was neglecting himself. I sat reading this book called Raising the Only Child as a Single Parent. There were chapters on discipline, on nourishment, on hygiene, and on problems of communication and affection. I read the line: Never allow the child into bed with you. I read the line: Things to Say When in Doubt. It was a list, an actual list of little taglines that were supposed to lead to deeper conversation, or to a richer sense, for the child, of the parent's undivided attention. When the child shows you a drawing, it said, look for specific things to praise— the way part of the drawing is colored or shaped. Refrain from simple expressions of generalized praise. And then later, that night, *when, thinking of anything else, I brought him a drawing I'd done, of a cat on the ledge of a red brick building, and he looked at me with the seriousness of his love and said,* You know, I think I like the red brick best of all—*I remembered the book on his nightstand and felt vaguely disappointed and embarrassed, lied to, though I know quite well that he was trying to be what all the books said he should be. What I mean by this is that there's nothing for it. We love the best way we can. He and I were all there was in the house for a long, long time.*

I was two years old when my mother died. I don't have much in the way of a clear memory of her. What I do have is a sense of something always about to be taken away from me—and the feeling that I wanted to run somewhere, anywhere. When I was around two—sometime shortly after her death—I remember that I woke in the night and the fact of her absence, the reality that she would not come home, would never come home, hit me like some sort of interior storm. I remember that night, and I remember that I didn't cry out or scream or ask to be taken into his bed. I simply lay there trembling in the sudden chill of knowing I was alone. That night, he was up; I could hear him turning the pages of a book. The house was that quiet. But I didn't move, and I'm not sure it was because I was so afraid. I don't remember how long I lay like that, or if he later came in to check on me—as he often did. I just remember the frozen sense of that aloneness. And that's what I learned. For all his effort and his love and the blinding power of his attention, I learned that I was alone.

Do you understand me? He did nothing so gravely wrong. He made mistakes, like anyone, and they were all the mistakes of wanting more than he could have: perfection, a fatherhood that obliterated the possibilities for unhappiness, misunderstanding, unintentional cruelty, failure. He worked at it and I grew up resisting him at every turn, almost as though that were what I had been assigned to do in the world, and we had a sense of humor about it, like friendly adversaries in a continual argument or debate—we understood this about ourselves at least. And in a way we enjoyed being together alone. There were many lovely moments. The world outside the house was big and dark, and terrible, but we were safe and warm, and we had each other. And yet when Cole came along—with that cavalier easygoing boy's way and those looks—I wanted nothing more than to be out of James Field's house forever. I felt as though I had been given some strange new intoxicating air to breathe, and I'm not talking about the drugs now, either. That was really only serious later. Then, we smoked pot, like everyone else; we did coke once or twice. It was all just to keep the party going, and I wasn't aware that Cole was as deep into it as he was. It was just a party, then, wanting more than my days as they were, as if I craved a life that was as far away as Mars. Space trips away from the house on North Superior Street, where we had been boarded up together, my father and I, still somehow feeling the effects of a loss I had no clear memory of.

It was not morbidity, either, really: he kept no mementos or pictures around; he saw other women; he took me places and we had fun and laughed. I was allowed to bring friends over to visit and spend the night, and I roughhoused and played like any other little girl; I took piano lessons, and studied the flute, and ballet, and he took me to concerts and plays and movies; we spent many hours at various sights of interest in the upper Midwest, and one summer we traveled east to New York and Boston and Washington. I had all the time with him I could have wanted, and, growing up, I wanted a lot. I would never have believed that I would one day long to be away from him as much as I had ever longed to be with him. And I would never have believed that he would fight me about it like a possessive, jilted lover. Which was exactly the way he behaved, even undersanding that Cole frightened him—even understanding that he saw through Cole, saw the ice under Cole's skin, that would never change. Finally I don't know what I became for him, then. I knew that I had to stay as far away as I could, though. Even loving him as I still did—even feeling that I had hurt him badly. Even knowing that he was drinking too much, and that I'd taken

*the heart out of him somehow. There was something vaguely hu-
miliating about it all, and for years after Cole and I were settled in
Savoy, after I'd had Linda, and had begun to see what a mistake
I'd made marrying someone like that, and it was quite clear that
things were never going to be any different—even then, for a long
time I couldn't bring myself to think about what I might say
to my father over the telephone or even in a letter. And even when
the time came that I knew I had to get out, knew I couldn't stay
with Cole another day, it was all I could manage just sending a
telegram announcing my arrival. I had never been so nervous in
my life.*

*I have had a recurring dream since I was very small. In this dream,
I seem to be standing somewhere in the high, rocky bluffs above the
city, except that I'm also, in the odd logic of what happens in sleep,
right at the level of the lake. It is winter. The city of Duluth lies
before me in a ghostlike descent into ice; it sparkles with its lighted
windows, and then it fades, seems to dissolve. I'm alone, and I feel
this with a forlorn and shaken sense of having been abandoned; it
is almost a sense of betrayal, except that there are elements of frus-
tration and fear in it, too. For now, in the distance, where the sky
and the lake merge into one smoky color, I see a wall of blowing
snow come roiling out of an ashen mountain of cloud; it is advancing
toward me across the frozen water, and everything is gray and cold
and the wind howls. I stand there shivering, naked, or barely clothed,
the wind moans as if trying to say a name to me, and off in the
snowing distance, obscured by the moving cloud, something is approaching, coming at me, something I know or will recognize—
any second I'll be able to discern its shape. But then I wake up, and
I'm cold, no matter what I'm wearing or how many blankets I'm
wrapped in; I lie there and shiver. There have been times in my life
when I found it easy to think this dream was somehow about my
mother, but last night I told Louis that when I have this dream, I
wonder if I'm not standing somehow in the very heart of my true
self.*

All I want now is to learn how to be happy without being selfish . . .

. . .

As soon as I got to work, though I was ten minutes late, I called Dr. Naillin's office and made the appointment. I made it for eleven o'clock, and then couldn't concentrate on anything else. Mrs. Bradford, the head librarian, made a catty little comment about how love is blind, but she dearly wished it wouldn't be forgetful and distracted, as well. She's exactly the kind of horrible, vulgar but somehow virginal, aggressive, pants-suit-wearing, cigarette-smoking, late-middle-aged woman that has always reacted to me with the force of some sort of moral objection, as though just by looking at me they can tell that I'm not religious, that I've done things they would never do—and that I am in some strange unspoken way the enemy.

At twenty minutes to eleven I stood in the entrance to her office waiting for her to look up from what she was doing; she had some folders open in front of her and was writing. When she looked up, she smiled, then removed her glasses. A cigarette was burning in the ashtray at her elbow.

"I have a doctor's appointment," I told her. "I won't take lunch."

"A doctor's appointment. We're not sick, are we?"

"No," I said.

She went back to her writing, and I knew I was to take this as her answer—as *exactly* her answer: just enough displeasure not to say anything at all, just enough of a nod for me to know I had her reluctant permission. I got my jacket and headed out of the building without saying anything to the others in the office. I didn't look, but I felt sure she watched me from her window as I crossed the parking lot.

Dr. Naillin's office was in a modest little rambler off Michigan Street—it was the first house Dr. Naillin and his wife owned, back in 1946, after he got out of the navy. It sat back off the road in a stand of birches and its windows were shaded by big green awnings. But for the sign out on the curb, it might as well have been a private residence. I had come there the first time back when I was going around with Cole: I wanted to get a prescription for birth control pills, but hadn't the courage to say anything to the good doctor, and had instead complained of headaches. In fact I was afraid I might be pregnant, and when he began to ask me about the headaches, I remember I thought he might have seen something in my face—and I suppose I left him a little puzzled. The waiting room was in what had been the living room. There were chairs along the walls, and a fireplace with a wide white mantel on which magazines were stacked. On one side was a picture window. The walls in the hallway leading to the examination room were festooned with photographs of all the babies he had delivered over the years.

When I went in there I was as usual almost woozy with recognition, looking at those rows of photographs and remembering how it felt to suspect that I was pregnant, in trouble, nineteen years old. Dr. Naillin himself called me into the examining room and took my hands into his own. "So good to see you again," he said. I had come in for a routine exam only a year previous to this, but I let him look me over in this way, still holding my hands, his eyes trailing over my face as if gauging the effects of time on me. "Well," he said, "you look none the worse for wear."

"I think I'm pregnant," I said.

"Of course," he said. This seemed to bear no relation to anything. He turned and took something from a drawer, and asked. "Have you missed any monthly cycles?"

"This last one," I said, and then his nurse came in—the same one, too, Miss Waple, showing the years in her hair and around her middle, cheerful and smiling and motherly, though as I recalled she was a single woman with no plans to have children ever. She looked past having them now, though I found myself imagining that perhaps she'd changed her mind at some point over the last ten years and, without saying anything to anyone, peopled a house with her own babies. This was impossible, of course: she was a fixture in this office; if she had ever been pregnant, I would've known. Even so, I looked at her and thought about a house full of squawling babies somewhere in hiding, and then she looked at me with that nurturing smile and said, "How are we this morning?"

"We think we're pregnant," I said.

She helped me get ready and comfortable, and then she sat by while Dr. Naillin went about the business of examining me. He hummed half to himself, an old man murmuring under his breath, through the whole procedure—it was something new about him, or a thing I hadn't ever noticed—and I watched his clear eyes shining under thick, furry brows, wondering if he could sense how much *he* was a type: Wise Old Friendly Doctor. It was odd. I felt suddenly quite cold and clear and observant, as though I were not in my body but were watching from somewhere else: the way I imagine life always looked to Cole— everything as mere phenomena. I trickled a little into a pink sample-bottle, and then waited in the examining room, sitting, fully clothed, on the table and looking out the window at the trees and rocks behind Dr. Naillin's old house. He had told me once that it was his honeymoon cottage, and how his wife refused to part with it, even though he was now semiretired, and only saw his patients twice a week there. Now he sidled back into the room and stood staring at me.

"Well," he said.

I said, "Well?"

"It's true," he said.

I waited.

"You are pregnant." Now he smiled. He was apparently under the impression that I would be happy to hear it.

"How far along?" I said, controlling my voice.

"About five weeks."

I looked out the window again. I had suspected it—I had in

fact been pretty certain of it—and now that it was confirmed, I felt stupid. I couldn't believe it.

"Do you want to talk?" he said.

"No," I said. He seemed to be waiting for me to go on, and I suppose I almost told him, almost said it out, that I did not want to be pregnant, that I couldn't be pregnant, not now, not by Louis, who is fifty-two, and not like this—not, for God's sweet sake, by accident. The whole thing was humiliating. I was thinking about this, feeling the heat of deep embarrassment all over my skin, exactly as if I'd been doused in hot water, thinking I could not allow such a ridiculous thing to happen to me, and gazing into the old eyes of Dr. Naillin, whose face had begun to show something of uncertainty. Then, quite without my knowing it would happen, I was smiling like an idiot, deciding in that instant to hide what I really felt, because of course he was not the sort of person you spoke to about these things: he was too much in the mold of the grandfatherly general practitioner to hear what I was already thinking. I might as well have said I was thinking of jumping out a window. Old Dr. Naillin wouldn't know what to do with such a confession; he'd say, "You're a little under the weather. Go home, take a nap. You'll feel better." Dr. Naillin had a central idea of the world, and it was plastered all over the walls of his waiting room: he had brought more than seven thousand babies into the world.

So I smiled, and allowed him to attribute my trembling to nervousness.

He handed me a sample bottle of prenatal vitamins. "You know what I have to say, don't you? Plenty of rest. These vitamins. Come see me in a month, and bring another urine sample. Miss Waple will give you some things to read, and she'll set up the appointment."

"Thank you," I said.

And he actually hugged me. "Now you take good care of yourself," he said.

I said I would.

Later, I walked down the cracked sidewalk leading to the parking lot outside, and a scary gust of wind blew down out of the sky, like a stray soul. I remember thinking that it was like something alive, that wanted me to notice it. It stung my face and then was gone, and I got into the car, shaking. I sat there, shaking. The morning was cloudless and very bright, and the leaves were flying everywhere, leaves of an astonishing sunny yellow color. I watched them, sitting behind the wheel of the car. And deciding that I hadn't really thought through marrying Louis. I hadn't really thought it through carefully enough. Not having a child with him. I don't know how long I sat there thinking this.

I remembered when I first realized the enormity of the mistake I'd made with Cole. We were living with his mother in Savoy, in that big old farmhouse. She had gone into town to do some shopping, and we were alone with the baby. We had the whole house to wander in, without Selena's garrulous talk to listen to. We put Linda in the crib in her room with some stuffed toys, then went into our room and made love, Linda crying and whining through the whole thing, and I thought how the true business of adults, when it's being transacted, has nothing to do with children. We had smoked a little, and he was doing coke pretty regularly, keeping it from his mother, and probably keeping some of it from me, too, hiding in the bathroom, using his straight razor and my hand mirror and a little drink straw, the kind you stir your drink with. But this time we had made love and he was very fierce-eyed with dope, his eyes showing that unnatural brightness, and I was feeling it, too, feeling quite separate from Linda, crying in her room. I had lost time for a few seconds, and then I had this funny little moment of recognizing that even if there were something seriously wrong with Linda, I wasn't going to get up and go to her. The thought scared me in a way I can't express, and I made myself stir.

"Come on," Cole said, flopping over on his stomach, reaching for me.

We had already begun to have some trouble—I had discovered that Cole didn't really know how to *be* with someone—but on this day things had been hilarious; we had made love. I thought we were happy enough, and I *had* thought I could work everything out if I was persistent; and I believed that I loved him. Something had been nagging at me underneath for a long time, but I wasn't thinking of it. I was thinking how frightening it was to mentally abandon your baby to whatever might happen. She was crying loud, building up a shriek, and I hurried in to see that she was all right, feeling guilty and fake somehow, as if I didn't really mean it. I heard Cole say my name out, casually, loud enough for me to hear him and turn. Through the small space of the upstairs hall, where we were, I could see him on the rumpled sheets of the bed. He lay there on his belly, smiling, looking at me. We had the rest of the afternoon together, and I can't explain it, but I had the sudden feeling that the rest of the day would pull me in the direction of the something in me that had acceded to the prospect of the loss of the child I held in my arms at that moment.

And I shivered with fear.

Standing there holding Linda, I looked into the white room where Cole lay staring at me, and found myself hoping to be able to hide, to shield myself in care of my baby. "Hey," Cole said, "put her down. Come on."

But I didn't want to go in there, didn't want to have to listen to him talk, or try to keep myself straight all day in his company. I carried Linda into the bathroom, and made the excuse that if she had a warm bath she would sleep, not waiting for him to answer or object. I was still shaking with what I had stared at in my own being, and when I looked into Linda's eyes, into the little toothless, crying mouth, I wanted to run away, run far away with her, where no one could find us. It dawned on me that I was high, that I was about to climb into a bathtub with a five-month-old baby, and I hadn't even got towels for us, or made the water ready. I had just turned twenty-one, and I was living in the home of a man I couldn't imagine anymore for the fright of knowing where we were headed. He talked from the other room, said my name and the baby's; he was happy in his lazy, boy's way of being happy, and he didn't exist, quite. He was someone I didn't know and I was at a place I had never dreamed of, and though this happened long ago, I sometimes think my soul was burned white by that moment. Linda was still crying. Cole came down the hall, impatient, wanting to know what I thought I was doing. He was ripped. He wanted to get back to sex with me. I sat in the hot light of the bathroom, holding my little girl and fearing that I might harm her.

I remembered all that, sitting behind the wheel of the Volks-wagen in the brightness, and then I put the car in gear and drove myself back to the library, my job, what I knew would be Mrs. Bradford's little knowing glances. I wasn't going to be able to do it. When I walked into the central lobby, there was Louis, sitting against the far wall with a magazine in his lap, waiting for me. He smiled. I had almost turned to go—almost seized the half second before he looked up, to duck out of his line of sight. But I was frozen there in the middle of the foyer, and he was out of his seat, folding the magazine tight in his big, dark hands, smiling at me and, I knew, feeling nervous, tentative.

"Is everything okay?" he said. "Mrs. Bradford said you went to see a doctor."

"Mrs. Bradford made it sound serious, too, right?" I couldn't look back in his eyes, and I knew he was noticing it. *Oh, Lou.* I took his elbow and then let go. "I'm fine," I said. "It was just my usual yearly exam."

"But I thought—" He stopped. He had one hand out, his mouth open.

"Lou," I said.

"I thought you'd already gone."

"Look," I said. "it's nothing."

"Honey, you look upset." He followed me past the circulation desk, and upstairs to my office. We went by Mrs. Bradford's open door and she called hello to Lou, her voice simply dripping with her own special brand of scornful amusement, as if we made a welcome spectacle, a welcome interruption of the dull routine of her day. In my office, Lou put his arms around me, and I felt myself hide there for a moment, breathing the faint, clean, bay-rum-scented odor of him. But then I remembered what was happening inside me, that I was so confused and afraid about, and removed myself from him. I tried to do it gently, but Louis is not the sort of man on whom little falterings of demeanor and stance are lost.

"Annie," he said, "if there's something you want me to do, I—" He trailed off. He was standing on one side of the desk and I was standing on the other. I looked at his face, wondering if I could have talked myself into loving him. In that moment, I felt sorry for him until I realized that the sorrow came from the possibility that I might deprive him of myself. Then I was just irritable and I wanted him to back up a little, give me some room to think. I didn't say this. I made some excuse about being swamped with work, having a headache, and when he suggested that perhaps we ought to call off the evening, I said I'd have to see how I felt. The look on his face made me wish I was dead for ever letting him get close enough for me to hurt him. I said, "Maybe if I go home early and take a nap."

"It isn't—"

"What?" I said, keeping still, managing to look at him.

"Anything else?"

"What?" I said, trying to seem gently exasperated. I just wanted to get away from everyone for a time, and decide.

"Should I wait and call you?" he said. He was holding the magazine in both hands like a wrung piece of cloth, or a crumpled hat. I looked at those hands, with the soft, ropelike suggestions of veins in them, then reached over and touched one of them.

"Lou," I said.

But when he started toward me I couldn't help the step I took away from him. I picked something up from my desk and said, as calmly as I could, "Just come to the house this evening— you know. As planned."

Nothing.

I didn't want to turn around. I glanced out my window at the street, people walking there—lives in order, everyone going along in the stream of unappreciated days when the problems are manageable and mistakes are reversible or harmless. *Lou, if you only knew me, if you only knew what it's been. I can't have a baby now*

"Seven-thirty?" he said.

"Sure," I heard myself say.

"We—we don't have to go to the hotel, afterward. I mean I understand—"

I interrupted him. "Oh, can't we talk about it tonight?"

"Tonight," he said. "All right."

When I looked at him now, I saw anger. His jaw moved, the way it does when he clenches it against his temper. I sat down behind my desk and tried to let my nerves and my unhappiness seem produced by the work there. He leaned over the desk and kissed me on the forehead, then murmured, "Why don't you take your coat off." When I looked up, he had turned and was gone. A moment later, I heard the ever-watchful Mrs. Bradford's musical little sarcastic hello. She would come strolling down the hall to say whatever she would say, and, knowing I couldn't bear it if she did, I got up and closed the door to my office— leaned against it, trying to breathe, trying to control myself. I had let him kiss me that way, without kissing him back and without saying anything, and now I caught myself wondering what it would take to drive him away. Mrs. Bradford's knock startled me, and when I could control my voice, I said, "Yes."

"Open up," she said.

I wiped my eyes and wrapped the coat tight around myself, then opened the door wide. "I'm going home early," I said before she could speak.

"Is everything all right?" she wanted to know.

"I'm just going to take a little comp time, Mrs. Bradford. I've got a headache."

"Well, for goodness sake, honey—take sick leave. You want to be able to go have fun on comp time." She was looking at me now with serious, sad eyes, and I thought about how she really meant only generous things. It wasn't her fault that her way of being friendly, of trying to be witty and familiar, frayed the edges of my nerves, and I felt sorry for having been so intolerant of her.

"Thanks," I said.

"You go home and take a nap," she said, walking with me to the stairs. There was something so motherly and sweet about the way she waited at the top of the stairs and watched me go down.

"I'll see you on Monday," she said. And then, with emphasis, "If you feel better."

I nodded at her, tried to mean my smile of gratitude, but when I got outside in the sun I felt as though I were coming up for air from a long time in some deep, suffocating cavern. It was getting colder all the time, even with the sun bright over what little was visible of the lake from here. I got into the car and drove home. Ellen was sitting in the kitchen with her feet in a tub of water, and a book on her lap.

"You're home early," she said.

I almost told her. In some strange way I was afraid it would trouble her too much. For all her understanding, and our early confidences, our sisterly feeling for each other during the divorce, I had done things in the time before I met Louis that she couldn't quite be at peace with in her own mind, and we had begun to drift into something less than the intimate friends we'd been. There were times when I had sought the company of someone for not much more than a night's pleasantness, and while I had kept it well from my father—while he studiously refused to see what must have been obvious to anyone else—I had thought, mistakenly, that Ellen would at least understand it if she did not condone it. The first time I let it out, though, she retreated back into an almost childlike befuddlement and upset—or it would've seemed childlike if it hadn't also been rather weirdly pietistic and full of retribution and anger. I had come home from a five-day vacation I'd taken alone in New York. It was one of those travel agency packages, and I'd saved for it. I went sightseeing with a young man I'd met on the plane, and in the evening I went to his hotel room. At the time, I needed what he had to offer, including the Quaaludes he had in his suitcase. I was tired and alone, and bored, and I let it happen. When I told Ellen about it, wanting to confide in her, and needing to talk about it with someone, she stared at me a moment and then said, "You stayed with him?"

I nodded.

"Annie, that's a blatant sin."

For a moment, I couldn't say anything. I thought perhaps she was joking. She had never shown me such a pinched, outraged expression.

"Well?" she said, and I knew she was serious.

"Do you think God is disturbed?" I asked.

"I think you've made a terrible mistake," she said. "Do you know what that young man thinks of you now?"

I didn't want to argue or discuss it. I had in fact been more worried about doing the Quaaludes, and I'd known all along I wasn't going to tell her about that. So I tried to look chastened enough for her to feel that her work was done, and in any case I was vaguely grateful for her displeasure: it felt good. I believe it gave me an inkling of what it would be like to have her, or someone like her, as my mother. But after that, my sporadic little adventures into the nightlife were always in the air between us, like a gauze we had to look through.

Now she sat there with her feet soaking in that pan, and watched me fish a cup and spoon out of the soapy water in the sink. I rinsed them, dried them. I was going to make tea. My hands shook.

"Well?" she said.

"I have a headache," I told her.

"I'll get you something for it," she said, rising.

I said, "Sit down."

She waited. I put the water on to boil, then took an aspirin, realizing as I swallowed it that my headache was merely something I was conjuring to explain the pressure under my scalp, the knowledge of what had started in me. *Oh, Lou. I can't be pregnant. I just can't. Not now, not like this*

"Make me some, too?" Ellen said.

I stared at her.

"Tea."

"Oh, sure."

"Your headache's got you pretty distracted," she said.

"Yes," I said. I waited for the water to boil. *Watched pot never boils* went through my mind and repeated itself twice, like absurdity itself. Then I thought of the hours ahead of me—just that day's waning hours. When the water had boiled and I had made the tea, I sat down heavily across from her, thinking of myself as someone toppling with exhaustion.

"Maybe you've got a touch of the flu," she said.

I looked at my hands cradling the cup of tea. "Maybe so," I said.

When she came home to stay, Annie sent me a wire: Linda and I arriving for good on train 5:30 PM Wednesday, Annie. *It was the middle of winter. Snow had been blowing across the lake all morning as though the whole great north was coming down the side of the world. I had spent the early afternoon shoveling the walk and the porch steps, and had finally given up. I was sound asleep on the sofa in the living room when the telegram came—I'll remember that moment if I live to be a hundred and ten: the weak little light in the hall, and Ellen standing under it, remarking how even a bad storm, as this was, couldn't keep a telegram from being delivered. The news that Annie was coming home filled me with a shameful sense of vindication: I had been right about everything, of course, and of course one of the things to learn about this life is it's no great accomplishment to be right. It might even be an accident. And so when Wednesday afternoon arrived, clear and almost warm enough for thawing, I walked down to the depot in the cold, my mind working the ways I could keep myself as plainly accepting and incurious as possible, concentrating on the fact that I was glad she was coming home after almost five years away.*

I waited on the platform as the train pulled in, and it huffed and steamed and screeched. It felt like an element of the cold, somehow. Anyway, I was colder, watching it roll into place next to the platform. There were only a few people meeting this train, and even so I didn't recognize her right away. She wore a big blue parka, and had Linda wrapped up inside it. Her face was partly obscured by the hood of the parka. Apparently she'd been standing in the vestibule between the cars as the train pulled into Duluth: her face was an angry red from the cold.

"Well, I'm back," she said.

I took a shaking step toward her, kissed her on the cheek, then took Linda from her. She stood very close, talking to Linda, telling her who I was. She wanted to know if Linda remembered me from the pictures. Linda was tired and sleepy and cold. She stared at me the way a child stares, with that plain, appraising look. Her eyes were deep blue and sleep-clouded. I brought her close and kissed her cheek. My throat constricted: I couldn't say anything. I held Linda tight, eyes closed, everything blotted out but the fact that I was holding her. I wanted to hold my own daughter that way, and of course I couldn't. When I looked at her I saw that she was studying me in that way she always had of seeming to read me. I couldn't return the look. "Annie," I said.

"Here we are," she said.

Then we were both watching Linda. I saw that Linda was heavy in the legs, and very round-faced, with small, puffy lips and an upturned nose. It was strange, seeing her this way, and I couldn't help measuring her against her photographs. Linda turned in a small circle, looking at her own shadow on the floor. I watched the light change in the whiteness of her face. Her hair was almost red.

"Duluth," Annie said, shivering.

Trying to concentrate on the practical matter of getting her bags from the porter, I was crying, just like that, without warning. There were only two bags, and they weren't particulary heavy or unwieldy, but I made use of them for a minute's worth of hiding my face from her. Linda wanted a doll from the smaller bag, and I fished it out for her. Then I was standing, and my one daughter was staring at me. Her hair was pushed back, matted at the sides of her face by the hood of the parka. She'd been on the train for two days. She needed tending to, needed tenderness. I reached for her, and she recoiled as though I had given her an electric shock. I put my hands into the pockets of my coat.

"I'm tired," she said. "And irritable. Sorry."

I told her I understood, but of course I was broken.

"I'm a mess, you know." She stepped back. It was clear to me that she wanted no affection at all. She held one hand up as if to fend something off.

"Annie," I said. "What in the world."

"I'm tired," she said. "Don't make a big thing out of it."

Thirty years ago, the evening of the day before I was to marry her mother, I took a walk up my street—the old main street of Point Royal, Virginia. It was a quiet place, with small clapboard houses set back in the trees that bordered the road. The road led on to the two-story, red-brick building where I had gone to elementary school. I hadn't looked at it in years. I was twenty-nine, about to turn thirty, and I was going to marry someone with whom I *believed I wanted to spend the rest of my life. On this night I am remembering, I walked across the playground of that school, and sat in one of the swings and breathed the air. I supposed I wanted a family. What I wanted more than anything was to make love to this young woman who was going to be my wife. And sitting there in the dust of the playground, I thought of another girl I had known there, who had moved, with her family, to Florida before I was ten years old. I had heard somewhere that this girl had died in Florida, or been killed. I don't remember where I heard it, or even if, hearing it, I quite believed it; there were always stories going around about children who had moved away. But that twilight I thought of her, and in my thoughts, she was dead. She had gone out of the world, the gorgeous, astonishing world that was ticking away even as I sat there looking at the ground where I had run and wrestled, wearing the body of a boy. I thought of her, and then I guess I reveled in the fact that I was alive, and that everyone I knew and loved was alive. The world was like a wonderful, spacious room, that I was very comfortable in, and there were gifts waiting.*

That afternoon at the depot, I had a flash of remembering that twilight, and everything that had happened to me since then, and I said, "It is a big thing, Annie."

She stared.

I wiped my eyes and just stood there.

"Linda, stop whining," she said.

I hadn't heard Linda making a sound.

"Look," Annie said. And then she came close to me, put her arm across my back, and kissed me on the cheek. I could see that she'd begun to cry, too.

"It's going to be fine," I said. "It's going to be okay."

"Where's my daddy?" Linda said, then.

We didn't say anything for a time. We just stood there, almost shoulder to shoulder, while Linda muttered and mumbled to herself, sitting on one of the suitcases and turning the pages of a comic book

she'd pulled from the pocket of her coat. Annie looked around us.
"Home," she said. "And the wounded have arrived."
I didn't even ask. . . .

All morning I spent at my desk in the upstairs window of
the Duluth Savings Bank, watching the street and worrying.
I'm not sure what I thought I might see; I didn't see anything.
Annie had written Cole, and that bothered me, even though I
understood the legal aspects of the situation: the law required
her to notify Linda's father that adoption proceedings would
soon be under way. And I don't suppose I had any real idea
what Cole might do, even if he did decide to come north. It
was possible that he might try to contest any adoption through
the courts, though that seemed an absurd possibility, given his
record as a provider. It was also possible—it was in fact probable,
I thought when I could shake my nerves—that he would do
nothing. At any rate, this was what I wanted to feel certain of.
Yet I was increasingly uneasy, and a little past noon I walked
down the street, to Louis's shop, thinking, I suppose, that I
might reassure myself simply by going on as though nothing
was wrong. I had often stopped to see him after he and Annie
became engaged, and while I wasn't as yet completely comfortable with him—as I'm sure he wasn't with me—we had
managed, over the past few weeks, to achieve something like
an affection for each other. The truth was that I liked him, and
when I could forget that he was going to be my son-in-law, I
enjoyed his company. We would sit in the back room of his
shop and drink coffee and talk about sports, or music, or the
news. There were times when I felt we had a bond, given our
relative nearness in age, and considering the circumstances under
which we had come to this relationship: I was even tempted to
tease him about that now and again, but of course I never gave
in to the temptation, since there was about Louis the feeling

that one could hurt him easily enough. Besides, he was always so nervous.

That early afternoon, I walked down to the Stardust Shop, and was surprised to find it closed. I knocked on the door, just in case Louis was in back, and then I saw him come down from the parking lot on Lake View. He paused on the corner, saw me, then started across against the light. There wasn't any traffic to speak of. The wind that sailed down from the bright sunlight along the rooftops above me was cold, and I folded my arms against the chill, watching him come—taking the opportunity to regard him, with his heavy arms and stout, blocky figure; his oddly graceful, balanced, athletic gait, that made me think of a fighter slightly out of training.

"I was just at the library," he said, and seemed to shake his head, putting the key in the door and opening it. I wasn't sure of the gesture, so I said nothing. We went into the shop, and straight to the back, where he hung his coat up and put the coffee on.

"I can only stay a while," I said.

"Is something up?" He was standing on the other side of his desk, holding a magazine in one hand, rolled tightly. He'd had it with him when he came from the parking lot.

"What's that?" I said.

He looked at it, then set it down on his desk. "Nothing. I don't even remember where I got it."

"Is something wrong?" I said.

At this, he frowned, and I was sure this time that he shook his head. "Usual worries," he said, putting his hands in his pockets.

"Business?" I asked.

He merely repeated it, as if muttering to himself. "Business."

I said, "You've had busier days here, I know that."

"I don't need much business here."

A moment later, he said, "Is Annie all right?"

The question surprised me, until I realized that, in some way

I hadn't been quite conscious of, I had been compelled to come here, to seek him out—precisely because there existed the possibility that we might have this conversation. "Something was bothering her this morning," I said. "She wouldn't talk about it with me."

He frowned again, and looked worried, and now I felt heartless: for the very clear possibility was that her distraction and trouble consisted of no longer wanting to be Louis's wife. We seemed both to have this thought at the same moment. He glanced at me and then turned his attention to the coffee, with another almost imperceptible shake of his head.

We drank the coffee and talked about the World Series. It was absurd, but we seemed to be avoiding the subject of Annie now.

"Well," I said, finally. "I ought to go." Then: "I'm sure there's nothing to worry about."

He gave me a gentle, disbelieving look. "I guess so," he said. "We'll see."

When I got back, I found work to do, but I was restless, so I took the afternoon off and drove toward home. On an impulse, not even aware at first that I was going to do it but feeling no surprise at having done it, I drove on up to Linda's school and parked across the street from the playground, where I could watch for her. I was too early for afternoon recess, but I was willing to wait. I wanted to see her among the other children. I have always been the sort of man whose picture-taking and gathering of mementos, whose acts of sentiment—if that is what they may be called—are not the product of a desire to remember or savor as much as they are attempts to provide myself with something against the cold that is always approaching, and has always been gathering itself on my horizon, since I was a very small boy. I believed, even when I was little, that one day I would be left alone, with nothing but what I had been able to save among the things I prized, or could collect, or keep, or write down, or make a record of. Photographs, letters, notes in a journal, objects of sentimental attachment, places where the memories leaped up, were never matters of nostalgia, but were a kind of salvage to a man like me.

So I sat there in the car and watched the empty playground, and fixed the look of that grassy, windblown lawn in my mind, planning to have it right when I chose to remember the afternoon, toward the end of my time as her acting father, that I went to watch my granddaughter in the flux of an hour's play. It was, I suppose, a kind of spying. I didn't analyze it. The sun went behind clouds, and I was watching the doors of the school, and when the first group of children came bolting out, I almost ducked below the dashboard of the car. They all seemed to look right at me. But they went on about the serious business of their games and horseplay, and Linda was not among them. I watched for almost an hour, and other groups of children came out; I thought I recognized a few of them as being classmates or friends, but I never caught sight of Linda. The bells rang. The playground monitors divided the children into small lines and filed them back into the building, and in a while I was simply staring at the lifting dust of the bare places on empty ground.

I drove home. Annie's car was parked along the curb. It was just past two in the afternoon. I went up the walk and onto the porch, hurrying, imagining all sorts of bad scenarios. I was certain that Linda had come home. But Annie was sitting in the kitchen with Ellen, drinking tea. She, too, had come home early from work.

"Is everything all right?" I asked.

"Everything's fine," she said. But she looked away when she said it.

"Is Linda home?"

"Why would Linda be home?"

"I went over to school to watch her on the playground, and she never came out. It looked like all the other children were out there."

Ellen looked at the clock. "Her recess is an hour earlier. They don't all take recess at the same time, James."

"It looked like the whole school was out there," I said.

"I'm going upstairs," Annie said, rising.

I followed her down the hall to the stairs. "Hey," I said.

She turned. "Linda's fine. Why don't you walk up to meet her if you're worried about her. She gets out in forty minutes."

"Are *you* all right," I said.

"Got a little headache."

I touched her forehead. "No fever."

"I'm fine, Dad." She squeezed my elbow.

"You know," I said, "I went down and stopped in on Louis earlier this afternoon."

She simply returned my gaze.

"He said he'd been over to see you."

"Yes?" she said.

I had taught myself not to pry; I had never learned not to seem curious.

"Dad, my head is going to crack right here if I don't do something about this headache."

"I'm sorry," I said, and kissed her forehead.

She brushed the hair away from her cheek and I saw something pass over her face, almost like a shadow; it hardened the features, made her eyes look somehow more than haggard, or pinched with headache. It was as if she were holding something in with all her strength, and the effort was killing her.

"Annie," I said, "you can talk to me."

She looked at me with those eyes. I thought she might say something, might tell me. But she only squeezed my elbow again, and went on up the stairs.

In the kitchen, Ellen was leaning against the sink with a dish towel in her hands. When I walked back in there we stood for a moment and gazed at each other.

"Nerves?" she said finally.

I said, "Hell, I don't know."

"It's nerves."

I went into the living room and sat for a time on the sofa. I didn't know what I was waiting for. And then I did know: I was going to walk up to the school to meet my granddaughter. Putting my jacket on, I padded across the foyer and up the stairs to Annie's room, and called to her. "I'll walk up and meet Linda," I said.

She made a little conceding sound, an almost inaudible "Mm."

"You try to take a nap," I said.

Nothing.

PART THREE

PART THREE

The Progress of
Various Lives

At school, during recess, Linda waits in the bathroom—sits in the last stall, near the windows, and listens for the bell calling everyone back. Other girls come in, and some of them smoke, or write on the walls, but mostly she's alone. The room makes its water-dropping sounds, the pipes flute and sigh and groan, and in the other bathroom, the boys' room, the toilets flush. She hears voices there, voices in the halls, and the cries of her classmates on the asphalt outside. She hides here as long as she can, and today when her teacher, Mrs. Phillips, comes in looking for her, she pretends to have been using the toilet.

"My word, child—you are a regular one, aren't you." Mrs. Phillips gives her a look. It's clear that she knows Linda has come here to hide, and the whole thing becomes something like a game between them: Linda flushes the toilet and takes time washing her hands, knowing Mrs. Phillips will never speak directly about having found her hiding here. Mrs. Phillips is waiting for Linda to say something about it, and Linda will do no such thing. She's content to have had the fifteen minutes of quiet to herself, time away from the cold, measuring eyes of the other children, and she knows that when Monday's recess comes, she'll be hiding here again.

"You don't want to miss one of the last pretty days of the
year, do you?" Mrs. Phillips says.

"No."

"I didn't think so."

Linda follows her out into the chilly sunlight, where some of
the children are engaged in a game of kickball.

"Why don't you join in?" Mrs. Phillips says.

"I'd rather play on the sliding board," says Linda.

Mrs. Phillips lets her wander off, lose herself in the confusion
of rough-and-tumble games. Linda watches two boys take turns
climbing the gleaming aluminum sliding board surface, only to
turn and glide down on their bellies, looking like those television
films of otters slipping into a stream. Now and then one of the
boys glances at her, but they're having too much fun to really
notice she's there. This is the way she prefers things to be. And
now one of the room mothers, a tall thin woman with sun lines
in her face and a thick brushed mane of gray-streaked hair,
comes over to ask her if she wants to play kickball. "No, thank
you," Linda says.

"You're a watcher, aren't you," the woman says.

Linda looks at her, trying to decide how she means this, then
shrugs.

"I saw you coming out of the school with Mrs. Phillips. Are
you in her class?"

"Yes, ma'am."

"Well, that's nice. Are you sure you don't want to play kickball?"

Linda nods, looking off at the street.

"Would you like a jump rope or something to do?"

"I'm fine," Linda tells her.

"Well," the woman says, moving away, "have fun."

Linda watches her cross the lot to the swings. Several younger
children are playing in the little bare places in the grass there.
In the kickball game, an uproar starts. It is as Linda gazes at
this that she sees her father walking toward her from the other

side of the street. Her father is wary, looking around, but advancing all the same. She faces him, waits. He comes on. And then something happens that she can't understand. Pausing, he looks over his shoulder, stops. The children in the kickball game move through her field of vision, and when she steps to one side to keep him in view, she sees that he is retreating, running away. His back is turned, his light blue denim jacket flying; it's clear he doesn't know she's seen him. He ducks behind a parked car, and Linda moves through the scrabbling and wrestling of the playground to see him, perhaps even to follow him. But she's lost him in the line of parked cars on that side of the street. She waits, staring. The shouts of the others behind her seem to come from a long way off. Finally, her father appears again, farther down, beyond the end of the block. Now he's pulling some woman by the hand, ducking down, and almost immediately he's out of sight, but there's no doubt in Linda's mind. It's her father, all right; and she's sure of something else, too: his desire not to be seen. This knowledge goes through her with a chill, and she turns quickly, pretends to be watching the boys on the slide. She wonders if she can get back into the building, to the bathroom, the window there, where she can watch the whole playground, and wait for him to show himself again, if that's what he's planning to do. The two boys on the slide have grown tired of their game, and they go chasing off to the swings, and so now she's alone here. Carefully, she steals a glance back at the cars across the street. He's gone. She scans the grounds, the houses along Duluth Avenue, the bushes that grow at the base of the playground fence. Mrs. Phillips is standing in the entrance of the school, arms folded, gazing out at the kickball game. It is getting near the end of recess. Linda makes her way slowly across to her teacher, then takes one more look at the street; a car going by might or might not have her father sitting behind the wheel. She doesn't know, and then she does; she's certain: two people, a man and a woman, the car nosing on around the corner and out of sight—one of them is her father.

"Hey," Mrs. Phillips says. "What're you doing here. You've got another five minutes of recess."

"I don't feel like recess," she says. She feels her teacher's warm, rough hand on her forehead. "I'm not sick."

"Honey, why don't you go play."

"It's time to go in anyway."

Mrs. Phillips stops the game by putting two fingers in her mouth and giving forth a shrill, startling whistle, and begins to say something about the recess being over. Then she turns to Linda. "Sweetie, would you like a chance to kick the ball?"

"No," Linda says.

Everyone seems to have stopped; everyone's looking at her.

"All right everybody, just go about your business," Mrs. Phillips says.

"Why did you do that," Linda says to her.

"I didn't mean for anybody to hear me. I was going to pitch one to you myself after everyone went in."

"I don't want to kick the ball," Linda says, and walks fast into the building, along the fluorescent and polished hall crowded with others, past rooms where still others study and talk and play, until she reaches her own classroom. Here, she closes her books and her desk, and under the scrutiny of the others, moves to the closet to put away her coat. But then Mrs. Phillips is there, and gently walks her out into the hall. "Good Lord, girl, will you give a person a chance? I thought you might be feeling left out."

"I want to be left out."

"Why?"

"I don't know."

"Do you think anyone wants to leave you out?"

She shakes her head. She's trying not to cry.

"All right," Mrs. Phillips says after a pause. "We'll just say you don't like kickball, then."

"Okay." Linda can't return her gaze.

"I hate it, too, of course."

"You do?"

"Oh, I was *never* any good at it."

"I can't run fast," Linda says. "I'm too—big."

"I don't know. I wouldn't say you were that big."

"You're just saying that."

"No, I'm not—and it's not very charitable of you to suggest that I am. Perhaps you'll be in a better mood after the weekend," Mrs. Phillips tells her.

Linda nods, but she wants to say this isn't any mood she's in. This has nothing to do with anything that passes. She sits at her desk near Mrs. Phillips's desk, and while Mrs. Phillips talks to the class about addition in her rich, smoker's voice, she tries to conjure the clearest possible image of her father when he came to Duluth the last time, after she and her mother had taken the long train ride north. She remembers the train—a dream of swaying motion, the slow gliding by of the distances outside, and the backs of apartment buildings as they'd passed through Chicago: laundry lines like wires connecting the yards; bicycles leaning against walls, or left out in the weather; porches and curtained windows, dumpsters and bare, empty playgrounds in wintry light, under cover of snow. She remembers arriving, the first sight of the frozen eternity of the lake, and the station with its noise and outcry, the barely human voice ringing from the walls. She remembers seeing her grandfather from a fold of her mother's woolen wrap, how he knelt down to look at her, and to put his big hands on her shoulders. All this is clear enough in her mind, and if much of the time between then and now is lost, she remembers with tantalizing clarity the afternoon of the first spring they were in Duluth, when her father came driving up to the house, and was allowed to take her out for ice cream. It is an hour of her life she has replayed many times, like a daydream, trying to keep it exactly as it was: her father pulls up and gets out, looking for her. She's sitting in the middle of a sandbox in the front yard, and, seeing him, runs to him. She remembers tremendous unease among the grown-ups, and oddly she feels her father as being with her in some sort of natural opposition to them. He picks her up and she puts her arms around his neck, breathes the unfamiliar odor of cologne. His hair is cut shorter than usual, and he's wearing a sportcoat and tie. There's a lot of shifting, talk among the grownups, and now her father is with them, speaking to her mother in tones Linda recognizes but has no words for: the old, cajoling, earnest, meaningful tones of the end of trouble. Her mother's responses are polite and definite, and there's no discernible emotion in them: it's the voice she uses with strangers. Linda wishes she could hear them. In a while she doesn't care, because her father has her by the hand and is leading her to the car.

"We'll go get an ice cream cone," he says.

In the car, she rides close to him, away from the passenger window, and he asks if she wants to sit over there to look out. "No," she says, and smiles at him. He smiles back, then is watching the road. She looks at the side of his face, and sees a small cut on his cheek. "What's that?" she says.

"What?"

She touches the place.

"Cut myself shaving," he says.

"Are you going to live with us?" she asks him.

This makes him smile. "I'm going to visit a lot. All the time."

She rides along trying to understand this. She knows there has been something bad between him and her mother; she knows *he* was bad. But she can't decide *how* he was bad, and she can't imagine that it could still be going on. "Why can't you live with us?" she says to him.

"It's not allowed," he says.

"Why?"

"Just isn't."

"You could stay in my room," she says.

"That would be very nice," he says. "But it's not allowed."

She ponders this for a moment. It seems strange to her that he's permitted to take her for ice cream, and is free to come and talk and visit, but can't stay in the house. It seems to her that whatever her mother was angry about should be put aside now, as it has always been put aside before. "Is Mommy still mad at you?" she asks him.

"Hey," he says, glancing down at her. "Are we going to spend the whole time talking about this?"

She shakes her head no, but she feels unhappy now, and exasperated. They stop at a frozen custard stand near the north shore. He buys two chocolate cones, and they sit and eat in the cool, breezy shade of a small picnic area adjacent to the stand. She watches him nibble at the bottom of his cone and then begin to suck the frozen custard out that way, intent, obviously thinking about nothing else; she studies his face. She doesn't know what to say to him, but finds that she doesn't need to say anything. It's easy and peaceful, and seems quite normal that they should be here together. Everything else recedes into the background. They talk for a while about Grandmother Selena, and how much she misses Linda, and he buys two more cones, vanilla this time. They sit quietly for a little while, and he begins to clown for her, pretending to be unable to get the cone in his mouth, smearing his face with the frozen custard. She laughs from deep down, watching him. At one point, he dips his chin in the custard and makes a white beard for himself, mugging for her, raising his eyebrows and looking, with the pointed beard, like a magician. She's laughing so hard she's crying. He pats the top of her head, smiling, beaming at her, the beard melting away, dripping onto the grass between his feet. He wipes it off, finally, finishes his cone, and then is waiting for her to finish. Others come to sit and eat, three children about Linda's age— who smirk at her and make faces—and two women, one of whom is pregnant. The children argue and laugh, while the women talk in voices too low to distinguish. One of the women, the one not pregnant, glances over at Linda's father and gives him the trace of a smile. Linda's father nods.

"Nice day," he says to them.

"Yes," the pregnant one says, with an unfriendly look.

"I like nice days," says Linda's father, simply, smiling at them. And it strikes her that it is exactly that. She looks off through the thousand shades of green in the trees bordering the north shore, and sees the slate-colored, prehistoric rocks jutting into the water, which is white-capped and moving in the wind, and she knows she'll never forget this moment in her life, if she lives a hundred years.

Now, after keeping it inside and fighting to preserve it all this time, she can't put the memory to use anymore, can't call it up for solace, or for the simple pleasure of hoping for something like it again. It won't match what has just happened. Now when she thinks of that day, her mind presents her with the image of her father scurrying away from her in the street. All afternoon she broods on this.

After school lets out she makes her way back around to the playground again, with some obscure, wordless notion of arranging the experience in her mind; she wants to look at the angles again, stand in the place where she saw him. But as she's crossing toward the kickball diamond she loses heart, and turns around. It's true all right; she knows she hasn't imagined it. She walks through the empty school, out the front doors, and finds her grandfather waiting.

"You're always the last one out," he says.

She nods, then starts with him toward home.

"Hey," he says.

"What."

"Can't you say hello?"

She manages a smile. "Hello."

"How was school?"

"Fine."

When a car comes by them she turns with what she hopes is a casual motion and looks at it, but it's a big Cadillac with blinding chrome on the sides. It goes by. Her grandfather has stopped a few paces ahead of her, and is standing there waiting, his hands on his hips. "What," she says to him.

"Who're you looking for?"

She shrugs, remembers with a jolt of anger and bewilderment that her father's voice over the telephone in the morning had asked her to keep his presence a secret between them. "Nothing," she says. "I thought I saw Stephanie."

"The one who's moving away?"

She nods, returning his gaze, wondering if he's guessed everything somehow, the way grown-ups sometimes do. "I'm going to miss Stephanie," she says. This is true, of course, though it has nothing to do with what is wrong. He seems convinced; he reassures her about the persistence, the strength, of good friendships, and as she allows him to take her hand, it occurs to her with a species of sour elation that she's learned something important, something useful about the world; she has acquired the knowledge, quite by accident but with the certainty of inspiration, that at the right time and in the right circumstances it is possible, it is in fact desirable, effective, and very easy, to tell a bald lie by using some version of the truth.

In the evening, while he showered and dressed, Louis tried not to let himself think about the change in his fiancé. If Annie was planning to tell him the marriage was off, if she had stopped loving him or realized that she hadn't loved him in the first place, then he wanted her to say so; there could be no use in dragging everything out. She should make a clean break, as the ridiculous phrase went, and get it over and done with. But the thought of losing her made him feel weak in the back of his knees, and took all the moisture from his mouth. Looking at himself in the mirror on his bedroom wall, he felt shaky, miserably unglamorous—a man too ordinary to notice. Here he was, tying his tie, his fingers shaking, his chin in the air, his

whole bearing appearing to his own eye to be stuffy and overly
fastidious, faintly silly. He untied the tie and threw it on the
bed, then adjusted the collar open; this only served to accentuate
the girth of his chest, the wattled skin of his throat—and there
were age spots just below the line of his neck. He stared at
himself, cursed under his breath, and retrieved the tie. "I am,
goddammit, what I am," he muttered.

Roger went by in the hall, then came back and looked at him
from the open doorway. "You're dressed and ready to go and
it's not even six-thirty."

"Are you going with us?"

"Sure."

"You don't have to if Fran wants to do something else."

"No, we'll go." It was impossible to gauge the younger man's
true reactions about almost anything lately, especially the present
situation: Louis yearned to find out what his son thought about
it all without embarrassing either of them. What he did know,
he told himself now, was that the boy's very reluctance to approach the subject of his father and Annie was an admission of
a kind: he was pretty sure his son saw him as being in the grip
of some foolish, late-middle-aged quest for youth.

He tied the tie, then stood back and evaluated himself: he
could not imagine what Annie saw in him.

"You look great," Roger said. "What'll you do, now—stand
in a corner until it's time to go?"

"Just *you* don't be late if you're going."

"We're going," his son told him, and crossed the hall to the
bathroom.

He went downstairs and fixed himself a whiskey, then stood
at the window in the front door, sipping the drink and gazing
out at the street. It was quiet; everything was in dusk, now.
The street lamps were on, and the wind moved the shadows of
the tree branches. His son sang badly off-tune in the shower, a
happy boy with no idea in the world what he would ever do
with himself. The shower stopped, but Roger went on singing.

A moment later, he was in the back bedroom, still singing, getting ready. Louis wondered if he himself had ever been so uncomplicatedly happy, and when the unpleasant thought arose in his mind that his son's happiness was a species of simple-mindedness, he consciously worked to remember the boy's accomplishments as a precocious child.

He passed the time in this fashion, worrying about everything, checking the clock, pacing, looking out the window.

Finally his vigilance yielded Roger's date, Fran, pulling up in front of the house. She turned the ceiling light on in the car, and spent a moment looking at herself in the rearview mirror, touching the corner of her lip with one pinky finger. Not wanting her to see that he had been watching, Louis stepped back a little when she got out. She came up the walk and onto the porch. He opened the door.

"Chilly," she said, coming in.

"It's getting that way," he said.

She kissed his cheek, then walked into the living room, removing her coat; there was something almost studiedly languid about the way she moved.

"Can I get you something to drink?"

She didn't want anything. She sat down on the sofa, smoothed her skirt over her thighs, and gazed at the room while he settled in the chair across from her. He was quite aware of the fact that he made her nervous, and it was difficult to keep from doing things to exaggerate her unease: he knew from his son's several clumsy attempts to cover for her that she disapproved of him for his relationship with Annie. Now, sitting across from him, she smoothed the skirt again and crossed her legs primly. She was an attractive girl, with wide, long-lashed innocent blue eyes, and bright blond hair, which she had arranged in a low sweep across her pale forehead. If there was a flaw in her features, he thought, it was well hidden in makeup, and there was something about the perfection of her appearance that made you think of flaws—that made you think in those terms. He looked away from her, hummed softly, half consciously, part of a measure of the song Roger had been singing in the shower. She cleared her throat, shifted slightly. He breathed the rosy fragrance of her perfume. A flaw: she was wearing too much of it. It seemed to Louis that at this moment it was taking all the oxygen out of the air. He sighed, took the last of his drink.

"So. My son was too lazy to pick you up tonight."

She smiled, but her expression was finally a little bewildered. They spent another moment looking at the room.

"I guess we're all going to a movie," Louis said.

And her smile changed.

"Roger didn't tell you?"

"It's okay," she said. "I didn't know—but it's fine. We can do that."

"Did you have other plans?"

"No—a movie's fine. No problem at all." She kept the smile, sat back, and again smoothed the cloth of her skirt.

Roger came into the room, walked over, and bent down to kiss her, then straightened, folded his arms, and regarded her as though she were a work of sculpture with some puzzling idiosyncrasy of design.

"You're dressy," he said to her.

"I sure am."

There was a pause.

"What's up?" he asked.

"Fran didn't know we were going to a movie," Louis said.

"Sure she did."

"Roger, I did not."

"Oh, come on, Fran. We talked about it this morning. Don't say we didn't talk about it."

It was now apparent to Louis that they might well be about to have an argument. He said, "Well, you guys settle this. I'm going to make myself another drink."

"Would you make me one, too?" Fran said.

"What would you like?"

"Vodka on ice."

"You don't drink," said Roger.

Louis said, "I'll make you whatever you want."

"Vodka on ice," she said.

Louis looked at his son. "You?"

"Sure, okay. Vodka," said Roger, with ill-disguised annoyance.

"All right," Louis said. He left them to their quarrel, whatever it was. As he mixed the drinks, the thought struck him that if Annie continued in her own unhappy mood, it might be a very long evening indeed. After the drinks were mixed, he waited a while, wanting to give them every chance to solve their difficulty. When he returned they were on opposite sides of the room, Roger staring out the window, his back to her. She had remained on the couch, but she was sitting slightly forward, as though she had been importuning him about something, and, hearing Louis's approach, stopped in mid-sentence. He hesitated a moment in the doorway, then walked over and handed her the vodka. Roger met him over the coffee table for his own drink, and they all sat down in the increasingly awkward quiet.

"Look, you two. Get over it—whatever it is."

Fran now seemed to be musing about something very far away. She was holding her drink high, and she hadn't taken any of it yet. Roger rattled the ice in his glass, and, drinking, gave forth a small sigh of satisfaction. Louis watched Fran put her own glass to her lips. She started to swallow, then stopped, looked as though she were about to choke, and now both men were standing over her, trying to attend to her. Somehow she hadn't spilled the drink, but she was having a bad time trying to keep from spitting out what she had apparently failed to swallow. Her cheeks bulged, and she held one hand, the delicately polished tips of the fingers, over her lips. Finally she gulped, breathed, shaking her head and patting her chest as if to indicate where the vodka had lodged, like a solid knot of something, on its way down. Roger put his hand on her shoulder, took the drink from her and set it on the coffee table. He did so with a gentleness that Louis was proud of, then came back and stood over her, and when she had managed to compose herself, leaned down and said, "Why don't you drink it all down, Fran."

"Oh, for Christ's sake," said Louis, "you sound like a bad marriage."

"What's wrong with wanting to try something once in a while," she said, obviously fighting off tears.

"I'm going," Louis said.

"It's early," said his son.

"Finish your drink and let's go," Fran said. "I want to go."

"Let's go," said Louis.

In the car, riding through what had become a fine mist, they were quiet, and it was not an awkward quiet, now; it was miserable and intentional, and there was no pressure at all to speak: all pretense of even tempers and cordial relations was gone. They were like three members of a family after a period of bickering. Louis put the radio on—the professional cheer of a woman disk jockey predicting a continuation of unusually warm weather. He ventured that it was difficult to believe such sunny optimism now, looking at things, and in the silence that followed realized that both of them might have interpreted the remark as aimed at them. He turned to Fran, seated next to him in the front seat, and asked if she was warm enough in her light jacket.

"I'm fine," she said. Then, after a pause: "Thank you."

"Don't mention it," Louis said.

"We're way early," said his son from the backseat.

"Okay, so we're early, then."

They drove the rest of the way in silence. The radio voice was abruptly mixed with strains of music from another station; it died in static, and Louis turned it off. The borderline of trees to their left seemed to fall away as they ascended the long hill, and beyond the dark configuration of more trees in the distance, a single white spire stood out like a marker. The road angled off to the right, and took them away from this view of far-off Wisconsin, and up another incline, along a row of tall houses, the fourth of which was James Field's house.

"It's only seven-ten, Dad."

"I know what time it is."

"What'll we do now?"

"Come on," Louis said.

They went up the sidewalk to the porch in a confusion of muttered speculation about what they ought to do: Roger wanted to drive around a while, or wait in the car, and Fran said something about finding a place to have another drink. Louis was tired of them both. He knocked on the door and waited, beginning to feel the network of swollen, hypersensitive nerves lining his stomach. Linda opened the door and gave him an expression that bordered on rudeness.

"We're early, aren't we, honey," Louis said, inwardly preparing himself to be turned away.

"My mother's not ready."

Mr. Field's sister came down the corridor, wiping her hands on a dishcloth and peering at them. "Oh, good Lord," she said. "Come in. Linda, don't make them stand out on the porch."

"We're early, I know," Louis said.

They all filed into the living room, where James Field had apparently been dozing over the newspaper. He was standing in front of his easy chair now, and part of the newspaper was on the floor at his feet. The television was on, someone offering opinions about the taste of coffee. Field offered his hand to Roger, nodded at Fran, and patted Louis on the shoulder. They all sat down and gazed at each other, glowing with goodwill, beaming with it, making the effort, and Louis felt like a fool: he had caught the household off guard, and it was this rudeness that everyone was having to overcome.

"I'm really very sorry," he said. "I don't know what I was thinking of."

Mr. Field leaned down and picked up the fallen part of his

newspaper. "Tell you the truth," he said, smiling, "I thought you were late. Can I get anyone a drink?"

"I'd like a vodka on ice," Fran said.

"I'm making the drinks," said Ellen from the entrance to the dining room. But then she paused, for she had caught sight of the expression on Roger's face. "I'm not making the drinks?"

Roger stared at his date. "Fran."

"What?"

"She just almost choked to death on vodka and ice," Roger announced to the room.

For a moment no one said anything.

Fran smiled, crossed her legs, and touched the crossing knee with the lavender tips of the fingers of one hand—a small, graceful brushing movement before she brought the hand up to her chin. Louis thought it was a masterful demonstration of poise and confidence, and there was something alluringly vivacious about it, too, even knowing that it was done in anger, that it had come from a wish to retaliate and to cause embarrassment to her companion for the evening. "I would love a vodka on ice, if it's all right with our hosts," she said.

"I'll have an old-fashioned," said Field.

"Anyone else?" Ellen asked, looking at Roger, who simply stared at his hands. "Okay," she said, and went through the dining room into the kitchen. She closed the kitchen door behind her, but it opened again almost on the instant, and Linda came out, moving slowly, ruminating, into the living room, eyes down. Louis reached over and touched her elbow as she walked by him, and she gave him a fleeting little smile. She went to the front window and peered out at the night. Her dress rode up on the backs of her thick, babylike thighs.

"See anything, honey?" Louis said.

She didn't respond; apparently she hadn't heard him.

"Linda," said Mr. Field.

She turned.

"Louis is talking to you."

"I just asked if you could see anything," Louis told her.

She shook her head.

"Is there something the matter, sweetie?" Fran said.

"She's thinking about a friend of hers in school," said Field.

"Come here, honey," Louis said to the child.

"I have to go help my mother get ready."

"Go give Louis a hug," Mr. Field said. "Where're your manners?"

She walked over and allowed herself to be held a moment, standing with her arms at her sides. Then she said, "Excuse me," and left the room. Louis watched her go, keeping the pleasant smile on his face, aware of the others in the room, of their eyes on him, and feeling more fraudulent every minute: no doubt her mother was upstairs preparing to tell him she didn't want to see him anymore; he was certain of it. He was certain that this was the explanation for the child's odd, distant, dreamy behavior.

"I heard the first winter storm is on the way," Field said.

"We heard on the radio that the weather would stay warm for a while," said Fran. "Didn't we, Roger?"

Roger said nothing, and this brought everyone to a halt. For an uncomfortable moment they were all unable to look at one another, or say anything.

"Every year I think about moving south," Field said.

A little later, Annie came down, wearing slacks and a sweater, her hair tied into a single ropy braid in back. Louis stood as she entered, and she kissed him on the cheek, then helped Ellen with the drinks, giving Fran her vodka and ice.

Fran put the glass to her lips and sipped from it with a casual but somehow controlled air. "Delicious," she said, her voice only minimally altered by what she had this time successfully swallowed.

"I'll make my own," said Annie. She stepped around Louis and headed through the dining room. He followed. In the kitchen, she brought the whiskey out from the cabinet over the refrigerator and poured a liberal amount of it into a water glass.

"Hey," he said. "Go easy."

"I'm putting ice in it. I'll cut it with water."

"Are you okay?" he asked. Lately it seemed the only question.

"I'm cagey," she said. "I'm shrewd and full of cunning."

He took her arms just below the shoulder. "Annie."

"Don't," she said.

He let go. She opened the refrigerator and got out the ice tray, put two cubes into the glass of whiskey.

"What is it?" he said.

Sipping her drink, she seemed to be having some sort of inner dialogue with herself. But she simply turned to him and patted his wrist. "I'm sorry. I'm in a bad mood."

"We don't have to go to the movies," he said.

Somehow, though she smiled at him, her features gave him what was nevertheless a troubled expression: there was nothing of mirth in it. "I'm pregnant."

He waited, coming to believe that he had heard the words clearly, and finding himself perfectly incapable of speech. He could not have imagined what anyone would say.

"Don't tell anybody, all right?" She looked as though she might begin to cry.

"Oh," he said, reaching for her.

"No," she told him, removing herself. "You don't understand."

"Annie," he said.

"Please," she said, "you've got to understand. Please."

They were standing perhaps five feet apart now, and she was fighting tears, not looking at him. He was afraid to move, afraid to try to speak.

"You just don't understand," she said, mastering herself, taking more of the drink. Then she was moving toward him. "Don't look at me like that."

"I thought you—I thought—" he stammered, "I thought it was something else."

"No, please," Annie told him. "You don't understand. You don't understand at all."

Mr. Field saw as they came out of the kitchen that something had transpired between them. Annie carried her drink high, and was being rather automatically charming, as though in an effort to distract anyone from noting that she was flushed and wet-eyed, and that poor Louis Wolfe, his face the color of the ashes in the fireplace, looked as if his knees might buckle any minute. Field pretended an interest in the time, stared at his watch, wound it, let things settle a moment. He supposed he would know what this was, soon enough, and he wondered if Ellen already knew. He watched his sister bustle around the room, making sure of everybody's comfort. No. She was apparently as much in the dark as he was.

"I guess we should get started," Annie said. She was standing by the entrance to the foyer, and she finished her whiskey in a series of gulps, as though it were water.

"Annie, you're going to make yourself sick," Louis said with a kind of strained jollity.

"I'd like another vodka and ice," Fran announced.

Everyone looked at her.

"Of course," said Ellen, who crossed the room to collect the girl's empty glass. Louis Wolfe's son, sitting on the hassock across from her, lowered his head slightly, looking at the floor.

"Have we decided on a movie?" Field asked the room.

No one answered. There was the sound of Ellen breaking ice out of the tray in the kitchen.

"I think *I'd* like another drink," Annie said, but she didn't move.

Field looked at Louis, saw him draw in a deep breath. There was a little shimmer of sweat in a line down the side of his face next to the ear. While Field watched him, he took out a handkerchief and wiped it away, then put the handkerchief back.

Then he leaned toward Field's daughter and murmured something, which she nodded to.

"If we're going to a movie," Roger said, "we ought to go
soon."

"The question is what movie," said his date. "I mean I think
it's very strange just deciding to go to the movies without any
idea what you want to see." Her demeanor was faintly indignant,
as though by telling him this she had scored a blow for some
sort of moral imperative.

Field wanted them all to leave. He stood. "I'll go see what
choices we have."

The newspaper was in the hallway, on the telephone stand,
but he took it on into the kitchen and closed the door. Ellen
was there, pouring Fran's drink. Field watched her fill the glass
with water, then touch the top of it with a few drops of vodka.

"Did you do that to the first one?"

She nodded, suppressing a laugh with two fingers. "Poor girl
hasn't had more than a teaspoon of it."

"Why?"

His sister shrugged. "I saw the look on that boy's face when
she asked for it."

"Well, she thinks she's drunk."

Ellen laughed, put her hand to her mouth. "Wait." She opened
the door and went out. Field poured himself a shot of whiskey,
drank it down. Ellen came back in and rolled her eyes at the
ceiling, one hand over her chest. He had a moment of being
quite plainly glad of her, and he touched the small of her back
as she went by him to sit in the breakfast nook with her own
drink—a vodka tonic.

"I'm supposed to be looking for a movie we can all agree on,"
he said.

She sipped the drink.

For a moment, neither of them spoke or looked at each other.
When he turned to her, she was staring into the ice in her glass.
"So," he said.

She said, "So."

"Something's up."

She nodded. Then, in response to his questioning look, she said, "Not me."

"You think maybe Annie's changed her mind?"

"Is *that* it?"

"I was asking you."

Ellen shook her head.

"Well, something's up," he told her.

He stood at the counter and opened the newspaper to the movie section. She went on sipping her drink. From the other room came the sound of Roger's date going on about slash movies as the products of obscene invention.

"What were you arguing about this morning?" Ellen wanted to know.

"We didn't argue, really. Something's bothering her, that's all. I suppose she'll tell us what it is when she's ready."

"She doesn't tell me anything anymore," said Ellen.

"She tells Louis."

Ellen nodded.

"Poor Louis. He looks pretty stunned."

"I saw."

"Do you suppose our interest has gone beyond familial concern?" Field asked.

"I don't understand."

He left a little pause. "Well, would you say our interest has entered the province of simple gossip?"

"I'm worried about Annie, if that's what you mean."

"Your interest doesn't go beyond that."

"Of course it doesn't—James, what in the world are you getting at?"

"I don't know. I seem to be the auditor of my daughter's life in some way. It seems to be just interest by itself, somehow. Like waiting to see that poor girl out there make an idiot out of herself getting drunk on water and ice."

"I know this," Ellen said, "I know if she *is* breaking it off with Louis it'll make us both very happy."

"I never denied it," Field said. "I never made any bones about it. And I like Louis, too."

They said nothing for a moment. Mr. Field stared at the newspaper, at the names of theaters and movies and starting times, none of it quite registering. The voices in the other room were louder now; something was at issue—something was being all too politely discussed. A moment later, the door opened and Annie walked in. She put her empty glass down on the counter, and faced them. "Listen," she said to Field, "I think Louis and I are just going to take off alone. Would you mind if we did the movie another night?"

"What about Roger and his girlfriend?" Ellen wanted to know.

"She's drunk," Annie said. "She drank that second vodka down like it was water."

Field and his sister exchanged a look, and then they were laughing.

"What," Annie said. "Tell me."

Field held one hand up to hush her, leaning against the counter and laughing. Ellen had her head down on the table in the breakfast nook, and Annie stood between the two of them, turning from one to the other.

"Tell me, will you?"

"It *was* water," Ellen explained.

Annie stared at her, then at Field. "You didn't."

Field had got control of himself, and he pretended a grave seriousness, nodding at her as though he were answering her worst fears.

She put both hands to her face and her lovely laugh came forth, high and musical and rich. "Oh, that's wonderful," she said, laughing. "I love it." Field put his arms around her and rocked with her, and he could feel the valves of his own heart expanding with the ache and happiness of it.

"Louis will die when I tell him," she said, her eyes tearing up. "Will you two watch Linda for us?" She dabbed at her eyes and took a breath, and her countenance was already losing the look of lightness and mirth it had worn.

"You wouldn't want to leave her with that drunk out there," Ellen said, and laughed again.

"We'll watch Linda," Field said.

And now Louis came in, acting sheepish and embarrassed, the lines in his face showing in the overhead light, and causing Field to think of him with a kind of pity: he didn't want anyone to be sorry tonight.

"Tell Louis," he said to Annie.

And he watched Annie whisper in Louis's ear.

Louis seemed tremendously relieved, but he didn't laugh. He walked over to Ellen and very stiffly and formally offered her his hand, then bowed at the waist to kiss the back of hers in a gesture obviously intended to contribute to the evening's humor. For some reason, it only embarrassed Ellen, who tried to cover her discomfort with another joke, asking him if he wanted water and water and ice.

He said he would, still affecting the formal demeanor, and Annie took him by the arm. "I just told them we'd go—just the two of us," she said to him.

"We have to drop Roger and the souse at home," said Louis. "They came with me."

"Well," Field said, trying another joke, "don't stay out too late." Apparently no one had quite heard him. Annie was kissing Ellen on the side of the face, and Louis had opened the door into the hallway, was waiting there.

"I don't know how long we'll be," Annie said, moving to join him. "So don't wait up, Dad."

"You know me," Field said, feeling a sudden ache of emotion in his throat.

When they were gone, Ellen went in and sat in front of the television with a bowl of popcorn and another drink. Linda sat in the chair by the living room window, now and then moving the curtain aside to look out. Field fixed himself some coffee, then sat in the kitchen reading the papers. For a long time there was just the sound of the television. When Linda crossed the hallway on her way up to bed, he swallowed the last of his coffee, put the empty mug in the sink, and went up after her. She had settled on her bed, legs folded, with a book open in her lap.

"Hey," he said.

"Hey," she answered.

"We'll all go to the movies another time," he told her.

She shrugged this off, and turned her attention to her book.

"Linda," he said.

"What."

"That is not the word you use when you're addressed by an adult, young lady."

She said, "Yes, Granddad."

"Don't be a pouter."

"Yes," she said, smirking.

"And don't take that tone of voice."

She turned the pages of the book.

"What's the book?" he said, trying to use a friendlier tone.

"Nothing. A story."

"What's it about?"

"A kid that thinks she looks like a goat."

"Want to read it to me?" Sometimes at night when she was smaller, he would let her sit on the edge of his bed and read to him, and he would pretend to fall asleep; she would tuck him in, kiss his forehead, and go to bed herself. He would wait a moment, then get up and return the favor, reading to her until she actually did fall asleep. "Well?" he said.

She gave him a sardonic expression as if to say that she was far too old for such games. "Granddad please."

"All right," he said, turning. "I'll be downstairs."

"Granddad," she said.

And he heard something urgent in her voice. He went in to stand by her bed. "What is it?"

"I saw my father at school today."

Mr. Field sat down on the bed and took her plump, dimpled hands into his own. "Did he say anything to you?"

"He didn't want me to see," she said, beginning to cry. "He was sneaking around—like he was afraid or something."

"Did he *say* anything, Linda."

She spoke, but he couldn't understand it all through her crying. He thought she said something about secrets, but then she shook her head and, making an effort to get control of herself, looked at him and said, "He just ran away."

Field drew her in against his chest, feeling as though he ought to get up and pull the window shades down, close the curtain. "It's all right," he heard himself say, patting her shoulder. "You have to listen to me now. You can't let him near you. Do you understand? You can't let him get close enough to put his hands on you."

"He's my father."

He held her. "I know, I know."

"He runs away," she said, crying, wiping her eyes with the backs of her hands.

"Where was he—did he come into the school?"

She went on crying, saying something about spying, hiding behind cars.

"Linda, listen to me," he said. "Did you tell your mother?"

She shook her head.

"I've got to tell her about this, Linda."

"I know."

He put his hand on the side of her face and cradled her, swaying slightly there on the bed. "There," he kept whispering. "There. It's all right."

Presently she put the book on her nightstand, got to her feet, and pulled her dress up over her shoulders. "I'm glad I told you," she said. "I didn't know I was going to."

"It's going to be fine," he said.

"I've got a stomachache." She sobbed.

He reached for her again. "Honey, I'm so sorry."

"You hate him."

Field patted the back of her head.

"I wish I wasn't me," she said, sniffling.

He bent down and tried to look into her face. She wouldn't look back. "Linda, look at me."

"What."

"Linda."

"My head hurts."

"I'll get you something for it in a minute. Listen to me."

"What," she said.

"You must not let him get near enough to put his hands on you—no matter how much you want him to. Do you understand?"

"You told me," she said.

"Well—but you have to promise me. Otherwise you might wind up somewhere you don't want to be. Away from your mother and Aunt Ellen and this house."

"He wants to see me."

"He spoke to you?"

She closed her mouth tight, gave forth a little breath of determination, then told him in a firm voice that she had spoken to her father on the telephone. Field listened to her, filled with a kind of admiration for her, for the way she had managed things all day. She sniffled, telling him, then she stepped away, holding herself erect—she was a person marshaling her strength—and crawled into bed. Pulling the blankets over herself, she said, "But he doesn't want me."

Field watched her arrange herself on the pillow, and something toppled in his chest. Her face shone with tears. She put her hands to her mouth as if to breathe warmth into them, and he reached over to tuck her in.

"You—you want a Tylenol?"

She shook her head.

"I'll read to you if you want."

"No."

"You know, I love you," he said.

"I know," she answered.

"Want me to stay here?"

"If you want to."

"I'll stay here," he said.

He sat in a chair against the wall, while she slept, or seemed to sleep. She lay very still. He gazed at her posters of movie stars and rock singers, at the dark window, his own aging hands, and when he leaned his head back, closing his eyes, wanting only to rest them a little, the sharply defined edges of consciousness began unexpectedly to wear smooth. Time ended. He was gone in the sensation of being deeply pillowed, of softly floating, falling through, and then for a moment he seemed to be awake. He was awake and staring into a moving glow. Annie was here, six years old. Field came to know this, and it seemed very natural that she should be so small again—a skinny, quick-moving, nervous girl—come to stand before him in this strange, timeless, placeless glow.

Ellen awakened him, standing in the doorway, whispering that she was going to bed. She was gone, she had been gone some time, and Field finally woke up for good, got to his feet, confused, obscurely aware of something he should be worried about. The house was quiet; it was past ten o'clock, and, realizing this he was abruptly wide, wide awake. Linda lay with her hands folded on her chest, her mouth open slightly. He kissed her forehead, watched for a moment the faint rise and fall of her chest, hearing the slow, rhythmic susurration of her breath in sleep. Before he left her there, he decided that he didn't like the morbid look of her hands lying on her chest, and he gently uncrossed them.

She opened her eyes, and he kissed them closed again.

"Go to sleep," he murmued. "Love you." Then he crept out of the room and shut the door.

Alice Minneford complained about the cold, and being hungry. What she wanted was to cross over into Superior, where her uncle and his family were probably back from wherever they had gone, and would now be sitting down to dinner. Gilbertson paid no attention to her, and she went on talking; she didn't see what good it did to sit in a car shivering and watching people go in and out of a house. Any more than she could understand why a man would sneak away from the daughter he had come eight hundred miles to see, after having conspired with her over the telephone only hours before.

"Shut up," Gilbertson said, finally.

They waited. What he was really hoping for was another glimpse of Annie. He had seen the record shop owner go into the house with a young couple, and he had caught a fleeting glance of Linda in the door. There had been nothing since.

"Come on," Alice said. "Jesus. Can't we at least listen to the radio?"

"Be quiet."

She opened her purse, brought out one of her vials of pills, and took one.

"What's that."

"Aspirin," she said.

"Bullshit."

"It's aspirin, goddammit."

They waited, and at length the door opened. The young couple traversed the porch unsteadily, arm in arm. They seemed to be arguing.

"Look," Cole said, and cracked the window. He couldn't make out what they were saying, but it was clear that they were angry with each other. The young woman was unsteady on her feet.

They were in shadow at the edge of the porch. A moment later, the shop owner came out, telling them to wait a minute, he would take them home. There would be no something, and that was that, said the shop owner. Gilbertson heard the phrase "Cool off." The door closed, and the young couple stood facing away from each other, not speaking. In a little while the door opened again, and here was Annie, stepping out of the light. Gilbertson wiped his own breath away from his window and peered at her, putting his hands on either side of his face to blot out any light but the light she was standing in, moving through. He almost opened the car door and called out to her. She was even wearing a jacket he thought he recognized. The shop owner moved to accompany her, one hand on her elbow, as though he had produced her out of nothing.

"Jesus," he said to Alice. "Look at him. Jesus Chirst."

"He looks nice," Alice said. "At least he looks like a gentleman."

"Maybe he's just going to be a hurting gentleman, too."

"For Christ's sake—you're divorced."

Gilbertson started the car.

"What now," Alice said. "I'm starved."

"We're going to follow them."

"Oh, come on, Cole. You're ripped. Leave it alone, will you? You said we could go to Superior."

"Just shut up. Will you shut up?"

"I don't believe this," she said.

He eased the brake off, and as the other car glided away from the curb, he followed at a safe distance. Nothing could be easier. He kept four or five car lengths behind them, and when at last they stopped, and two of them got out, he pulled by them. Annie and the shop owner were staying in the car. He drove to the corner and turned right, and then sped to make it back around the block.

"Great," Alice Minneford said. "Just fucking great."

He pulled back onto the street, inched over, and stopped. The other car was still idling in front of the house, which was a two-story, Victorian-looking place with a porch and bay windows; it did not look particularly like the house of a wealthy man. Gilbertson watched the windows, the door, thinking the other two would come back out, but then the other car edged away from the curb, and he was following it again, trying to keep a reasonable distance. They wound through descending streets to the business district, and then climbed back toward Annie's father's house. He went by them again, pulled over at the corner below them, and waited, keeping them in his side-view mirror.

"This is the goddamnedest bullshit thing I ever did," Alice said.

He turned to her. "Say one more thing and I'll knock you into the backseat."

The other car came coasting toward them, and he ducked down. "Get down," he said to her. But Alice sat straight, arms folded stubbornly. The other car went by, and again he was following it, muttering curses at her under his breath. Once more they descended into the business district, and then along Michigan Street, with its closed shops and lighted nighttime establishments—bars, video stores, and movie theaters, and, next to the old USO building, a mission called the Serviceman's Home Center which, when he'd arrived here in 1976, had been tended by two old women who laid out trays of homemade cookies and distributed religious articles and pamphlets to penniless and homesick young soldiers. They stopped at the old Royal Duluth Hotel. "Christ," he said, parking across the street from the entrance. "You believe that shit?"

"They'll probably have champagne and eggs Benedict for breakfast," Alice said. "Yeah, I believe it."

"I don't believe she's actually fucking the old bastard."

"I bet the beds are soft."

He turned the car around and headed back down the street.

"Come on, I thought we were going to Superior," she said.

"Not tonight," said Gilbertson. "Tomorrow morning. Okay?" He spoke the last word through his teeth, hitting the steering wheel with both hands.

A moment later, she said, "Just let me get somewhere other than the front seat of this car."

He nodded, looking out at the road. "That's more like it."

On the way to Louis's house, Fran talked foolishly of what she imagined she was experiencing—the world was moving round and round, she said, and she felt giddy, everything looked funny. Her hilarity had the effect of darkening Roger's already sour mood, and he sat staring out the window, as far over on the seat as he could get. Now and again Annie and Louis exchanged a look, but they had also gone beyond the joke now, and their expressions were almost rueful about it. When they reached Louis's house, he slowed at the curb and stopped, and for a moment no one spoke. Then Fran giggled, and Roger opened his door to get out.

"Where's everybody going?" Fran said.

Annie put her arm over the seat back and shifted to look at her. "Why don't you go on with Roger?"

"Where's he going? God, I'm reeling."

Roger leaned in the open door. "Christ—will you come on?"

"I don't think I can walk. I want another vodka."

"Roger will fix you one inside," Annie told her.

"Roger's a stick in the mud, isn't he?"

"Will you come on," Roger said.

"Old stick in the mud," Fran said, waving him away as she slid across the seat. When she was out, Roger slammed the door, and the two of them walked off toward the house.

In the quiet that followed, Annie said, "Poor girl."

"What," Louis said.

"She's in for a surprise if Roger fixes her the real thing."

"She's a prig," Louis said. "And in this instance, life is fair."

Annie breathed into her hands, settling lower in the seat. "What're we waiting for?"

"I don't know where to go now," he said.

She had closed her eyes, and for what seemed a long time she didn't respond. Then she sighed, straightened a little, pulled her coat around herself. "Where do you want to go?"

"Anywhere you say, Annie."

She sat there considering for another moment, after which she appeared to come to herself, as if just realizing that he was waiting for a response. "Just drive, why don't you."

He took the brake off, and started in the direction of Twenty-first Avenue.

"We can just ride around and talk," he said. But there wasn't anything he could think of to say. He sifted through everything in his memory, all the phrases of happiness and wonder and love—even entertaining, for a fleeting few seconds, the absurd idea of congratulating her—and everything felt wrong to him. Everything failed before the steady brooding seriousness of her gaze.

"Well?" she said.

"Annie," he said, "give it a chance, will you?"

She was silent again.

He drove on into the center of town. All lights and traffic, and people waiting to cross at intersections—winter was on the way. Everybody wanted to walk out in the night while it was still possible to do so. Couples strolled along in front of shop windows, and in the small open square off Wilson Lane he saw people sitting on benches facing the far off harbor lights, which made huddling shadows out of them.

"Just take me home," she said.

"Home."

"I understand, Louis."

"No, you don't understand."

"Where are we going?" she asked.

"I thought we might go to the hotel."

"Are we going to talk at the hotel?"

"Look," he said, "I really don't know what you want from me. I'm just trying to do what you want. I thought you wanted to get out alone, so we could talk."

"Oh, Jesus," she said, shifting uncomfortably, again pulling her coat around her.

"All right, now, look. You're pregnant. Let's start with that."

"When I told you," she said, "your face went white as a sheet."

"Annie, you can't pretend to believe I wouldn't be surprised by the news."

She said nothing to this.

"Of course I was surprised. I thought you were breaking off the engagement or something."

"Maybe I am," she muttered.

At this, he was silent. He had made the turn, and was heading back to her father's house.

"Maybe it's all been a mistake, Louis."

"Look," he said. "I'm pushing fifty-three. I just didn't think we'd have a child. What do you want me to say? It's a little frightening for someone my age and you'll just have to understand that."

"I understand it, all right. I feel the same way."

"Well, then what're we arguing about?"

"Please," she said, "I don't want to talk about it anymore. I have to decide what I'm going to do." She had begun to cry. She was sitting low in the seat as if in an attempt not to be seen.

He looked out at the street, the parked cars, the people walking by on the sidewalks. He had lived here all his life. He was driving by his own shop now, and the sight of it made him feel queasy.

"I'm sorry," she said.

He made the turn up the hill toward Superior Street.

"Look," she said, "what if we get married and I have this baby and then what if—what if something happens to you.

Something could happen, right? I mean—it's not like you're twenty-seven, Louis. Or thirty-seven. I'd be alone with *two* children."

"People die at all ages, Annie."

"And don't talk to me like I'm a child. I'm not a child."

They didn't speak again until he slowed the car and came even with the curb in front of the house. Lights were on in the downstairs windows—there was the shifting glow of the television in the living room. He said, "I hope you'll forgive me for pointing out that I was telling you something you've apparently overlooked, and if that's talking to you like a child then maybe you're thinking like one a little."

"I don't want this baby," she said in an almost eerily emotionless voice. It appeared that her mind was made up.

"Is this because of my reaction?" he said.

"It's because I don't want this baby." She looked at the house, crying, sniffling, touching her nose with the back of her hand.

"I'll take care of you," he told her.

She shook her head.

"I will. I'll take care of you and Linda and the—and our baby."

"Please," she said.

He touched her shoulder, but she moved a little as if to get out from under his fingers, and he took his hand away.

Presently, she said, "I can't go in there." She straightened again. Appeared to gather herself. "Let's get out of here. Let's go to the hotel."

He put the car in gear. "You're sure?"

"For God's sake," she said.

"There's nothing to be unhappy about," Louis said. "I love you, Annie."

She had covered her face with her hands now, and again he touched her shoulder. "Oh, please, Lou. I can't think."

He gripped the wheel and drove down into the city once more, heading toward the hotel.

The lobby was crowded and noisy. There was a convention of orthodontists from the upper Midwest, and at this hour, the end of the dinner hour, many of them were convening near the front desk to make arrangements for the coming night. Louis waited in line to speak to the clerk about the room he had reserved, while Annie sat in a red velvet wing chair against the wall, daubing her eyes with a handkerchief and nervously smoking a cigarette without inhaling it. The air was layered with cigar and pipe smoke, with the various odors of cologne, hair spray, perfume, and perspiration. Standing in line, Louis thought about the fact that she was carrying his child. He thought of his first wife, all those years ago, sitting in a chair in the living room of a house not five miles from where he now stood, gingerly touching her moving abdomen and smiling proudly at him. *Oh, darling.* Two decades; two decades. When he turned to look at Annie he saw only discouragement and anxiety in her face, and even so he experienced a quick surging in his blood; he would find the right things to tell her. After all, he told himself, she had wanted to come *here,* to this old, tiered-cake of a hotel, the scene of their early passion. He felt strong; he was still vital. There were things he could say and do, and he was going to be a father again. He looked at the other men in the line, feeling competent and ready for anything, and then he saw a man about his own age reach into his jacket pocket for a handkerchief to wipe the sweat from his face. The man was fiftyish, heavy around the middle, balding, tired-looking. Because he was of a certain age, Louis could assume some things about him: that he remembered Korea, for instance, that he had been a boy during the war; that he had acquaintance with certain forms of expression, with certain songs, certain aspects of popular culture, and with shifts in the social fabric. He was a man who knew what it felt like to turn forty, and forty-five, and fifty, and his losses were grafted to him in the discolorations, the marks and scars and failings, of his body. In some odd, mysterious way that had to do with his own natural objectivity about himself and how

he must appear to others, the sight of this man, this contem-
porary, had the effect of leeching all the energy out of him, as
though someone had shouted him down for the presumption of
his own good feeling.

The room he'd reserved was on the second floor, and in the
adjacent suite there was a party going on—more orthodontists,
apparently. Someone sang a ditty about incisors, and others were
shrieking with the high-pitched, hysterical, boozy laughter of
late hours.

It wasn't even eight-thirty.

"Friday at the Royal Duluth," Louis said.

Annie got undressed and into the bed, and, with sad eyes,
beckoned to him. They made love without speaking, and then
she lay in his arms, curled against him like a little girl. He was
quiet, listening to the raucous sound through the walls, trying
to recover something of the strength he had felt downstairs in
the lobby.

She moved, sighed. "When I was small, I was afraid to go to
sleep at night because it was night. I mean it didn't matter that
I had my light on and the lights in the house were all on. The
idea of the dark itself—that the whole world could be dark—
that terrified me."

"The silence of these infinite spaces," Louis said.

"Oh God—not Pascal. Not now."

"I don't know who that is."

She said, "Anyway, I was terrified of the dark. Nothing else.
But my father wanted an explanation of it. I think—I think he
needed one, somehow. And so I made something up and scared
the hell out of myself. I mean I hadn't thought about anything
else, you know? Just the dark."

"What're you afraid of now?" Louis asked.

"Everything."

"Even these idiots on the other side of the wall?"

"No."

They were quiet for a time. They listened to the voices.

"I can't stand the thought of what he'll say—the way he'll look at me—if I tell him I'm pregnant."

"It's not really any business of his, Annie."

"I feel so stupid."

"Don't," he said.

She nestled; her hair touched his cheek.

"I'm happy about it," he said.

She said, "Let's go to sleep."

A moment later, he said, "We'll make a nice family. You and me and Linda and Roger and the baby."

"Louis, please."

"I love you," he said.

"Aren't you sleepy?" she asked.

He felt it slipping away; he was losing her, and he had to try something. He put his hand on her abdomen. "I'm in love."

She lay still, breathing as if in sleep.

"You've gone to sleep," he said.

"No."

"I'm sorry."

"It's not you. It's the hyenas on the other side of the wall."

"Well," he said, "bless them. Bless them and everyone else this night on earth."

She snuggled closer to him, and he was momentarily encouraged.

"Do you feel protected?" he asked.

"Mmmm."

"I'll fight off the bad things," he said.

"That's what my father used to say. He did the best he could."

"That's all anyone has a right to ask."

"It wasn't good enough. He loved me like hell and it wasn't enough."

"That's just the way you feel now, talking."

"When I think of all the things he did because he loved me—

what people visit on each other out of something like love. It's enough for all the world's woe, Louis. You don't even need hate to have a perfectly miserable time."

"Go to sleep," he said. "Maybe we'll both feel better in the morning."

She was quiet a long time. Then she removed herself from him, slid to the edge of the bed, and stood. "Have to pee," she said.

He tried to joke: "You just thought you'd keep me informed."

But she went on into the bathroom and closed the door. She was in there a long time. He got up and moved to the window to look out at the city, the distant lights of Superior. It was a clear night, at last. All the clouds had moved off to the west. Somewhere—not in the next room—he could hear Benny Goodman's "Moonglow." He strained to listen. When she came out of the bathroom he was still at the window, his head cocked to hear the music.

"Hear that?" he said.

She gazed at him—at his body. It made him want to cover himself. He felt his love of the music—this willingness to stand here in the chill of the window casement and strive to hear something he knew by heart and had heard at least a thousand times in his life—as somehow an element of his nakedness: it was as if this devotion were a part of the configuration of his flesh, as if it marked him in a way he couldn't help, like scars, or blotches in his skin.

"Annie?" he said.

"Let's go down and have something to drink at the bar," she said.

"Shouldn't you—should you be drinking?"

Flopping down on the bed, she began pulling her stockings on, her back to him. "I can't sleep. Are you coming?"

"Why don't we just call room service?"

"I don't want to be here, right now, Louis. Please."

So they got dressed and went down to the lounge. It was

crowded, there weren't any open tables, and they had to sit side by side at the bar, looking at each other in the candlelit shimmer of the mirror behind the rows of bottles. The bartender was a woman in black leotards and a bright red vest over a luminous white blouse; her lips looked bruised in the light, and her hair was teased in the style of the mid-sixties. She took their orders without appearing to notice them at all, her thick imitation lashes hiding her eyes. Annie ordered a whiskey sour, and Louis, as if to compensate for this apparent breech of all the medical indications concerning pregnancy and alcohol, asked for soda water. The barmaid went about the business of making the drinks, and Louis watched her, sitting with his hands folded in front of him, while Annie opened her purse and, bringing out a small compact, began to apply makeup to her cheeks. "I look like death." She gazed into the little mirror.

"You look fine," said Louis.

"I'm sorry, but I don't want this. I never wanted this."

"You mean us?" he said.

She looked at him. "You know what I mean." She put everything back into her purse, and in a little while the bartender brought their drinks. Louis paid for them. Annie drank immediately from hers, then set the glass down on the bar and looked at it. They sat there quietly, amid all the noise and confusion of the place, people arriving and departing, and everyone seeming to know everyone else. "Let's go," she said, finally.

Back in the room, she lay down on the bed and buried her face in her hands. He stood over her. "Maybe I should leave," he said.

"We've got the room all night." Her voice was devoid of feeling.

"Annie, I love you and I want to make a family with you. Beyond that, I don't know what I'm supposed to do. Why don't you tell me what you want."

"I want you to stop talking," she said.

He put one knee on the bed, leaned down to give her a chaste

kiss on the cheek, and she moved as if to avoid contact with
him. At this, he hauled himself across the room, gathered his
coat and made a show of putting it on, half hoping she would
say something to call him back. Yet when he opened the door
into the noise of the hall, some part of him abruptly realized
that he wanted time away from the complications in the room
behind him. He turned. She had come to a sitting position in
the middle of the bed, leaning back on her hands, one leg slightly
bent at the knee. It might have been an erotic pose if her face
were not so unhappy and troubled. "Will you be all right?" he
said to her.

"You're leaving?"

"You seem to want me to."

She sighed. "No." Then: "I don't know what I want."

He'd had enough. "When you decide, why don't you let me
know. You know where you can find me."

Now she simply stared at him.

"Look," he said, "I'll call you tomorrow morning. Is that all
right?"

"Of course it's all right. Don't be ridiculous."

He closed the door.

Certain Testimony

A little more than a year after her mother died, I started going out with someone I'd met at the bank—a very kindhearted and good-humored woman named Kitty, who owned an old green Pontiac and used to drive me home in the evenings. It was a friendship. She had known my wife, and we'd spent some time together at various social gatherings put on in those days by the bank. In her own recent past, there was a bad divorce; she lived in a small apartment by herself, was lonely, like me, and quickly enough our friendship became something else; Kitty started coming into the house with me, started sleeping over. Annie wasn't much past three years old when it began, and of course she was suspicious of Kitty—would look at me with plain outrage that I could bring this stranger into the house. She started making difficulty in the nights, and it wasn't long before Kitty decided that she needed her sleep more than she needed me. At any rate, Kitty deemed that unglamorous fact important enough to list as the first of her many reasons for breaking things off between us. I don't recall that I felt any great regret over her decision—the truth of the matter was that she struck a deeply unpleasant note in her voice whenever she laughed, and her interests very rapidly showed themselves to be far from mine—but I did feel that something in what happened with Kitty was bound to happen over again, because I was a man with a child. I remember feeling unhappy about this—unhappy and very lonely. But I would hold Annie, I would hold that baby girl, feeling the soft, small weight of her in my arms, and everything else seemed unimportant.

I was happy, then. I didn't know how happy.

And of course, all my worries and responsibilities were leading me away from that simplest of the aspects of peace.

Nights when I can't sleep now, I count failures, and my soul turns on regret. That I didn't appreciate it enough; that I wasn't glad enough for the privilege; that I couldn't love excellently, and that I failed to keep from expecting more than I had a right to expect.

Long ago, now, there is a night—only one of many nights—in which I get up, tired and frustrated and needing the forgetfulness of sleep, to go down the hall and speak to a little girl in bed there. Annie, lying awake under the room light. I am a man nearing forty, trying to raise a child alone, and worried about whether or not I'm up to it. She's not quite six. She's lying quite stiff, with her hands closed tight on the edges of the blanket.

"What's wrong?" I say to her.

And she whimpers something I can't understand.

"Tell me, honey."

"The window."

"What about the window."

"It's dark."

"All right," I say. "Let's close the curtain." And I do so. When I face her again, I see that she's begun to cry. "Honey," I say, "I closed it."

"But it's still dark."

"What is," I say.

"Outside."

"I closed the curtain."

"I know."

"Then it's all better, right?"

She shakes her head.

"Annie, I don't know what you want me to do."

"I don't like the dark," she says.

"Tell me what you don't like about it."

"It's dark."

"There's nothing in the dark that isn't there in the light."

"Can I come to bed with you?"

"No—now this is silly," I tell her. *"You have your light on. Go to sleep."* I recall that the books say to be firm.

She closes her eyes while I watch, and I wait a few minutes. When I believe she must be sleeping, I go quietly to my own room. It's late, past midnight. I have to get up early, and, trying to go to sleep, the worries keep me awake. I lie there in the bath of light from her open doorway across the hall, and now I hear her begin to cry.

"Annie," I say. *"Go to sleep. I'm right here."*

She's quiet again. But only for a few minutes. It's like all the other nights. All those nights when she stopped Kitty from anything and kept us both irritable and awake. Now I get out of my bed, stand for a minute in the cluttered, desolate half-dark of the room, thinking about how my own life is circumscribed, every night the same struggle to get her to fall asleep. And my patience starts to snap. I'm alone, a widower; sleep is precious, won't ever come easily again; I lack the energy to do anything in the house or at my job; things are piling up and there are money problems and my life is getting away from me. I walk into my daughter's room, stand over her, feeling my own height like a threat—and abruptly I become a man in a fit, exasperated and sarcastic and mad, gesticulating wildly as I talk.

"All right, let's just get to the bottom of this. Let's look at this a minute. Just what is it that makes you afraid? What is it that scares you? Suppose you tell me right now. Suppose you tell me what you think is the matter."

"It's dark."

"It's not dark. The light is on. See this? This is a light. It's on."

"I'm scared."

"Did you have a bad dream?"

"No." She looks at me, her chin lowered into her neck, her hands clutching the blanket there.

"Look," I say, feeling sick. "Honey," I say. "What're you afraid of in the dark?"

When she speaks now it's as if she's admitting something she's held in for a long time. "Monsters."

I hear myself telling her there's no such thing.

She nods, pouting at me.

"So you don't have to be afraid," I go on and say.

"Can I come to bed with you?"

"Annie, I'm right here across the hall. Okay? I'm right here. Nothing can hurt you while I'm here. Now just close your eyes and go to sleep."

"Can I cuddle with you?"

I remember what the books say. "Honey, this is where you sleep."

"Can I please cuddle with you?"

And I can feel the anger returning. I'm thinking about what all the books say and how useless they really are. "There's no such thing as monsters," I say, firmly and definitely. "You go to sleep."

But she keeps crying, and finally I'm standing over her again. I'm towering with reason. "All right, look, you're almost six years old. Count it all up why don't you. Count up all the nights in six years. Six times almost four hundred nights, right? That's almost two thousand four hundred nights. And in all that time, have you ever seen a single solitary monster?"

She simply stares at me.

"What makes you think you'll see one tonight?"

"I don't know."

"You don't know. You don't know. Look." I move to the light and turn it off, and she utters a little cry of alarm. It enrages me. "Now it's dark, right? What's here in the dark." I turn the light on again. "I am. See? Nothing else."

She nods, pouting, and I tuck her in, can't help the way my hands move. I tuck the blanket tight and then put my hands on her shoulders as if to hold her down. "Now for the last time, Annie. Go to sleep."

Her eyes are closed, but she whimpers. I stamp back to my own room and collapse on my bed as if from the sheer weight of failure. She's quiet. I expect any moment to hear her, but there's nothing, and perhaps my mind lurches toward sleep again. An hour passes and I wake knowing myself to be wrong, so awfully wrong that my heart feels swollen. Getting up, I falter to the entrance of her room— and see that she's wide awake, lying there staring at the curtained window. The anger comes back with all the force of an attack, and I storm into the room, lift her from the bed and carry her downstairs, out the front door, to the edge of the porch. It is a cool, moonless summer night. There are street lamps and little islands of light out in the dark, and lights wink on and off in the big blackness of the lake. I kneel beside her, my hands tight on her arms. "See this?" I say, pointing to the yard, "this is where you play all day. See over there, your bike? See it? See the sandbox and the toys? It's all there just like it is in the daylight, only it's dark. Do you see it, Annie?"

"Yes," she says. "Yes." And she keeps on saying it, crying. "Yes. Yes."

I lift her again, my little girl, carry her back inside, feeling her solidness and the shudder that goes through her, and I begin to know again how bad this is—what a mistake I have made. When we get back to her room I sit down on the edge of her bed and hold her on my lap, rocking with her, knowing it's not enough, knowing it's entirely possible that nothing will ever make up for it and thinking that even so, somehow, I'll have to try. She's sobbing, still trembling.

"There now," I say, hating myself, crying, too, now. "There. It's all right," I say. "I'm here. Daddy's here, Annie. Don't cry, my baby. I'm sorry," I tell her, rocking slightly, crying, looking at her pictures on the wall, those big drawn cartoon faces, and the one crayon drawing of the house, with a red sun and dark green grass, me standing on the porch. DADDY: a tall, leaning figure in bright blue. . . .

· · ·

I watched television for a time, then went out for a walk. I
wasn't sure what I thought I'd find. The street was quiet, though
it wasn't extremely late—not much past ten o'clock. I looked
at each parked car as I walked, half expecting something to
move in one of them. It was chilly, and the wind had picked
up again. I went on down to the corner and stood in the light
there, then turned up the street, to the Stop 'n' Shop. Four
teenagers were standing under the light of the sign, smoking
and drinking something from a bottle they kept passing back
and forth. They watched me carefully as I came past them, and
I heard one say something about going home. Inside, in the
brightness, a young, bright-looking man with a mane of un-
combed hair the color of pennies, lifted his gaze from a magazine
and smiled at me. I must have returned the favor, because he
was encouraged to ask me how I liked the chill in the air and
whether or not I thought the snow would be worse this year
than it was last year. I said I sure didn't know, bought a pack
of chewing gum and some aspirin, and he asked if I wanted
anything else.

"If I wanted to buy a gun, where would I go?" I said. I hadn't
known I would say it.

The clerk looked at me with wide, innocent green eyes. "A
gun?"

"Right," I said.

"No, sir."

"You don't know."

He shook his head, and stared.

I had gone half a block back in the direction of the house
before I realized that I had frightened him, probably very badly.
I almost turned around to go assure him he had nothing to fear
from me, but a part of me felt almost good about it, too; and
of course I didn't examine the feeling much beyond accepting
the fact that an aging man never minds indications of how others

still take him seriously. I am old, I might say to someone like that, but I can be fearsome.

And having said all this, let us go on to point out that I am, for instance, very good at terrorizing little girls.

I went back to the house, walked through the rooms of the downstairs: the den, with its shelves of books and its record albums leaning against each other along the wall; the living room, cluttered with the objects of daily comfort, and the signs of hospitality and company—the empty glasses on the coffee table; the cigarettes in the ashtray on the mantelpiece. I cleared these things away, being quiet, waiting for Annie to come home, and thinking about how it must have been to be a child in my house. A little girl alone with a worried man. It had begun to seem to me that during all those years of her growing up, even in the many moments of simple loveliness, of a tranquil and ordinary charm—father and daughter taking an evening walk, or sitting in the dining room of the house on a rainy day, playing cards, or cuddling together on the big, threadbare sofa in the den, watching televison—I had somehow unwittingly managed to communicate the coloration of anxiety and the fear of harm, an idea of the threatening world outside—like a fever, an uncannily subtle delirium.

I got myself ready to retire for the night, cleaned my teeth, chose a book to read, and pulled the blankets back from my bed. And then I went downstairs and looked out the window in the front door again. The street was still, might have been a painting of an empty street at night. I wanted to talk to Annie I wanted to get to the bottom of things, say things I had never said to her. *Annie, I loved you so, and was afraid. The world is such that these two things are always somehow true between a parent and a child, a father and a little girl*

I went into the kitchen and made myself a pot of coffee, then didn't want any. My stomach was sour. I was too nervous: something was happening. Cole Gilbertson was back, and I wanted to be awake when Annie came home. I wanted to talk to her about it, wanted to warn her against anything he might try to do. I stood again at the front door window, watching for the lightening arc of headlamps in the fixed, sharp shadows of the street. Annie was going to be gone, I knew, all night. And even so I was waiting up, worrying, giving in to my old habit of imagining what might happen to ruin my life.

Cole was back, as I had supposed he would be, and the last time I had seen him he was dressed in a muted, brown suit and tie, a man in the process of revising himself, perfectly reasonable and friendly and contrite. There was no reason to suspect that he might be different this time. *Then,* he had driven up to the house as Annie had said he would, unannounced, in the middle of the day—a pleasant, late spring day—having come all the way from Illinois to stand on my lawn and very gently ask Annie if they might have a little talk. Annie and I had been sitting on the porch, watching Linda play in the sandbox I'd bought for her only that morning, and now Linda, having seen her father, made a run for him out of the sand. He swept her up and swung her around, and Annie looked at me.

I stood.

"No," she said to me. "Wait."

Gilbertson walked up to the foot of the porch steps, holding Linda high on his shoulder. He had sand all over the front of him.

"How's Selena?" Annie said.

"She's okay."

"You can tell her I miss her sometimes."

He shuffled his feet a little, looking like someone trying to get his nerve up to ask for a date. "You know," he said, "I waited to come here, honey. I wanted to get turned around. Get myself straightened up. I got a motel room. You know, Annie. You know what motel. I can stay for a while, anyway. And I thought we could talk a little bit."

I stood and came to the top porch step, next to Annie.

"I got some presents for you, sweetie," Gilbertson was saying to Linda, putting her down and bending to look into her eyes. He made a gesture of asking for our tolerance, then lifted her again and moved toward the street, his car.

"You wait a minute," I said.

Annie took my wrist. "Let him," she said, low.

Gilbertson opened the car and reached in, and Linda climbed down out of his arms, sliding along his outstretched leg, to take one bright package into her dimpled hands. He brought out another, larger one, and the two of them walked back up to the porch. After a pause, Annie suggested that we all go into the house, and we did so. I held the door for them all, and when Gilbertson sidled past me something hot moved in my chest. His hair was trimmed, close-cut, almost like a military cut. He looked prosperous and disciplined. In the living room, he bothered to comment about how things hadn't changed, how nice it was to be there, and even so he seemed to be looking at everything as if for the first time. He put his large package on the sofa and then offered to shake hands with me.

I did so with a sullenness I couldn't control, and then we all watched Linda tear at her brightly wrapped, profusely ribboned presents: one was a doll, the other was a Big Wheels tricycle.

"Amazing," Gilbertson said, watching her with the doll. He looked pale. His hands shook when he reached to untangle one of the ribbons from the yellow handle bar of the trike. "Selena wrapped them," he said, and I felt a little stir of pity for him, thinking without wanting to about how he had cost himself everything. It struck me, watching him gaze at his daughter, that he and I might begin to seem similar enough to anyone looking on. I took myself into the kitchen, where I suppose I meant to stay until he was gone, and a moment later Ellen came in, having walked straight down the hall from the front door.

"I don't believe it," she said.

"Believe it," I told her.

"What's she going to do?"

"You tell me."

"Poor Annie."

"If she gives an inch, so help me—" I began.

Ellen interrupted me. "I just glanced in and saw him as I went by in the hall—is he wearing a tie?"

I nodded. "Did you hear what they were talking about?"

"They were petting Linda. They looked like a young family at Christmas. It's none of our business."

"Dad," Annie called from the living room. "Aunt Ellen—what're you doing in there?"

"Your move," Ellen said to me.

She stayed behind. In the living room, Annie was seated on the sofa with Linda in her lap, and Gilbertson was standing across the room, his back to the sunny window there, which made a shadowed outline of him.

"Will you take Linda?" Annie said to me.

I went to her and lifted the child from her lap. The doll lay face down in its fold of wrapping paper, and she picked it up and held it out to me as I sat down.

"She hasn't really seen this work yet," she said.

I took the doll.

"I saw Aunt Ellen come through—is she hiding or something?"

"I don't think she's hiding, Annie."

"Well, we're going out on the porch for a few minutes."

I nodded.

She gazed at me. "Is that okay with you?"

"Yes," I said, trying to get the agitation out of my voice.

Gilbertson came forward a little, reached down to touch his daughter's hair. It was a very tender gesture, yet there was something almost ingratiating about it; it made me want to push his hand away. When they had left the room, were outside on the porch, I smoothed Linda's hair down where he had touched it, the furious and somehow satisfying thought gusting through me like some secret mistral that I might as well be trying to remove a soil or stain.

"Look," Linda said, holding up the doll.

Through the window, I saw the shadows they made; they were standing close enough to touch, but neither of them moved. Linda wanted to go out to them, so I tried to distract her with the doll, which cried real tears and talked when you pulled a small cord that drooped from its neck. She pulled the cord and the doll said inane, vaguely commercial things, while the shadows moved in the window, in the brightness there. Cole was gesturing, making small, Italianate motions with his hands as he talked. And now Ellen walked in from the kitchen, and sat in the wing chair by the window, her hands folded primly in her lap.

"Don't sit there," I said to her.

"I can't hear anything," she said.

"Ellen."

She stood. "I swear."

Linda pulled the cord on the doll, and it spoke in a tinny little voice about being Tanya the talking doll.

Ellen stared at it, and Linda pulled the cord again.

The doll voice expressed automatic, unspecific affection.

"My God," Ellen said.

Linda pulled at the cord, but there was a snag in it now, and the doll's voice was garbled—and there came from the window something oddly similar: garbled; a kind of pleading, an emphasis.

"It's broken," Linda said.

Ellen tried it, and the little voice shook through an almost seductive plea to be taken in. "Won't you take me home with you?" it said.

We were watching it, and whatever was taking place out on the front porch was taking place.

Finally Annie came in alone, and took Linda up in her arms. "He wants to spend some time with his daughter," she said to me.

"Yes?" I said. I thought there had been something almost aggressive in the way she spoke, as if she were somehow confronting me with it.

"So I told him he could."

"All right," I said. And even as I felt the surgings of protest rise in my blood, I found that I could admire her—could see her as the grown woman she was, apart from me, alone and strong and knowing what she wanted. I said, "Fine."

"No," Annie said. "Not particularly fine. But it'll have to do for now."

"Annie," I said. "Have you wondered about the possibility that he might take her south with him?"

"He won't."

"Can you be sure he won't?"

"Yes."

"Are you telling me you think you can take the risk?"

"I'm telling you my husband—from whom I'm separated— wants to spend some time with his daughter. You ought to be able to understand that, right?" She went out, and I was standing alone there with Ellen, the two of us in attitudes suggesting arrested motion, as though the thing that had just taken place was something pathological or supernatural.

I straightened a little, pressed my hands into the small of my back. "Well?" I said.

Ellen seemed irritated. "I don't know anything," she told me. I said. "You're the one who's been talking to her, Ellen."

"Look," my sister said, "I'm not in this—this is none of my business."

The door opened and Annie came in without Linda. I went to the window in time to see Gilbertson drive away.

"Jesus Christ, I don't believe it."

"He took her to get some ice cream," Annie said.

"I can't fathom your simplicity in this," I told her.

The look she gave me was almost amused—as though I were an innocent form of entertainment. "I'm going out on the porch and wait for them."

In a little while Gilbertson returned, of course, and for a time he and Annie stood under the shade of the willow in the yard, talking. Linda played happily on the porch, and I sat in the window, watching it all. When the wind stirred, the light changed, and the sun shone on Gilbertson's tanned, handsome face. He stood with his arms folded, leaning slightly to one side, while Annie talked and ran her fingers through her own dark hair. There was a life between them; years of going through the days—days that had nothing whatever to do with me. And watching them I still felt as though I should go out there and break in on their talk, stop him from saying the things that might convince her to capitulate, might entice her into taking him back. I'm aware that this thought miserably failed to credit my daughter as an adult, capable of deciding in a responsible way what was in her own best interest; but seeing Gilbertson again had opened all the wounds we had been trying to heal over those difficult weeks, and I had in my mind, quite vividly, the recklessness of Annie's first decision—the one that had got her where she now was (I now believe the truth of the matter was simply that I could justify my own wish to insinuate myself simply by recalling the one time I hadn't done so with enough force to effect a change in the outcome). So I made my way down the porch steps and ambled across the sunny lawn to stand within a few feet of where they were standing, neither of them talking now, but simply staring out at the far blue vistas of the lake.

"Well," I said.

Gilbertson looked at me and said, "Well."

"Would you excuse us, please?" Annie said to me.

"Annie," I began, "I don't think you're going to solve much by standing out here in the yard—"

"Man," Gilbertson said, not looking at me. "You just won't be satisfied."

"Be quiet," said Annie. "Please."

He faced me, and I saw that his lips were white. "We might've made it if it wasn't for you."

"No," Annie said. "Stop. It has nothing to do with anything." She took me by the wrist, tight. "Will you please leave us alone."

"Come out here putting your shit into the equation," Gilbertson said, muttering, shaking his head.

"You haven't done much growing up," I said to him. But I felt wrong. I was wrong.

"Cole, this decision is my own," Annie said, actually pushing me away. "It has nothing to do with anything else but us."

"I'm going to see my little girl," he said. "She's mine, and nobody can do a thing about it."

"You want her like a—like something you'd wear," I said to him. "You want her without having any responsibility for her."

"Coming down here adding your shit," he said, muttered, looking away again.

Annie stepped between us and put her hands on my arms just above the elbows. "If you don't go back to the house right now, I swear I'll never forgive it."

I wanted to find something to tell her, something to let her know she had my love and my support and that she shouldn't let herself be charmed or bullied by him, and then it struck me how much strain I had put on her with my meddling. It was in the troubled, exasperated mask of her face.

"I'm sorry," I said.

She said, "Please."

And I went back up to the house. Ellen had come out, and was sitting in the rocker on the porch, watching Linda play in the sandbox. My granddaughter seemed to understand that all this agitation going on around her was adult business, not to be interrupted or even attended to. I went up the steps of the porch, turned to look back at Linda and Cole, who had moved off toward the street.

"Did you study to be such an idiot?" Ellen said to me.

"I have natural talent," I told her, spitting the words out with my anger at myself.

Then, not a minute later, Gilbertson got into his car and drove off in the usual roar and cloud of exhaust. Linda sat in the middle of the sandbox watching him go, and her mother walked over and took her hand, then walked with her up onto the porch, swinging the hand slightly, bending slightly to accomplish it, and seeming calm and untroubled, almost relieved. She turned, swept her hair back away from her face.

"I told him he could see Linda any time he wants to," she said. Then she sighed. "Poor Cole. He was really kind of sweet when you consider that I didn't even leave him a note to say I was leaving him. And he knows he's in no position to take care of anything. He's having a hard time realizing that he's in the middle of a divorce."

I said nothing.

Ellen had gone back into the house, but she was standing there on the other side of the screen door. "That's that?" she said.

Annie sighed again. "That, as they say, is that."

That evening I watched the sun fade and redden at the bottom of the sky, and caught myself thinking about how in many houses this was the natural close of a lazy uncomplicated summer day. Across the street, down the hill, a man was cutting his grass. He wore ridiculously loud bermuda shorts, a white T-shirt with something emblazoned across the front of it. I watched him toil in the dusk, and heard Annie putting her little girl to bed, heard Ellen's television show and the beginning of the crickets' song in my own uncut grass. For the first time since Annie had come back home I felt confident that the long anguish between us over Cole Gilbertson was ending.

. . .

Nights Cole was gone, his mother and I sat in the living room of that old run-down house in Savoy and watched television. Selena knew all the shows. She was the only person I've ever known who actually kept a correspondence up with a television character: she'd been writing that Jack something who starred in the series about the tough motorcycle cop, whose name was also Jack. This being so, the actor answered her letters as the cop. I never learned how or why it came about; for Selena the whole thing was as normal as writing a cousin, though she was very proud of it, and at times seemed a little confused about the difference between a real cop and an actor who played a cop. I was pregnant then, too. And scared, too. Part of me wanting to run. If the baby was a boy, Selena said, we'd name him Jack. Cole was off on some scheme or scam—taking the short way around, as he put it, meaning laws were being skirted or broken. He was always going to make a fast dollar some way, selling drugs, working one scheme or another: once, he loaded a five-pound bag of marijuana into the trunk of the car, and sold it all in two days; he was going to go big time, he said, and start dealing scag; he knew someone who could bring it in from Mexico; he had got the pot from him, from this very resourceful guy, and then the resourceful guy went to jail, and for weeks Cole lived in back of the garage, afraid the police would come any minute to arrest him. Another time, he went to Indiana to steal a truck, so the person he stole it from, who happened also to be his accomplice, could claim it for insurance, while collecting for the sale of it privately in Illinois. Cole followed the plan to the letter, boosted the truck in the early morning before light, and on the way to the state line, got into an accident, and wound up running away from the police and the accomplice both. The police caught up with the whole thing, and Cole got probation after being charged as an accessory to insurance fraud and for car theft. He got off easy because he could claim that he didn't know why the man wanted him to take the truck. But he

*spent weeks away during the trial, and I had images of myself
bringing a baby to jail to visit him.*

*And how cruel it was that I had thought we were magic. He
made me laugh. He was beautiful to look at and he made me laugh.
He was just very clever and free with himself, completely unself-
conscious. He'd ingest some of his toot, and in no time at all he was
all energy and fun. At least when I first knew him. But then we
were in Illinois and I found out I was going to have a baby, and I
had to change: there was this other person I was carrying, and I
couldn't just go day to day—which was one of his expressions. What
it meant to him was that you did what you wanted and you took
each day as an opportunity for more of the same. The way to approach
life was simply that whatever came, you dealt with it, and you didn't
worry about consequences or effects. I was carrying a little conse-
quence around inside me, and was changing in a way that made
him want to be gone a lot—so he was gone a lot. And Selena and
I spent the nights together.*

*Before I ever saw him, there used to be a house my father and I
drove by at night on the way home from shopping, or a movie, or
something at school. It was one of the millions of boxlike ramblers
they built after World War II, with a little fenced yard and a couple
of small trees and a sidewalk. This house always had lights in the
windows and sometimes, going by in warm weather, I saw a young
woman—someone not much older than I—standing out at the gate,
talking to a neighbor, or simply watching the traffic go past. I never
got a clear look at her face, and I never really thought about her
except as in some way being exactly what I would soon be, somehow.
I mean that when I thought of myself in any future, I saw that
woman standing at the gate outside the little house. I wanted, then,
not much more than that. A warm little house, like a cottage, where
I could live with someone who loved me and where I might have
children. I was a little girl who could not remember her mother
very well, and often felt a tremendous loneliness about it, and this
fantasy of mine was soothing, in its way. It was what I envisioned*

for myself; it became a kind of possession, something I owned because I never told anyone about it. I never gave the real woman a second's thought, either, not even when, going by one evening, I saw her standing in her doorway, crying, while someone—a man, very tall, very heavy—waved his arms and shouted at her from the lawn. That small, tree-shaded cottage in my mind, like the false-front television houses where perfect ladies performed perfectly reasonable daily miracles of mediation and tranquillity, stood up to all the assaults upon it from the complicated and messy facts of existence. And in the long nights down in Savoy, while I was carrying Linda, and Cole was gone, I would lie awake and think of that inviolate little knot of expectation in myself, that could still yearn for that unreal house. Oh, how I wanted it! And how I wanted to be out of the querulous Selena's rooms, much as I liked her, and liked being with her during the long days, when all I could be was pregnant, and Cole was out making his torturous way through the legal code of another state. I lay there dreaming it all up, amazed at my own persistence in it, until the moment when I would catch myself, see it for what it was—a baby's daydream, a fraud—and I would remember that I was pregnant, that I had never known my own mother. Then I would feel oddly as though I were about to be given some new perception concerning her, as though, having become pregnant, I had entered some province where she could be felt and even, in some way, heard. I thought I might even begin to hear voices. But this was merely another kind of fantasy, and the only voices were those of Selena's late-night talk shows. When I finally went to sleep I had dreams that I was just where I was: in Savoy, Illinois, alone with a woman who wrote letters to television characters. . . .

There wasn't any reason to stay in the room, and anyway it was too noisy, so I went down to the lobby and bought a pack of cigarettes. In the lounge, now, a bad male vocalist was laboring through something vaguely jazzy—a medley of songs I didn't quite recognize, but of which others in the crowd seemed to have an intimate, sing-along knowledge. Everybody seemed quite happy and content to be there. I didn't feel like going home; I knew he would be waiting up for me, and I would have to get through the goodnights without explaining anything to him, without confiding in him, or seeking his love and help. And I thought, goddamn Louis for leaving me here.

I drank part of a vodka tonic, then returned to the room, and sat by the window looking out at the street below. The window looked out past the dark humps of coal beyond the old depot, and a ship was coming into the harbor, its lights winking in the swells of the water. There was a moon, with white striations of cloud breaking up along its bottom edge. Someone laughed like a hyena in the next room. I smoked the cigarette, and lighted another. When the knock came at the door, I jumped, then tried to be calm, wanting control, wanting Louis to find me quite sufficient and quite simply furious with him. But it wasn't Louis.

It was Cole.

I peered at him through the round magnified lens of the peephole in the door, and a sound escaped me, a little gasping yell, just as, in the next room, the hyena laugh broke forth again, this time with the clatter of breaking glass. I watched my own hand on the doorknob, watched it turn, and then I was standing there under his dispassionately evaluating gaze. He looked bad, sleepless and nervous and completely paranoid, but his eyes were cold. He stared at me, his hands in his pockets.

"Hey," he said.

"How did you—" I began.

"Pretty fancy," he said, looking beyond me at the room.

"Look," I said.

He held his hands up, palms toward me—a gesture of surrender. "Just wanted to say hi."

I simply stood there.

"Can I come in?"

"No," I said.

He looked down, put his hands back in his pockets. "I scored some pills down in the lobby of this very hotel," he said. "You believe it? Apparently the whole fucking country's involved. Whole thing's falling apart. I'm kind of fucked up."

"What're you doing here, Cole."

"I saw you down in the lounge. I was in the lounge."

I just stared at him.

"Selena died."

At this, I took a small step back, gave him the indication, merely by shifting my weight, that he could enter the room. He came past me and walked all the way to the window.

"Pretty view," he said.

I lighted another cigarette and kept my place by the door.

When he turned around, he seemed to go off for a moment. "I got a traveling companion," he said, looking at the walls. "She's down in the lounge."

"You got my letter," I said.

He nodded. He was moving in a little circle at the center of the room, his hands still in his pockets. "Kind of like to see Linda."

"After four years," I said, "suddenly you're interested?"

He didn't respond to this. Quietly, as if not wishing to disturb the noisy crowd on the other side of the wall, he moved to the bed and sat down.

"Cole."

"We never had it this fancy," he said, smoothing the sheet with one shaking hand.

"Jesus, Cole—will you get out of here?"

"I came to see my daughter." His voice now was full of anger and determination; it was the wild determination of whatever he was on, I knew, and so I didn't argue with him—I would only be arguing with *it*—whatever it was. I said, "No one's kept you from seeing her."

He looked at me, and appeared to be trying to concentrate

on my face. Then he smiled; it was an interested, crazy smile. "Why'd you stay in your daddy's house so long?"

"I think you'd better leave." I opened the door wider.

"Four fucking years," he said.

"Get out."

"Just want to see my daughter."

I waited.

He stood, wavered slightly, then abruptly began running in place, not looking at me, concentrating, huffing and blowing and speeding up. When he stopped, he was out of breath, and he sat down again. "Man," he said, "this is very scary stuff. Very scary and good."

"Cole," I said, "please leave us alone."

He just sat there breathing heavy, looking down. And then a woman came along the hallway outside the door, carrying a small, leather purse with both hands and appearing quite tentative. She looked past me into the room, then straightened. "I'm sorry," she said. "Excuse me."

I let her go by me. She stood over Cole, still holding her purse with both hands, and merely watched him for a time.

"Please," I said, "if you could both just leave."

"Jelly," the woman said, looking at me. "He's just made of jelly." Then she turned to him. "Aren't you, Cole."

Cole was communing with himself, holding his stomach and beginning to rock back and forth.

"Jesus Christ," the woman said. "Drink all that whiskey and then take pills on top of it."

"Can you please get him out of here?" I said.

"I'm not going to carry him."

I told her I was going to call the police.

"You hear that, Cole?" she said.

Cole shook his head. His face had gone a sick, bluish white, and his eyes were bright and round and dry as marbles. "My little girl," he said.

The woman looked at me. "He was full of all these plans—

what he was going to say to you and all about his little girl. And look at him. I'll tell you it's the story of my life, who I get hooked up with. Just look at him."

He breathed quite shallowly, staring at nothing. His elbows were resting on his thighs, his hands limp between his knees.

"I got an uncle over in Superior," the woman said. "We're going over there for a few days." She put her purse under one arm, then reached down and took his elbow, and he looked up at her. There was a doglike trustingness about the expression on his face, and it hurt me to see it.

"God, Cole," I said.

"What's left of him," said the woman. She walked him toward me, and then he seemed to gather enough of his own power to step ahead of her. He came past me, his mind apparently fixed on simply getting through the opening the door offered, out into the wide hallway. The woman stopped to offer me her hand. "I'm Alice. I hope we didn't disturb you. Now maybe we can get past all this and get a firm footing on something."

"I don't understand you," I said.

"I just mean I don't think he'll bother you again."

I looked past her at Cole, who was muttering to himself and smiling, standing with his back against the opposite wall, his hands in his pockets again.

"What is he on," I said.

"Hard stuff," said Alice. "Whiskey, mostly, tonight."

"He said he got some pills."

"Oh, yeah. He's into that stuff all right. He's on pills, all right."

And it dawned on me that she was, too. That she hadn't had any alcohol, but was certainly going along under the influence of the same pills Cole had ingested; there was an indefiniteness, a kind of bright blur, in the irises of her eyes. She apologized again, gathering him into the wing of her arm and beginning to edge along the wall with him.

"Come on," she said. "Jesus."

"Tell him I'm calling the police," I said.

She stopped, looked over her shoulder. "Hey."

"Cole," I said, loud enough for him to hear me in his rarefied, dizzy, pill-induced heights, "I'm calling the police."

They both turned and stared. He had straightened, and though he was now standing without her support, his whole frame seemed about to sag to the floor. It was his eyes that were changing, now, showing the reaction in him to what I had said. The woman merely looked puzzled.

I spoke to her. "He must've told you that he's wanted in this state. Nonpayment of child support."

"Can't take my little girl away from me, can they?" he said to his companion, as if she were invested with the authority to tell him the answer, one way or the other.

"Cole," I said. "Don't stay around here, I mean it."

He stared at me, and his eyelids drew down, a narrowing that seemed almost lazy but for the freezing hatred in the eyes themselves—this was a new level of animosity.

"I mean it, Cole," I said, barely able to control my voice.

"Come on," said the woman, trying to turn him around.

But he came toward me, staggered toward me, so that I moved quickly into the room and behind the door, holding it open just enough to see that he had stopped, and was leaning against the opposite wall, glaring at me, showing his teeth. "Maybe you're fucking Daddy," he said. "Maybe I'll tell the lawyers you're fucking Daddy."

"I'm going," the woman said. "Cole. You hear me?"

He pointed at her. "You shut the fuck up." He turned to me again, his face registering some sort of perverse satisfaction, as though he were confident that he had touched a nerve in me.

"I'm calling the police," I said. "You'd better run."

"Fuck the police."

"You tell them that," I said, and, closing the door on him, went to the phone and asked the hotel operator for the police. My hands shook; I could feel my throat going dry.

Cole beat on the door twice, cursing, and I shouted twice, then yelled into the phone for someone to get me the police. The clerk said he'd ring me through, and while I waited, crying, still shaking, I realized that I didn't hear Cole anymore. When the police came on the line I managed enough control over my voice to report that a man on whom there was an outstanding warrant had been beating on my door not two minutes ago. I gave the name of the hotel and the room number, and Cole's name, and the policeman on the other end, a younger man from the sound of his voice, said he'd dispatch a unit right away. I said I didn't think that was necessary—anyway, the man was gone now. But the warrant was outstanding, and Cole Gilbertson was back in the jurisdiction. The officer didn't quite know what to do about a three-year-old warrant at that hour of the night, and he promised to send someone over to speak with me. "No," I said. "I just want to report that he's in the state. He's here, and there's been a warrant out on him for failure to pay child support. Just put it on Sergeant Reeves's desk and he'll handle it in the morning."

"Sergeant Reeves isn't with us anymore," the voice said.

"Well, someone handles these things, right?"

"Sure," the voice said, sounding anything but sure.

"Good. I'll come in and file a new complaint in the morning."

"Yes, ma'am. That's what you'll have to do, I think."

I hung the phone up, and went to the door to listen. There was the sound of the party still going on next door, and nothing else. Through the peephole, I saw empty hallway, and very carefully, warily, opened the door. Cole had been sick on the wall next to the door, a small dark splash, which emitted a terrible odor of what he had drunk. It was a petty little trick, part of the childish, tantrum-throwing aspect of his temper, and yet there was something so pathologically hate-filled about it that it sent me trembling back into the room, where I locked the door and, turning the lights off, sat in the dark by the telephone, wanting to call Louis, or my father, wanting to call the police again, and finding myself unable to muster the will to do anything at all except sit there stewing, worrying, beginning to be afraid for what would happen next. I don't know how long I remained that way. There are hours of the night in which any action seems colored with extremity; Cole had come and I had sent him away. I had called the police. Surely there was nothing he could do: I was thinking of lawyers and courtrooms, and how no judge would allow a man so obviously unfit for carrying the responsibility of parenthood to block a legal move to adopt that man's biological child. And then, almost as if against my will, as if the thought were thrust upon me from some outside force, I remembered that Louis and I were in question, too, now; and finally the whole night seemed freighted with everything I had been running away from since that chilly dawn, when I first climbed onto the train north out of Champaign—having seen and done things that made my old daydream of the little yard and the cottage seem so much beside the point as to be embarrassing; having had everything go so badly, so impossibly wrong, that I was left too empty and frightened to do much but travel from one day to the next—and here I was, these years later, still living in my father's house.

Once, when we had been married about three years, and there had been a week of unhappy silence between us, I woke from a late afternoon nap with a feeling of unspecific fear, like waking from a nightmare you can't remember, except that I knew this was not the source of my fear; and then I was sitting up in the bed, facing Cole, who was standing over me with his father's shotgun, looking down at it and lightly rubbing the smooth, blue-oiled double barrels.

I said, "Cole." I said, "What are you doing?" I said, "Don't."

Then he took a small step to one side, exactly as if he were moving to let someone or something pass.

"Cole," I said, "for God's sake."

When he looked at me, there was something almost playful in his eyes. He was flying high, and reaching some level of paranoia that I hadn't seen yet.

"Put it down," I said.

"I was wondering if you might want to tell me one or two things," he said. "Like where the fuck the rest of my stash is."

I hadn't done anything with him in a long time, and of course I had no idea where anything was that he was using. I said, "You know I don't use it anymore."

"Maybe you're selling it."

This was a bad indication of just how far gone he was. It brought me up out of the bed, to stand close to him, the shotgun almost caught between us. "Honey, I don't have *any* use for it. I've got Linda to think about."

From the other room came the sound of Selena's television, and he turned his head slightly to look in there.

"Please, Cole—nobody took anything of yours."

"You know how good my father was at firearms?" he said. "Used to tell me about it all night. Great shot. Shot all sorts of wildlife and big game and bad guys, just like in the movies. He was in the war to end all wars."

"Cole," I said, and gently took hold of the gun.

When he wrenched free, I whimpered—it just came out of me—and he stepped back and pointed the gun at me. I moaned again. "Bang," he said. "Bang, bang, bang."

"Please," I said, turning and covering my face with my hands, feeling the inside of my skin like something burning. "Please."

With the end of the gun barrels, he moved my hands away, smiled at me as though there were some conspiratorial joke between us, then turned and walked out of the room. I heard him saying something over the nervous, disapproving voice of Selena, and in a little while he was outside, across the road, firing the gun at birds in the field there, and, according to Selena's grumbled remark from the other room, hitting nothing at all.

It was the only moment in the whole time I lived with him that I felt there was anything at all to fear from him, and while Selena was quick to put the best face on it—talking about his harmlessness and how he'd wept secretly to her once because his father had made him shoot a squirrel—and while I myself had as an example his usual affable demeanor, even in the midst of our worst failures together, the plain facts of the matter were that I could no longer stay in that house—not with a child to think about, and not with Cole's increasingly frequent use of drugs, of all the intoxicating and mood-altering substances: alcohol, mushrooms, dope, pills, coke, and, during the last summer I was in Champaign, heroin. Needles. I came home early one evening after working all day as a temporary at the university, trying to make money because he was out of work again, and when I entered the house I caught him cooking the stuff in one of Selena's measuring spoons over a candle. He was too far gone to care that it was time for me to get home, too far gone to worry about being caught at all. He had the syringe laid out on the table, and the little length of rubber, the tie off, already loosely wrapped around his arm.

"Cole," I said, "Jesus God."

"Unbelievable," he said. "You'll never believe it."

I watched him tie his arm off, and inject himself, and then he sat staring at me. "Come on," he said. "Don't get religious all of a sudden." He sat straighter, came to his feet, moved to the wall and eased himself down, leaning against it. "Ohh," he said. "Jesus. Mmmm."

I stood over him. Linda began to cry and complain upstairs. "Where's Selena?" I said.

He was shaking his head, eyes closed, his hands clasped over his up-raised knees. "Good God almighty," he said. "My God."

I went upstairs. Linda was standing in her crib, where, I was soon to find out, she had been since Selena left the house, sometime in the morning. Her diaper was falling off in strips, and the whole bed was smeared with shit. I lifted her out of the mess and took her into the bathroom, planning just how I would walk out of there and take her with me—and even so, it was four months, most of the fall and winter, before I finally had the nerve to go through with it. There's an inertia which happens to you in such a situation; it makes you hesitate, makes you think you can find some way to fix things, save something, make it work. You keep trying, and it's quite obvious to everyone that you're long past helping, that every hesitation is a surrender of a kind, a capitulation and a denial.

I grew up in a man's house, a man who wanted me to go to college and have a career.

When I saw Cole again, that time just after I'd left him and brought Linda with me to Duluth, I felt something for him again; it was odd. I had expected him to come, had dreaded it, and when he did drive up, looking all groomed and straight— off the drugs, he told me, since he'd stumbled into Selena's house to find me and the baby gone—I was surprised at the warmth that flowed through me, looking at him, still so handsome, the two of us standing out in the yard, talking about nothing for the few minutes we took to be cordial with each other before he began to question me about my plans.

"I miss you and Linda," he said.

"Cole," I said, "it's no good."

"I'm clean, Annie. Look at me."

"I'm happy for you," I told him.

"Isn't it funny," he said. "I drove all the way here to see my daughter—just like your father when we first got married."

"He was wrong to do what he did," I said. "And you were right to do this. But the outcome is going to be the same."

"I have to be able to see my baby," he said.

"I won't keep you from seeing her," I told him.

"I was hoping I could see you, too."

"No," I said.

"Just like that? You won't even think about it?"

I shook my head. I was denying him and I was denying

something in myself, a pull in his direction. In my mind was the memory of speeding down Highway 53 with him, streaming away from the dingy red-bricked confines of Duluth, my hair flying in the wind, my blood racing, a late spring day in 1976, when I was wildly, deliciously free, completely irresponsible, guilty and frightened and—I thought—on my own at last.

PART FOUR

PART FOUR

Closing the Stardust Shop

Louis opened the shop, shivering in the wind, and when he was inside he stood for a while by the space heater, huddled over, watching his breathing on the air. He had stopped at the hotel, but finally hadn't been able to bring himself to go in: it was impossible to shake the feeling that to do so would be to give up his dignity somehow, as though in Annie's eyes he might begin to seem abject; perhaps he already had, in fact. Whatever she was going to decide about him, she would decide it without any more embarrassing scenes. When he thought about the baby, something faltered in his heart, and he almost changed his mind: for a time he sat there in the car and imagined himself storming into the room to plead with her for the life they might have together, for the hope of love. But then the whole scenario seemed rather strangely melodramatic to him, and he decided to take himself to work; he had always believed in going ahead with the daily things. In a while he would call her—though now he kept catching himself glancing out the shop window, his mind wandering to the possibility that he might see her coming along in the slanting shadows of the street.

It wasn't quite late enough for Saturday shoppers, yet there were people strolling through the pockets of shade across the way. He watched them for a while, then pulled the space heater around behind the counter, and seated himself on the high stool there, from which he had a better view of the street. On the corner, an armored car idled in front of the bank, its back lights blinking; two gray-uniformed guards stood by and stamped their feet in the cold shade, while two others loaded bags of money onto a cart. Beyond this, a frozen-food supply truck was broadside in the street, backing toward an open gate in the sidewalk. It looked warm up that way, sunny and bright, but the guards were breathing clouds of condensation, stamping their feet, and the small puddles in the dips and gulleys of the road surface were iced over; people walking by the shop were holding their coat collars tight against their throats. Louis wanted to suppose that if Annie came to him and found him doing his daily work, she might be reassured, somehow, might feel his willingness to leave her alone as a kind of trust. In the next moment, going over this possibility in his mind, he wondered if she might not interpret it differently—it could appear to her that he was being overconfident, even in some way complacent. He went into the back of the store and picked up the phone on the desk there. Hesitating, wavering, he dialed the hotel, then hung up. He sat at the desk, his head in his hands, trying to think it all through clearly, and then he picked up the phone and dialed the number again. It rang twice, and again he hung up. On the desk, lying flat, was a cardboard matted photograph of him and Annie and Linda at Park Point, taken during one of their outings in the late spring. He brought it under the light of the desk lamp and stared at it. It had been a windy, bright day, and they were all smiling, their hair disarranged by the wind, their faces burnished by the sun. Annie looked beautifully, uncomplicatedly happy. Behind them a sky of the deepest, purest blue trailed down the north, meeting, in a gradually whitening haze, the far rim of the lake. Louis sighed, propped the photograph against the base of the lamp, then got to his feet, hearing the small ding of the bell out front. Customers.

When he entered the shop, he was rather unpleasantly surprised to see the same pair that had come in yesterday—the man wearing the same workshirt, the same faded jeans. Louis moved to the counter and the man stood leaning on the end of it, gazing at him. The eyes were indeed an extraordinary shade of blue; but, whereas yesterday, he had looked edgy and nervous, this morning he looked sick; the small pouches of skin under the eyes were of an unhealthy yellow cast, and around the softening edges of the jaw was a fishy discoloration, almost like lividity.

The woman seemed bothered with the same agitation she had exhibited before, her hands moving aimlessly about her face and neck, except that now there was something of anger about it. When she looked at her companion, she glowered, and the expression stayed in her face as she turned her attention to Louis.

"You get rid of your headache?" he said to her.

"Chilly out," said the man.

"Can I help you with something?" Louis said.

"Maybe." The man looked at him.

"Something you're looking for?"

"Yeah."

Louis waited.

"You married?" the man said.

"Am I married?"

"Yeah. Just—just wondering."

"My wife died some years ago."

"Mind my asking how old you are?"

"I don't understand," Louis said.

The other man shrugged this off. "Just making conversation."

"That's pretty personal conversation, if you don't mind my saying so."

"No offense intended."

"I'm not offended," said Louis. "Look—this shop does very little business in a week. There's not enough money here to feed a man for a whole day, you know?"

"What—you think we're robbers or something?"

"What is it that you two people need from me," Louis said.

The woman took her companion by the sleeve. "Come on, Cole."

Louis stared.

"You just keep the store as a hobby," the man said. "Is that it?"

"You're just making conversation," said Louis. "Right?"

"Sure."

"He's a terrific conversationalist," the woman said, sardonically. "You must've noticed by now."

"And he's just curious," said Louis.

"Sure," the man said. "I guess."

"And your name is Cole."

"Cole—yeah." He shot a glance at the woman. "Right. Cole."

"I wonder, would that be your first or last name?"

"It's the last name," he answered, in exactly the same moment that the woman said, "First name."

"Excuse me?" Louis said to her.

"Well, I guess it is the first name," said Cole. "Isn't it, honey."

The woman looked down at her hands on the counter. "That's what I said. I said it was the first name." She looked at Louis, and then at Cole, then turned and marched out of the store.

"She gets confused," Cole said.

Louis said, "What can you possibly hope to accomplish by coming here?"

The other man strolled over to the door and peered out. The woman was standing at the curb, her back to the windows.

"You've been bothering Annie the last few days, too, haven't you?" Louis said.

"Man, I don't know what you're talking about," said Cole. "I just wanted to look at some old records." He put emphasis on the word "old."

"All right, well you've had your look. Now get the hell out of my shop."

"No hard feelings, pal."

"No, no feelings at all." Louis said. "Pal."

Cole hesitated a moment, seemed about to say something more. But then he simply opened the door and went out. Louis stayed behind the counter, and watched him walk, with the woman, on up the street. At the corner he turned and looked back, and though Louis knew the reflection of the sun made it impossible to see anything through this window, he still withdrew a little. A moment later, he was dialing the hotel. He believed he had the answer to Annie's recent unrest; and in any case, he felt like a lover with questions on his mind. It was time for him to place a demand or two; time to require some explanation. He was already formulating what he would say to her— *you don't have to keep secrets from me, Annie, I'm supposed to be your friend, too, you know.*

The line to her room was busy.

He tried twice more in the next few minutes, and then he tried to call his house—that line was busy, too.

At some point during all this, two women had come into the shop. They stood in the doorway talking, obstructing his view of the intersection outside. They were wearing sweat suits and shiny windbreakers of the same olive color; the taller one, a redhead, wore a dark blue scarf, and her ruddy cheeks were flushed to a violet color, as though something of the scarf had seeped down into her face. They chatted a moment about someone they knew, but soon they were marveling at what was in the bins, holding the records up to show each other and sounding exactly like the type of customer who merely looked, merely paused and remarked about things, as a tourist responds to the objects behind glass in a museum.

"Look at this," said the one with no scarf.

"I know."

"I fell in love and got married over this one."

"My goodness," said the tall one. "Destroy it immediately."

They went on, putting each record back after commenting

on it, or swooning over it, and Louis sat watching them, feeling trapped. The line in Annie's room was still busy. He kept dialing the hotel number, kept asking the front desk clerk to ring it through. Finally he tried Annie's house, and Field's sister answered. "Everybody's still asleep," she said.

"Ellen, have you talked to Annie, this morning?"

"She's still asleep," Ellen said.

"She's home?"

"I *guess* so. Isn't she? Where is she, Louis?"

"I'm sorry," Louis said. "I didn't mean to wake you."

He tried the hotel again. The line in the room was still busy. It had been almost forty minutes now. And his two customers were still musing and cooing over the bins.

"Okay, ladies," he said. "Everybody out. We're closing up for a while today."

The two women stared at him.

"I'm sorry?" the tall one said.

"We're closing up today."

"You—you want us to leave?"

Stepping around the counter, he opened the door and waited for them to pass through. "Sorry," he said, "a little family situation here." They each gave him the sort of searching look that—without meaning to, without even being aware of it— people give other people when there is trouble. He nodded at them and smiled, and when they were gone he tried calling the hotel one more time. Again the line to Annie's room was busy.

"All right," Louis said to no one. He closed the store and drove in the cold, windy sun over to the hotel. Inside, the lobby was empty; all the drapes were pulled wide, the day's brightness pouring in on the expanse of faded red carpet. He walked through to the stairs and up, along the thickly carpeted hallway. The air here smelled of cleanser, and something faintly sour, as though the cleanser had been used to mask other, stronger, odors. The heavy door to the room was slightly ajar. "Annie?" he said, stepping a few paces in. On the other side of the bed, framed in the brightness of the window, a dark young woman in a maid's uniform stood, holding a pillow to her chest as though to shield herself.

"Nobody here," she said in a deep accent he did not recognize.

"Where is the woman who was in this room?"

"Nobody here."

He looked at the telephone on the bureau. The receiver was off the hook, its wire running down into the closed drawer. He walked over to the bureau, opened the drawer, and brought the receiver out. "Look at this," he said. "For God's sake. Don't you even look at a room when you come into it?"

The young woman said nothing.

"How long have you been here?"

"Nobody here, please."

He hung the phone up. "Didn't you see the phone was off the hook?"

"Please, all gone," the young woman said firmly. "Nobody *here*."

Downstairs, the clerk yawned and told him a woman fitting Annie's description had checked out shortly after eight o'clock in the morning.

"Why the hell did you put all my calls through?" Louis said.

"I don't answer the phone. We have somebody who does that."

"Yeah, well they ought to be able to tell when somebody's checked out."

"They're supposed to be able to."

"Are you sure she left that early?"

"She's the only woman I saw, sir."

He went out onto the sidewalk in front of the building, and looked up and down the street. There was a small coffee shop at the end of the block, a place where he and Annie had often stopped for breakfast after a night at the hotel. He walked down to look in the windows of the place, and a row of strangers looked back at him. In the cold—shivering, tired, and anxious, beginning to feel that scratchiness in his throat that signaled the onset of flu—he made his way to the car and drove home. The house was quiet. He assumed that Roger was still asleep. He found him sitting in the kitchen, with Fran.

"I was just going to get dressed and come to the store," Roger said.

Louis had paused in the doorway. Though he did not look at Fran, he could see out of the corner of his vision that she was wearing one of his bathrobes. "Did Annie call here earlier?"

"Nobody called."

"I tried to call here a while back and the line was busy."

"Fran called her parents."

"I have to get home," Fran said, rising.

"Stay there," said Louis.

"No, she really does have to," Roger said.

Standing now, Fran touched one hand to the back of her hair, looking away from Louis—a nervous motion that she was apparently unaware of at first, and then it appeared to embarrass her.

"You really don't have to do anything on my account," Louis said.

"Dad," said his son.

"I have to get ready," Fran said.

Louis stepped back from the door and watched as she hurried upstairs.

"Well?" Roger sad.

"Well, what, son."

"I didn't hear you come home last night."

Louis said nothing.

"It surprised me when I heard you moving around this morning."

"I bet it did."

"Are you angry?"

"You're a grown-up," Louis said. "I'd appreciate it if you were a little more discreet about some things."

"I thought you'd be at the hotel all night."

"Forget it," Louis said.

They were quiet for a time. They heard Fran cross the hall upstairs. It wasn't even ten o'clock in the morning, and though Louis felt as if he had already been through a complicated and busy day, and nothing of it was remotely available as a subject for talk, he felt the need to clarify things, to speak to his son in a way that would make him understand something he had begun, just now, to see—something that was coming to him with all the authority of recognition, but which he knew would not easily yield itself up in words. He waited. He was quiet; it went through him: a strange, nerve-tingling sense of kinship beyond that of blood and circumstance—a kind of sympathy, coupled with a deep, inarticulate yearning. He would have said he wanted his son to see him as Louis Wolfe, yet it would not have been exactly what he *meant*. When he could speak at all, he said, "I'm not a young man anymore," trying to control his voice, "but I feel—I don't feel any different than you do, son." And the moment of recognition, of understanding, whatever it was, had passed. He had heard it leak out in the words as he spoke them. It seemed to him now that it was all nothing more profound than the wish to be taken as what he was.

"I know that," Roger was saying. "Don't you think I know that?"

"Well."

They were not looking at each other now. Louis wanted to say, *Listen, I think Annie may be seeing her ex-husband behind my back. I'm afraid she's changing her mind. She's pregnant. She's going to abort it. Jesus Christ.*

Something fell and broke upstairs, and there was the small sound of Fran cursing low.

"She's a little upset," Roger said. "This is all kind of new to her."

Louis was silent.

Roger sat back, arms folded, and stared out the window at the lawn in back of the house. Tall weeds stood in it, and there was a litter of tree branches lying around in blown leaves, looking like the aftermath of a storm. He sighed, then turned to Louis again. "Where's Annie?" he said.

The Heads of Animals

Alice Minneford's uncle Ellis and his wife lived in a sprawling rambler behind a school yard on the south side of the town of Superior. The school was an old two-story red-brick building with canvas chutes attached to the top windows, and a playground that had apparently been a casualty of the school's decline: most of the swings were broken or off, the sliding board lay over on its side, and the sandboxes, two of them, were flat depressions of dried mud with clumps of grass standing up in them. There were monkey bars, and an old fire truck that Uncle Ellis's children liked to climb on, and now, watching three of them do so, Cole Gilbertson took a deep, rasping breath of the cold air, and cursed, low.

Alice, standing next to him, said, "Watch your language, for Christ's sake. They'll hear you."

He said, "I'm going to need something quick, here."

"You can leave any time." She walked away from him, to the fire truck mired in the blowing dust, and the children, who were ranged across its surface like birds on the back of a rhino. The children—two boys and a girl—were all very close in age, and they all had the same plump-cheeked, round-eyed faces. They got their round eyes from Alice's uncle Ellis, who otherwise was tall and vaguely funny-looking, with ears that stuck straight out from his blond head, and a long neck with an Adam's apple lodged in it like something he'd tried unsuccessfully to swallow.

The fact was that Uncle Ellis's looks frightened Gilbertson. There was something uncanny about the way the features came together to form the round, pink-cheeked mask that so upset Gilbertson's sense of shape, as though the man had walked into his mind out of a nightmare. They had come from the Stardust Record Shop to find Uncle Ellis home alone with the children— his wife, Maureen, had gone off to do the week's grocery shopping—sitting in his living room with a baby in his lap, and four other children lying among blankets and pillows on the floor at his feet. The children were watching cartoons on television, and still another baby stood in the playpen in the middle of the room. Alice had walked up to the door and in, as if she lived there, and Gilbertson had followed, feeling that he should duck into the room, it seemed so crowded and close—not just with children and pillows and blankets and toys, but with furniture: a ratty sofa with cushions disarranged and frayed; a La-Z-Boy lounge chair and two easy chairs; a coffee table piled high with magazines and books; and a rocking chair, in which Ellis sat, smiling. Gilbertson had never seen such a face; he hung back as Alice stirred up the noise, greeting the children, wending her way through them, reaching for her uncle and talking through his talk—how pretty the baby was and how he shouldn't get up. The children were saying Alice's name, and everything was confused. She greeted them; it dawned on Gilbertson that somehow she had got complete charge of everything. She had taken over, and now he was just waiting for the next thing she would tell him to do. He looked at Uncle Ellis's face and shivered deep in himself. He thought of how he'd backed down from the man in the record store, and the memory of it scraped the inside of him.

"Well, Cole?" Alice said, looking at him almost grimly. "Aren't you going to shake hands?"

"It's all right with me," he answered. He heard himself, and had a scary moment of not recognizing the voice. He needed to calm down and do something on the level of normal citizenship.

"Cole," said Alice, under her breath.

Uncle Ellis seemed to study him—but no, there was just the smile. That weird, unlined friendly face with its choking Adam's apple in the neck and its skull faintly visible under the skin. It sent little paroxysms of terror through him. He shook hands, and then shivered again.

"We haven't slept much," Alice explained, looking at him.

The television blared on, but the children were mostly watching Gilbertson now. "Kind of worn out," he managed.

"We—we drove all night," Alice lied.

"You just did catch us," Uncle Ellis said. "We were up in the wilderness a few days. Just did get back last night." He nodded at Gilbertson, and smiled again, and his teeth led on back up into bone. The eyes sat in sockets.

The baby began to shriek.

"Boy it sure can get loud in here, can't it," Gilbertson said.

"How long can you stay?" Uncle Ellis asked.

"Can't," said Gilbertson.

Alice had spoken at the same time: "Couple weeks." Her skull had begun to show through as well. She went on talking. "I'll be staying a couple weeks, anyway—if it's all right."

"You know me, honey," her uncle said. "I like a lot of people in the house."

Gilbertson moved to the doorway, feeling the need for air, and Alice said, "Who wants to go out to the playground?"

A shriek went up—a piercing yell that made all the noise of before seem like a part of quiet.

Gilbertson put his hands over his ears.

Uncle Ellis spoke. "Billy. Liz. Ronny. You can go. Todd has to stay and finish his homework."

"Aw, Dad."

"I know all I have to do is mention it to you, son."

And then it was quiet a moment. The air seemed almost muffled now. At the hotel, last night, Gilbertson had waited and planned what he might do, sitting in the lounge, drinking, with Alice muttering and complaining across the table, and when Annie and the record store owner walked in, he almost cried out. Then, too, there had been a muffled feeling in the air, as though it were coming against him in invisible smothering waves, blocking out sound and oxygen, too. In Uncle Ellis's living room, he took a deep breath, and opened the front door.

"Cole," Alice said to him.

He went out into the cold sun of the porch. Across the street was the playground and the school, the high, sun-bright windows with the chutes angling down from them. He crossed the street, the grassy lot, and looked into the mouth of one of the chutes. The wind blew and made a whistling sound. There was the smell of tents, and a mildewy something in the little stir of wind that murmured down through the dark chute. He took one of the pills, and for a bad minute it wouldn't go down. When it had, he stood waiting for the rush, and then he was looking up into the dark chute again. He almost crawled in. Somewhere he had heard about a man climbing into a tunnel and out of it to another world.

"You're a mess, Cole."

He turned. Alice was standing there with her hands in the pockets of her coat, her hair blowing across her face. The rush had hit him with deep, satisfying force, though he was, somewhere in himself, worried about his heartbeat. His heart seemed to be thrashing around in his chest. He said, "This is the tunnel to the other world."

"Jesus, there's nothing left of you is there."

"Don't mess with me," he told her. "I'm standing in a great wind."

"Just don't show it to these kids," she said.

They were all crossing the street, running, their scarves flying. Gilbertson watched them, and felt himself to be totally outside, a traveler, a man of such dark thoughts. It was exactly as if he were intending to do harm to everyone. This idea came to him with a kind of resignation, as though things had been set into motion by the thought itself. It was all part of the coming retribution.

Now Alice was perched on the driver's seat in the dull red wheelless hulk of the fire engine, and the children were all climbing down. They ambled over to the broken swings, and the sandbox, the older girl holding the plump, babylike hand of the youngest boy. None of them was more than ten years old. Alice sat in the fire engine and held the wheel, looking out as if at some imaginary scene or vista—other worlds. Gilbertson walked over to her, put his hand on the low-swung side door. "It's time to decide," he said.

"Decide what?"

"Fate."

"Cole, will you please."

Last night in the hotel lounge, he had looked through the doorway out into the lobby, and seen a transaction. The one who had things for sale was a tall pale man in a brown coat, who wore thick horn-rimmed glasses and had his hair combed like Buddy Holly. Gilbertson went out to where he was apparently waiting for someone else, and though it took a little while to build the man's confidence, he managed to purchase enough speed to get him through the next day or two, and had even engineered the possibility of purchasing more coke. It had been through the surge of confidence and energy the speed gave him that he had decided—upon seeing the record store owner leaving the hotel, and subsequently watching Annie come into the bar for cigarettes—that he would confront her, speak to her. He had worked himself into believing that she might want to make love after all the years of absence: she had come so far down, going around with a man like that, desperate and lonely, and wanting love. He felt supremely confident, following her, making his way to the door of the room. And then later, having gone back to the motel with Alice (having been guided back there in his half-mad state) he had failed miserably with her, too—had been unable to do anything at all, turning in the bed, so dizzy and sick, and his heart bumping around in his throat and stomach, as if it had broken out of its stall. He had looked upon the gray hours of dawn in a spiraling mood of desperation and anger, and had decided that he would hurt the record store owner. He'd fully planned to do the man some injury; to bring him the kind of trouble that would frighten him away from Annie forever.

And he'd failed that, too.

The rush was almost nothing; it hadn't moved him enough. He took another pill, turning from Alice, feeling the wind blow. It was a gale, coming from somewhere under his skin. Alice was watching the children, ignoring him, and he looked at the skull under her skin.

"Oh," he said. "Oh, God. There's no plan of action. He's taking my little girl away from me, and then I got nothing left."

She stared off at the children.

"You know what their plan of action is?"

"Cole—yesterday, at the school—why didn't we just go up and talk to your daughter?"

He watched her face return to its normal configuration. But deciding whether or not to look away was hard.

"Well?" she said.

"This is out of my control," he said. As he spoke, the children set up a racket and began running across the playground in the direction of the house.

"Look," Alice said to him, "just please don't do anything crazy now."

Her aunt had arrived from the grocery store, and was lifting bags out of the trunk of the car—an old, low-to-the-ground Chevrolet, with a serrated line of rust along the bottom edges and climbing from the wheel wells. Uncle Ellis had come down the walk to help her. Alice and the children crossed the street and for a moment everyone was gathered around Alice's aunt, who seemed a little confused and troubled, looking around as if expecting more surprises. She hugged Alice, and cried some, wiping her eyes with a big white handkerchief. Gilbertson waited at the curb, hands in his pockets. The second rush had hit him. He was thinking of vengeance. He had an image of himself hiding, and quite abruptly remembered walking out into the open to show himself to his daughter, walking toward her in the street, and losing his nerve, quailing and shivering inside and then ducking away. He would not turn any lights on this in his head. He shut the light off. All the years, it had been that things got in his way, stopped him from getting down to the business of straightening the details out and finding a way back to her, the one good and lovely thing in his whole life. Now, watching Uncle Ellis burden himself down with bags of groceries, he had a moment of something worse than regret or loss, worse than dread. It burned him, then was gone. He was unbelievably quiet and empty inside, looking out; the trees in the yard were like the twisted shapes of anguish, and there were sick gray patterns of color in the windows of the house. It was all in the other world, outside him. He closed his eyes, swallowed, tried to breathe. Everything was falling apart.

Alice called to him. She was standing there with her hands on her hips.

"Come on, Cole. Lend a hand."

He crossed the street, hands still in his pockets. The children stared at him, and he thought of them as species—the cold made their skin almost perfectly transparent, and there were the bones showing beneath.

"He drove me here, Aunt Maureen. He's a little groggy from the drive. Right, Cole?"

He thought he must've nodded.

"Right?"

"Right," he said.

"Young man, you are positively white at the gills," said Aunt Maureen. "You go inside and lie down, why don't you."

Gilbertson looked at her—a big, tired woman, with shadows under her eyes and deep lines on either side of her mouth. She seemed to grimace at him.

"Well, go on," she said.

He went up the sidewalk and into the house. He was the angel of death, entering a happy home. The thought rattled around in his mind and then dropped out of sight. He went on into the kitchen, which was all light—there were floor-to-ceiling windows in one wall—and apparently newly remodeled; everything looked new. It made him sick. Uncle Ellis came in with his mask of a face and set bags down on the table.

"Well," he said.

"Well," said Gilbertson.

"You all right, son?"

"Yeah, fine."

"Can I get you something? A drink?"

Gilbertson couldn't look at his face. "I need a little whiskey if you have it around."

"I do. It's awful early for whiskey," Ellis said, moving to a sideboard in the hall. "But I guess you know what's best for you." He brought the bottle back into the kitchen, and poured a shot glass full.

Gilbertson drank it down, turning slightly when the women

came in with more groceries, and when they had gone back out, he asked for another.

"You sure?"

"I'm wired. I need to calm down."

"Okay."

The second glass made him want to gag, but he suppressed it.

"I just put this kitchen in," Ellis said. "After ten years of saving and scrimping to do it. The old kitchen is through there." He pointed down a hallway. "Not big enough to turn around in. You want to take your coat off?"

"Got to go," Gilbertson said.

Aunt Maureen hurried in, almost dropping two more bags. Ellis took one from her, and then the other. "I'm sorry, dear," he said. "I got so damn tied up being a host. I'll get the rest of it."

"You," she said to Gilbertson. "Come here."

She led him down the hallway Ellis had pointed out as leading to the old kitchen. The passage was dark, and seemed to Gilbertson to be giving forth vistas of blackness. He put his hands out and ran his fingers along the walls. She led him out into dim light. She had just turned it on, a lamp on a table next to the opening. The room was small, close, with a stiflingly low ceiling, and a yellow Formica counter along one wall, on which were several rifles in various stages of dismantlement. There were rifles on the walls, too, and, Gilbertson saw to his utter horror, the head of a deer, a caribou, a bear. The caribou's mouth was open in what looked to him to be an attitude of choking, and, seeing it, he couldn't keep back a small, high-pitched murmur of alarm.

"Nervous—Lord," Aunt Maureen muttered, bending down to pick something up from the floor—a piece of wrapping paper her husband had apparently let fall. She crumpled it up and put it somewhere in her skirt. Then she faced him. "So," she said.

He waited. He was going to see what this was. It struck him that for some time now he had been merely waiting to see what would take place next.

"I know you're both of age and all that," she said. "And I don't even want to talk about it. But I want to know what your plans are."

"Plans," he said.

"That's right. If you're going to be staying here, I think I have a right to ask that question. Alice is my niece after all."

"I'm going," he said.

She stared at him.

"I've got to head out."

"I got the impression you might be staying with us awhile."

"No," he said.

"Where——" she seemed to be just getting it. He could see it dawning in her face. It was the only face with no skull showing under the skin, and he admired her for it.

"Right," he said.

"Look," said Aunt Maureen. "Wait here a minute." She went out, shaking her head and muttering to herself about younger people learning to make up their minds.

He stood in the center of the room, and all the other rooms were loud with activity—children calling, voices and running footsteps and the crackle of the grocery bags as Uncle Ellis emptied them. Alice was apparently in another part of the house, running with the younger children. Gilbertson took a step toward the yellow counter along the wall, and saw that amid the rifle parts were also three revolvers. He picked one of them up, a .22-caliber target model, small enough to fit into the pocket of his coat. Without thinking or consciously making the decision to do so, he opened the drawer under the table, found a box of cartridges, and loaded the pistol. If he hadn't found the cartridges he might simply have put the gun back; but here they were, like fate, and so he loaded the gun. It took less than a minute, everything going very smoothly, exactly as if he had planned it;

he even had time to look the other two revolvers over. Then he put the loaded one in his coat, and closed the table drawer. When he heard them coming down the hall, he got away from the counter, and kept both hands in his coat pockets, the one hand just cradling the stock of the pistol.

"Now," Aunt Maureen said, entering the room, leading Alice in behind her. She took Alice by the elbow and made her face him. Then she spoke: "Tell her what you just told me."

"He doesn't have to say anything," Alice said.

"Go on, tell her."

He looked at Alice. "Just said I had to be heading out."

"I don't get it," she said.

"He's leaving you here, honey."

Alice turned to her. "Yeah?"

"I have to get going," Gilbertson told them. "I have to set a plan of action."

"So go ahead, then," Alice said.

"I don't understand," said Aunt Maureen.

"He can go where he wants," Alice said.

"He's just walking away from you, honey."

"I knew that—I told him to."

"Well, I sure have misunderstood this situation," Aunt Maureen said.

"Can we have a few minutes alone?" Alice wanted to know.

"I'll be in the kitchen helping Ellis with the groceries."

When the older woman was gone, Alice walked over to the counter and looked at the guns and parts of guns there. "Ellis loves to hunt," she said.

He waited.

"I feel sorry for you, Cole."

He said nothing. It was incredibly quiet in his mind.

"I mean I'm not even going to miss you this time."

"Okay," he said.

"You know what I learned by coming here with you?" She gave him a moment to speak, then shook her head a little and seemed to smile. "I guess I really started to learn it when you ran away from your daughter, after all your talk. You don't have any bravery at all, and it's just that simple."

He wrapped his hand lightly around the small stock of the pistol. It was going to be with her that he would begin, if she kept on. He was thinking that she had better be very careful, talking this way to him.

"Your fatherly interest is just another ego thing. She's something you produced—something you invented in your mind. The real little girl couldn't be allowed to see you now because then she'd be the only one, the one you've made up would have to disappear. She'd be somebody that needed things from you and needed you to think of something besides yourself."

"You figured everything out to the utmost," he said, gripping the pistol tight. Any moment he would bring it out and begin.

"You're so good to look at," she said, "and you have all that pretty charm and you're dead inside, and it's as simple as that. You don't have anything inside you but you."

"You figured me up like math," he said. And let go of the pistol—brought his hand out of his pocket, feeling benevolent, kind. He might very well have brought it all down upon her.

"Like bad news," she said. "I'm staying here. I'll drop you at the bus station if you want, but then I'm coming right back here."

He pushed past her, into the hallway, to the kitchen, where Uncle Ellis and his wife sat in the light of the windows, on the same side of the breakfast nook. They nodded politely at him as he passed by, going out onto the front lawn, where two of their boys were now tossing a football back and forth. Alice had followed him to the door, and she held it open to watch him cross the lawn. "I said I'd ride you to the bus station."

He opened the car door and reached in for his travel bag.

"Can we go?" one of the boys asked.

"Watch out," said Cole, and pointed his finger at them. "Bang, bang."

Alice called them in. He went on up the sidewalk, then turned to look at her standing in the doorway. She was holding the door open to let the boys pass, looking like the lady of the house; she had narrowly missed it. She would never know how close she had come. He went on. He had turned his back on her. He was on his way to other things. He stopped at a gas station two blocks down the street and bought a can of root beer. At the corner, under the thin, spidery shade of an almost bare birch tree, he took out his supply of speed and swallowed two pills with the soft drink. Then he finished the can and hurled it into the piled leaves of the small park which bordered the road. The rush didn't come until he had almost crossed the grassy field of the park, and when it came, it stopped him. He stood in the center of the park, in the wintry sun, his hands on his knees, breathing, and whispering, "Now, okay. Jesus. Okay. Mmmm. Right, right." The wind blew. It was cold. He wrapped his arms about himself and headed on. He had a loaded revolver in his coat pocket, and he was wild and bad and mad. All sorts of things were going to happen now.

Waiting

On spring days, the first warm days after the storms of the long northern winters, Mr. Field had sometimes sat out on his porch with Annie and watched the wind play on the distant surfaces of the lake. They would sit in the porch swing and say nothing, merely watching everything: the traffic on Superior Street, and the bud-heavy branches of the trees as the wind moved them, soughing up from the white shore of Park Point; and the vessels coming and going in the harbor—oil tankers and freighters and the occasional sailboat, their progress some-times almost imperceptible, like the progress of stacked clouds across a bright summer sky. Annie would speculate about what people on the far shore might be doing: she liked to imagine that they were sitting on porch swings, looking out across the water, which was such a dark, deep, pelagic blue.

Now, sitting at his living room window in the glass-magnified heat of the late morning sun, watching his only grandchild rake leaves into neat piles on the front lawn, he remembered that when Annie was small there had been such peaceful, pleasant, uncomplicated times, even with a dirty war going on across the world and fires burning the cities—and he wished for the least of those times back. He had fallen asleep sitting in this chair looking out at the dark street, and had awakened to hear his sister talking to Louis Wolfe on the telephone.

"Annie's not with Louis?" Field had said when Ellen hung the phone up.

"I guess not."

Field stood out of the chair and felt the soreness of having slept sitting up. Something moved in his stomach, roiling, and he looked at Ellen standing in the entrance of the hall, her hair tied back in a knot. "Then where is she?"

"Maybe she's on her way here."

Very soon after this, Annie called from the Royal Duluth Hotel to say that she would not be home until later in the morning.

"Where've you been?" Field asked her.

"I said not to wait up," she told him.

"Yes, but—Annie."

"Look, I'm calling you now. All right? I'm all right."

"Annie, Cole Gilbertson's back."

"I know."

He said nothing.

"I'll be home later in the morning," she said.

He had heard something in her voice. "Annie, are you all right?"

"I'm all right."

"Can you—can you tell me where you're going to be?"

Silence.

"Annie?"

"Daddy, I'll be home later on this morning," she said, and broke the connection.

And so here he was again, waiting, staring out at the street. Ellen rattled dishes in the kitchen, clearing away the breakfast she'd made—that he hadn't been able to bring himself to eat— and making preparations for a day of baking bread. When her anxiety got bad enough, she took to the kitchen; she would spend all day there, mixing flour and butter and eggs, kneading dough, opening and closing the oven door. In the past, there had always been something about these sounds that soothed Mr. Field as well. But not this morning. This morning Annie had not come home, and James Field believed he knew why. He believed that wherever she was, she was with Cole Gilbertson—that the pattern of restlessness of the last few months had led her to a mistake with poor Louis Wolfe, and that now, with Gilbertson back, it was entirely possible that she might be giving herself up to the despair of being alone and unhappy, a woman still young and with a large appetite for living, caught at home with a child, and an old, doting, frightened man. Mr. Field saw himself as he must look from the street: an abject watcher in a window, and the image brought him to his feet.

"I can't find the vanilla," Ellen called from the kitchen.

He said, "I'm going out."

"What?" She came to the entrance of the living room. "Where are you going?"

"I'm going out to look for my daughter."

"James, why don't you go upstairs and lie down—read the newspaper or something."

"I'm going to ride around a little."

"Don't be ridiculous—you're being ridiculous. You're not going to go chasing around after her again, are you?"

"I can't just sit here."

"Don't, then. Go about your own business, James. And stop being a fool."

He had moved to the door and was putting on his jacket. Through the window there, he could see that Linda had begun to put one of the small piles of leaves into a plastic bag. She paused and seemed to forget for a moment what she was doing. Of course she was waiting, too. And it wasn't just Annie she was waiting for.

"James."

He took the coat off. Ellen came over and put her arms around him. It was a very odd, nervous moment, and he patted the wings of her shoulders, feeling the unsteadiness in her, the force of her own worry. "It's going to be fine," she said. "Now stop fretting and come help me find the vanilla."

Last night, very late, he had been standing at the kitchen sink, pouring out the coffee he hadn't drunk, when Ellen came in and startled him by putting one hand lightly on his shoulder. "What're you doing?" she said.

He could see that she was half asleep. He breathed a sigh, gathered the tattered cordage of his nerves, and said, "I thought I wanted some coffee."

"It must be three o'clock."

He said, "Cole Gilbertson's back."

She appeared not to have understood him at first. Then she put one hand to her mouth.

"Linda saw him at her school, for God's sake. He was ducking out of sight, like a goddamn spy or something."

"That poor child."

Field rubbed his eyes. "I wish Annie would stop this business, whatever it is, and come home."

Ellen said nothing. She was standing there with her hand now moving at the back of her neck.

"I can't sleep," he said.

"I probably won't be able to either."

"Go up and go to sleep," he said.

"You're the one who's pacing the floor at three o'clock in the morning."

He said nothing.

"I wonder where . . ." She had spoken almost as if to herself. "I mean I don't know how I managed to get here. Not from where I started."

"We got old," James said.

She took this lightly. "Yes—we sure did, didn't we?"

"Old and nervous," he said. He was remembering her as a girl, sixteen years old, standing in a room that they had come almost fifty years and a thousand miles away from, hanging underthings on a clothesline she had strung from one end to the other of the living room of that house—Point Royal, Virginia, 1939, and on the radio talk of the sit-down war in Europe, like a pause before the real storm. "I'm engaged," she was saying to him in this memory, and once again, as he had been then, he was embarrassed for her. He reached over and touched her shoulder. "Nervous and old," he said.

"You were always old and nervous," she said. "Even when you were a baby. You were always worried about the consequences of things and you always expected the worst outcome all the time."

They were quiet. This was the sort of talk he had always wanted to have with Annie—something forgiving and without any agendas, without anything to protect or keep back.

"You took everything to heart all the time," said his sister. "I used to wonder how you'd ever make it."

"I don't remember much about it," he told her.

"It used to manifest itself with money. You were always counting your money and worrying about it, and I thought you were miserly until I realized that you were that way with everything—that you were even hoarding little scraps of paper you'd found on the street. Do you remember that you wanted to keep everything and that you were always unhappy because you couldn't do it?"

"I wanted to save things," Mr. Field said. "I don't remember feeling much unhappiness about it."

"Yes, but you did. You used to cry when Dad threw away the paper our Christmas toys came wrapped in. The toys and the wrapping paper and the packages—it was all one to you. You wanted to keep everything."

Field looked at the old image of her in his mind, the skinny girl, thinking of weddings, putting up her slips and panties, and the training bras she was so proud of, holding clothespins in her mouth and standing on tiptoe. He remembered wanting to tease her, and then deciding not to; and he remembered knowing

that he would take this image of his older sister to the grave.
"As I recall," he said to her, standing in the kitchen of the house
in Duluth, all the years later, "they were awful good at throwing
things away."

"Mom and Dad?"

He nodded.

"Well, they had each other."

"They had each other and they didn't need anything else."

Ellen stood quiet, remembering.

He said, "I was just thinking of you telling me you were
engaged the first time."

"Really? When?"

"1939."

"I was—you're kidding."

"1939," he said.

"Well, I was a little ahead of myself, then."

"It's the clearest memory," he told her.

She smiled. "I have some of those, too. You getting caught at
things, mostly."

"I remember," he said, thinking of an instance in which she
had saved him from trouble: a story he had liked to tell Annie,
and that Annie had always liked to hear, about the time his
father found out he was smoking. The old man had come to
see Field play in the opening basketball game at the high school,
which turned out to be a fast-breaking, wild, high-scoring affair
that the boy had been brilliant in, playing, Field would modestly
say, beyond himself, scoring more than thirty points, his father
sitting in the crowd and witnessing everything, especially how
winded and out of breath Field was during the pauses in the
action; and when James had come home that night, Ellen had
been waiting for him, sitting in the dark on the stairs opposite
the front door, with her dress pulled down over her still skinny
knees. "Daddy knows you smoke," she told him as he came
singing into the house. The one thing you could never do in
that house was tell a lie, and so Field had walked into the kitchen

and his father had said, "You'd do better if you laid off those cigarettes," and Field had known enough, thanks to his sister, to say, "I guess so, sir."

In the night, standing in the kitchen with her, he felt the odd desire to thank her for that long-ago favor.

"What?" she said.

"I was just thinking of that time you saved me about the smoking."

"That's Annie's favorite story about us."

He was silent.

She sighed. "I think it represents what she always missed here, and . . . I don't mean anything by that, James. She would've liked a brother or sister. She told me once that she thought about it a lot, waking in the night. Well—that she felt alone, anyway."

"Ellen, why won't she ever talk to me?"

"She talks to you, James."

"You know what I mean."

She said, "Sometimes I think it's like with the pennies and the pieces of paper."

He looked at her.

"It's just that you don't let go, James."

"Is that what Annie thinks?"

"I told you it was sometimes what *I* thought."

"All right," he said. "But do you think Annie feels that way? That it's something—I don't know—miserly in me?"

"Don't say miserly. That is not what I meant at all, and you know it."

He didn't say anything for a moment.

"She doesn't confide in me, James. It was only in those first days after she came home that she told me anything at all— and then it really wasn't much. You always made more out of it than it really was."

"Apparently I do that with a lot of things," he said.

"Now don't start feeling sorry for yourself."

He bowed slightly. "I stand where I have been put," he said. "In my place."

"Come on," she said. "Let's give it all a rest. We'll talk to Annie in the morning and see that everything's fine. You'll see."

They had gone up to their respective rooms. Mr. Field got into his bed and turned the light off, but then he couldn't lie still, and he could hear Ellen moving around in her room—it was, he knew with an ache, the restlessness of the hypothetically sick—and finally he rose, dressed, and padded quietly down to the living room in the dark, to sit in the chair and wait, even as sleep began to steal into his worry and his wakefulness, for the light in the street, the door-closing sound that would mean his daughter had come home again, had made her way inside his house, out of the turning winds of the world, and was safe.

Now Ellen walked away from him, back into her kitchen to search for the missing vanilla. Her movement, her bustling from one room to the other, pushing her sleeves up to begin the work ahead, seemed an expression of a kind of faith; that it was just a Saturday morning in October, and all worries were unfounded. He stood by the front door and looked at his granddaughter, who was raking the leaves, and who still paused from time to time to watch the road. This morning, everything felt like a pretext. He was about to turn from the window, when a taxi pulled along the curb, and Annie got out. Field breathed a sigh, watching her pay the cabbie. She turned and talked to Linda for a moment, hugged her, and then looked up and down the street.

"She's here," Field said to his sister.

Ellen came through the pantry and down the hall to him. Her face was flushed with the heat of the kitchen, and with something else—relief, gratitude, excitement.

"My very dear and always right Miss Ellen," Field said.

She smiled, and her eyes swam.

He opened the door and went out onto the porch. Annie was on the steps, looking up the street. She seemed calm—merely interested. "I was worried," Field said to her.

"It's the condition of this life," she said, smiling at him.

"Where have you been all morning?"

She hesitated a moment. "I—went over to the library for a while. I thought I'd make up for several late mornings by showing myself there—and it was something to do. I didn't feel like being cheerful for anybody who particularly needed it, you know?" She looked at Ellen. "Has Lou called?"

"First thing."

"Before *you* called," Mr. Field said.

"Poor Lou."

"Why poor Lou?" Field wanted to know.

She shrugged. "I guess that's how I feel."

Linda came up onto the porch now, and put her arms around her mother, then went on inside.

"See if you can find the vanilla," Ellen said after her. "Will you, darling?"

"You know she saw Cole at school yesterday?" Field said to Annie.

Annie nodded. "I just heard." Looking off up the street again, she said, "I wonder what he thinks he can do."

"Annie, how did you know he was back?"

She simply returned his gaze for a moment, then spoke very evenly, almost casually. "He paid me a little visit last night at the hotel."

Field waited for her to go on.

"He thinks he's come to stop the adoption. You should see him." She started inside. "I better call Louis."

"Annie?" said her father. But when she paused, waiting for him to speak, he could find nothing to say.

"I sent him away, if that's what's worrying you."

"I—I just wanted to know if you're all right."

"I'm fine," she said. "I really am, oddly enough."

"I waited up—" Field began, but then he stopped himself.

She regarded him with something like satisfaction. "You only want to protect me," she said. "I know."

He followed her into the house.

The Passing
of Various Lives

Linda makes her way back outside in the chilly sun to pretend an interest in the raked leaves. She, too, is waiting, and she doesn't know quite what she'll do yet. Everything about the way the adults are behaving tells her that something is about to happen.

Last night, she had awakened to find her grandfather dozing, his head back against the wall, his mouth wide open. And she'd heard Ellen laughing softly downstairs in the busy sound of the television. She lay awake longing for her mother's return from wherever she had gone with Louis, and then she began to think about these people who looked after her, watched over her life. She loved them all. She'd spent many nights—while wind and snow blasted at the windows of the house and kept her awake—praying that nothing bad would happen to any of them. From somewhere before she could quite remember, she'd received the impression that everything was in a kind of jeopardy, though she hadn't known the word until recently. The first time she heard it and understood it, she had a small shock of recognition, as though it were a thing she had always known—or had known and then forgotten somehow. Her grandfather snored, moaned and shifted slightly, seemed to be waking up, then was still again. Linda stared at his face, at the swelling of his body around the middle, the way his plump hands lay folded in his lap. It was strange looking at him this way; it made her feel his separateness from her, and at the same time it made her want to crawl up in his arms and cry. He had begun to dream, and his hands moved, jumped a little, almost as if to grasp something, then were still. For a moment, his breathing ceased, and she thought of getting up to touch his shoulder, wake him. But soon he was snoring again. Turning a little in the bed, she listened to him. She was abruptly visited by a wave of fear so strong it took her own breath away. She shook, held on, found she could breathe in but not out. The quiet seemed thick, as though it would settle over her and muffle everything—air, light, sound, strength. Her memory of the night is of staring at the ceiling, hearing her grandfather's slow, throat-rasping breath, and wishing for daylight.

Now she looks off down the street, through the leaf-blowing shade and sun. Day has brought little relief from the fear, which has settled deep in her bones, and she doesn't know how to think about it, what it means. She crosses the lawn, begins to sweep at the leaves matted under the hedge there, pausing now and again to look at the street. When she hears the sound of an engine, she stops and stares at the place where the road curves out of sight up the long hill toward school, and a small truck comes rumbling down, with one driver. She watches it pass, sees that the driver is a woman.

"Linda," her grandfather calls from the porch.

"What?"

"Why don't you come inside."

"I don't want to."

"Would you like to go to a movie this afternoon?"

"I don't know."

"Maybe we'll go somewhere."

She shades her eyes with one hand and looks at him. "No."

"Well, come on inside, all right?"

"In a minute," she says.

He's looking off at the sky. "Hardly looks like snow."

She follows his gaze. The sky is a blinding shade of light blue, almost white.

"Big storm coming, sweetheart—be here by nightfall." He comes to the edge of the porch steps and looks down the street. "Why don't you come on inside and watch some television."

"I will in a little bit."

"You want to talk about anything?"

She looks at him, means to show him her calm face, and sees that he's become intent on something beyond and behind her. Almost in the same instant she hears the whir of an engine, the whisper of tires. She turns. The car slows, stops. It's here. The sun is on the windshield, the reflection of tree limbs and leaves and wires, showing through and around some writing in white crayon. Linda sees that there is a price written across the bottom left side of the windshield of the car. The shape inside is her father, who gets out and walks around to stand at the edge of the sidewalk.

"Hey," he says, "little girl."

She's standing in the yard, holding the rake, and her grandfather is coming down the porch steps.

"Hey, doll," Linda's father says.

He looks scarily ragged and shaky, standing there, his hair flying in the wind and sun, his hands moving in and out of his coat pockets; there's something nervous and broken about him.

"Don't you recognize me, little girl?"

She nods.

"Sure you do."

Her grandfather has come to stand behind her, and he lays his hands lightly on her shoulders. She feels nothing of restraint in the way his heavy fingers close on the bones there, as if to reassure her. She puts her hands on top of his.

Her father looks at her grandfather. "Well, now, here I am after all these years coming after *my* daughter."

The hands on her shoulders tighten, just slightly, and something inside her understands that it's tension, not something meant to communicate anything to her.

"Seems like it's you and me, Mr. Field. Seems like it's always been you and me."

Her grandfather says nothing.

"You're in the way of truth and justice, old man. *You* couldn't do it—what makes you think *I'm* going to let somebody take my little girl away from me."

The hands on her shoulder move slightly, as if to caress. "No, Gilbertson—you gave her up. You gave her up and you know it, too, son."

Her father looks at her again. "Linda. Come here, sweetie."

She tries to breathe, feels her knees begin to pulse, as if each has a separate heart. It's dawning on her that what she wants more than anything is to stay where she is—that any change, going to Europe with Louis, or moving into his house down the road, or riding off into the sun with her father, is more than she can begin to stand. She doesn't want to move from the house whose shadow she now stands in, because it's all she's ever known of safety and warmth and the hands that understood her, tucking her into the blankets in the cold nights, and the waking up to voices she recognized that soothed her with the simple predictability of their various music, and knowing what the day will be and not having to worry about strangers so much.

And she understands without words, in her nerves, that this is home; that it means everything.

"Linda."

"No," she says, and knows it's barely audible.

"Sweetie," he says, and takes a step toward her.

She screams, "No!" and, breaking free of her grandfather,

runs to the porch steps, scrabbles up to the front door and into the house. She's in the foyer, and there's confusion and a lot of noise, her mother's arms surrounding her, Aunt Ellen kneeling to look into her face.

"My baby," Aunt Ellen says, shouts.

Because now everything is shattering.

Some time later—he no longer had time down—Gilbertson was driving in his boosted car down North Shore Drive, trying to remember where the record shop was, what exact street. He felt good. In a weird way he felt quite all right. He had watched Linda run into the house, had seen the look of relief and satisfaction on James Field's face, and when he brought the pistol out of his coat, he saw that look change to surprise and fear. He hadn't decided whether or not he would actually go through with anything, and he was just standing there enjoying the sense of victory it gave him to watch the old man try to speak, and hearing Annie's voice shouting his name—the voice that used to moan and whisper that name in the deep secretiveness of lovemaking in the house in Savoy—when it all seemed to come crashing down on him, an avalanche, that he had squirreled out of everything on this journey, had come up against the thing he meant to do and faltered, and so now he brought himself up, stood straight, meaning to take hold, remembering that he had boosted a car, had walked up to the man standing in the used car lot with the keys and just politely asked for them, pointing the gun (the way he was pointing it now, raising the hand that held it slightly), and then he had driven himself away, heading to the moment when he stood with James Field in his sights, and he would go through with it, he would go through with something.

"You ruined everything," he said. "Right from the start."

"No," Field said.

"You turned her against me."

"This is your failure, not mine," said Field, seeming less afraid.

He should not feel less afraid, Gilbertson thought, and the gun went off, exactly as though it had decided for him—it went off, and James Field went down, and the barrel of the gun followed. It was all simply happening. It was the next thing. The pistol went off again. Annie came out onto the porch, and he waited for her, while the old man groaned and lay still. She was screaming. Gilbertson fired once in the direction of the porch, heard a window break. Then he looked at James Field. He felt wonderful. Field lay with one arm at an odd angle over his side, his face registering surprise and terror, even in unconsciousness, his foot twitching in a funny way, as if everything that was his life had retreated there and were thrashing around. Annie was crouched behind the railing of the porch, screaming and crying.

"Okay," Gilbertson said, "I'm going to ruin it all, now." He hoped she could hear him. "I'm going to fuck everything up good, Annie. Hear? This is justice. This is for taking my little girl away from me." He fired once more at the porch, and the bullet splattered wood, kicked up a little puff of dust. He couldn't see Annie anymore. It didn't matter. He had reached into his own destiny, and he felt very good. He walked slow around the car, got in, set the pistol on the seat next to him, and drove away. It was almost casual. He drove down to the end of the block, turned around and came back past the house. Annie was kneeling and crying over her father on the lawn. People were coming out of their houses to look at what had taken place. Gilbertson drove by. He put his radio on, and headed back toward the lake, listening to a man talk about the storm that was on its way. The first storm of the new winter.

"I am the fucking storm," he said. He was flying. He was ready for whatever weather could do. Nothing could have prepared him for the exhilaration and satisfaction that coursed like heat through him now, mixed with an overwhelming sensation of certainty and peace, as though the arc of his life had been completed. He was perfectly aware of the enormity of what he had done, but almost immediately after it had been accomplished, all the desperation and anger and helpless rage that had led to it were gone, and for a few minutes he just drove up and down the streets of the city, looking out at the houses and rooftops and trees and lawns with all the peaceful benign proprietary pleasure of an emperor or a God. He pulled down toward where he remembered having found Annie's storekeeper in the morning, finding himself very clear, very capable of remembering the street now, making the right turn, flying, waiting for the next thing.

And then he was visited by a sudden, terrifying, pervasive feeling of abandonment. It was as though some force, God, had been breathing in him, and had now left him in this quiet car, engine stopped, everything dead and gone, crashed and burned. He swallowed another of the speed pills and waited a moment, but nothing happened. He took another. He was in front of the Stardust Record Shop. He got out. There were three shots left. Reaching into his pocket, he put his hand on the pistol. He was going to do this, too. This was also next. Opening the door to the place, he heard the little ding of the bell, and stopped. There was a young man behind the counter.

"Yes?" he said.

"Where's the old guy—the owner."

"I'm the owner."

"You're the owner?"

"Well." The young man smiled. "I'm the owner's son." His face was innocent and friendly and he had probably never been more than five miles away from home, and Gilbertson hated him suddenly with a fierce, hot, reasonless hate.

"Where's your father at?"

"Why?"

He brought the pistol out.

"Jesus," the young man said, raising his hands. His face went irritatingly white. There was something about the way it emptied

of color; there was something about the solidness of his body—
what were probably his several smells, odors, damps, bumps,
warts, and imperfections. There was something about the bulk
and sweat of him.

"I want to know where your father is, boy."

"He's not here. Look, there's money in the register."

Gilbertson stared at him, then raised the pistol and fired. He
had known he would do it this time, and there was no feeling
of elation. The young man went down behind the counter, and
began to crawl away. His voice made a helpless, disbelieving
sound. Then he was still. Gilbertson went out into the street.
He had actually done all this, and here it was: he had actually
got here. Looking at the gun, he thought of Annie, thought of
going back to the house to see her and try to explain. There
were people running in the street. He turned and watched
them—two women, one of whom had dropped what she was
carrying, and a man with a little boy—all of them running away
from him. They were all frightened of him, exactly as he thought
they always should have been, all the time. What the woman
had dropped was a bag with toys in it; the bag had broken, and
a stuffed doll, a cartoon-faced bear, lay out on the pavement,
its button eyes staring at nothing. Gilbertson put the barrel of
the gun in his mouth. It was a simple thing to get into his stolen
car and drive away, drive until someone stopped him. But he
was empty now, broken, it was all coming to pieces, and there
wasn't anything else or anywhere. He waited a moment. There
seemed to be no sound in all the world, not even his own
breathing. And, what he had done—he had shot two people.
He was somebody out of the dark, sailing down. And in this
minute he wanted to hear some sound other than himself. Up
the street, two men in suits had come to peer at him from the
protection of a clothing store sign, and looking at them he
thought of the ones who had come to kill him, so far ago, in
Illinois. Perhaps they had followed him here, and now they saw
how dangerous he was. He waited for them to move, step out

of cover, aim at him, come get him. He said, over the barrel of
the gun, "Come get me." And the men ducked back out of
sight. "I am danger," Gilbertson said, his words garbled by the
gun barrel. In the periphery of his vision, he saw something like
a uniform. He turned a little, looked at it—a man in a blue
coat, no badge. He took the barrel of the pistol out of his mouth.

"Hello," he said.

The man said nothing.

"Watch," Gilbertson said.

But the man had dropped behind a parked car.

"Time to go," said Gilbertson, and put the end of the gun
barrel under his chin. He turned to look at the street, the blue
shade falling. Lightly, he squeezed the trigger. The only sound
was himself, and the emptiness, vistas of it, opening in him—
all the long frightened passages of life and all the lonely rages,
the useless span of it traveling outward from something inside
him, like a kind of falling through the dark—and now he
seemed to hear something from a long way off. He thought of
his father, big and talking at him in the stifling heat of some
lost summer night that had gone on like eternity; it was a vivid
scene in his mind, and it raked through him like the knowledge
of death. He looked at it and then denied it, refused it. Another
moment passed. He didn't know it, now. He was falling backward, surprised. There had been the beginning of another sound,
and for a tiny space he tried to remember what it was, flying
all apart, hitting something sudden and coming to a stop. He
had always been so confident of his looks. He had always been
so pretty. Pretty boy, his mother would coo, pursing her lips, so
pleased, so willing to give him anything. Pretty boy. The thought
traced somewhere through him and was lost, was somehow
about another child far away, and he turned in himself, or
seemed to turn, staring at something blinding, a light, or something like light, that took his vision away in a blaze and then
while he gazed blind straight into it, he could feel it begin to
shift, leech out, fading. He stretched for it, knew that this was

dying, this was his death, and then—rather too quickly, while he lay thinking about the fact, looking at the fact of his own death almost curiously from a distance—any knowing at all ended, forever.

That morning, after riding by the house several times, Louis had driven over to the library, had gone in and browsed distractedly among the rows of books, hoping Annie might be there and see him, but lacking the nerve to ask for her. The library was surprisingly crowded at this hour, mostly with children and their mothers, who were apparently involved in some Saturday morning reading program that included movies and cartoons. There was a lot of noise from the children's side of the place, which was an alcove in the wall beyond the reference section. Louis sat in one of the microfilm booths and idly turned the knob, looking at lists of author's names, aware of this as an all too obvious pretext. He wanted to talk to Annie. Finally he went to the desk and asked for her. The woman there, whom he vaguely knew—a kindly old woman with glasses on a black strand draped over the back of her neck—told him that Annie would be in on Monday.

"Office staff are on Monday through Friday, sir." She looked beyond him to the next customer.

"Excuse me," Louis said, "are you sure she didn't just come in on her own?"

The woman looked at him as though he had cursed at her.

"Have you *seen* her?" he said.

"No, sir—I haven't. She works Monday through Friday."

Sick of himself and truly discouraged, he went out and got into his car and sat there staring through the windshield at the traffic going by on Michigan Street. Everyone was heading for something definite, something planned; they all looked so settled into the patterns of life, so much at peace and so happy. It was a beautiful, sunny, cold morning. The light flew at him from every angle, from the metal sides of cars and from the windows of the shops across the street. People were walking along the sidewalk, and he watched them for a time, trying to decide what he should do next. He believed he should have the discipline to simply go on with his daily affairs, and stop chasing all over the city looking for her; but he couldn't shake the feeling that he must try to head her off, must get to her before she did anything that both of them might regret.

He drove by her house again, and saw that someone had been raking leaves in the yard. He drove on, feeling angry now, things going on so normally in that house, as though Louis Wolfe had never existed or been in love with the woman who lived there. He wasn't hungry, but he drove to the north shore for something to eat. Roger had volunteered to keep the store all day, as if the store mattered. Nothing mattered to him now but finding Annie and arriving at some understanding about things. Yet he was afraid that his nervousness about her feelings had been working against him somehow, crowding her, putting her off. He wanted to find the right way to approach her, and then he was thinking about the fact that she was pregnant. That had changed everything, and surely it had been the pregnancy that had altered the way she behaved with him.

He couldn't eat. She was out there terminating the pregnancy, and there was nothing he could do to stop it.

He went home. He changed into a pair of blue jeans and a sweatshirt, and then he took the phone from its place along the wall at the base of the stairs and lay down on the sofa, the phone in his lap. He started to dial the number, then hung up. If she was there, she could call him: she had sent him away the night before, and it was her place to call. But wasn't he letting pride make him act foolishly? Wasn't it pride, rather than dignity? He began to dial the number again, and again he hung up. He should not seem to be hectoring her; the tack to use was of a loving but independent distance for the time being. He should appear to be wanting to give her the room to move in that she apparently craved.

He lay there going back and forth with himself. The scratchy feeling in his throat was increasing, and he had begun to feel sluggish, vaguely woozy and out of breath. He was coming down with something, and he cursed it, waiting for the phone to ring. Annie called, finally, twice. The first time, she was whispery and teasing, said she felt so much better in the light of day. He could tell that someone—Ellen or Linda or James Field—was in the room with her, and she couldn't talk as freely as she might have. They talked about Cole Gilbertson, and he told her not to worry; at any rate, *he* was no longer worried. He was too happy about the baby to let anything bother him, and he almost said this to her, too. Somehow, it didn't seem quite appropriate, and so he held it back.

The second time Annie called, she called from Mercy Hospital, and he couldn't understand her. He had fallen asleep, was beginning to be feverish, and she was crying; it astonished and frightened him. He sat up on the sofa with the receiver at his ear and heard her broken voice and thought about the baby.

"Annie what is it—tell me."

She wanted him to come quickly, something terrible. "My father," she said, "shot."

"Shot." He stood. His legs seemed to go out from under him. Something seemed to fall nearby; it made a shattering sound: it was a small statuette, a woman in an attitude of pagan worship of her own slender form that Roger had bought for him a year ago; he had pulled it off the phone table with the wire when he sat back down.

"Please hurry, Lou. Please."

He said through her crying that he was on his way, and wasn't certain whether she had heard him or not. She had broken the connection. He put the phone back on its table, stepping over the broken pieces of the statuette, and was on his way out the door when the phone rang again. He let it ring. Outside, there were sirens, far off, many of them. The whole city seemed to be in a state of alarm. He got into the car and drove toward the hospital, thinking about the fact that Annie's father might be dead. Then thinking of Annie depending on him, reaching for him in her grief. Finally he tried very hard to empty his mind, understood that this was fever, and that these importunate thoughts were a function of being agitated and feverish. "Oh, Lord," he prayed. "Please help James Field." His throat was hurting now, and the sweat poured from his brow; he was beginning to feel dizzy. Before him the road wavered and went on, seemed to be unraveling itself under the hood of the car.

Mercy Hospital was a big, white, odd-looking building above Lake View Drive. It had once been a complex of buildings making up a single, almost outlandishly palatial mansion, the property of one of the steel barons who had lived in that part of Duluth back in the days of the iron boom. The buildings were all tin-roofed and there were only two floors in all of them, the steel-baron owner and builder being, according to the lore of the place, inordinately afraid of dying in a fire. He had built everything on a level from which a man could easily jump, and he had lived to his ninety-second year, and then died of a heart attack while watching a play in the Palace Theater in Duluth, back in 1935. Louis pulled into the emergency room parking lot, and couldn't find a place. He drove through it, then turned around and came back, and at last he left the car in the middle of the lot with the emergency flashers on. At the entrance of the building an ambulance was backed up, its roof lights revolving, the engine idling. Two attendants stood in the open back door, smoking cigarettes.

"Fucking holocaust," one of them said to the other, blowing smoke.

Louis went by them, into the drear light of the waiting room. There were people sitting in chairs around the curved wall, all in various stages of impatience and suffering: a woman held a bloody rag over her fist; a man sat gingerly stroking a badly sprained ankle. Louis scanned the room, walking toward the center of it, and then he heard his name. He turned. Ellen and Linda were sitting in one of the sheeted cubicles inside the main suite of rooms; they were just visible from where he stood, and they had seen him. A moment later, Annie stepped around the row of desks on that side of the room and came to him—walked, crying, into his arms.

"Is he—?" Louis began.

"Oh, Lou—you don't know."

"Annie, he lived to see you happy again." Louis heard himself, and wondered at the hollow sound of it.

"No," she said. "Dad's—he's in surgery. He—it's his hip, and his leg."

"He's going to be all right, then?"

"You don't know," she said, crying. "Oh, Lou."

"I know," he heard himself say.

She had rested her head against his breastbone, and she had his coat in her fists. Very lightly her forehead came against him twice, three times. "No," she said and looked at him. "You don't understand. Oh, honey. It was Cole. Cole just went crazy."

Louis Wolfe looked at her—knowing quite abruptly, with the heat of his rising fever, and out of some unendurably delirious part of his mind, that this, whatever it was, would be news he couldn't stand. "Tell me," he said, "just please tell me now."

During the funeral, Linda is blank, staring, quiet. There's nothing to say about anything: the man who was her real father started shooting at people, and then turned the gun on himself. The television news people called it a shooting spree, which sounds eerily like some kind of celebration or party, like a jamboree, or gala. At poor Roger Wolfe's funeral she watches Louis cover his red face, sniffling, sweating, suffering the flu along with what has happened to him, and thinks about the fact that her father's body is on a train back to Illinois, back to be claimed by authorities of Champaign County because that is where his home is, and all of his belongings. Linda thinks of him coming north, leaving everything, and she doesn't know what to do with the knowledge. She waits for something to come to her, some way of thinking about everything; her mother is so careful of her, and Aunt Ellen hovers around her, worrying and fidgeting.

"I think it's bad," Ellen had said. "I'll stay home with her."

And Linda's mother had looked at her. "I want you to do what you want."

"I want to go," Linda said.

"It's bad," said Aunt Ellen. "I just think it's very, very bad."

"If she wants to go I'm not going to stop her," Linda's mother said.

"I want to go," said Linda.

Because she did want to go. And now that she's here, she wishes Aunt Ellen would stop looking at her as if she expected her to break into pieces all of a sudden. She straightens a little, squares her shoulders to show that she can stand it, and Aunt Ellen looks away.

Roger's Fran sits with her parents in the front row of the church, looking stunned, and, as the ceremony is about to begin, she gets up, walks over to Louis, and puts her arms around him, crying. The ceremony is a plain and simple affair, presided over by a round, balding man with a red beard and small nervous hands, who talks about the mysterious ways of God, how it is not possible that anyone could understand this event, since it is beyond understanding. Linda watches everything, and feels as if it all extends from herself somehow, remembering that she had spent many nights dreaming about her father's return. Outside, it snows and snows, a heavy, wet snow: branches have broken in the trees from the weight of it. Linda stands in the cold and watches her mother embrace Louis in the open doorway of the second car, the limousine. The snow has gathered on their shoulders, and in their hair. Louis looks old, his face is without any color at all. Linda gets into the backseat of the car with Aunt Ellen, sits watching the snow melt on the front of her long coat. Then her mother and Louis are there, Louis shifting himself in the middle seat, getting over to the window. Her mother gets in and the door is shut. Her mother clears her throat, coughs into her fist. Louis sneezes twice, wipes his nose and face with a ragged handkerchief. The car idles. A young man in a visored cap gets in at the wheel, and begins to remove tight white gloves from his hands. No one says anything. The young man puts the car in gear, rests both hands on the wheel. The procession moves slowly. Aunt Ellen sniffles and holds a handkerchief to her mouth, staring out at the snowy street. Then for a long time there's just the steady thrumming of the windshield wipers.

"I told them we'd stop by the hospital this afternoon," Louis says.

"I know," says her mother.

"I told them it might be late."

They are silent again. Perhaps two minutes go by.

"Boy was in the complete dark about what he wanted to do," Louis says, low. He seems not to be talking to anyone in particular, but Linda's mother answers.

"Lou," she says, reaching over to touch his arm.

"He thought college—"

Linda's mother moves closer to him, reaches her arm over his shoulder.

"I wish the son of a bitch had found me," Louis says.

"Don't, Lou."

"I wish he had."

Linda thinks about her father, and begins to cry.

Her mother looks over the seat and says, "Ellen." And so Ellen wipes Linda's face with her handkerchief, pulls her over against her wide hip.

"There's a girl," she says.

Linda is crying about her father, and feels divided, wrong, watching Louis's head sink against her mother's shoulder. Everything is confusing and hurting, and when Louis turns to look at her with his wet, reddened eyes, and, laying his big hand on her forehead, says her name, she thinks she might begin to scream. But she doesn't. She keeps it down inside herself. The procession reaches the cemetery, and everyone files out into the snow. In a gathering of black umbrellas, in the cloud of their collective breathing, they pray for the repose of the soul of Louis R. Wolfe, Jr. Linda stands at her mother's side, looking at the faces of the others. She feels quite suddenly the odd sensation that they are all somehow a part of what she will have for shelter in her life. It comes to her with a feeling like helplessness. She looks at the snowing sky as though it is alive and burdened with all the possible ways she can come to harm. Then the feeling changes, becomes something else, as the prayers are recited, and she watches the snow swirl and settle on their shoulders. Her mind reels with it. She looks at the sky again, where the snow is like a fading curtain of shade, and begins once more to cry, only now, though she thinks of her father, she senses that she's crying for him in a different way. She feels herself begin to shift inside, and she knows, without any way to quite express it, that she's changing, that her sorrow is changing—that it includes everyone now, and in some unfathomable way has begun to draw her more deeply into this knot of bewildered people standing on a hillside in the snow. It all comes to her as a kind of recognition and memory, all the faces looking strangely, almost pleasantly familiar to her. In only a moment, this feeling changes, too—is replaced by a shivering wave of loneliness—and she's confused again; she can't remember. She stares from face to face, trying to recover herself as she was only seconds ago. The voices are all murmuring the last prayer now, the Lord's Prayer, and now, from some bottomless well of her being, without knowing she would do it, not even really acceding to it inwardly, she reaches across the small space between them and takes Louis's hand. It is a movement she watches herself make, and when he kneels down to wrap her in his arms she feels a small, transitory thrill of surprise.

She hears Aunt Ellen's voice with the others, "... but deliver us from evil ..."

And Louis hugs her, his strong arms around her middle. She buries her face in the cold, snow-dusted cloth of his coat and cries with him, thinking finally, blessedly, of nothing else. Her mind is quiet now. She's hearing the sound go out of her, of her crying, and it seems to be exactly what she feels. He rises with her. She closes her eyes and is carried back to the line of waiting cars.

Certain Testimony

I have a memory of her that I couldn't begin to explain: because I couldn't have been there. It is like a vision, and takes place in Savoy, perhaps a week before she decided to come home again. Its clarity is doubtless the result of what I came finally to know about the woman who happens to be my daughter. But I must describe for you, if I can, the way she looks on this day I'm remembering, when she wakes up a thousand miles from me and dresses Linda. I watch her small hands moving the soft cloth of the child's coat. Linda is four years old and complains about the coat; it is old and the zipper comes loose all the time, and she wants to go without a coat. Annie's quick, practical hands get her zipped up and she says with the plain authority of knowing what she'll do and not do, "It's cold. You need something on. Now quit whining about everything."

"I'm hungry," Linda says.

"We'll get something in a little while," says my daughter, who lifts the child and carries her on her hip through the house. Perhaps my daughter's hair is tied back in a chignon; perhaps it is under a bandanna. She takes Linda out to the car and puts her in the infant seat, then gets in and drives toward Champaign. The weather is cold and gray, and there's a mist in the air. The oncoming cars have their headlights on. Annie puts her own on, and the radio, and begins looking for some music.

"Where're we going," Linda wants to know.

And Annie tells her. "Shopping."

They are in fact going to buy a new coat for Linda, and then they'll ride over to the train station and look at the scheduled times for departures. It will be the fifth or sixth time they have done this, taken this little ride into Champaign and, after following some small pretext or completing some errand, wound up standing in the high-ceilinged, mostly empty lobby of the train station, staring at the television screen with its white letters: DEPARTURES. My daughter, this time, drives onto the campus and stops at a small thrift store on Florida Avenue. She gets out of the car and reaches in for the baby. She has trouble with the clasp on the belt, but she manages it and, in the wind and chilly fog, makes her way into the store. Her life is mostly made up of trouble: husband drifting into vagrancy and crime; serious and myriad financial difficulties—creditors calling all day, mail full of threatening letters. Law firms are marshaling themselves against her. She goes into the little shop and jokes with the women who run it, two very kind Baptist ladies, who know her from earlier visits. She buys a good clean secondhand coat for her daughter, and then she simply passes the time with the two ladies, talking about weather, babies, day care, men. The two ladies—one is sixty, the other forty-three—are both married and they seem happy enough. Their jokes are about time: the time their husbands don't spend with them; the football games on Sunday and the poker games on weekend nights; the fishing and hunting trips; the trips to stock car races. They smile good-naturedly and they talk about their husbands as though they are difficult but lovable children; it's clear that they have learned to accept these things in their marriages, and Annie finds ways to change the subject. She can't say, "My husband is trying to sell a trunkful of drugs at this very moment." She lets Linda show off for them awhile, and then she bundles her out to the car again. The mist has become rain—an icy wave of needles coming out of the northwest. Linda doesn't want to sit in the car seat, and she won't put her legs down, keeps blocking her mother's efforts to get her seated. So Annie hauls her out to the curb and stands her there.

"Walk," she says.

Linda cries.

Annie storms back to the car and gets in, starts it up. It's one of Cole's odd investments—a Ford Comet with a V-8 engine that's running on five cylinders, if that—and it roars, smokes in the rain. Annie closes the door and then rolls the window down to look back at where Linda stands, crying, on the curb. She backs the car up a little, stops, looks back again. Then she gets out of the car and crosses to her daughter, picks her up, and carries her to the open door of the car.

"In the car seat," she says.

And Linda obliges, somehow without taking her thumb out of her mouth. Annie straps her in, then gets in herself. They are both shivering with anger. She looks into the rearview mirror at her daughter's tear- and rain-streaked face and says, "I'm not Grandmama. You do what I say."

The rain is now mixed with heavy snowflakes, like wet tissue paper slapping the windshield, but she drives to the train station, gets out with Linda, carries her into the quiet lobby, which is well lighted and pine-smelling from the floor cleaner a man with a mop is pushing around in puddles near the counters. Several people are sitting on the ranked benches, which always remind her of church pews. A balding black man in a three-piece suit, with soft, dark, wide eyes and astonishingly white teeth, gives her a wonderful friendly smile, and out of an impulse, Annie sits down next to him.

"Traveling to Chicago?" she asks him.

"Milwaukee," he says. "Visiting my grandson in college there." He pauses, then seems to see that further explanation is called for, and, leaning slightly toward her, as though this were a sort of confiding, says, "It's parents' week at Marquette, and I'm afraid both his parents have passed." His voice is rich with kindness and somehow *with experience, too, as though it has been polished and aged by travel and time: there is an elegant, sonorous music in it. Now he looks at the windows. "I hope this weather lets up."*

"Do you live here?" Annie asks him.

He nods. "Are you going to Chicago?"

"No," my daughter tells him, and then finds that she can't speak. She looks across the room, at the man pushing the mop around, and knows that she's starting to cry.

There is a girl, sitting in a train station with her child on her lap, wearing, say, a red bandanna and a denim jacket and jeans, looking off and crying, because she's alone, and has no one at all to turn to and still keep her good strong prideful sense of herself.

"Are you all right?" the kindly man at her side asks.

And she gets up, hauls herself to her feet. "It's late," she tells him. "I have to go."

He stands. "Miss, I—"

But she's already heading to the doors and out. She gets into the car and works her child into the straps of the car seat, then sits crying, looking through the sliding surface of almost melted flakes at the facade of the station, the figure of the gentle, balding man standing in the window, gazing out at her. She tells herself she will. She will. She tells herself there's only so much a person is supposed to stand. She's crying, pulling the car out of the lot, heading herself home, to the house where her mother-in-law, Selena, is already working on dinner. Selena admires the new coat and there's not the slightest implication that anything could be wrong with the fact that it is a secondhand coat bought with scrape money. Selena has been home from her visit with a neighbor friend for perhaps an hour, and she's already in what she'll wear to bed tonight. Annie sits at the kitchen table with her and pulls the wet bandanna from her hair. She's my baby, my little girl, in this life I never planned for her, that I somehow drove her to, and she's beginning to know that she'll have the courage to manage another day. Tomorrow, perhaps, she'll find something to do that will change everything and still keep it together: she has her own little girl to think of and Linda adores her father. In this vision, I see mother and child in the gray light of the kitchen in that house, with rainy snow falling against the windows, and an old woman muttering to them about dinner. My daughter shakes the rain from her hair, and Selena smiles at her with haggard, lonely eyes from across the room. Annie smiles back....

Sometime during the first night in the hospital, I awakened to find that I couldn't move. I was alive. I could feel my legs and arms, there was pain deep in my side and down low, in my pelvis. I had discomfort in the bottoms of my feet, though I couldn't begin to imagine why. And there was a tube in my arm. I could turn in the half-light of the room and look at it. I was alive. With a species of wonder, I took a breath, looked at the room, the apparatus above me in the bed. I couldn't remember exactly what had happened, why I was there. Next to me, partly obscured by a heavy gray curtain, was another bed, empty. Beyond the bed was a window looking out on darkness, winking lights far off. The room was quiet. I listened for a while to my own breathing, wondered where Annie was, and Linda, and when I thought of Linda I began to recall the moments just before I had looked down the little barrel of Cole's madness. Then I seemed to remember Annie and I, in that room, in the smell of antiseptic and cleanser and the faint traces of blood and sweat, talking. I had a moment of seeing her quite clearly, sitting at my side, brushing tears from her eyes as I spoke.

"Annie," I said. "It was me, wasn't it. All the time."

"Quiet," she said. But she was nodding.

"When you came home and stayed. For me, wasn't it," I said. "Something you were doing for me."

"Don't talk," she said. But it was in her eyes, the years she had given me as some half-conscious form of expiation for the pain of her running away; the thing she had decided to do out of what she had perceived as my neediness. I could see it in her eyes and in the way she began to turn away from it, telling me to quiet down, rest, stop agitating myself. I could see that she was realizing it, too, and perhaps even trying to reject it. And something else began to come to me, that I wished not to look at, either.

Now I tried to recall what it had been.

There was something larger, waiting for me behind the plain truth that I had badly misunderstood everything. Annie, I wanted to say, have we been so mysterious to each other?

I remembered seeing Louis Wolfe standing in the light of a doorway, his face strangely lit up and crying; and I remembered Ellen looming above me, apologizing as if the whole thing had been her fault. I looked at daylight out the windows and was puzzled by the fact that only seconds ago it had been the winking lights of a radio tower in the distance: the tower was there, but it was only a pair of spiny shadows on the whiteness. I saw snow falling, and then I saw sunlight. I blinked, and there were stars. And then slowly I began to realize that the first night's waking, the first time I lay trying to recall everything and remembering Annie telling me not to speak, was days ago. I had been in the bed for days, and people had come and gone. Something very bad had gone on unfolding beyond me, outside the walls of the room. I came to know this, and in the night when I was alone and awake again, not sure how much more time had gone by, I cried for it all. I remembered once having said I would kill Cole Gilbertson. I saw myself in the hysterical, alcohol-hazy moment of pointing at him through the windshield of a car and shouting that. In a strange way this seemed more recent than being shot and realizing I had been shot, lying in a room and realizing it, as I was beginning to realize my own part in it. I was out of the stream of time, perhaps dying in this bed, and now Annie became more vivid. Annie sat in a chair near me and looked terrible, and I told her so. I turned my head, feeling the stiffness of my neck, and said, "You look terrible."

"So do you," she said.

And the second thing, the thing larger, hit me. I said, "You would've come home sooner, wouldn't you."

She stared.

"If I hadn't chased you that way."

"That's all so long ago," she said, trying not to cry.

"I left you with no place to go."

"Don't be silly," she said.

"No. Because we were as close as we were. I left you nowhere to go."

She came to the side of the bed, and time seemed to bend toward her; it narrowed out and caved in, and I was in some other moment. This moment, I said to myself, with Annie resting her head lightly on the bed at my shoulder, her hands on my arm. "I was so scared," she said.

"It's going to be all right, now," I told her.

She went on crying, and I looked at the tiny asterisk of scalp in her dark hair. "Annie," I said. "Annie."

Then it was dark again. I had been asleep again. Something was wrong with my recovery. I seemed to have heard that something was wrong with my recovery: fever, infection; my own attitude. They were putting things into me, and others stood around the bed, lifting me, putting me back. Annie seemed to float in the air behind them, and once I thought I saw Linda. My mind ached for what I couldn't ask or know. I was a body being moved and handled and prodded and wrapped. I had a dream of being slowly lowered into the ground, and I jerked awake, gasping, feeling the heat of fever in my face and neck, the pillow under me soaked and cold. Night followed night, and there didn't seem to be any days between. I lay dreaming of Ellen, sick, on a deathbed in a room I didn't recognize. I saw my mother and father sitting together in a big easy chair, cooing at each other and being in love. They were young, and something almost stupidly innocent about their faces made me want to shout at them, "I'm shot. I've been shot."

"James?"

I opened my eyes and looked into the face of my sister. "What time is it?" I said.

"It's three."

"Night or day." There was light at the window, but it didn't look like real light.

"Day," she said.

"I'm dying," I said. "Right?"

"You had us scared you would."

"I'm sick, Ellen. I feel sick."

"There's no fever now. You had an infection, but it's over now."

"Did anybody go after him?"

Ellen said, "Don't worry about anything now."

"Did he get Linda or Annie?" I asked in the sudden wave of fear that came: that everything of the past few days had been delirium.

"No," she said.

"I'm shot," I told her, and heard myself beginning to cry again.

Ellen touched my face. I remembered that she had been worried about the little sore spot on the back of her neck.

"Ellen," I said, "I'm so glad to see you."

"I'll go get Annie," she said.

"Annie's all right?"

"Yes. I told you."

And I remembered to say, "I've got a sore place on the back of my neck."

I don't think she understood; I don't think she remembered her own trouble. She touched my forehead again and said, "You've been lying here for almost three weeks."

"Three weeks," I said to the room, watching her go out.

A moment later, my daughter came in. She wore dark colors,

dark skirt and blouse—a shade of blue almost funereal. Her
eyes were washed out and troubled. She had Linda at her side,
her arm lightly over the girl's rounded shoulders. When I looked
at Linda, my heartbeat changed: she stared at me with concern
and fright and hope, out of eyes from which all the child had
been driven out; they were adult eyes, old eyes, the eyes of
someone with the ageless, unwanted knowledge.

"Honey," I said, and reached for her hand.

She came over and kissed my cheek, then went back to stand
behind her mother. Annie looked at Ellen, shook her head
slightly.

"Well," Ellen said, "I'm going to take Linda down to the
cafeteria for something to eat."

No one said anything, and, for a moment, no one moved.

"I'm not going to be crippled, am I?" I said.

Ellen said. "A cane." And that was enough.

I looked at Annie. "But you have something to tell me."

"I have a lot to tell you," she said in a trembling voice, looking
at the others.

*When I was in my teens, many nights I couldn't sleep for the
restless feeling that I was about to experience something grand. At
school, boys noticed me and were clumsy, and I would lie awake,
listening to the sounds the house made, and planning whole lifetimes,
glamorous futures as well as the one pretty little domestic one, and
finally I would begin to hear him moaning in his sleep; at first it
was a noise like sighing, interspersed with his snores, but soon enough
it grew to sound like hurt: little exhausted moans, tinged with fear.
I would lie awake hearing it, and then, thinking of the howling
dark outside the windows of the house (often in Duluth, the dark
howls just as awfully as anyone ever could've meant the phrase), I
would begin to feel terribly small and fragile. I'd shiver, not from
cold, and finally I would just be lying there praying, "Please, God,*

don't let my father die. Please, don't let anything happen to us. Please, God, let us live a long time." Sometimes this went on for hours, long after he had stopped the moaning or the sighing or whatever it was. And then in the mornings he was always so cheerful that I never looked at it in daylight as anything but the sounds he made in sleep; it never dawned on me that he might be glad in the mornings for the end of another bad night's dreaming, and I never asked him about it, either. It was just one of the things I knew about him.

One night I woke after my own nightmare—I dreamed my frozen dream of the lake in winter—to see him standing in his pajamas in my doorway, the light of the hall making a big shadow of him there. I didn't say anything, and, for a moment, neither did he. Then he said my name, and I could tell from the way he said it that he had been saying it, trying to wake me.

"Yes?" I said.

"You awake?"

"Yes," I told him.

"Say my name."

"Daddy," I said.

"Say your name."

"Annie."

"You were yelling."

"Really?" I said. "What?"

"I couldn't make it out."

I turned in the bed.

"You all right, honey?"

"I'm fine," I said.

And he came to the edge of the bed, leaned over, and kissed the side of my face. The shade he put me in was like something I could wrap myself in for warmth. "Sleep tight," he said.

Then he was gone. He was in his own room and the furnace kicked on; the dark changed slightly when the wind blew the lamps on the street, and in a little while I could hear him breathing—in

*a little while those broken sighs began from him, and for some reason
I remembered the morning, perhaps three years earlier, when, nervous, bumbling, obviously frightened, he had come to my room with
a pamphlet called* Beginning to Be a Woman, *and with a quaver
in his voice, put it in my hands. "Honey, now, I want you to read
this, and then if you have any questions, I'll be glad to talk to you
about it." I had already seen most of the material at school, and I
almost laughed. Instead, I took the pamphlet as though it were some
grave mystery to me, and said, "Okay."*

*The children on our street had taught me words and gestures that
all meant one thing, and for a long time I'd tried to keep the
knowledge of it from him, thinking I had to protect him from it,
somehow, as though it were new information, or were such a clear
advance on whatever he might know that the shock of it might be
too much. I felt so much older than he, watching him make his
embarrassed way out of my room, and later I went down to where
he was in the kitchen and poured myself a glass of milk, waiting
for him to ask me if I had any further questions.*

He said, "Well?"

*I turned, held the glass up and drank, then smiled at him. "Well
what?"*

"Any questions?"

"None," I said.

*He breathed a sigh. "I guess the book pretty well explains it."
And I realized that his voice was sad—I heard all this sadness in
his voice. He went on, looking away from me, his hands clasped
tight over his knees. "Most girls have their mother to explain these
things."*

*I walked over to him and put my arms around his neck. "Daddy,"
I said. The look on his face told me I had done the right thing, but
then he was up, moving across the room, getting busy. It was the
first time I felt as though he needed my care as much as I had always
needed his.*

*In the night, listening to him in his hard sleep, I decided to go
stand in his doorway and say his name. It was a favor I could*

return. So I crossed the hall on tiptoe, not wanting to disturb or waken any of the old, imagined monsters of my little girl–hood, and turned the hall light on; and when I had come to his door I stood for a few minutes, breathing the night odors of that room—talcum and soap from his shower; his clothes with their faint traces of aftershave and cologne, and somehow all the slowed processes of his body, too—and quite suddenly he sat straight up in the bed and looked at me. "What?" he said.

I said, "You were dreaming."

"No I wasn't."

"You were making a noise."

"Was I snoring?"

"No," I said, "moaning."

He lay back down. "Your mother used to wake me for it."

"I'm sorry," I said.

"Pay no attention to it, honey. It's just the way I sleep."

I went to his bed and leaned down and kissed him, thinking of the shadow I now made on him.

" 'Night," I said.

"Goodnight, my good grown girl," he said.

I went out and turned the hall light off, and returned to my room, feeling tall and calm and adult, feeling the always present harm that was possible in the world in night, or that made itself felt anyway in the night, and choosing to put it away from me, choosing not to lie awake and pray for my father's safety, as I had done so many times before, but to get into bed and pull the blankets high over my shoulder, and try to notice how sweetly my own warmth collected in the little nest I'd made in the bed. I remember having the thought, that night, that I would soon make my own cold sheets warm as love. . . .

When they put him in the ambulance, and I had got in with him, I looked through the side window, through the letters EUCSER in bright red, and I saw the house: there was Linda standing on the porch with Ellen. If they hadn't looked so forlorn and stunned and afraid, and if there weren't police in the yard, it might have been a homely little scene of farewell. I watched them as we pulled away, and then I was watching the house, that old place, with its one broken window, like a wound, and its wide porch, beyond which you could see the distant thicket of masts in St. Louis Bay Marina. I heard the siren begin, that awful futuristic sound, and felt us gathering speed, and then I reached down and took his hand. He was breathing. The paramedic had put him on oxygen and he was breathing. They had stanched the flow of blood, and they had him stable, unconscious. I looked at his face under the mask, and knew he would die. There were all the things we had never resolved. I had come so far with him, and always there had been the feeling that one day, when we had the time and were past all the worry and strife and pride, we would finally see each other as we were and not as we wished we were; we would finally arrive at the answer to each other, the puzzle we had made out of everything—I could tell him that I loved him, and have it clean, no longer freighted with everything I had done to hurt him; he could take me by the hand without thinking of his mistakes and failures; we could stop evaluating each other all the time because we would have aged enough to be past the need for it, somehow, and past the memory of whatever it was we thought we needed from each other, and couldn't give. I put my hand on the crown of his head, almost as if to hold him up, and the paramedic gave me a discouraging look.

"You don't understand," I wanted to say. "This is my father."

But of course he did understand, and he let me alone. I kept my hand where it was, and leaned close, watching the small sign of breathing in the mask. "Daddy," I said. "Please." I couldn't believe it would end here, and then I thought of Cole, out there driving around with his madness and his gun. I put my hands over my mouth and looked out the window, thinking about what else he might do, and even as I was thinking this I believe I began to hear the call coming in over the ambulance radio, and the paramedics talking about how there had been more shooting.

"At my house?" I said. "At my house?"

"No, ma'am."

As for the rest of that day and night, things blur. I remember standing over the bed he lay in, thinking about a time when I was a little girl and had drawn a picture in school with the help of the teacher—how I went home and took his praise for the picture, letting him believe it was my work, and that what he liked about it was my idea. It seemed to me, standing in that quiet hospital room, that in this deception I had wronged him beyond help for it, and I remember thinking how the difference between us was always what he didn't know about me. Oh, I wanted the chance to ask him to forgive me, as I already had forgiven him—for being human and complicated and badly flawed. The rest of it is confusion: I remember somber yellow light on the walls of the waiting room; I remember knowing that poor Roger was dead and that Cole had finished himself; and I remember being sure my father would die, too, and worrying about Linda, watching it all settle in her face.

There was a moment, after the hours of the night had worn on and the first hopeful reports came through, when Louis, who had just spent the necessary hours making arrangements for the burial of his son, stood in the little cove where the water fountain was and wrung his hands, seeming to pray, his head bowed, his face streaked with tears. I tried to comfort him, and couldn't, because nothing could. And when we went home, late morning of the next day, we were surprised to find that it had snowed four inches, and was still snowing.

We clung to each other, all of us. We went to the house and into the living room, which was cold from the big star-shaped hole in the window, and Louis said, "I'll get something to cover it," his voice sounding small and quite ordinary. It was oddly as though we had been married for twenty years. Ellen took Linda upstairs, and I waited in the living room, standing in the stream of chilly air, but needing it then, I thought, to breathe. Louis came back from the kitchen, carrying a box of cellophane and a roll of masking tape. It struck me that he knew the house almost as well as I did. We worked together to tape the window up, and then we went into the kitchen to put coffee on. He sat at the kitchen table and put his head in his hands and cried. I stood with him for a time, and then I left him, went upstairs, and tucked Linda into bed. Ellen was in her room, with music on, and though I stood outside her door a moment, I didn't knock. Downstairs, I found Louis as I had left him. I went to his side and put my hands on his shoulders. He went on crying.

The morning of the shootings, I had taken a cab to a clinic in Superior—a tall, sealed building with wide areas of glass in its sides, like some sort of colorless mosaic. The windows were all different shapes and sizes, and the patterns of brick were various. It all looked faintly jumbled to me, as though it were something I had dreamed. I went in and got on the elevator to the fifth floor. I hadn't slept very well after the pathological minutes with Cole in the hotel, and the elevator seemed to be carrying me toward some procedural badness, like surgery or punishment: for a moment it was not as though I had pushed the button for any floor, but was being traduced, had been caught and was beyond my own will and strength.

The clinic was in an office at the end of a hallway. There was plenty of time to think, heading down that blank space of white wall with black featureless doors in it to the one door. I thought about having another baby, and about being married to Louis. I thought about being in love and not being in love. It was as though I could tell the difference, just thinking. I said: I am in love with Louis. I said: he is almost twice my age. I said: I don't feel the way I did with Cole. Then I was looking

at my own hand turn the knob, and the door at the end of the
hall opened. There was a woman behind a desk, talking quietly
into a telephone. Behind her, along the wall, were filing cabinets
and windows. The queerly shaped windows looking out on the
parking lot, and the intricate tracery of iron on the skyline in
the distance: Duluth. The lifting bridge. Home.

The woman put the receiver in its cradle, and smiled at me.
"Yes?" she said.

"I want to talk to someone about aborting a pregnancy."

She handed me a clipboard with a card on it, which asked
for the basic information: my name and address; my family
doctor; the name of my insurance company. I filled it out and
handed it back to her. She looked it over, then folded her hands
and stared at me a moment. She had a squarish face, wide-apart
little green eyes with too much makeup, but she smiled kindly,
and when she spoke her voice was gravelly with decades of
smoked cigarettes: "You want to terminate a pregnancy, Ann?"

"I want to talk to somebody about an abortion, yes."

"All right. One moment, please."

She pushed her chair back and, opening one of the file drawers,
pulled out a sheaf of papers. "Here," she said. "There are a few
more things to be filled out."

I took the papers from her, and said, "I wanted to talk to
someone."

She seemed to hesitate, then nodded. "Yes. Just a minute,
please."

And she left me there. I sat quiet, with the sheaf of papers
on my lap. I found that I couldn't bring myself to look at
them, so I crossed my legs and waited. The wind blew and
battered against the strange windows. Out in the morning,
Cole was lurching toward murder and suicide, and I didn't
even think of him except to suppose that he was lying somewhere sick, with his traveling companion. I didn't even entertain the possibility that he might try to take Linda, because I
knew how frightened he was of ever being truly responsible

to anyone. I just waited, and in a little while the woman came back.

"Someone will see you now."

"Thank you," I said.

She showed me into another hallway. This time, the door opened off to one side of it, issuing into a small room with a little writing desk, a sink, a slablike examining table, and a single straight-backed chair. There were no stirrups on the examining table. I put the forms down on the writing desk, settled into the chair, crossed my legs, and waited, thinking about how I could be somewhere awaiting an interview for a job; or how this could be a dental office—a general practitioner's. There were drawings on the wall of women and babies, and, weirdly, of farm animals. Above the sink was a mirror. I stood and gazed into it. My eyes were red, circled. I did not look particularly in charge of myself. I ran my fingers through my hair, then turned and dug my hairbrush out of the chaos in my purse. I was standing there brushing my hair when the door opened, and a man Louis's age entered, wearing a white coat and carrying the clipboard with my filled-out card on it.

"Hello, Ann," he said.

I stuffed the hairbrush back into my purse and sat down with the purse on my lap.

"I'm Dr. Mackinley," he said. Then he put the clipboard down, and leaned on the examining table. "You're sure you're pregnant?"

I nodded.

"And you're sure you want to terminate?"

"No," I said.

"You want to talk about it."

Again, I nodded.

"Have you seen a doctor yet?"

"Yes," I said.

"Have you talked with *him* about this?"

"No."

"Well," he said, and shifted a little.

"I came here to talk," I said.

"Okay."

"If I decide to abort, can I get it done now?"

"No," he said.

"Why not?"

"That's just the way we go about it. How does the father feel about it?"

"The father?" I said.

He waited, looking at me with gentle, concerned, honest eyes. I couldn't look back at him, so I opened and closed my purse, then simply fiddled with it. "Maybe that isn't the right question," he said.

"No," I told him. "It's the right question."

Once more, he waited.

"The father wasn't happy."

"*Wasn't* happy?"

"I don't think I want to talk about it," I said.

"Are you married?" he wanted to know, and when I didn't answer right away, he said, "The forms will ask for this information anyway, you know."

"I'm engaged," I said, and felt ridiculous, as if I were a little girl again, playing at being a grown-up.

"And your fiancé wasn't happy to hear that you're pregnant."

"No."

"Did you give him a little time to adjust to the idea?"

"Look," I said. "This is my decision. My problem."

"Does he feel that way?"

I said, "I'm quite certain that question isn't on any of these forms."

"No. That's right. But I thought you wanted to talk to someone."

I couldn't think of an answer to this.

"Do you?" he said.

I did. But what was I to say? Oh, please, yes, I want to talk to someone. I'm afraid I'm not in love enough. I think I may be out of love. And my dear, dear friend, with whom I have made this child, is old enough to be my father. Tell me what I am to do, because the man who *is* my father and whose presence looms over my life exactly as strangely as grief will look at me with eyes that wonder why, and I know what all the psychologists will say, and I don't know how to answer it. Even if I wanted to.

None of this made sense to me in any way that would permit me to say it out. So I said nothing.

"All right," said the doctor, "you need time to think. Would that be a safe thing to say?"

"I came here to find out what I have to do," I said.

"Right," he said.

"I believe I want an abortion."

"All right," he said.

"It's that simple?" I asked.

"No."

"Right," I said. "The forms."

"We try to counsel people to take other options first," he said.

"Yes."

"And the forms are a way of looking at the whole situation carefully."

"I understand."

He stepped away from the table, and unfolded his arms. He picked up one of the forms, seemed to study it—but he was thinking, going over something in his mind. "I do think you ought to talk to the father again before you decide anything."

I said nothing. I was watching him.

"It's been my experience anyway that ambivalence often means people don't really want to terminate."

"How can anyone be anything but ambivalent about it?" I asked.

He shrugged. "I guess not."

"Well, then, what do you mean?"

"I guess I'm responding to what I'm able to infer here," he said. "If you'll forgive me."

"Forgive you."

"Look," he said, "I'm just trying to give you the best advice I can, given what you seem to need."

"What do you think I need," I said.

"Time."

I took the forms and went out into the main office, where now there were three other women—one of whom was very pregnant—waiting to see the doctor. I went out, down the hall toward the elevators, and the woman from behind the desk called to me from the open door. "Ann," she said. "You forgot to pay."

"You'll have to bill me," I said, and got into the first elevator.

Out in the parking lot, I looked at the bright sun, and decided what to do next. I was aware of myself confining the decision to the next few moments, the next two hours or so, and yet as I waited for another cab, thinking of calling Louis and asking him to come get me, the idea of carrying his child seemed rather suddenly like an idea I was accustomed to: it was better somehow than the idea of futuristic buildings with odd windows and smooth, silent elevators that went too fast. It was a plain, very ordinary idea, as neutral and factual as the sun blazing on the high, billowing, impossibly white clouds to the north. I was tired and frightened and empty, and it was all right. When the cab came, it was the same cab, the same driver, and I took that as a positive sign. I got in and almost told him I was pregnant. I imagined it, watching the back of his head—black curls, lines in the neck, and a pair of ears that stood out like open doors: I'm pregnant, I said. He looked back over his shoulder and smiled at the news; he would see it as something to celebrate.

Now, in the kitchen of the house, with a snowstorm at the windows and the wind driving at the eaves, I took Louis's hand and put it on my breast. "We'll have the baby," I told him.

"Don't," he said. "No. I won't have you do this out of pity."

"Not pity," I said. "No."

"Annie, please."

"Louis," I said.

"I think we should wait a year," he said. "I think we should wait and not do anything right now. Not like this."

"I'm going to have a baby," I said. "That won't wait."

"Annie," he said, turning to me, putting his arms around me. I held him. I held him a long time.

That night, when I slept, I had my snow dream again; it was all rolling toward me across the ice—a single, moving wall of cloud behind which someone or something waited to say my name. I woke knowing Louis was next to me in the bed, and even so the feeling of aloneness was with me like an old, bad ghost. I breathed and moved closer to Louis, wanting his warmth, needing it in a way I could not have thought would ever be so complete, and then I remembered my father, thought of him waking up in a hospital room. For some reason, it was then that I could believe he would live, and it was then that something of what we had always been for each other seemed to move through the dark rooms of the house, calming me, just as his big shadow had when he had leaned down to tuck me in for the night. I thought of him awake in his hospital room, maybe thinking this, too, that we must be terribly careful of each other, all the time, always.

Off in another part of the house Aunt Ellen played her music, her sound to ward off fears and ghosts and the bad future— being old, being alone, being wrong, or sick, or ridiculous, or in pain. I touched my abdomen, where I knew the baby was, and caught myself worrying that something might happen to stop it. I didn't want it to stop now.

Night, and the snow blowing outside, a prodigious storm ramming the house, and I was not afraid, but full of grief for us all, and still, in the middle of that hurt, praying for what was mine in the world—asking that I might be blessed enough to appreciate it, and to keep it for a time in the simple gratitude